## Also by Laura Griffin

# WHISPER OF WARNING

## LAURA GRIFFIN

POCKET BOOKS

New York   London   Toronto   Sydney   New Delhi

Pocket Books
A Division of Simon & Schuster, Inc.
1230 Avenue of the Americas
New York, NY 10020

This book is a work of fiction. Any references to historical events, real people, or real places are used fictitiously. Other names, characters, places, and events are products of the author's imagination, and any resemblance to actual events or places or persons, living or dead, is entirely coincidental.

This Pocket Books paperback edition March 2014

POCKET and colophon are registered trademarks of Simon & Schuster, Inc.

For information about special discounts for bulk purchases, please contact Simon & Schuster Special Sales at 1-866-506-1949 or business@simonandschuster.com.

The Simon & Schuster Speakers Bureau can bring authors to your live event. For more information or to book an event, contact the Simon & Schuster Speakers Bureau at 1-866-248-3049 or visit our website at www.simonspeakers.com.

Cover design by Jae Song
Cover photo © David Tejada/Getty Images

Manufactured in the United States of America

10  9  8  7  6  5  4  3  2  1

ISBN 978-1-4767-6387-3
ISBN 978-1-4165-7075-2 (ebook)

For my sisters

## ACKNOWLEDGMENTS

So many people answered questions for me as I wrote this story. Thanks to Kristin Isaac, Frank M. Ahearn, Barbara Castillo Noyes, Jessica Dawson, and Jen Nollkamper for sharing expertise in everything from firearms to scissors.

I especially want to thank the team at Pocket: Abby Zidle, Lisa Litwack, Jessica Silvester, and everyone else who worked so hard on this book. And finally, thank you to Kevan Lyon for her unwavering support.

# WHISPER
# OF
# WARNING

# CHAPTER

# I

Courtney Glass whipped into the gravel lot and cursed the man toad who'd invited her here. This was August. Texas. It was ninety-nine degrees outside, and any halfway sane person was holed up in an air-conditioned building right now, not parked at a deserted hike-and-bike trail, hoping to score after lunch.

Did he think this was romantic? Spontaneous, maybe? Despite the Ivy League diploma, John David Alvin could be a real idiot.

Courtney huffed out a breath and flipped down the vanity mirror. Idiot or not, she wanted to look good. Looking good was the best revenge, especially when it came to ex-boyfriends.

But the Beauty Gods weren't smiling on her today. The humidity had turned her hair limp, and her makeup was practically melting off. She dug through her purse, seeking inspiration but finding little. She blotted her forehead with a tissue and fluffed her hair. She started to put on lipstick, then decided to hell with it. Who cared if she impressed David? He was the last person she wanted to see right now. She shouldn't even be here, really, but his insistent messages were driving her crazy. They needed to hash this thing out, once and for all.

A flash of movement in the rearview mirror caught her eye. He was here. She watched the black Porsche Cayenne glide up alongside her. He'd traded in the red Carrera, apparently, which shouldn't have come as a surprise. Suddenly nervous, she cast a glance around her Buick Skylark, a hulking testament to the emptiness of her bank account. Courtney could work wonders with drugstore cosmetics, and she was a bloodhound for treasures in a thrift shop, but this car was beyond help. Until she climbed out of credit card debt, she was stuck in a '98 clunker with a temperamental AC. She turned up the power now and adjusted the vents.

David sat in his SUV, but didn't get out. Courtney could feel his gaze on her while she cleared clutter off the front seat. She refused to make eye contact. This was *his* meeting, and he was going to have to come to her. She didn't relish the thought of talking to him in her heap, but she wasn't stupid enough to give up her home field advantage by getting into his Porsche.

From the corner of her eye, she saw him exit the car and fist his hands on his hips. She set her chin. She could match wills with him any day of the week. Sweat beaded between her breasts as she waited, silently, gazing through the windshield at the dragonflies playing in the sunshine.

Finally the Buick's door squeaked open, and he slid into the passenger seat. He wore a crisp white shirt with monogrammed cuffs, a red power tie, and his usual dark pants. In an instant, the Skylark smelled like Drakkar Noir.

Courtney looked at him with disgust as she rolled down her window.

*"Well?"*

"Well, what?" she shot back. "You called me."

"I most certainly did not."

"Text message. Whatever." God, he was such a prick. Just smelling him again made her want to retch.

He gave her an annoyed look. "I don't have time for this shit. This is bordering on harassment."

"*Harassment?*"

Suddenly the back door jerked open. Courtney turned around and found herself face-to-face with a black ski mask.

The man pulled a gun out of his pants and pointed it at David's nose. "Gimme your phone."

All the breath whooshed out of Courtney's lungs. She gaped at the gray eyes glaring out from holes in the mask.

He jabbed the gun at David's neck. "Now, asshole!"

She glanced at her ex-boyfriend. His arrogance had morphed into fear, and he wasn't moving. *Do it!* She tried to tell him mentally, but he was frozen. At last, he braced a hand on the dashboard and jammed the other into his front pocket.

She cast a panicked look outside. No one. This was unreal. It was the middle of the *day*. Granted, it was hotter than hell outside, but there had to be someone—

The barrel swung toward her, and her stomach dropped out.

"Yours, too."

She stared at the twisting pink mouth and tried to process the words. Hers, too. Her phone. He wanted her phone. Did he want her money, also? Her phone was in her purse, along with her Mace.

"Come on!"

David tossed his phone at the guy, and it landed with a

clatter on the back floorboard. The man scooped it up and shoved it in the pocket of his tracksuit.

Then the masked head turned toward her. "*Now*, or I'll blow his fucking brains out."

David went pale. He sent her a desperate look. "*Hurry, Courtney!*"

Her purse was near her feet. On the floor. And her Mace was in there. She dragged the bag into her lap and thrust her hand inside. She groped for the tube of pepper spray but couldn't find it amid all the junk she lugged around. *I can't die yet. There's so much I haven't done.*

"*Now!*" The eyes watching her through the cutouts squinted.

Her clammy fingers closed around the phone, and she pulled it free. She held it out to him.

Time stretched out as the phone hovered there in her trembling hand. He reached for it. He wore tight black gloves, and she knew—with sudden certainty—this was going to end badly.

He squeezed her wrist, and the phone dropped to the floor. He didn't let go her hand.

"Take my wallet," David said, yanking it loose from his back pocket. "Take whatever you want."

Courtney watched, transfixed, as the black-gloved hand pried open her fingers. Did he want her ring? The cheap silver trinket from Santa Fe?

"I've got cash." David's voice hitched. "I've got a Rolex."

The pistol slapped into her palm. The thick black fingers squeezed her hand around the grip. Suddenly she realized what was happening. She tried to yank her arm away, but couldn't.

*"No!"* she shrieked, pulling her arm until her shoulder burned.

David's gaze met hers.

*Pop!*

Their bodies jerked in unison. Surprise flickered in his eyes as red bloomed on his white shirt. He sagged sideways, thunking his head against the windshield.

Courtney's ears rang. A high-pitched noise rasped in and out of her throat as she stared at the gun in her hand. The gloved fingers closed around hers again, and she thrashed sideways, trying to wrench her arm away.

*"No!"* She used her free hand to punch at the ski mask as hard as she could. Her whole arm reverberated from the blow.

*Pop!*

The windshield exploded. Screaming, she hunched down in her seat. Her gaze landed on her purse, wedged between her leg and the door. The Mace was there, peeking out from inside the bag. Her right hand was being crushed as the man forced her unwilling fingers around the grip. With her left, she grabbed the Mace. Her wrist twisted painfully. The gun barrel turned toward her.

Her thumb found the top of the vial. A stream shot out, straight at the ugly pink mouth in the hole of the mask.

*"Fuck!"*

She crashed backward into the steering wheel as her arm was released. Curses and moans filled the car as she clawed frantically at the door latch. The door popped open, and she pitched sideways onto the gravel. She tasted dust and jerked her legs free from the car. She glanced back over her shoulder and saw David slumped against the dashboard.

The back door squeaked open.

She scrambled to her feet and ran.

Nathan Devereaux fed a few quarters into the hospital vending machine and ordered up some lunch. His tour had started at 2:00 this morning, and he'd been running for fourteen hours straight on nothing but coffee.

"Want anything?" He glanced over his shoulder at his partner, who stood on the other side of the waiting room. The guy was peering through the miniblinds at the traffic on North Lamar. Either he didn't hear the question, or he was being an asshole. Nathan had known Will Hodges less than forty-eight hours, but his money was on the latter.

"*Hodges!*"

The guy's gaze shot up. "Yeah?"

"You want anything?"

"No."

Asshole it was. Nathan fished his Mars Bar from the vending machine and wandered toward the hallway, hoping to see the forensic artist they were waiting on. No sign of her. It had been nearly an hour, and the door to Room 632 was still shut, meaning that she was still in there interviewing his witness for the suspect sketch.

Nathan ripped open his lunch. On days like this, he really felt his age. He hadn't even hit forty yet, but ten years as a homicide detective and a steady diet of junk food hadn't exactly kept him in peak condition. He still looked good enough to get his share of come-ons at bars, but his energy wasn't what it used to be.

He watched his new partner from across the room. The kid looked like he could bench-press a VW. He probably ate protein shakes for breakfast and made it to the gym six times a week.

Give him a year.

Nathan chomped into his candy bar and glanced at his watch.

"We're finished."

He turned around at the familiar voice. Fiona Glass stood in the doorway holding her battered leather art case and a sheet of paper. She wore a conservative beige pantsuit and had her reddish-blond hair pulled neatly back in a headband.

Nathan crossed the room to take the sketch she held out to him. One look at it had his gut twisting.

"A profile? That's all she saw?"

"She says he grabbed her from behind and the only real glimpse she got was when he fled the scene."

Nathan heard the edge in her voice and glanced up. "What's the deal?"

She darted her gaze around the waiting room, as if to make sure no one else could overhear. She paused briefly on Hodges, and Nathan knew she didn't trust him yet. Fiona was slow to warm up to people, and Hodges had been with Austin PD less than a week.

"What's the problem?" Nathan prompted.

"Everything." She nodded at the drawing. "What does that look like to you?"

"I don't know. Black male. Twenty-five. Average features."

"And his expression?"

He stared down at the picture. She had drawn it in charcoal on a sheet of thick gray art paper. He could smell the fixative on it, which meant the witness had declared it finished.

Nathan studied the face of the man who had attacked a prominent judge and her husband in their carport shortly after midnight. "He looks bored," Nathan stated.

"Precisely."

He met Fiona's gaze and remembered why he loved working with her. She had the eye of an artist, but she thought like a detective.

"He robbed two people at gunpoint and shot one of them in the face," she said. "I'd expect to see aggression, nerves, panic. Anything but boredom."

"You think we got a false alligator?"

"The angle bothers me, too," she continued, avoiding the question. Nathan knew why. The witness was a municipal judge. If Nathan suggested she might be lying about who shot her husband, the result would be a virtual shit storm.

"The angle. You mean because it's a profile?"

"It's very rare to get only a side view, particularly the right side."

Nathan frowned at the drawing. "You're saying it should have been a left-side profile?"

She shrugged. "No, it's just more common."

"Why?"

"Bank robberies."

Nathan glanced over at Hodges. He still stood beside the window, but apparently he'd been paying attention. "What's that?"

"If a witness only sees a profile, it's usually the getaway driver," Hodges said.

Wow, an entire sentence. Nathan glanced at Fiona. She

was staring at his new partner again, looking impressed now, but still distrustful.

She turned back to Nathan. "So based on the interview, and the information provided, and the information *not* provided, I'd say your witness has a credibility problem."

Just what he needed. A well-respected judge with a credibility problem. He couldn't wait to run this up the flagpole.

He decided to play devil's advocate. "What about her injuries? She claims she was knocked to the ground, and she's got a concussion to back that up."

"I don't know who knocked her to the ground," Fiona said. "It could have been someone she knew."

Nathan's head started to pound. He had to unravel this murder case, deal with the politics, and train a rookie detective all at the same time. This case was going to suck.

Fiona took out a manila envelope, slid the drawing inside, and handed it to him. The sketch was eight inches by fourteen, just the right size to fit in his case file. She paid attention to details like that.

"Call me if you need anything else." She turned to Hodges. "Welcome to Austin. It was nice meeting you."

She disappeared into an elevator, and Nathan looked at Hodges, who was still standing on the other side of the room.

"You get all that?"

He gave a slight nod.

"You agree with her?"

Another nod. Not much of a talker, this guy. It was going to be a party teaching him to elicit a confession.

A buzz sounded, and Nathan reached for the phone clipped to his hip, just beneath his side holster. "Devereaux."

"We've got a Code 37 at Zilker Park."

"I'm at Seton Hospital on the Goodwin interview. Give it to Webb."

"He's still in court. You and Hodges are it."

Could this day get any worse? Nathan pulled out his notepad and jotted down a few details before hanging up. Then he made a call and arranged for a uniform to hightail it over, just in case the Honorable Judge Goodwin decided to check herself out of the hospital. Finally, he turned to his partner.

"We got a shooting at Zilker." He lobbed the rest of his stale candy bar into a trash can. "I'm driving."

Ten minutes later, they were in an unmarked unit en route to Austin's largest park. Hodges had said nothing since leaving the hospital. Nathan slid a glance at him. His short haircut reminded Nathan he'd been in the military not so long ago. He decided to make more of an effort.

"You ever work homicide before now?"

"Narcotics."

"Well, there's three rules once we get to the scene: Don't touch anything. Don't touch anything. And don't fucking touch anything."

Hodges kept his eyes trained on the road.

"And you can pretty much bet that the least competent jackass we got wearing a badge is going to be the first responder. It never fails. And it's been that kind of day."

Nathan swung onto Barton Springs Road, the four-lane street that cut straight through the park. He could already see the congestion up ahead, where a uniform had diverted traffic away from the parking lot serving the hike-and-bike trail that paralleled Town Lake. Nathan off-roaded it for a few hundred feet and then flashed his ID at the guy manning the blockade. He started to move the wooden barrier, but Nathan swerved around it and saved him the trouble. The narrow road wound down closer to the water and ended at a gravel parking lot surrounded by dense foliage.

Nathan jogged here sometimes and knew the area well. Typically, this lot would be filling up right now, despite the oppressive heat. But the only cars parked here today were police units, a crime-scene van, and a silent yellow ambulance. No news crews yet, but it wouldn't take long. Nathan pulled up beside the ambulance and waved at a paramedic he knew vaguely.

They parked and made their way over to the crime scene, which had already been taped off. Inside the cordoned-off area, on a tree-shaded patch of gravel, sat a blue Buick Skylark and a black Porsche Cayenne. Both vehicles faced a thicket of mesquite and mulberry bushes. The Cayenne's doors were closed. The two doors on the Buick's left side stood open, and a photographer knelt between them now, taking a picture.

Nathan approached the dour policewoman standing beside the sawhorse that marked the crime scene's southeast corner. He'd been right about the jackass thing.

He nodded. "Brenda."

She nodded back, then squinted at Hodges.

"This is Will Hodges," Nathan said. "He just came on board."

"Victim's name is John David Alvin," she announced proudly. "Age forty-two. Six-eighty-nine Sunset Cove."

"You rifled his wallet?"

Her face fell. "Uh, no. I just—"

"Never move the victim."

"I didn't. His wallet's sitting open right there on the floor. I saw his ID through the window."

Nathan took the clipboard she held out to him and scrawled his name and badge number on the crime-scene log—which consisted of a torn slip of paper. Hodges followed suit, and they both ducked under the tape.

John Alvin. The name rang a bell, but Nathan didn't know why. Alvin. Alvin. Where had he heard that name before?

He walked up behind the photographer and peered inside the Buick. The smell of fresh death wafted out from the roasting car, and a swarm of flies was already busy. Sometimes Nathan longed for a job in Minnesota. Or Vancouver. Anyplace where it took insects longer than twelve seconds to go to work on a corpse.

"Hey, Bart." Nathan crouched down beside him. The photographer's olfactory nerves had gone numb already, and he was snapping away with his camera, oblivious to the smell. Nathan needed a minute.

"Close range," Bart said. "I'd say about one meter."

Nathan ducked his head lower to get a better angle. He could just barely make out the face. . . .

John David Alvin. Attorney-at-law. Nathan had met the man back in January.

"Shit," he muttered, standing up. He was getting a very bad feeling about this. He walked around to the back of the vehicle and looked at the tag.

"We have a witness, Detective. Says she was in the car with the victim when he was shot."

His feeling went from bad to very bad. He turned

around to face the patrol officer, who stood flushed and dripping in the late-afternoon sun. He was fair-skinned and overweight, and the pits of his uniform were soaked through.

"*In* the car?" Nathan asked.

"Yep. Sounds like a robbery."

"Where is she?"

The officer nodded toward a unit parked on the far-eastern edge of the lot. The back door of the car was open, and a woman sat there, barefoot, her elbows propped on her knees, her head buried in her hands.

"Shit."

"What?" Hodges walked up and his gaze followed Nathan's to the car. The witness waiting to be interviewed had long black hair streaked with vibrant red. She was hunched over her knees and looked to be massaging her temples. Nathan couldn't see her face.

But he didn't need to. He took one look at those mile-long legs and knew exactly who she was.

"*Shit,*" he repeated, too thrown off even to curse creatively.

"Who is she?"

He glanced at Hodges. "You know the artist you just met?"

"The suit at the hospital?"

"Yep."

"What about her?"

"Brace yourself," Nathan told him. "You're about to meet her sister."

# CHAPTER

## 2

Flies streamed in and out of the Skylark.

Courtney tried like hell to ignore them, but she couldn't stop looking. They were in there with David. He was *dead*. And if she'd been just a little bit stronger, a little quicker to understand, he'd be alive right now, and she wouldn't be hearing this weird buzzing noise and looking at all those flies.

She dragged her gaze away from the car. The skin between her shoulder blades tickled, and she had the disconcerting feeling she was being watched. She cast a glance over her shoulder and wondered, for the hundredth time, what had become of the man in the ski mask. Who was he? And where was he now? Had he scuttled off to nurse his wounds, or was he somewhere close, watching her?

"Miss Glass?"

She jerked her head around. It was that cop again, the fat one with the flattop. McCoy? Mahoney? She'd given him her story, and he'd told her to wait here, that more people would want to talk to her.

He flipped open a notebook. "I need to get down some additional information."

She watched his mouth as he talked. He had pink lips

and light skin. He was short and bulky. The ski-mask guy had been bulky—

"Full name?"

She checked his eyes. Blue-gray. They weren't gray enough. And she was losing her mind even to consider that this potbellied cop might have held her at gunpoint.

"Ma'am?"

"Courtney Jane Glass."

"Address?"

"Nine-twenty-five Oak Trail, Apartment B."

The questions droned on, and she recited answers. Her gaze drifted back to the car, *her* car, where a man in white coveralls had climbed inside with a black case. What was he doing in there? A shudder moved through her.

She scanned the surrounding area. There were so many trees. So many places to hide. He could be anywhere. He could be watching. Her stomach knotted at the thought, and she wondered whether police cars had bulletproof windows. She glanced around the lot, where a group of uniformed men were huddled off to the side. A guy in street clothes stood near them, his back to her, having a heated conversation on his cell phone. Yet another man leaned back against the trunk of one of the police cars. He wore street clothes, too, and had a gun plastered to his hip.

He was watching her.

"Miss Glass?"

Her attention snapped back to the cop. Those gray eyes peered down at her. She shuddered again. "Sorry. What?"

"Could you tell me what time you arrived at the park?"

What time had she arrived at the park?

"I don't know. Three-thirty? He'd asked me to meet him at three-thirty."

Her gaze wandered back to her car. There was a stretcher there now, just beside the passenger door.

"Miss Glass?"

*"What?"* God, what was wrong with this jerk? Did they have to do this *now*? She could barely think straight.

The officer's brow furrowed. "I have a few more questions—"

"Time for a break." The street-clothes guy, the one with the gun, came up and slapped the cop on the back.

"Who are you?" he demanded.

"Detective Hodges." He held a blue windbreaker out to Courtney. "Cold?"

She realized she was freezing. She had on a flimsy lime green sundress, and her whole body was shivering.

"It's a hundred degrees out," the cop protested.

The detective turned to him. "Why don't you go grab a couple of waters? EMS should have some."

It was an order, not a request. The uniform snapped his notebook shut, then trudged off toward the ambulance.

Courtney took the windbreaker. It was lined with gray flannel and had APD printed on the back in yellow block letters. She slid her arms inside the sleeves and felt better immediately, a little more protected from the chill and all the male gazes surrounding her.

The detective crouched down beside her. They were at eye level now, but he looked out at the lake, not at her. His silence continued, and she could hear the cicadas buzzing.

Or maybe it was that same relentless buzzing she'd been hearing since the gun went off.

"Tic Tac?"

She glanced over. *Tic Tac?* "No, thanks."

He rattled a few mints into his spacious palm and popped them in his mouth.

"You like to bike here?"

The question put her on guard again. "No."

"Not much of a biker myself."

This guy wasn't from Austin. The town was full of Lance Armstrong wannabes who liked to "ride" and were "into cycling." Bikers around here rode Harleys.

She didn't say anything. The interview would start up again. Or maybe this *was* the interview. Maybe he was fishing for information. Do you like to bike? Jog? Did you shoot your ex-boyfriend in the chest?

Courtney shuddered.

"You're in shock."

"Huh?" She looked up at him and felt a twinge of relief. His eyes were brown, like amber, and even if they hadn't been, his build was nothing like her assailant's.

"Shock. Throws your system off. Heart rate, temperature, everything."

She looked away. This detective wasn't here to chat. He wanted something, probably answers to a long list of questions.

He shifted slightly and pulled something from his pocket. A neatly folded white handkerchief. He nodded at her scraped knees.

She took it from him. The only man she knew who carried handkerchiefs was her grandfather, and he was eighty-one years old.

She dabbed at her cuts, wiping away the dust and gravel.

She had cuts on her arms, too, and probably her face from when she'd plunged into the woods to get away from the hideous ski mask. She'd run until it felt like her heart would burst, tripping over vines and roots, not hazarding a single glance backward until she'd reached the trailhead and found a blue emergency phone.

Her cuts needed cleaning. She had some hand sanitizer in her purse, but that was back in the Skylark. With David.

She stood up and stuffed the handkerchief in her pocket. She couldn't do this. She couldn't stay here even a minute longer.

"I need to get home."

The detective stood, too, and she got the full effect of his height and heft. She considered herself fairly tall at five-ten, but she had to tilt her head back to look at him. She squared her shoulders and tried not to seem intimidated.

"Can I go?"

He didn't say anything. His gaze moved over her slowly, and she could feel him taking in her bare feet, her dirty knees, the rapid rise and fall of her chest.

"Are we done here?" she asked, straining to keep her voice even.

No response.

Why wouldn't he answer? She had rights. Goddamn it, she had all kinds of rights! They couldn't just keep her here indefinitely. Frustration burned in her throat, and she swallowed it down. She wouldn't lose it. She would *not* lose it. Not in front of these cops, anyway.

The freckle-faced one plodded up to them wearing a sour expression. He offered her a bottle of water.

"I'm fine." Actually, she was parched, but her thirst wasn't nearly as pressing as her need to leave.

The cop shot the detective a glare and then turned to Courtney. "Ma'am. We need to take you to the station now to get a formal statement."

*A formal statement.*

"Do I have a choice?"

His eyebrows snapped together. "You're saying you won't go?"

"I didn't say I *wouldn't,* I just asked if I had a choice."

"We could probably do it here," the detective said blandly, "if you really want."

She looked around. The thought of being stuck at a police station for the next few hours made her head throb. But she couldn't stay here. She felt rattled and vulnerable, and she needed a chance to pull herself together.

"Fine." She crossed her arms. "But someone better give me a ride, because my car's occupied."

Her car was a crime scene. She glanced over at it, just as those men in coveralls lowered David's body onto a black bag that had been spread out atop the stretcher. They tucked his arms close to his sides. One of them reached for the zipper—

"Whoa."

A hand clamped around her elbow as she swayed backward. Her vision blurred at the edges.

"Easy, now." The detective frowned down at her. His fingers gripped her arm, holding her up.

She pushed away from him and used the car door for support. "Sorry." What the *hell?* She'd never fainted in her life.

"You'd better sit down," he said.

"No."

"I think you need some water."

"I'm fine." As long as she didn't look at her car again.

"You sure?"

"Let's just *go*," she said. "I want to get this over with."

Will left the witness in Interview 2 and went off to find a vending machine. He took the long route, stopping by his desk first to check phone messages and e-mail. He wanted her to stew for a while. And he needed some information before he and Devereaux began their interrogation.

After combing the first floor for a few minutes, he found a break room with a machine that took dollars. He bought two Cokes, one for himself and one for Courtney Glass. He'd bet she drank Diet Coke, but her system needed sugar. And he knew better than to bring a woman a diet drink when she hadn't asked for it.

Cans in hand, he rode up the elevator and wove his way through the maze of cubes and corridors back to his department. He recognized the detective slouched against the doorway to the lieutenant's office. Will made his footsteps silent as he walked up on him.

"Yeah, that's because he's twelve."

He identified Devereaux's voice inside the room.

"Twenty-nine." This from the lieutenant. "And he's a war veteran."

"I don't give a shit what he is; he's never worked a homicide."

Will stopped in the doorway, startling Webb, whom he'd met for the first time yesterday. He scanned the expressions.

They ranged from pissed off (his partner) to stressed out (the lieutenant) to mildly entertained (Webb).

"Witness is in Two," Will reported. "McElroy's on the door."

Lieutenant Cernak cleared his throat. "Someone's got to take this girl's statement. You're it."

"All right. Why me?"

"She seems to like you. And Devereaux's been reassigned."

Will glanced at his partner. Devereaux's jaw tightened, and he looked away.

"She waived her right to an attorney," Cernak continued. "Looks like she's in a hurry to get home. You need to get her talking, then pin down every goddamn detail."

"Yes, sir."

Devereaux crossed his arms. "Don't fuck this up."

Will gritted his teeth.

"Flirt with her, if you have to," the lieutenant said. "Do whatever you need to to make her trust you."

"You want to brief me on what's going on?" Will asked.

Cernak exchanged a look with Devereaux.

"Her story's hinky," the lieutenant said. "The GSR test, the 911 call. And so far we got no physical evidence that puts some ski-mask guy in the car."

"You think she's lying."

Devereaux's shoulders tensed at Will's statement. Clearly, he had a conflict of interest here, and Will guessed it had to do with the forensic artist.

"I'm saying it doesn't hang together. And this is a sensitive case." Cernak stroked a meaty hand over his head, as if to comb his nonexistent hair. "Vic's a high-powered trial lawyer. Wife's from big money. And the witness's sister works freelance for us."

Will filed all that away. Was this a love triangle? An affair gone bad? That presented some complications for the random-robbery scenario. Not that he'd given that much credence anyway.

Cernak stood up, a clear dismissal. "Any questions?"

*Yeah, plenty.* "No, sir."

"Go get her talking." He glanced at his watch. "And do it quick, before the news comes on and my phone starts ringing off the hook."

McElroy stood outside the door with his arms folded over his chest. He didn't look happy. He'd had a tedious afternoon and probably faced an evening filled with paperwork. And preseason football was on tonight.

Will handed him a Coke.

"She's all yours," McElroy said, and stalked off.

Will entered the room and immediately noticed the change. The wobbly, distracted woman from the crime scene had disappeared. The new-and-improved Courtney sat in a plastic chair at the end of the conference table, her legs crossed and tilted at an eye-catching angle. She was filing her fingernails with one of those sandpaper things and took a few seconds to glance up from the task.

"Ma'am. Thanks for waiting."

She raised a brow at the "ma'am," but stayed silent. Her dark hair was smooth and shiny now, and her lips, which had looked bloodless back at the park, were a deep, dewy red. She wasn't beautiful, but she did a good imitation.

He popped open the remaining Coke and slid it in

front of her. The can was the same color as the streaks in her hair.

"Mind?" He pulled out a chair and sat down next to her. She looked surprised, as if she'd expected him to stand over her, scowling and reeling off questions.

She watched him warily as she took a sip of the soft drink. The smudges were gone from under her eyes now. He noted the backpack at her feet, the one he'd retrieved for her out of the Buick's trunk. He knew—because he'd searched the bag himself—that it contained a crapload of makeup, a striped blue bikini, and an iPod. The jeweled flip-flops that had been in it were on her feet now.

"Thank you for your time, ma'am." He produced a small tape recorder and placed it on the table. "You don't mind if I record this, do you? My handwriting's terrible." Without waiting for an answer, he activated the device.

She put the Coke down and glanced at the recorder. He could tell it made her uneasy, but she shrugged. "Do whatever you want."

He recited the date, the time, and both their names while she returned her attention to her glossy red nails.

"So let's start at the beginning." He scooted his chair closer, and she leaned back fractionally. "What time did you arrive at the park this afternoon?"

"Three-thirty."

"And you were there why?"

"David had sent me a text message—several, actually—asking me to meet him."

"John David Alvin."

"Yes." She huffed out a breath. "Look, I already went

through all this with Officer Macaroni. Don't you guys talk to each other?"

He ignored the question. "So you showed up at three-thirty. Then what?"

She put down the nail file. She took a deep breath and focused on something over his shoulder, probably the video camera mounted up near the ceiling.

"I waited," she said. "It was just a minute or two, and then he pulled up."

"In the Porsche Cayenne."

"Yes."

"You two meet there a lot?"

Her gaze snapped to his. "No."

"You ever met there before today? Maybe at night?"

She bristled. "I haven't met him anywhere since we broke up six months ago."

"And why did you break up?"

She glanced at the recorder. "I found out he was married."

"You didn't know that when you started going out with him?"

She crossed her arms beneath her breasts. "No."

Will stared at her for a moment, waiting to see whether she'd squirm. She looked annoyed, but calm.

"So Mr. Alvin lied to you? About his marital status?"

She scoffed. "He lied about everything. He told me his name was David, that he was down from Dallas working on a case. I didn't even know his first name, or that he lived in Austin, until I googled him and found his law firm."

Will gave her a long, hard look. He had a knack for

knowing when people were lying. It was something he'd picked up in Afghanistan, back when the ability to detect a lie was a survival skill, every bit as important as the ability to fire an M4.

And this woman appeared to be telling the truth, at least for now. He decided to switch topics.

"You remember him leaving the car running?"

"The SUV?" She frowned. "I don't know. Why?"

"His keys were in the ignition. Anyway, so you were saying? He pulled up?"

"He got in my car. And almost the same moment, this guy jumped in the back. He had a ski mask on. I—" she cleared her throat. "It scared me to death."

The fear in her eyes looked genuine. She had olive green eyes. Her skin was fair, but tanned slightly and freckled, like she'd been in the sun all summer. He figured her natural hair color for a rusty brown.

"Are you sure about the timing?" he asked.

"What do you mean?"

"I mean when this man got in the car with the two of you. Are you sure it hadn't been a few minutes?"

"It was right after David got in. We exchanged, like, two words, and then suddenly this guy jumps in and pulls a gun on us."

This was one of the places where her story didn't line up with the witness account. A woman walking her dog on the trail had seen a couple arguing in the Buick a few *minutes* before hearing the gunshots. The dog walker claimed she was thirty or forty yards down the path at the time of the noise.

But Will didn't want to focus on that just yet. "Could you describe him for me?"

She took a deep breath. "Black ski mask. Dark blue tracksuit. Black leather gloves."

She tapped the nail file on the table. Witnesses typically got agitated recalling their attacker.

Or when fabricating a story.

"You notice his build? Big? Small?"

"He was bulky," she said firmly.

"Bulky."

"You know, *bulky*." She gave him a once-over. "Not like you or anything. Like, *soft*. He had a beer gut."

"And his height?" he asked, fully aware he was being manipulated.

"Shorter than I am. Maybe five-eight? I couldn't tell for sure."

"Race?"

"Caucasian. And his eyes were gray. I could see them through the mask."

"Okay, then what?"

She took another deep breath. "He said, 'Gimme your phone,' and David froze up. Then he said it again, and David did it. That's when he turned the gun on me and said, 'Yours, too.'"

Will nodded.

"I remembered my Mace that I keep in my purse. So while I was digging through there for the phone, I grabbed hold of it." She swallowed and looked down. Will waited.

"Then suddenly he just *shot* David. Out of nowhere. I

don't know why he did it, either. He'd just given him the phone and he was getting out his wallet."

"Maybe he thought David was reaching for a gun," Will suggested.

"I don't know. Maybe." The nail file was in motion again, a rapid staccato against the faux wood.

"And then?"

She gulped. Looked down. Seemed to notice the tapping and stilled her hand. "And the rest is a blur, really. Next thing I knew, we were struggling with the gun."

"You tried to get the weapon away from him?" Will leaned forward, resting his elbow on the table. This part struck him as odd. When faced with a fight or flight situation, most women chose flight unless there was a child involved. And based on her description, this attacker probably outweighed her by fifty pounds, minimum.

"I . . . I don't know how it happened, really. I just panicked, I guess, after he shot David. I thought, 'I'm next.'"

"Show me."

"What?" Her eyes widened.

"Show me how you struggled with him." Will needed to understand why the gunshot residue test she'd submitted to in the field had come back positive.

She inched back, as if she was afraid of him. "I can't really remember, exactly. I just—"

"Try your best." He scooted his chair around, positioning himself behind her. "Pretend I'm in the backseat. Was he right- or left-handed?"

She turned to look at him, and he knew she was way out of her comfort zone. She bit her lip and stared at his chest for a moment.

"Right, I guess. He held the gun in his right hand."

"Do you remember the weapon?"

"Not really. Something black."

"Let me know if you recall any more details. We could use a description of it." Will pretended to be holding a gun and pointed it at the hypothetical front passenger. "Okay, now show me what you did."

After a brief hesitation, she reached over and cupped her hand around his. Her fingers were soft and cool.

"I don't remember, exactly. I guess I did this." She squeezed his hand and tried to push it down. He resisted. She winced. He glanced at her wrist and saw the angry purple welt there.

"Then the gun went off again. And I pulled the Mace up and pointed it at his face." She demonstrated with her left.

"Where was his other hand?"

Her eyebrows arched. "Huh?"

"His left hand? While you were struggling with the weapon."

"I don't remember. The windshield shattered, and then I sprayed the Mace, and he let go. All I could think about was getting out."

She dropped her hands now and scraped her chair back a few inches. She blew out a breath and folded her arms over her chest.

Will moved his chair around to face her. His knees almost touched hers, and he nodded at the abrasions there.

"And you got those . . . ?"

"From the gravel. I got the door open and fell out onto the parking lot. He was cursing and moaning. Then I heard the back door open and I ran."

"To the emergency phone."

"That's right. I ran into the bushes. I tripped on all the vines and everything and lost my shoes, but it was easier to run without them, and I just kept going until I found the phone."

"You went straight there? Or did you stop, maybe to look for your shoes?"

She pursed her lips. "I had an armed maniac after me. I didn't care about my shoes."

He nodded and leaned back in his chair. She seemed relieved to get him out of her personal space.

"And then what?"

"I called 911. I told the operator everything. And then I waited there until I heard sirens."

"You ever think to go back to the car? See if David needed CPR?" It was a cheap shot, but he needed her reaction.

"He was dead." Her voice quivered, but she looked him directly in the eye. "I could tell. And I didn't know where the ski-mask guy was, so I waited for the sirens. Actually, I hid. In a clump of trees."

"You hid."

"Yes, damn it! I *hid*. I was scared, okay? You try running for your life from some armed psycho! I wanted to get out of sight."

Will watched her. If her story was true, she'd done the logical thing. But that was a pretty big *if*.

"Then what happened?"

"When the sirens sounded really loud, like there were lots of police, that's when I went back to my car."

She reached for her Coke and took a long gulp. He watched her slender throat as she drank, noting all the scratches on it. She had scratches on her arms, too. They corroborated at least part of her story, but there were still lots of holes.

She plunked the can on the table.

He stood up and switched off the recorder. "All right, ma'am. That should do it."

Her eyebrows shot up. "That's it?"

"That's it for now."

"I'm free to go?"

"Just some paperwork to fill out, then you can head home." He pulled her chair out for her. The APD windbreaker was draped over it, and he planned to check later to see if that bloody handkerchief was still in the pocket.

She turned toward him, her face a mix of relief and confusion. "Okay. Thanks."

"Oh, just one more thing." He reached around her to open the door.

"What's that?"

"Don't plan on leaving town."

Courtney slid her hand behind the drainpipe leading down from the gutter and found the magnetic box that held her spare key. She unlocked the front door to her side of the duplex, stepped into the foyer, and took what seemed like her first breath of air in hours.

She could feel herself decompressing as she kicked off her flip-flops and tossed her backpack on the floor. She walked across the living room, grateful for the familiarity of home—the smell of lantana outside, the soft carpet beneath her feet, the hum of her neighbor's television through the shared wall.

The entire bus ride home, Courtney had been fantasizing about a glass of ice water, but now all she could think of was the need to get clean. She made a beeline for the bathroom, unbuttoning her sundress on the way and shedding it in the hall. Before today, it had been her favorite summer outfit—light, breezy, with a flirty, fluttery skirt. Now she wanted to burn it. She twisted the shower knob to hot and stood in front of the mirror as the bathroom filled with steam.

She looked like hell. The quick repairs she'd made to her makeup while waiting in the interview room had done almost nothing to help. Tiny, hairline cuts covered her neck and arms, and her eyes were bloodshot. She turned away from her reflection and stepped into the shower. The scalding water sluiced over her, and she reached for her most textured loofah. She scrubbed every inch of her body in a manic—and futile—attempt to wash off the day. After double shampooing her hair and using a moisturizing conditioner, she stepped out of the shower and grabbed a fresh towel from the linen cabinet. She wrapped it around herself and went into the bedroom.

The room was dark. She sank down onto the corner of her queen-size bed and stared at her closet.

David was dead.

No matter how much she tried to distract herself, she couldn't get his expression out of her mind. Surprise. Just before he'd slumped over.

Courtney shuddered. The tension that had drained away in the shower returned, and she felt a muscle spasm at the base of her neck. She reached over and switched on the bedside lamp. She opened the top drawer of her nightstand.

Empty.

For a moment, she just stared at the drawer. She slid her hand to the back, but turned up nothing more than an old book of matches and a packet of sandalwood incense. She went to her closet and hunted through a few purses until she found a vial of pepper spray. Her fingers curled around the cool, smooth tube.

Someone had tried to kill her. Why, she did not know. But she had a deep-rooted feeling it had very little to do with a robbery.

She placed the Mace on her nightstand and switched off the light. She eased back against the spongy bank of pillows and tried to clear her mind. Nervous energy hummed through her veins. She felt exhausted, but knew sleep would never come. And then there was Fiona. Her sister was sure to call, or more likely show up, the moment she got wind of what had happened. Courtney didn't want to deal with it.

She got up and tugged open a dresser drawer. In the dark she felt around for clothes—panties, a T-shirt, yoga pants. She pulled on the most comfortable clothing she owned and went into the kitchen. Just the thought of food repelled her, but her body needed nourishment.

She jerked open the refrigerator and searched its contents. Diet Coke, cottage cheese, a tub of pasta salad from Whole Foods. Her gaze settled on a pack of shaved ham, and she decided to make a sandwich. She lined the ingredients up on the counter and started going through the motions.

David was dead. He'd been a lying, cheating son of a bitch, but now he was dead.

Courtney pitied his wife. She hadn't at first. When she'd first discovered the woman's existence, she'd felt nothing but anger toward David. In fact, *anger* was putting it mildly. She'd been practically blind with rage.

Hence the Porsche Carrera incident. Trashing David's car hadn't been one of her smarter impulses. Ever since then she'd been on a turn-over-a-new-leaf kick that included giving up smoking, partying, and men.

The smoking and partying had been surprisingly easy, but the men part was giving her trouble. Especially today. How else to explain a flare of attraction for a man who was completely and utterly *not* her type? She went for flashy guys. Guys with either looks or style or both. And with the exception of David—who had had looks and style, but no heart—they tended to be creative types, as in musicians or writers or aspiring artists.

Jacked-up military men were *not* her scene.

Courtney pulled out two slices of bread and noticed a spot of mold on one of the edges. She sighed. She'd been working extra hours this month, trying to put a dent in her credit card bill, and she'd hardly had time to get to the grocery store. She poked her head back in the fridge.

*I'll blow his fucking brains out.*

Goose bumps sprang up all over her arms as she remembered the twisted mouth, the spittle flying at her as he barked orders.

Her gaze landed on an expired six-pack of yogurt. Behind it was a salad kit full of wilted greens. She opened her pantry and pulled out the trash can.

*Thunk.* The yogurts were history. *Thunk. Thunk.* Ditto the expired mayo and a case of food poisoning disguised as ranch dressing. *Thud.* Year-old Pillsbury biscuits. *Thud. Thunk.* A tub of margarine and the Chinese mustard that had accompanied the egg rolls at last year's Christmas party.

She pitched and tossed her way through the entire refrigerator, and when she was done, she stepped back.

Diet Cokes. And a jar of jalapeños.

Courtney snagged a soft drink and took it into the living room. She slumped onto the sofa and stared blankly at the darkened television screen.

The doorbell rang, and she shot off the couch.

Who would be here? It was almost nine. It wasn't Fiona, because her sister always parked in the driveway and came to the back.

She tiptoed to the front door and peered through the peephole.

Amy Harris.

Courtney's shoulders sagged. God, she was losing it. She flipped the bolt and swung open the door.

"Hey," she said.

It wasn't just Amy, but her son Devon, too. The eight-year-old wore a Houston Rockets T-shirt and looked sullen. Courtney immediately knew the reason for her neighbor's visit.

"Sorry to drop in," Amy said. "But I was wondering if you might do us a favor?"

"Let me guess," Courtney said. "Someone needs a trim?"

Devon scowled down at his basketball shoes. He hated haircuts, but he was too proud to admit it.

"Would you mind?" Amy asked, mussing her son's hair. "It's getting so shaggy, and I can never seem to get off work in time to take him."

Courtney stepped back to motion them inside. They'd been through this before. Typically, it irked her when friends asked for free cuts, but tonight she didn't mind. She didn't particularly want to be alone right now, and a cut would get her mind off everything.

Amy steered Devon into the kitchen. Courtney pulled out one of her four dining chairs and retrieved the bean bag cushion she kept on the top shelf of her broom closet for occasions like these. She tossed it on the wooden seat.

"Hop up."

Devon complied, still looking mulish.

"Are you sure it's all right? I hate to bother you."

"It's no bother," Courtney said, although usually it was. She couldn't count the number of times she'd been to parties or friends' houses and someone had nudged her in the ribs and asked, 'Hey, did you bring your scissors?' It was incredibly rude, like her walking up to some doctor and asking if he'd mind giving her a quick checkup before the burgers came off the grill.

But Amy was different, sort of, because she had a nice kid and she was even more broke than Courtney.

"If you're okay here, I've got to run back and check something on the stove."

Courtney waved her off. "I've got it."

When she was gone, Courtney stepped back and looked Devon over. His hair was long all around, and she guessed he hadn't had it cut since the last freebie a couple months ago.

"What'll it be?" she asked gruffly, because that's what worked with this kid.

"I want a Mohawk."

She opened the drawer where she kept a spare pair of scissors. "That probably won't go over too well with your mom."

"So?"

"Sit up straight." She filled a spray bottle with warm water. "Sounds like you're mad at her."

He grunted.

"Shoulders back." It was difficult to get an even cut when the client was slouching, which was one reason she disliked working with teenagers.

That, and the ones who could afford the rates at Bella Donna were a bunch of spoiled brats.

She misted his hair. "How 'bout just a quick trim today?" she suggested, even though he needed way more than a trim. She avoided the word *cut* around kids because they seemed to take it literally, like she was going to *cut them*.

Devon nodded, visibly relieved.

"If you get your mom's permission, I'll give you a faux-hawk for Halloween."

He eyed her skeptically. "Is that, like, a wimpy Mohawk?"

For the first time in hours, she felt herself smile. "Not wimpy, just temporary. You comb all the hair up in the middle and spray it. Then it goes back to normal after you wash it. We can do some hair paint, too, if your mom says yes."

Devon brightened considerably at this prospect. For the next few minutes, Courtney snipped and combed as he debated possible colors. When her floor was littered with three-quarter-inch brown locks, she dusted off his neck with a dish towel.

"All done."

He hopped down from the chair. "Thanks. I'm gonna go tell my mom about Halloween."

And he was out the door, without even remembering the Tootsie Pop she usually gave him.

Courtney reached for her broom and began sweeping up hair. She captured some dust bunnies, too, and tried to recall the last time she'd cleaned her house.

The bell rang again.

She grabbed a Tootsie Pop from her pantry before going to the door. Out of habit, she checked the peephole.

It wasn't an eight-year-old boy but an oversize detective.

Was he here to arrest her? Her pulse started to race. Maybe she should pretend she wasn't home.

But then she spotted the bag in his hand and pulled open the door.

"I didn't know detectives made house calls," she said.

His gaze skimmed over her, lingering on her navel. She remembered she was in a midriff shirt and yoga pants.

"Come in." She gestured with an exaggerated motion to conceal how naked she suddenly felt. She wasn't even wearing a bra.

He stepped into her house, and she closed the door behind him. She considered locking it, then noticed the gun at his hip and decided she didn't need to. But then the ski mask flashed into her mind, and she flipped the bolt anyway. This guy was armed, but he might be a lousy shot.

"Detective Hodges, right?"

"Will." He eyed the lollipop in her hand. "Am I inter-
rupting dinner?"

"Not yet." She forced herself to keep her arms at her
sides instead of crossing them insecurely over her chest.

He held out the black leather handbag. It dangled from
his thick fingers, and she could tell the simple act of holding
a woman's purse made him uncomfortable.

She took it from him. "Thanks."

"No problem." His gaze roamed the room, picking up
details.

Her mammoth Visa bill sat open on the coffee table.
Courtney strode into the kitchen, casually snatching it up as
she went. She tucked the bill inside her purse and deposited
everything on the kitchen counter.

"Any word on my car?" Not that she ever wanted to see
it again, but she was searching for conversation.

"No."

"You want a drink or something?" She opened a cabinet
and pulled down two glasses.

"No."

She glanced over her shoulder at him. He was hovering
beside her CD tower, reading titles.

He looked up. "Thanks, but I'm still on the clock."

"I'm not." She fished several bottles out of her cabinet
and poured two fingers of Grey Goose into one of the
glasses, followed by a splash of lukewarm cranberry juice.

She went into the living room and made herself comfortable on the couch. Having a cop in her house didn't
faze her at all. She was perfectly at ease, not a thing to
hide.

He wore charcoal slacks and black dress shoes along with a plain white shirt. The top button was undone, and she could see the white T-shirt he wore underneath. Very wholesome. Not a scrap of individuality to the entire ensemble.

She took a sip of her drink and placed the glass on the table. "A little late, isn't it? Don't you need to get home to the wife?"

He glanced over, his face unreadable. "I'm not married." He nodded at the oil painting above her stereo cabinet, a desert landscape. "You paint this?"

"Fiona's the artist in the family. You've met her, haven't you?"

He grunted, which she took for a no.

"You will," she said. "They're always calling her in on murders and robberies, that kind of thing. She gets a lot of sexual assaults, too. She's good with people."

He didn't respond. But then, he hadn't come here to talk about Fiona. He sat down on the sofa arm, and Courtney's heart started pounding.

"I have some follow-up questions."

"Fire away." She tucked her feet beside her and noticed his noticing her toenails. Men liked red. She didn't know what it was.

"You said something earlier about your phone. How he asked you for it, and you reached in the purse for your defense spray."

"That's right." She smiled cooperatively.

"So how'd your phone get in the backseat?"

"Huh?"

"Your cell phone. It was recovered from the floor of the backseat."

Courtney thought back to the struggle. She'd given him the phone. Just before he'd forced the gun into her hand . . .

"I don't know."

His eyebrows arched.

"What? How should I know how it got there? Maybe he went through my purse after I ran away."

"With a face full of Mace?"

She surged to her feet. "He could have done anything, for all I know! Or maybe he had an accomplice. A getaway driver. You ever think of that?"

He cocked his head to the side and watched her. He was calm. She was not. She was getting far too emotional about a little blip in her story. She forced her shoulders to relax and tried to make her face neutral.

"What else can I answer for you?"

"Also, I was wondering about the timeline. How long do you think—"

*Pop!*

"Gun!" she shrieked, and dove for the floor.

## 3

Will gazed down at the woman sprawled flat on her stomach with her arms covering her head.

"Courtney." He crouched beside her. "That wasn't a gun."

She looked up at him with terrified eyes.

"What was it? That noise?"

He tried for a soothing voice. "I don't know. Something in your kitchen. It wasn't a gunshot."

She glanced at his sidearm. He hadn't even reached for it, that's how certain he was that they weren't in any danger. She seemed calmed by this, but then her cheeks flushed, and he knew she was embarrassed. He offered her a hand and pulled her to her feet.

"It sounded like an explosion." She peered into the kitchen. He doubted she realized she had a death grip on his fingers.

"Let me see," he said, tugging his hand away. She glanced down and flushed even redder.

He stepped into the tiny kitchen. A broom was propped up against the counter, and wisps of hair covered the floor. He remembered she was a hairstylist at some place with a fancy Italian name. Apparently, she was moonlighting.

In the middle of the floor stood a trash can brimming

with bottles, jars, and plastic containers. An exploded tube of biscuit dough sat on top.

"Found the culprit." He picked up the can of dough.

She stood beside her breakfast table now, looking uncomfortable.

"It did sound kind of like a gunshot," he lied.

She brushed her hair out of her face and blew out a breath. Then she sank into a chair.

"Sorry." She closed her eyes. "My nerves are frayed."

Will picked up an empty glass on the counter. He filled it with tap water and placed it on the table in front of her.

This visit was netting more information than he'd expected. Her behavior was that of a victim, not a perpetrator. Yes, her story still had holes in it, but he was becoming more and more certain she hadn't killed her ex. The gunshot residue could have resulted from her struggle with the shooter.

Then again, maybe his brain was getting muddled by those tight pants she had on and the bra she wasn't wearing. He needed to keep his distance.

"You eaten anything tonight?" He leaned back against the counter.

"No." She sipped the water. She wouldn't make eye contact, and her cheeks were still pink.

"You should eat something. And get a good night's sleep."

The doorbell rang, and she jumped to her feet. She hurried into the living room, and he followed.

"Check who it is."

She glanced through the peephole. "My neighbor."

She went back into the kitchen and returned with a Tootsie Pop. She unlocked the door to reveal a grinning little boy of about seven or eight. She handed him the lollipop and said something Will couldn't hear.

After the kid was gone, she kept her hand on the doorknob and turned to face him. "Thanks for bringing over my purse."

She was done talking. Which was okay. She obviously needed some rest, and he'd already learned more than he'd expected. He could come at her again later. In his experience, questioning a person on different occasions was more effective than hammering away for hours. It was especially useful to catch people off guard. They got flustered when they weren't expecting to see you, making it more difficult to lie.

As he stepped over the threshold, he examined her door. It had a sturdy latch and a dead bolt.

"You have an alarm system?" he asked.

"No."

He glanced up and down the block. It wasn't a great neighborhood, but it wasn't terrible. The streetlights glowed brightly, and the lawns appeared reasonably well maintained.

He looked her in the eye. "Lock up behind me."

"I will."

When he was halfway down the sidewalk, he glanced back at her over his shoulder. It was probably his imagination, but she seemed sorry to see him go.

Courtney Glass was in trouble again, and Nathan had the colossally stupid urge to help her. He watched APD's newest recruit cross the parking lot. Hodges stopped beside the unmarked Taurus, looking none too happy to see him.

"Thought you were on the Goodwin case."

"Waiting on labs," Nathan said. "Figured I'd give you a hand this morning."

They got in the Taurus, and Hodges didn't say anything as they pulled out of the lot.

"Take Lamar to Ranch Road 2222," Nathan advised. "You'll miss the traffic on Loop 1."

Hodges didn't comment, but followed the instructions. The tension in the car was thick, and Nathan was getting some definite hostility.

"You and Webb got a list of suspects yet?" Nathan asked.

A microscopic nod.

"You want to tell me who's on it?"

Hodges reached into the back and retrieved a brown accordion file from the floor. Nathan opened it. Under a tab labeled POI, he found a thick sheaf of papers. Nathan combed through. The Persons of Interest included two middle-aged males who had been arrested for armed robbery in various local parks. Also included were three women: the most recent Mrs. Alvin, Courtney Glass, and Alvin's ex-wife, who had gotten royally screwed in their divorce.

"You guys thinking murder for hire?" Nathan asked, examining the ex-wife's driver's license photo. With the exception of a ten-year-old DUI, she'd never been in trouble with the law.

"Don't know," Hodges said.

Nathan skimmed the info on Courtney. He felt the weight of Hodges's gaze on him as he reached the last page.

"Funny, you didn't mention her arrest back in January," Hodges said.

"Jail supervisor released her just after she came in. There's no paperwork. How'd you find out about this?"

"Lopez told me."

Nathan nodded. Lopez had been one of the beat cops patrolling Austin's bar district when an extremely intoxicated Courtney took a hammer and a can of spray paint to Alvin's red Porsche Carrera.

"Don't pull that crap again," Hodges said. "You got something relevant to this case, you tell me."

Nathan closed the file. The kid was right. And once again, Nathan regretted calling in favors to get Fiona's sister off the hook. At the time, he'd thought he was doing a good deed for a mixed-up young woman and a personal favor for Fiona, who had gone the extra mile for him more times than he could count. And since Alvin had wanted everything kept quiet, it had been a relatively easy favor to pull off.

He should have known it would come back to bite him in the ass.

"You're right, I should've said something," Nathan admitted. "And I see where you're going with this, but I gotta tell you, I don't think she did it."

Hodges kept his eyes on the road. "Either way, it's relevant. If you're boning her sister, I don't want to know about it, but don't hold out on me again."

Nathan shook his head. "I'm not boning her sister. Hell, I'm the best man in her wedding next month. You should be worried about yourself, not me. That woman's manipulative. She's also volatile, and she lies like a rug."

"But you don't think she did it."

"That's right," Nathan said. "I understand you need to

look at her, but don't waste all your time there. There's more to this thing than a mugging or a pissed-off ex-girlfriend."

Hodges clenched his jaw but stayed silent. He didn't seem to like getting advice, but Nathan didn't much care. This was an important case, and he didn't want it fucked up.

Ranch Road 2222 snaked through the hills of west Austin. The hot, hazy morning promised a sweat-drenched afternoon, and here they were, dressed for the occasion in dark suits so they wouldn't stand out among the mourners.

"This thing's gonna be a Who's Who of big Democrats," Nathan said, moving on to an easier subject. "Alvin was a hot-shot plaintiff's attorney. Won a hundred-million-dollar lawsuit against a tractor company about two years ago. This winter he won another sixty mil in some pharmaceutical case. Wife's family is in the meat-processing business. They call her the Weenie Queenie."

Hodges shot him a look.

"I kid you not. Woman's worth a fortune."

Hodges turned left at a light, indicating that he hadn't needed Nathan's directions to find the church.

Alvin and his wife were members of a small Episcopal congregation in Lakeway. Once upon a time, the town had been a haven for retirees who liked to play golf, but Austin's recent population boom had expanded the city boundaries, and Lakeway was now practically a suburb. Many of the houses there were expensive custom-built mansions with views of Lake Travis. Alvin's home had been purchased after his big windfall two years ago, and the most recent appraisal put the property at $3.5 million.

Hodges pulled into a parking lot surrounded by white

crepe myrtles. The funeral didn't begin for another half hour, but the lot had started to fill up. So far, the cars were a mix of Lexuses, BMWs, and suped-up SUVs. The gray Taurus would stick out, and Hodges had the sense to park it in the shade of a tree where it would be less noticeable. From their vantage point, they had an unobstructed view of people filing into the church.

Hodges retrieved the accordion file from the floor at Nathan's feet.

"See that man right there?"

Hodges glanced up. "Gray suit?"

"Yeah. He's the CEO of FireBreaker, that big software company."

"Security software?"

"That's the one," Nathan said. "And that blonde in the dark blue? She's a litigator with Wilkers and Riley, Alvin's firm."

Nathan's gaze lingered on the attorney. She probably played well in front of any jury that included red-blooded men.

But Hodges was too busy scanning the area to admire her. So far, this guy was an ice man. The only thing he'd reacted to so far, really, was being cut out of a piece of information.

"Who's the guy in the seersucker suit?" he asked.

Nathan followed his gaze. "No idea."

"And the short guy near the door?"

"Don't recognize him."

"What about the woman in red? Three o'clock."

Nathan looked over. "Well, what do you know? It's Alvin's ex."

The forty-one-year-old barely resembled her driver's license photo. She had short dark hair. She wore a neatly tailored red suit and low-heeled shoes. Everything about her looked understated, except the color she'd chosen, which seemed to broadcast her feelings about the deceased. A teenager shuffled along beside her in khaki pants and an ill-fitting navy blazer.

"Doesn't look like she's grieving much," Hodges observed.

"Ah, you wouldn't expect her to. She supported him all through law school teaching kindergarten. Then he dumped her flat when he landed a job at Wilkers and Riley."

"Traded her in for the hot-dog heiress?"

"Nah, she came later."

"So that's Alvin's first kid." Hodges glanced at the file. "According to the will, he'll inherit ten million dollars on his twenty-fifth birthday."

Nathan whistled. "Wow."

"Yep."

He turned to Hodges, impressed. "You got a warrant for the will?"

"Executor of the estate filed it the day after the murder. It's a public record."

"Usually takes longer to get the probate wheels turning," Nathan said. "Guess someone's in a hurry to divvy up that money."

"Ex-wife's the trustee on the kid's funds until he hits twenty-five."

Nathan considered the possibility.

"Who's that?"

He followed Hodge's gaze up the sidewalk. A tall guy

with a trim build and a shock of white hair stood at the door glad-handing people as they filed in.

"That's Jim Wilkers," Nathan said. "Founding partner at Alvin's firm."

"He doesn't look too broken up."

"Nope. Fact, doesn't look like anybody's doing much grieving."

At last the hearse pulled up to the church. A black limousine rolled to a stop just behind it. Several men in dark suits got out, followed by a petite woman in a slim-fitting black dress. Hodges had met her Monday when he and Webb had performed the miserable duty of informing her that her husband was dead.

A little girl clambered out of the car. She wore a lavender dress and white shoes. She had the same golden hair as her mother, only hers was natural.

"You meet Mackenzie yet?" Nathan asked.

"No."

"She's his only other child, that we know of," Nathan said, watching the four-year-old cling to her mother's leg. "And I'll never understand why rich people name their kids after consulting firms."

Hodges's attention was focused on the side mirror. Nathan checked the one on his side and noticed the white hatchback parked on the other end of the lot. It was under a tree, just like the Taurus.

"Know who that is?" Hodges asked.

Nathan studied the driver's silhouette. It appeared to be a woman with short-cropped hair and sunglasses. She didn't seem in a hurry to go into the church.

"Nope."

"Can you read the tag?" Hodges asked.

"Not from this distance. We can get it on the way out."

The hearse was open now, and a casket was being removed from the back by half a dozen men who ranged in age from thirty to sixty. Nathan recognized a local judge, but the other pallbearers weren't familiar. Their names had been in the paper, though, and Hodges could add the obit to the file, if he hadn't already.

The young detective's phone buzzed, and he jerked it from his pocket. Nathan waited, learning virtually nothing from this end of the conversation. Hodges had a talent for keeping things to himself.

Finally he ended the call and tucked the phone away. "That was Webb."

"Yeah?"

"A jogger stumbled across our murder weapon at Zilker Park."

Six months without a sip of alcohol, and now Courtney had had three vodka cranberries in five days. She didn't need to keep track, really, but it had become a habit. One of the defining goals of her life was to avoid ending up like her mother.

"Another Cape Cod?"

The bartender flashed her a smile and nodded at the empty glass.

"No, thanks." She returned the smile, but stopped just short of flirting. She wasn't in the mood right now, and her head was killing her.

Where the hell was Jordan?

When her friend had asked her out for drinks and tapas at Emilio's, Courtney had initially said no. But Jordan kept repeating the invitation, and Courtney knew it was hopeless. Jordan was determined to take her out for her birthday, and Courtney was tired of being at home. She hadn't slept well all week, and the unending nights alone were starting to make her crazy.

Courtney heard a few bars of Gwen Stefani and pulled her cell from her purse. The sleek flip phone was a recent purchase, a little early birthday present to perk her up after an extremely crappy week.

"Omigod, I'm *so* sorry!" Jordan's voice filled her ear.

"Where are you?"

"Have you been there long?"

"Almost an hour," Courtney said. "I'm on my third bowl of olives."

"Briana made me stay and do inventory!" Jordan wailed. "I'm going to be here all *night*. Did you know we were changing lines?"

"I heard this morning."

Briana, the salon owner, had recently decided to switch product lines after the main one they stocked began appearing in grocery stores. Bella Donna was nothing if not exclusive. Courtney had seen the floor-to-ceiling boxes in her boss's office this afternoon and was grateful she hadn't gotten stuck there with Jordan.

"You need a hand?" she asked anyway. She couldn't stand the thought of going back to her empty house. In the past four nights, Courtney had organized every closet and cabinet in her tiny home. She'd caulked her shower. She'd given herself facials. She was fresh out of projects, and if she watched one more minute of reality television, she was going to need a padded cell.

"Absolutely not," Jordan said. "*No* one should have to spend their Thursday evening this way. It's cruel and unusual punishment. We're supposed to be celebrating!"

"Don't worry about it," Courtney said. "My real birthday's not until next week, anyway." She motioned the bartender to bring her check as Jordan ranted about their boss. After voicing her sympathy, Courtney managed to get off the phone.

"My birthday's next week, too."

She glanced over. The guy beside her had been eyeing her for fifteen minutes and evidently thought he'd found an opening.

"Oh, yeah?" She smiled at him, trying to guesstimate how much gel he must have used to get his hair to look like an otter's. He had his BMW key chain in plain view on the bar, and she deducted points for cheesiness. "So you're a Sagittarius? Or a Capricorn?"

His looked confused for a second. "Uh, Capricorn."

Of course. She fished a twenty from her purse and slid it under her glass.

"And what about you?" He smiled and leaned closer. "What's your sign?"

She shouldered her bag and slid off the stool. "Do not disturb."

"Hey, wait." Beamer Man was determined. "Let me buy you another round."

"No, thanks."

"Come on, it's your birthday."

"No. Thank you." She turned away and nearly smacked into a big, broad chest.

"You're leaving." Will Hodges gazed down at her with those whiskey brown eyes.

"Trying to."

He sent a very scary look over her head at the guy with the otter hair.

"Come on." He took her elbow. "I'll give you a ride."

Before she could respond, he steered her through the crowd and pulled open the heavy wooden door. They stepped out of the noisy bar into the damp August night.

"What are you doing here?" she asked, supremely aware of his hand on her arm.

"Looking for you."

"Yes, but why?"

"I need to talk to you."

Her feet moved down the sidewalk, and she started to get uneasy. How had he known she was here? And was she being arrested? Taken in for more questioning? Her relief at seeing him turned to nerves.

"So talk." She pulled her arm away and pivoted to face him. He wore a dark suit and a stern expression. He rested his hands on his hips, and she noticed the butt of his gun poking out from the jacket.

"You changed your hair."

"Very good, Detective," she said, crossing her arms. She'd abandoned ebony with scarlet highlights in favor of a cool claret. She'd needed a change. Jordan had given her a trim, too, freshening up her long layers. "So what did you want to talk about? Besides my hair?"

He glanced up and down the sidewalk. "Not here."

"Fine. Let's go back inside." Anywhere but the police station. She hated that place. She'd been there twice in the past six months, and just the thought of returning made her queasy.

He reached over and opened the door of an ancient Chevy Suburban. "Get in. I'll drive you home."

"This is your car?"

He nodded.

She pursed her lips and looked it over. The tan truck had three dings on the passenger's side alone. It was rare to meet someone who drove a car older than hers.

She got in, marveling at the cracked vinyl seats. Will obviously wasn't a man who used cars to impress women, and she felt strangely grateful.

"Watch your feet." The door squeaked as he pushed it shut.

She smoothed her hair and tugged at her hemline as he went around to the driver's side. The black halter dress had seemed perfect for hanging out at Emilio's with Jordan, but now Courtney felt too exposed. She was getting goose bumps up and down her arms, and it wasn't the slightest bit cool out.

Maybe it was Will. He radiated testosterone, and she'd been going through withdrawal. Every time he came near her, her senses went on alert.

Will got behind the wheel and fired up the truck with surprisingly little trouble.

"How did you know I was here?" she asked him.

"Your sister told me."

So he'd been talking to Fiona. She didn't know if this was good or bad. Fiona had left a message on her cell phone about an hour ago, and Courtney wished now she'd taken the time to listen to it.

"How'd you know I needed a ride?"

"You don't have a car."

This was true, but she could have rented one. Had he been checking up on her?

Of course he had. He was an investigator. She was part of his case. Courtney folded her hands in her lap and struggled not to fidget. She sensed the interrogation coming and tried to steel herself.

"What did you do today?" he asked, pulling into traffic.

"I worked."

"What else?" He slid a glance at her legs, and she felt a hint of satisfaction knowing this big Robocop was actually human.

"Some chores around the house." She pulled her purse into her lap and rooted around for a lip gloss.

"What else?"

She looked at him. His gaze was fixed on the road now, and she had a chance to study his profile. He had a strong, square jaw and a straight nose. His neck was thick, and his arms strained the fabric of his jacket as he steered the Suburban. This man was very big and very intimidating, although it wasn't his size that made her uncomfortable.

"That's about it." She flipped down the visor. No mirror, of course, so she glossed her lips without one. She'd gone with pouty lips tonight, which required maintenance, and dramatic, smoky eyes. It was her go-to evening look.

They stopped at an intersection, and he glanced at her. His gaze strayed down to her mouth.

"What?" She dropped the tube back into her purse.

"I'm trying to figure out why you're lying."

"I'm not lying. And what the hell business is it of yours how I spent my day?"

"You were at Alvin's funeral," he said. "I saw you."

She tossed her purse on the floor and looked straight ahead. "Light's green."

Then they were moving again. They cruised down the street in his hulking Suburban, and she tried to pinpoint how he'd spotted her. She'd spent *hours* getting ready. Her wig was fabulous. Her own sister would have had trouble recognizing her.

"Why are you lying to me?" He glanced at her.

"Who says I'm lying?"

He shook his head slightly. Her stomach tightened, and she felt fear bubbling up. He could see through her. He could see everything. Somehow he knew what had really happened, and she was going to go to jail.

"Just be honest, okay? You'll be doing yourself a favor."

She bit her lip, contemplating the possibility. *Just be honest.* Easy for him to say. He wasn't under suspicion of murder. He hadn't been targeted by a killer. He wasn't spending his nights going room to room in a tiny duplex, switching on lamps and listening for prowlers.

"So I was there. So what? It's a free country." She crossed her arms and dared him to challenge her. Going to someone's funeral wasn't a felony.

"The question is, *why* were you there? And why the *Alias* costume?"

She didn't want to look at him. "Several reasons."

He waited, and the only sound was the rumble of the old engine.

"I wanted to see his daughter," she said.

This was the truth, but she felt weird saying it. Why should she have any interest in some little girl she'd never met? A little girl whose family she'd nearly wrecked by having an affair with her self-absorbed father?

"You wanted to see Mackenzie Alvin."

"Yes."

"Why?"

This was the weird part. "I don't know." She shrugged. "I just feel, I don't know, connected with her or something."

He glanced at her. "Connected how?"

"My dad died when I was little. I guess I just empathize with her." She sighed and folded her hands in her lap. "But she looked good. I watched her mom with her, and I feel better now. I think she's going to be okay."

Unlike Courtney had been. And Fiona. When their dad had died, their mom had pretty much gone to pieces. She'd jerked her kids out of school, moved off to California to "get a fresh start," and then proceeded to go from man to man, looking for the next love of her life. When she wasn't on the hunt for a guy, she was consoling herself with alcohol while Fiona tried to raise a kid sister. Fiona was only a few years older than Courtney, but she'd been a mother to her most of her life.

It had taken more than twenty years and a cross-country move for Fiona and Courtney to get away from the mess their mom had made of their lives following their father's death.

But Mackenzie's mother seemed to have her act together. And she had money, too, which would help. At least she wouldn't be desperately seeking a husband to help support her.

Courtney glanced over at Will. He was staring at the road again. Maybe he thought she was full of crap.

"Why else?" he asked.

"Why what?"

"You said 'several' reasons."

She looked out the window. Familiar houses flew by, and they were almost to her street. If she made up a lie, she could be finished with this conversation in a matter of minutes. If she made it a *believable* lie, he might just leave her alone for a few days.

Before he hauled her back in for more questions. She tugged at her hemline again and cleared her throat. "I thought I might see him," she said, going with the truth.

"See who?"

"The man who attacked us. I thought he might be there."

He pulled up to the curb just in front of her house. Amy's white Hyundai sat in the driveway, and Courtney realized how Will had recognized her at the funeral. It had been there Monday, too, and he was observant.

Parked behind the Hyundai was the pickup belonging to Amy's boyfriend, and Courtney guessed they'd kissed and made up after the argument she'd overheard earlier this evening. That was the thing about living in a duplex—you were in your neighbors' business whether you wanted to be or not.

"Why would he come to the funeral, Courtney?"

She brought her gaze back to Will. He seemed to be searching her face for answers. He knew she was hiding something.

"It wasn't a random robbery, was it?"

"I don't think so," she said.

It hadn't been a robbery at all. The ski-mask guy had tried to kill David and make it look like a murder-suicide. Someone wanted them both dead, and Courtney blamed for it. She'd been racking her brain for days trying to come up with a plausible reason.

"And did you see him at the funeral?"

She shook her head. "I don't think so. I would have recognized his body and his eyes. At least, I think I would have. No one even looked close."

Will stared out the windshield, drumming his thumb on the steering wheel. He seemed deep in thought. Abruptly, he cut the engine and got out of the truck to come around to her side.

She was home. Another night alone. She was so wide-awake, it felt as if she'd spent the evening at a coffee shop instead of a bar.

The door squealed open, and she got out.

"Thanks for the lift," she said, as he slammed the door. He stood there, staring down at her, and she got the impression he wanted to read her thoughts. Was he trying to solve his case, or was it something else? His face gave nothing away until the brief instant when his gaze dropped to her mouth.

An impulse came over her. Maybe it was the vodka. Or the summer air. Or the girl in the lavender dress who reminded her how lonely she'd been as a kid.

Maybe it was lust.

Whatever it was, she gave in to it. She went up on her tiptoes and kissed him. He stood there, ramrod straight, holding her waist but not kissing her back, while she moved her mouth softly against his. She was getting to him, she knew. She could feel it in his tense response, in the tightness of his stubbled jaw under her fingertips. And then it wasn't the vodka making her mind swim, but the heady realization that she had an effect on this giant man. She licked the corner of his mouth, and his control broke, like she'd known it would. And then she was up, off her feet, kissing him, and he was kissing her back, as he gripped her hips and pressed her against the truck. His mouth felt hot and powerful, and he tasted faintly of peppermint.

Suddenly he stepped back, and her feet slid to the ground. She blinked up at him. His big chest heaved up and down.

"Come inside," she whispered.

He wanted to. Desire was written all over his face.

But then he seemed to shake it off. Just like that, his eyes went cool.

"I can't," he said.

She smiled up at him, that warm, coy smile she'd known for ages but hadn't practiced lately.

He looked away. "I'll walk you to the door."

"You don't have to."

Anger flashed in his eyes. "I will." He took her elbow and propelled her up the path, like a disobedient child on her way to time out.

"You don't need to *walk* me," she said, feeling pissy now. It was easier than feeling hurt.

"I need to get you in safely."

They reached the door and she plucked her keys from her purse. She unlocked the door, gritting her teeth while she did it because she could feel him next to her, this massive presence that didn't need to be there. She buried her temper and turned to him with a big smile.

She reached up to wipe the lipstick off his lower lip. He flinched at her touch, and she knew he was going to have a rough night. Good. She wouldn't be the only one. "Night, Detective," she purred. "Sleep tight."

She stepped into the house and pulled the door shut behind her.


He'd kissed his suspect.

And not just kissed—he'd come about five seconds away from dragging her off to bed.

Five years he'd worked to become a homicide detective. Now here it was, the first lap out of the gate, and he'd nearly fucked it up.

She was a suspect. He knew in his gut she didn't do it, but he was definitely in the minority with that opinion. Cernak was convinced she'd pulled the trigger, and he'd made it clear he expected Will to coax a confession out of her. But Will couldn't bring himself to coax because—despite the lies—he was 99.9 percent certain she was innocent.

But maybe he was wrong. Maybe the mere thought of having sex with a woman as hot as Courtney Glass was short-circuiting his brain.

No.

He'd been there the night of the biscuit dough. He'd listened to the 911 call. He'd seen her that afternoon at the park. She'd been truly, deathly afraid. She may have lied about how it went down—actually, he knew she had—but that didn't mean she'd killed the guy. He was close to certain she'd been one of two intended victims. He just needed to gather the evidence to exonerate her and figure out who was behind it all.

Then he could kiss her all he wanted. And drag her off to bed, too.

Christ, he was screwed up. Why had he allowed himself to be alone so long? Lifting weights was great, but there was only so much frustration he could work off at a gym. At some point, soon, he needed a good, soft woman.

Not that Courtney was good. Or soft. She'd probably hand a guy his nuts on a platter if he messed with her. Will couldn't visualize her as Alvin's trophy girlfriend, but he had no trouble at all imagining her trashing his Porsche.

He pulled into a parking space at his low-rise apartment complex on the south side of town. The building was generic. His one-bedroom unit was generic. His cheap furniture was generic. And he didn't really give a damn because for the past five years even the most mediocre accommodations, by American standards, had seemed like the Ritz to him. That's what three years of sleeping on the hard ground did to a person. Three years of dust, and cold, and trekking through the mountains, hunting men and being hunted. Three years of camping out among villagers who drank from the same irrigation ditches where they bathed, and washed dishes, and butchered meat.

He parked and made his way up the metal flight of stairs to his place. On his doorstep was a package, and he stooped to pick it up, instantly suspicious.

Cookies. Chocolate chip, from what he could see through the light blue Tupperware. Another luxury not common in Afghanistan.

He let himself into the apartment and tossed his keys on the table by the door. He threw the bolt. In the kitchen he saw the flashing message light of his answering machine. He pressed the button to listen while he opened the lid to the Tupperware and read the note tucked inside.

*Thanks! XOXO Lori.*

Mystery solved. The woman whose new TV he'd hauled up the stairs had made him cookies.

A telemarketer droned into the phone as Will pondered this new development. Lori from next door was single. Pretty. A little short for him, but big deal. He chomped into a cookie. She was a decent cook and had a brand-new HDTV with surround sound. What was he doing messing around with his suspect? It was beyond dumb.

He deleted the second telemarketer and condemned to hell whichever utility company had given out his number, which should have been unlisted. Nathan's voice came on, and Will stopped chewing.

"Hodges. Where are you? Your cell phone keeps kicking me to voice mail. Ballistics just came back and—"

Will pressed Callback. Nathan picked up immediately.

"Shit, man. The phone stays *on*. How am I supposed to reach you—"

"Tell me about the ballistics."

"We got a match. The Beretta and the slug."

They had their murder weapon. This was real progress.

"That's not all," Nathan said tightly.

"What else?"

"The weapon's registered to Courtney Glass."

# CHAPTER

# 4

Courtney was late.

She twisted her hair into a quick bun, secured it with a pair of black chopsticks, and checked her watch: 8:31. She glanced at the laptop computer on her unmade bed. According to the bus schedule she'd looked up, she had four minutes to get to the corner before the 10/20 made its next stop. If she missed it, she'd have to wait half an hour for the next one.

Where were her shoes? She scanned the bedroom for her strappy black sandals but didn't see them. She spotted her red ones beside the closet and opted for those instead. Not the best match with a black-and-white Japanese print skirt, but maybe it would look like she was going for contrast. She threw a red lipstick into her handbag and headed for the door.

As she locked up, her gaze darted over to Amy's side of the front porch. Amy hadn't been home yesterday when Courtney returned the car, and the keys still were sitting in the flowerpot where Courtney had left them. She'd spied the keys sitting there last night, too, when she'd left to meet Jordan, but she hadn't wanted to interrupt the lovers' quarrel going on next door.

Courtney checked her watch. Three minutes. She

stomped across the porch, scooped the keys out of the pot, and rang the doorbell.

Devon answered.

"What happened to you?" she asked, gaping at the bruise under his eye.

"Nothing." He glanced furtively over his shoulder. Courtney stood there, unable to move. Maybe he'd been in a fight at school. But why wouldn't he just say that?

"Is your mom home?"

"Who's there?" a male voice called from the back of the house.

Devon met her gaze, and she read the look on his face. She grabbed his hand.

"Come here," she said, pulling him onto the porch and tugging the door shut behind him. She quickly unlocked her front door and nudged him inside.

"Sit," she said, pointing to the armchair.

Courtney closed the door. Devon sat down and stared at his feet. He wore a T-shirt and sweatpants, which Courtney guessed constituted his sleepwear.

"Devon!" The male voice came through the wall beside them.

"Did he do that to you?" she asked.

Devon glanced up at her, then down at his feet again.

Courtney clenched her teeth. She made a valiant effort not to curse. Instead, she jerked her cell phone out of her purse and switched on the camera setting.

"Look up." He did, and she snapped a picture. "Now lock this door behind me. And don't open it again unless it's me or your mom."

He looked confused, but he nodded. She stepped outside

and listened for the *click* of her bolt. Then she descended the front steps while dialing 911. She approached the pickup at the end of the driveway and looked at the license plate. It was splattered with mud, just like the sides of the truck and the chrome running boards.

"I'm at 925 Oak Trail," she told the operator. "I need a police officer."

"What's the nature of your emergency?"

Courtney leaned over to wipe the dirt off the plate. She wasn't sure whether the camera feature worked during a phone conversation. *Snap.* Apparently, it did.

"A domestic disturbance," she said. "I need someone right now."

"Could you describe the disturbance?"

The front door swung open, and Courtney glanced up. "He's about five-ten. Buzz cut. Acne scars."

Amy's boyfriend barreled across the lawn wearing only blue jeans. "Hey! What're you doing?"

"That's 925 Oak Trail. Please hurry." She dropped the phone in her purse but kept the line open.

"Morning," she said to him, trying to remember his name.

"What are you doing to my truck?" He stopped in front of her and plunked his hands on his hips. Courtney's heels put her slightly above eye level with him.

"I'm just admiring it," she said. "I'm thinking of getting one."

"You took a picture of it!"

"Yes. I really like those tires. Very impressive."

He frowned down at the massive mudders.

"I've got this theory about men with big tires," she said. "I'll have to run it by Amy, see what she thinks."

He eyed her suspiciously. "Where's Devon?"

Courtney gazed down the empty street. No police car. No siren. Not one *single* cop at the Dunkin' Donuts on the corner, which had to be a first. Courtney's heart started to palpitate.

"I sent him out for doughnut holes," she said, smiling. "I'm sure he'll get you one."

His gaze zeroed in on her purse. "Hand over the camera."

She inched back. "It's not a camera."

"That phone thingie. I know what you're up to."

He reached for her bag, and she lurched backward. He thrust his arm out and jerked the purse right off her shoulder.

"Hey!" She made a grab for it, but he held her off with an elbow as he rummaged through. Her stuff rained down: sunglasses, lipsticks, a suede pouch containing an eight-hundred-dollar pair of scissors.

"Hands *off!* That's my property!" She grabbed the bag and tried to wrestle it away, and the next instant she landed hard on her butt in the middle of the street. Shock paralyzed her for a moment, but then she jumped to her feet. A gray sedan screeched to a stop in front of her house. Cops. *Finally.*

Will Hodges got out of the car, and Courtney stalked up to him. "Arrest this man! He assaulted me *and* my neighbor! And he stole my purse!"

"Bullshit!"

Will shot an icy look at Amy's boyfriend. The idiot was standing there holding Courtney's bag.

"Up against the car," Will ordered.

The boyfriend scowled. "Who the hell are you?"

Will whipped out his ID, and Courtney took the opportunity to snatch back her purse. She started picking up her things.

Will turned to her. "In the car."

"*What?*"

"In the car. Now. Or I'm going to arrest you."

"*Me?* What about *him?*"

Will turned his back on her. "Hands on the roof. Feet apart."

Amy's boyfriend looked like he knew the drill. "This is bullshit, man! She was vandalizing my truck!"

Will glowered at Courtney and pulled open the sedan's back door. "Don't make me tell you again."

She slid into the backseat. Her hands shook with outrage as she rummaged through her purse and clicked off her phone. Arrest *her*. What a joke. A siren sounded faintly in the distance and grew louder as Will frisked and cuffed the boyfriend. Courtney peered out the window and saw Amy and Devon standing on the porch, watching. Amy said something to her son, and he disappeared into the house. Then she made her way down the sidewalk, clutching the lapels of her terry-cloth robe together.

Courtney tried to open the door, but it was locked. Will must have heard her, because he shot her a warning look. Unbelievable.

Through the tinted window, she watched the two uniformed cops exchange words with the couple. Amy looked worried, but Courtney doubted it was because of Devon. More likely, she didn't want her boyfriend going downtown.

Courtney watched Will's back. She thought about those broad shoulders and how they'd felt under her hands last night. And she thought about how unlikely it was that the 911 operator would dispatch a homicide detective to a domestic disturbance. He'd been on his way over. Courtney's heart rate took another leap.

Finally, the officers led the boyfriend to the police car while Amy looked on, wringing her hands. One of the cops returned to Amy with a clipboard and pen.

Will slid behind the wheel of the Taurus.

"What's happening?" she demanded.

He started the engine without a word.

"Will? What's going on?"

He turned to face her and shook his head. "Are you *trying* to get arrested?"

Her jaw dropped.

"Do yourself a favor. Don't talk until we get to the station."

"You're taking *me* in?"

Instead of answering, he thrust the car in gear.

"Will? What the hell? That guy assaulted me, *and* Devon, and probably his mom, too!"

The car lurched forward as he met her gaze in the rearview mirror. "So what, the guy's dangerous, so you decide to pick a fight with him?"

"I didn't pick a fight! He stole my purse and knocked me down!"

He shook his head and muttered something.

"What?"

"Jesus, put a lid on it, would you?"

Courtney crossed her arms and glared at him in the mirror. "This is messed up, you know that? Our whole freaking legal system is pathetic."

He glared back at her but didn't say anything.

"I'm going to file harassment charges. Against APD."

He didn't respond.

"You'll be named first in the lawsuit."

"Courtney."

"What?"

"You've got enough trouble already. Do yourself a favor and just *stop talking*."

Will didn't get this girl. She was smack-dab in the middle of a homicide investigation, and yet all she could talk about was her neighbor's boyfriend.

"I said I'd see to it," Will told her as he ushered her into the interview room. He pulled out a chair for her, but she didn't sit.

"I mean it." She pointed a shiny red fingernail at his chest. "This better not fall through the cracks. If I see that dickhead around my house again, I'm calling the cops."

"I am the cops."

She muttered something that was probably an insult and sank her butt into the chair. Finally.

"I've got evidence," she went on. "I've got pictures, and you guys damn sure better do something with them."

Will flattened his palm on the table and gazed down at her. "Has it occurred to you that I didn't bring you here to talk about your neighbor? You're here about Alvin."

Her expression changed, but she pretended to shrug it off. "What do you want to know? I've already told you everything I remember."

Nathan was right. She lied like a rug. She'd been lying to him from the moment she first opened her mouth until she'd kissed him last night. And she was still doing it.

"I'm required to remind you that you can choose to have a lawyer present."

She crossed her legs and tipped her head to the side. "I'm not a big fan of lawyers."

"I'm *advising* you of your right to an attorney."

"Look," she said, glancing at her watch. "You've already made me late for work. Can we speed this along?"

He pulled out his tape recorder, activated it, and plunked it on the table. "Fine."

The door opened, and Cernak strolled in. Perfect. Will's new boss had been watching the interview on closed-circuit television. He'd probably just about had a heart attack watching Will encourage their suspect to lawyer up.

"Lieutenant Don Cernak," he said, reaching for Courtney's hand.

She took it. "Courtney Glass," she said coolly.

Cernak settled into a chair across from her and looked at Will. "Don't let me interrupt."

Will cleared his throat. "Miss Glass, I have a few more questions related to our investigation."

She raised her eyebrow at the formal tone. "Ask away, Detective."

"Have you ever owned a gun?"

"Yes."

"And when did you purchase it?"

Her ankle started to bounce. "I don't remember exactly."

"Try to estimate."

More bouncing. "Last summer, maybe? August, I think."

"Where did you purchase the weapon?"

"A sporting goods store off I-35. I forget the name."

He eyed her ankle, and she stopped moving it.

"And what kind of gun is it?"

"I don't remember."

"Shotgun? Handgun? Rifle?"

She hesitated a beat. "Handgun."

"What type of handgun?"

Her attention moved from Will to Cernak. "I don't remember."

"You don't remember?" Cernak asked, incredulous.

Courtney looked at Will. Then she glanced at the video camera behind him. Her breathing was shallow, and she seemed to be making an effort not to chew her lip.

"Miss Glass?" Cernak leaned forward on his elbows. "You don't remember what type of gun you bought? Are you sure?"

She leaned back in her chair. Her gaze shifted to Will.

"I've changed my mind," she said. "I want to talk to a lawyer."

Apparently if you had a bad suit and a law degree, you could charge five hundred dollars to say *this interview is over*.

After a ten-minute meeting in a supposedly private room, and after Courtney had written a check that she prayed wouldn't bounce, Ross Ackerman had delivered this simple message on her behalf to a stony-faced Lieutenant Cernak.

The two men had traded a few snippets of legalese, and then Ackerman had escorted Courtney out of the dimly lit police station into the blindingly bright sunlight.

They stood on the sidewalk now, facing each other.

"I'm late for court," he said, checking his chunky plastic

Ironman watch. Courtney had picked Ackerman's name out of a grimy phone book, and even though his receptionist had called him "fast" and "affordable," Courtney had waited nearly two hours for him to show up. Two nerve-racking hours.

"I'll be busy all day." He reached into his front suit pocket and pulled out a business card. "But let's talk again tonight. Maybe five-thirty? I need to hear about your case."

Courtney took the card he offered and looked him over. She put him at forty. He had male pattern baldness, but what he lacked hair-wise, he made up for with a trim build and a decent manicure.

"Is Ackerman your real name?" she asked, squinting at him under the broiling sun.

"Why?"

"It just seems really convenient. You know, in the phone book."

He smiled. "I thought about going with 'Aardvark' but my wife put her foot down."

Courtney tucked the card into her purse. He was truthful, and he was a family man. She could put up with his fashion limitations.

"I get off at six," she said, as a familiar white Honda rolled up to the curb.

"Let's meet then at my office." He reached out his hand. "Nice meeting you, Miss Glass. I look forward to helping you."

After he walked away, Courtney slid into the passenger seat of Fiona's car.

"Who was that?" her sister asked, watching him go in the rearview mirror.

"My attorney."

Fiona shot her a look. "You need a real attorney."

"He's affordable," Courtney said, unzipping her purse. She rooted around for a Slim Fast bar but had to settle for a piece of Trident.

Fiona pulled away from the curb. "Forget affordable; you need effective. I'll lend you the money. Where are we going?"

"The salon."

Her sister gaped at her. "You're going to *work?*"

"I've already lost half my morning. I can't afford to get fired."

Fiona shook her head as she pulled up to a stoplight. "You seem to be missing this. You're in *real* trouble, Court. They recovered your gun."

"Who told you that?" Courtney's heart started to race. Hearing her sister say it made it feel all the more real.

"Nathan. How did your gun end up near a homicide scene in Zilker Park?"

"What else did he say?"

"He said it's not looking good for you. He said the slug matches your Beretta, and they found gunshot residue on your fingers."

Courtney could see the strain in her sister's face. She was worried. And in typical Fiona fashion, she was trying to hide it under a matter-of-fact demeanor. "What else did he tell you?"

"That was pretty much it. What's going on, Courtney?"

"What's it look like? I was set up." She rubbed her temples, trying to rub away the headache. She didn't really want to play twenty questions with Fiona right now.

"I don't understand."

"Yeah, welcome to the club," she snapped. "I don't understand, either."

"Why would someone set you up?"

"How do I know?"

"And how'd they get your gun?"

"I have no idea. It was in my nightstand."

"Was your house broken into?"

Courtney sighed. "I don't know. I mean, it *was*, obviously. But I didn't realize it until after the murder."

Fiona gave Courtney a doubtful look. "This seems far-fetched."

"Far-*fetched*? What, you don't believe me?"

"That's not what I meant. It just . . . I mean, I'm just saying. It sounds so improbable."

A knot formed in Courtney's chest—all the fear and nerves and anxiety of the past few days tangled together. "Believe what you want."

"I didn't say I didn't believe you. I just—"

"What else did Nathan say?"

"Not much."

Courtney catalogued her problems. They had her gun. And her prints. And the gunshot residue on her fingers. Not to mention some witness who claimed to have seen her arguing in her car with David just before his death.

But someone else had been there. There had to be evidence of him. There had to be DNA, fibers, *something*.

"That was it?" Courtney asked. "That's all he told you?"

"That was it, but . . ."

"But what?"

Fiona hung a left onto the upscale shopping strip where Bella Donna was located.

"Spill it, Fiona. I need to know!"

"It's just that they must have something else. To back you up. Otherwise, you'd be under arrest right now."

Tears sprang into Courtney's eyes. They had something, something that supported her story. It was such a relief, she wanted to cry.

Instead, she gazed out the window as Fiona's car rolled to a stop.

"Courtney."

She turned to face her sister.

"You need to tell me what happened."

"I told you what happened."

"You didn't tell me about the gun."

Courtney glanced away. She hadn't been able to tell her. She hadn't been able to tell Will, either. It was too scary. It made the nightmare too real. Someone, somehow, had gotten hold of *her* gun and forced her to kill David with it.

It sounded surreal. It *felt* surreal. And yet it had happened, and Courtney had no idea why.

And now the police had irrefutable evidence that pointed to her.

She needed air. She pushed open the door.

"Courtney?"

"I'll call you after work."

"We have to discuss this! Do they know about Walter?"

Courtney's stomach clenched just hearing the name. "I have no idea," she told Fiona.

"Well, did you tell them?"

Courtney scoffed. "What do you think?"

"They're going to find out, you know."

And this, of course, was part of Fiona's stress. And Courtney's. Walter was one of the two main reasons Courtney had lied to the police. If some cop did enough digging, he'd find out Courtney had been investigated for murder once before. She'd never been arrested or charged, so it wasn't part of her record, but just the fact she'd been questioned in the suspicious death of her stepfather had to be in a file somewhere. A skilled investigator probably could track it down. Someone thorough and determined.

Someone like Will Hodges.

Courtney felt a rush of panic. "I can't deal with this right now."

"You're avoiding it."

Fiona the psychologist. Courtney didn't want to hear it.

She glanced at Bella Donna's ornate front door. She'd already missed two cuts and a color. And one of those appointments had been her best tipper.

"You need to talk to Jack," Fiona said. "He can help you."

"I'll think about it."

Fiona's fiancé was an ex-cop who now worked for the D.A.'s office, and he knew all about investigations and evidence and police procedure. He'd helped Courtney out of a few scrapes, just like Fiona and Nathan had. And each time, Courtney had felt like the messed-up kid sister who could never get her shit together.

"I'll handle it," she told Fiona now.

"Courtney, this is serious—"

"I know. That's why I hired an attorney."

Fiona gave her a "get-real" look, and Courtney knew she

needed to escape. She grabbed her purse and scooted out.

"Please don't go to work right now. We need to deal with this."

"I'm dealing with it," Courtney said with false confidence. "You can stop worrying."

Will's gaze scanned the array of cops seated around the conference table, all drinking stale coffee and hashing out theories in the Alvin homicide. Webb came across as competent, but overworked. Cernak was experienced, but he seemed more worried about the political ramifications of the case than anything else. And then there was Nathan Devereaux, who officially had been reassigned but who had logged more hours than Will running down leads in this case.

"It just doesn't fit," Devereaux said, stuck on the same point he'd been making all morning.

"It fits great," Webb countered. "Her boyfriend dumps her to go back to his moneybags wife. She gets jealous and takes the guy out. Maybe she planned on killing herself, too, and lost her nerve at the last minute."

"Their relationship ended six months ago," Devereaux said. "And anyway, she dumped *him*. And vandalized his car."

"That's *her* version," Cernak said pointedly. "We don't have Alvin's side, because there's no report."

Devereaux shook his head and stood up. He wandered to the window and shoved his hands in his pockets. Devereaux already had relayed what Alvin had told him that fateful night in January, and everything corroborated Courtney's version of the relationship. But Cernak didn't seem interested in anything that wouldn't withstand the sunshine test.

Will didn't blame him. If and when this thing ever went to trial, every detail would be scrutinized by the media, not to mention some defense attorney. That was why Will was most interested in the physical evidence.

He looked at Webb. "So explain the Mace. We've got traces of it all over the Buick's ceiling and the backseat upholstery."

"So she staged the scene," Webb answered. "Maybe she hired the hit, and then made it look like a holdup."

"And then planted her own gun?" Devereaux quipped from across the room.

"And what about the mucus?" Will added. "You're saying she planted that, too?"

Webb guzzled coffee from his Styrofoam cup while Cernak squinted at the dry-erase board where investigators had listed the physical evidence they had so far.

Traces of mucus had been found on the back floorboard of the car, as well as the back door handle. It would be great to run the DNA, see what popped up in the database. But DNA testing was costly and didn't typically happen until there was a suspect in custody to compare the sample against.

The mucus was key. It went a long way toward proving Courtney's statement that someone else had been in the backseat and that she'd Maced the son of a bitch.

"Maybe the wife hired the hit," Devereaux suggested. "You know, take out the cheating husband and the girlfriend at the same time. It's not like she needed the guy's income."

This was a promising theory, one Will intended to pursue in the near future by driving out to Lakeway. He wanted to see how the grieving widow was getting along.

"Why not just divorce him, though?" Webb asked.

Devereaux shrugged. "Maybe she loves her kid. Doesn't want to share custody."

"Doesn't add up," Webb said. "She loves her kid, so she makes her go through her dad getting murdered? In a car with some bimbo?"

Will bristled at the description of Courtney. He glanced around, hoping no one had noticed, but Devereaux was watching him.

Will shifted his attention to the whiteboard, where their potential suspects were listed. "What about the partner?"

"Which one?" Devereaux asked.

"Any of them. Riley. Wilkers. Take your pick. None of his colleagues looked too broken up at the funeral."

Devereaux shook his head. "I ran down Riley and Wilkers. They both have airtight alibis: one was on a plane, and the other was in a meeting with the state comptroller."

Will gritted his teeth. No one—with the obvious exception of Courtney—looked good for this crime. They needed to track down this mystery gunman, assuming he existed. Will thought back to some of the tactics he'd used working narcotics in Fort Worth. Confidential informants, although slimy, had been one of his best resources.

"We need to hit up some of our CIs," Will said. "See if there's anything on the street about someone shopping for a triggerman."

"You thinking Courtney Glass?" Cernak asked.

"Maybe," Will said. "I was also thinking about the ex.

Rachel Alvin. She still uses his name. Maybe she never got past their divorce. And maybe she hired a hit to get control over that ten million dollars that's about to go to her son."

"But how would she know about his estate plan?"

"Plenty of ways." Will shrugged. "He could have just told her about it."

"Or maybe Courtney was in cahoots with the ex," Webb put in. "Two pissed-off women out for revenge."

"We need to look up that dog walker," Devereaux said, smoothly changing the subject. "What's her name again?"

Will thumbed through his file. "Beatrice Moore. Twenty-eight. She's a waitress."

"Her timeline's off," Devereaux said. "Let's talk to her again. See if she remembers anything new about what she saw in that car."

Cernak pushed his chair back and stood up. He took a few steps toward the whiteboard and surveyed it with crossed arms. "I want Courtney Glass back here, too. Hodges?"

"Sir."

"You handle it." He turned and glared at Devereaux. "And you butt out. She's got some questions to answer."

"She's got a lawyer now," Webb reminded everyone.

"I know." The lieutenant's glare shifted to Will. "Go through that weasel attorney, if you have to, but talk to her again. She needs to explain that gun."

# CHAPTER

## 5

Jordan poked her head into the employee lounge as Courtney was about to leave.

"Thank *God*. I thought you'd left already."

"I have." Courtney pulled a tiny bottle from her leather backpack and squeezed a droplet of oil onto her Japanese scissors. She rubbed lubricant into the screw.

"Baby. Please. This is a *huge* emergency. You've got to help me."

Courtney tucked the scissors into their suede pouch and returned them to her backpack. "I'd love to, Jordan, but I've got a hot date."

"At four-thirty in the afternoon?"

"We're going rock climbing."

"Girl, come on. This is my best client. You've got to help me out here—"

"I don't do brides." Courtney shouldered her backpack, carefully avoiding Jordan's puppy-dog eyes.

"It's not the bride. I've got that covered. It's her sister—"

"I *definitely* don't do bridesmaids." She shot Jordan an irritated look and got her friend's beagle impression in return, complete with head tilt and soft whimper.

Courtney sighed. "What's the emergency? I really don't have time for a cut—"

"Her hair's done." Jordan took her hand and pulled her back out toward the floor. "We're dealing with a skin problem. It'll take twenty minutes, max. I'd do it myself but I've got back-to-back clients until six."

"I haven't done makeup in nearly a year," Courtney protested. "Get Erika to help you."

"She left already. You're my only hope." Jordan led her past the shampoo chairs and into Bella Donna's holy of holies, the gilded, sky-lit, granite-appointed studio where the salon's top artists performed breathtaking miracles on a daily basis. Courtney spotted a trio of immaculately coiffed women awaiting their turn at the altar. It was a mother and two daughters. Bridezilla wore a gauzy white veil, along with a button-down shirt and jeans, which no doubt would be traded for a designer gown in a few hours. Her sister, who wore a pink rose tucked into her chignon, looked about fourteen. Courtney immediately saw the emergency. Besides having abysmal posture and about thirty excess pounds, the younger girl had a terrible case of acne.

"The mom and bride have been booked for months, but no one thought to make an appointment for the sister," Jordan murmured in Courtney's ear. "Can you believe it? The poor thing needs help."

The teenager stood glumly off to the side, nibbling a hangnail while her mother and sister debated something.

The bride was beautiful—in an underfed Texas debutante sort of way—while her sister looked mousy at best. Their similar height and dark coloring only emphasized the differences between them. Courtney pictured the girl standing beside her older sibling, being scrutinized by a church full of people. She sighed.

"See what I mean?" Jordan asked.

Courtney mentally canceled her plans for the evening. The rock climbing, like the hot date, had been fictitious, but she'd really been looking forward to a soak in the tub and some *Project Runway* reruns.

She turned to Jordan. "This is the last time. You know I despise wedding parties."

"You're a lifesaver."

Courtney tossed her bag on the nearest empty stool. "And my makeup kit's at home. You're going to have to lend me your stuff."

"No problem." Jordan flashed her Naomi Campbell smile. "I've got everything you need. You'll be done in a blink."

Will tracked her down at a high-end beauty shop that looked like it had been decorated by King Midas. A gold chandelier hung over the entranceway, where an old-fashioned gold phone sat on a big glass table. The receptionist stationed there eyed him with naked curiosity as he walked in.

"May I help you?" She wore a low-cut white blouse over a pair of breasts that probably cost half his annual salary.

"I'm here to see Courtney Glass."

"She's with a client right now. Do you have an appointment?"

He flashed his creds. "Nope."

She lifted an eyebrow. "Right this way," she said, and sashayed out from behind the table.

She led him past a purple sofa thing that was shaped like a mushroom and littered with hair magazines. Giant mirrors framed with gold froufrou leaned against Roman columns all over the room. Will smelled something fruity he couldn't identify, along with the unmistakable scent of singed hair.

He spotted Courtney crouched in front of a barber chair, talking to a teenage girl. The girl nodded, apparently riveted by whatever Courtney was telling her. Courtney held a little jar of something in her hand. She dabbed at it with a paint-brush, applied it to the girl's lips, and then passed her a hand mirror. The kid broke into a big grin, displaying a mouthful of braces.

"Courtney? There's someone here to see you."

Courtney glanced over her shoulder and froze.

He hooked his thumbs through his belt loops of his jeans. "You got a minute?"

The receptionist hovered, obviously hoping to catch some gossip.

"Thanks, Jasmine." Courtney stood up and gave her a phony smile. "Would you mind ringing up this client for me? She's with the Bennett wedding." Then she turned to the girl. "Have fun tonight. You look beautiful."

The girl mumbled a thank-you and let Jasmine lead her away.

Courtney turned her back on him and started dropping makeup into a metal tackle box. "My attorney advised me not to talk to police outside his presence."

She wore a stretchy black T-shirt that stopped about an inch shy of her hip-hugger jeans. She had nice, round hips, and her back was turned, so he let himself look.

"Did you hear what I said?" She spun around. "No more interviews."

"I'm not here for an interview."

She rested her shapely butt against the granite counter. "Oh, I see." She pumped some liquid sanitizer into her palm and rubbed her hands together. "You're here for what? A cut and color?"

"How about just a cut?"

"You want *me* to cut your hair?"

"You know how to do men?"

She tilted her head to the side, smiling slightly. "Uh, *yeah*."

"Great." Will plunked himself down in the cushy chair that had just been vacated.

"You can't afford me."

"Sure I can."

She was smiling fully now. Or maybe it was more of a smirk. She pushed away from the counter and stepped toward him. "You're really serious."

"Sure. Gimme a trim." How bad could it be? In the army, he'd practically been sheared like a sheep.

She stepped on a pedal, and the chair sank a few inches, putting him directly at eye level with her breasts. He looked up. She reached out to touch his head, and he felt the first stirrings of alarm.

"You don't have a whole lot to work with here." She frowned down at him as her fingers combed through the hair above his ears. "I can crisp up your lines, though."

She smelled spicy—different from the rest of the room—and he pulled back slightly. Maybe this wasn't such a smart tactic.

"Just a trim."

"You're the boss." She fisted her hands on her hips. "But

I'm warning you, you start giving me the third degree, and that's it. You're at Supercuts."

She pulled open a drawer and whipped out a black cape, which she swished over him. Then she lifted some clippers off a hook beside the mirror.

"Use the twos."

She sent him a scornful look. "These are trimmers. For your *neck*. I'm not using clippers on your hair."

She moved behind him and rested a hand on his shoulder.

"What do you mean you're not using clippers?"

She buzzed over his skin with brisk downward strokes. "This isn't the mall. You're paying for a custom cut, and that's what you'll get."

When his neck was shaved smooth, she put the trimmers away.

"Where do you usually get your haircut?" she asked.

Supercuts.

"Wherever," he said. "What about you? You do your own hair?"

She smiled down at him. "Hairstylists have one cardinal rule: never cut the back of your own hair."

"Oh."

"I let Jordan do it, usually. And I do hers." She moved in front of him and adjusted his shoulders. "Put your feet flat on the floor. You're screwing up my reference points."

"Yes, ma'am." He flattened the soles of his work boots on the tile floor. She had reference points.

A pair of shiny silver scissors appeared in her hand and she moved around to the side. Her fingers combed through his hair again, and the scissors made a *shh-shh* sound.

"You ever thought about a new look? This is very Be All That You Can Be. I could update it for you."

*Shh–shh. Shh–shh.*

Maybe if he opened up some, he could get her talking. "I used to be in the army," he said.

"No kidding. Iraq?"

"Afghanistan."

She didn't say anything. Military service was a conversation stopper for some people.

"I've never been overseas," she said. "That must have been a trip. You should tell me about it sometime."

"Yeah." But he knew he wouldn't. He never talked about it with anyone, not even his brothers.

"You know, with a thick neck like yours, you might be better off with rounded lines."

"Rounded."

Her gaze met his in the mirror. "Instead of square."

He shifted in his seat. This wasn't going well. He wasn't here for a makeover; he was here on reconnaissance. "Just keep it the way it is."

"Aye-aye, sir."

"So how'd you get into this?" If he got her talking about her background, he could lead her around to Alvin and their history together.

She shrugged. "I've been at it since I was a teenager."

"What, cutting hair?"

"Hair, makeup, manicures. All of it. I had a couple friends in high school who let me try anything on them."

"And you like it?"

"Love it." She smiled at him in the mirror. "I think everyone deserves the chance to reinvent themselves."

Interesting philosophy.

She moved in front of him now and scrutinized his hair. He looked down at his boots.

"Anyway, I got my license in California, which has some of the strictest requirements. So it transferred down here pretty easily."

He remembered the case file. She'd had a Texas driver's license for nearly three years. Prior to that, she'd been in L.A. Devereaux had said she'd moved down with Fiona, and Will wondered now what had prompted them to leave.

Courtney's fingers glided through his hair. *Shh-shh. Shh-shh.* She was very efficient. And she seemed relaxed, too—the opposite of how she'd been at the police station.

"You get many men in here?" he asked.

"Sure, sometimes. Legislators mostly. Some lobbyists. A few lawyers."

"That how you met Alvin?"

Her hands paused, and she locked gazes with him in the mirror. She wasn't going to answer that.

"No," she said, surprising him. "We met on South Congress. You ever been to the Continental Club?"

"Nope."

"You must be new in town."

"Yep."

"I thought so. It's kind of a legendary live-music venue. David told me he was in Austin on business. He was working on a big case."

"He tell you what the case was?"

She pursed her lips and continued to clip his hair. He was definitely pissing her off now. He could tell by the set of her shoulders.

"Courtney?"

"Look down." She tilted his head forward, so his chin rested on his chest. The cool blade of the scissors scraped his neck. Then he felt her fingers rubbing the back of his head.

"You've got two cowlicks," she said. "I'll see if I can get them to lay flat."

"I haven't had a cowlick since I was ten."

She made little circles on his scalp, and he was grateful suddenly for this cape thing draped over him. She had to know the effect she had on guys sitting in this chair. Maybe that's why she'd agreed to this. He was on a mission to gain information, and she was on a mission to distract him.

"Cowlicks don't go away," she said. "And they're hereditary. Your dad probably has some, too. Right here."

She rubbed his head again, and he started to get annoyed. He looked up and watched her in the mirror.

"I believe you, you know."

Her gaze snapped to his in the glass.

"I know you lied about some of it, but I don't think you killed him."

She lifted an eyebrow. Then she moved around the chair and stood in front of him. She wouldn't look at his eyes as she reached out and combed her fingers through the sides of his hair.

He'd conducted hundreds of interviews, but this was a first. She had a beautiful body. She had to know that. She had to know what she was doing to him, standing so close and touching him and smelling the way she did. He kept his gaze on her face, but all he could think about was how much he wanted to pull her into his lap.

She moved around and started on his sideburns. "Straight across, right?"

"I want to help you," he said.

She scoffed.

"I mean it."

"Gee, you're such a nice guy. Let me guess, though. You want something in return."

"I want to know who did this. If your story's true—"

"You said you believed me."

"I do." Shit. "So that means there's someone out there right now who killed Alvin and tried to blame you."

"It was a setup." She moved behind him and worked on the part behind his ears.

"A setup?"

"I don't think David was the one who asked me to meet him."

Vhat makes you say that?"

She stared down at his head. She didn't want to look him in the eye. God, what was she doing? Her lawyer was going to hit the roof.

"It was all text messages and e-mails recently," she said. "We never had a live conversation."

"But they were coming from him? The messages?"

She shrugged. "I'm not sure. I assumed so. But now I think they weren't. Maybe someone else got ahold of his phone. Someone who was trying to get me to meet him that day."

Courtney's pulse pounded. She was doing it. She was telling him the truth. And he was hanging on every word.

"When David got in my car," she continued, "he said something—I can't remember the exact words—but it was like, 'Stop harassing me,' or something like that. So maybe he was getting the messages, too."

"Mind if I have a look at your computer?"

She tucked the scissors into her apron. To cover her nervousness, she reached for a brush and concentrated on dusting off his shoulders and his neck.

She wanted to trust him. She wanted him to help her. He had all sorts of resources she didn't—maybe he could figure out what was going on. Courtney had been trying to make sense of it, but it didn't make any sense. She didn't have all the information. And the information the police had all pointed to her.

"Courtney?"

"My attorney would tell you to get a warrant," she said.

"I'm not asking your attorney."

She finished dusting him and peeled off the cape. Then she leaned back against the counter and looked down at him. He had warm brown eyes. Trustworthy eyes. But they looked old, much older than the rest of him. She wondered if that was from being a soldier.

"I'll think about it," she said.

This wasn't the answer he wanted.

"How many messages did he send you?"

"I don't know. Five or six? He'd started to get pretty intense. After I blew off the first meeting—"

"What first meeting?"

Damn it. She hadn't meant to say that.

But maybe it was for the best. Maybe she should tell him everything, let him use all those police resources *for* her instead of against her.

"What first meeting?"

Or maybe she should get a brain and consult her attorney.

Shit. She was going to cave into impulse again. She could feel it.

He leaned forward in the chair. "Courtney?"

"He'd set up a previous meeting. At the Randolph Hotel."

"When?" Will's gaze sharpened.

"A couple weeks ago. July twenty-fifth."

"And you blew him off?"

"I told him I'd be there, and then I didn't show."

"And this was all through e-mail?"

"Yeah at first. After I skipped the meeting, he sent me a couple text messages."

"Why didn't you go?"

She bit her lip, feeling childish now. "I never intended to go. I was just screwing with him."

"Screwing with him?"

"You know, getting him all psyched up. So I could disappoint him."

His eyebrows tipped up.

"I guess you could say I have a vengeful streak."

The smallest trace of amusement flickered across his face, then disappeared. "So why'd you go to Zilker if you didn't really want to see him?"

She sighed. "His messages got more insistent. And then that last one just freaked me out."

"Why?"

"He said he planned to leave his wife. For *me*." She remembered how she'd felt, reading it. Her whole body had gone cold. "I just couldn't stand it. I agreed to see him so I could talk him out of it. The whole thing was nuts. I hadn't even laid eyes on him in six months."

Will leaned back in the chair, absorbing everything she'd said.

"Guess you really hit the mother lode, huh? Coming in for a haircut?"

He just watched her.

She looked away from him. "You caught me in a weak

moment. I've had a really crappy week. I can barely sleep—"

"You need to be careful. You threw a wrench in some-one's plan, you know."

She couldn't look at him. "I know."

He stood, and she cleared her throat, trying to clear away the lump. She needed him to leave now.

"Courtney."

She looked up at him, and the concern in his eyes brought the lump back. She'd never been one to lean on a man—that was her mother's specialty. But Will made her just want to lean into him and feel protected.

"I'm going to need access to your computer. One way or another."

She turned away from him and pulled open a drawer. She wrote up a bill, trying to compose herself.

"Here." She thrust it at him, and enjoyed his look of shock when he got a glimpse of the number.

"*Fifty* bucks?"

"I gave you the GI Joe discount. Feel free to tip me if you liked the service." This was better. She could do banter.

He shook his head slightly, then reached for his wallet.

"Don't pay me. Pay Jasmine."

He paused and stared at her a minute.

"I'll be back for that computer."

"I know."

"Be careful," he said firmly.

"I will."


The Randolph was a small but upscale hotel nestled on the north shore of Town Lake. Given its proximity to the business district and the capitol, Will expected a mix of executives, lawmakers, and other muckety-mucks, which was pretty much what he found when he tossed his keys to the valet and pushed through the Randolph's beveled-glass doors.

The hotel was decorated in the style Will thought of as Texas Bucks. A giant chandelier made of deer antlers hung in the lobby above an expensive-looking rug. On the west side of the lobby was a huge limestone fireplace with oversize leather furniture arranged in front of it. A couple of guys dressed in golf clothes lounged there, reading the Sunday sports section.

Will headed directly for the reception counter on the lobby's east side. A staffer there—female, mid-twenties— chatted with an older man while another hotel staffer— male, mid-thirties—checked in a nicely dressed woman.

Will picked the female clerk and pretended to be fooling with his cell phone until her counter opened up.

"May I help you, sir?"

He approached her counter and tried to seem friendly. "I'm with the Austin police," he said, and watched her brow furrow. "I need to find out if a particular person was registered here a few weeks ago."

"Is there something wrong?"

Will smiled. "Yes, but I doubt it has to do with your hotel. I just need to check on a name. For the night of July twenty-fifth."

She continued to look worried. "I should probably get my manager."

Will glanced at his watch. "I'm in kind of a hurry. You think you could just look it up for me?"

She bit her lip. "Who did you say you are?"

He fixed a reassuring smile on his face and pulled out his ID. "William Hodges. APD."

"And who is it you're looking for?"

He wasn't really looking for a dead guy, but he leaned closer. "John David Alvin. Or David Alvin. Either one."

Her pink-painted fingernails clacked over the keys as she pulled something up on her computer. "That was a Saturday. I was working that night, but I don't remember Mr. Alvin."

Sounded like she knew the guy. Maybe the Randolph was one of his frequent rendezvous spots. Maybe he'd spent the night here with Courtney. The thought put a sour taste in Will's mouth.

"I show he was here," she said.

The computer sat in the corner of the reception counter, arranged at a diagonal. Will couldn't read the screen because of the glare.

"It looks like he checked out early, though. That same night."

Alvin had checked in. And then left.

Or someone had checked in under his name.

"You say you were working that night?" Will shifted his position so he could better glimpse the screen.

She looked up. "That's right. I always work Saturdays."

"Can you tell me which room he was booked in?"

She chewed her lip. She darted her gaze to his ID, which was still on the counter. "Four-twenty-six."

Will nodded. "And can you tell whether he self-parked or used the valet?"

"He always uses the valet," she said without looking.

Alvin was a regular. The valet would probably know him, especially if he over- or undertipped.

"And do you remember anything unusual happening that night?"

"Unusual?"

"Maybe a noise complaint? A person who skipped the bill, something like that?"

Her fingers flew over the keys. "I don't remember anything like that. I've got nothing in the log."

Will glanced around the lobby. He noticed the dimly lit bar just off the elevator bank: THE LARIAT LOUNGE. An easel stood beside the entrance there. Will couldn't read the sign, but he guessed it advertised a singer or maybe a pianist.

"We did have another early checkout on that floor."

His attention snapped back to the clerk. "What was that?"

"Another early checkout. You said anything 'unusual,' and that's sort of unusual for us. The guest checked out about ten-thirty. Just after Mr. Alvin."

"What room was the guest booked in?"

"That would be four-forty-one."

"And what name was on the reservation?"

Will held his breath, praying for cooperation. He could get a warrant for this, but it would be a lot simpler if she volunteered the information.

"Beatrice Morris."

Beatrice Morris. Will's pulse spiked. "Are you sure it's Morris and not Moore?" It was all he could do not to hurdle the counter and see for himself.

"It says Morris."

Still, Beatrice was an odd name. And what were the chances of coming across a Beatrice Moore and a Beatrice Morris in the same investigation? Pretty damn low.

The clerk cast a nervous glance over her shoulder. "If you need anything further, I really am going to have to go get my manager."

"Please do that," Will said. "I'm definitely going to need something further."

The sun was setting on another triple-digit weekend when Courtney stepped off the 10/20 and strode down the sidewalk like a woman born in high heels. Will watched her from his booth inside the doughnut shop. He liked her shoes today. He liked all her shoes, but these were particularly hot. They had skinny heels and black ties around the ankles, and Will took a second to appreciate her legs before he pitched his coffee cup into the trash and left the store.

He followed her for half a block, expecting her to hang a left on Oak Trail, but she kept going. She jaywalked across a street and passed a shadowed alleyway before ducking in the exit door of a small-chain grocery store.

Will followed.

He'd intended to approach her right off the bat, but now he adjusted his strategy. You could learn a lot about someone from her shopping habits. Did she buy for herself or for company? How much did she drink? Did she purchase prescriptions or OTC drugs? Did she use cash or credit?

She snagged a red basket from the floor beside a fruit bin and grabbed a bunch of bananas. Then she zigzagged through the produce section, oblivious to the young stock boy checking out her ass. After snatching up a few items in dairy, she turned down the bread aisle.

Will tailed her through the store, becoming more annoyed with every step. He wasn't hiding. He wasn't even making an effort to hang back, yet she seemed to have no idea she was being followed. She paused in the skin-care aisle and spent an excruciatingly long time picking out face soap before heading for the register. She smiled at the cashier and grabbed a king-size Snickers off the candy shelf before swiping her credit card. Then she scooped up her three plastic bags and strode out.

Will followed closely, not making the slightest effort to conceal himself or the sound of his footsteps. Movement flickered in his peripheral vision as a lanky man with a frizzy gray beard loped across the street, moving straight for Courtney. Will's hand was on his holster until she stopped and smiled at the guy. They exchanged a few words as she dug through one of her bags and handed him the Snickers. He took it and shuffled off.

She resumed her course, and Will closed the gap between them in a few long strides.

"Hey!"

She whirled around. Her face went from frightened to irate in an instant. "Damn it, you scared me!"

"You always walk around alone at night?"

"You nearly gave me a heart attack! What the hell are you doing?"

"I need to talk to you."

"How long have you been following me?"

"Long enough." He stepped closer and peered down at her with his "be-afraid" look. He'd used it on gangbangers and CIs and even a few terrorists. But instead of looking intimidated, she looked pissed.

"So you're *spying* on me now? What is this, Big Brother?"

"You told me you'd be careful."

"I am careful."

"You're oblivious. I've had a tail on you for half an hour. You broke two traffic laws. You walked past a dark alley twice. You let some guy pick you up in the snack aisle. You stopped beside a Dumpster to talk to a homeless man—"

"I didn't let someone pick me up!"

"That beefcake by the chips. Don't tell me he wasn't hitting on you."

"He wasn't hitting on me!"

"Oh, yeah? What'd he say?"

Her mouth dropped open.

He took her groceries and started walking down the sidewalk toward her house.

"Hey!" she shouted after him.

He kept going, and finally he heard her heels on the sidewalk as she hurried to catch up.

"What are you doing?"

"Walking you home."

She walked beside him, almost matching his stride with those long legs. "For your information, I'm not *oblivious* to my safety. I've taken self-defense classes."

"Good."

"Not that it's any of your business."

They turned down her street, and he scanned the area. It was quiet. Dark except for the streetlamps. He liked that her across-the-street neighbor had a Doberman.

"You hear anything from Amy's boyfriend?"

"No." Her voice was calmer now.

He glanced at her. She wore a sleeveless black dress that

clung to everything. The only color on her today was her wine red hair and matching lips.

"What about Amy?" he asked.

"She's avoiding me. I haven't talked to her since the other day. I think she's embarrassed."

They came to her sidewalk, and he motioned for her to go first. She dug a key out of her roomy black purse and went up the steps. He followed her.

"That guy *was* hitting on you."

She shook her head and unlocked the door. Then she turned and gazed up at him. "You want to tell me why you're really here?"

"I've got a warrant for you."

Her chest tightened. "An *arrest* warrant?"

He walked into her kitchen and set all her bags on the table.

"Will?"

"A search warrant. You want these drinks in the fridge?" He started unloading groceries. She closed and locked the front door, giving herself a second to regroup before answering. He'd come for her computer. And maybe to search her house. She should probably call Ackerman.

She went into the kitchen and took the six pack of Diet Cokes out of his hand. "I'll do it."

She made quick work of unloading the bags while he leaned against her counter, watching her.

"I went to the Randolph," he said.

The Randolph. For some reason, hearing the name made her uncomfortable. She and David had spent the night there at least half a dozen times. It was their romantic hideaway, and Will the supersleuth had probably figured that out.

Courtney put away everything except the bread, the cheese, and the butter. She needed comfort food in a major way.

"What'd you find out?" she asked casually.

"A lot of interesting things." He crossed his arms over his chest.

She bent down and retrieved a nonstick skillet from the cabinet beneath the stove. She switched on the gas burner.

"Apparently you weren't the only person who knew John as 'David' Alvin. That's the name he used whenever he stayed at that hotel. He even had a credit card issued under that name."

Courtney unwrapped a stick of butter. She felt vindicated, at least somewhat. She'd never liked the fact that she'd bought into his lies.

Not that she'd completely bought in. The nagging sense that something wasn't right had prompted her to poke through his pockets and his BlackBerry and, finally, to go searching on the Internet until she came across a John David Alvin at the Austin law firm of Wilkers & Riley.

"He spent the night at that hotel sixteen times during the past year. When was the last time you were there?"

She watched a thick pat of butter go liquid in the pan. The edges started to bubble and brown. She opened the package of cheese and peeled off several slices. "January."

"You sure about that?"

She opened a fresh loaf of honey wheat bread. "Our entire relationship lasted less than a month. If he's been at the Randolph since January, it wasn't with me." She tilted the skillet, spreading the butter around, and then laid down two slices of bread. "You hungry?" She glanced at Will, whose attention was fixed on the pan.

"No. Thanks."

"I haven't eaten all day." She layered two slices of cheese on each piece of bread, and then topped them off with more honey wheat.

Not only had she skipped lunch, she hadn't taken so

much as a coffee break. She'd been on her feet since 10:00, and the salon had been unusually hectic for a Sunday. Thank God tomorrow was her day off. Courtney bent over to untie the straps of her sandals. She stepped out of them and sighed with relief as her soles rested flat against the cool linoleum floor. Much better.

She glanced up, and Will was watching her, frowning.

"Those things hurt?"

"Yeah."

"Why do you wear them?"

She smirked and tossed the shoes into a carpeted corner of the living room. "They look good, and I'm in the beauty business. Why do you wear a holster all the time?"

"It holds my gun."

"And it looks intimidating. Projects the tough-guy image."

He nodded at the pan. "I think that's done."

She took out a spatula and flipped the sandwiches. "What else did you find out at the Randolph?"

"A number of things."

She stepped toward him, and he drew back. She reached around him and opened the cabinet where she kept her plates.

She made him tense. It was the kiss, most likely. He still thought she was going to jump him. There was probably something in the Good Cop Handbook about getting busy with your prime suspect.

She took down two dinner plates and set them on the counter beside the stove. She transferred the sandwiches to the plates, sliced them in half diagonally, and then took some potato chips out of the pantry. She heaped a mountain of Ruffles beside Will's grilled cheese and handed him the plate.

"I said I wasn't hungry," he said, looking down at it hungrily.

"You lied."

She took two bottles of water from her fridge, plopped them on the table, and sank into a chair. She picked up a warm half sandwich. The cheese was all soft and melty, and she closed her eyes to enjoy the first bite.

Will scraped back a chair and sat down across from her. He picked up a chip.

"I would have figured you for Baked Lays. Or sunflower seeds or something."

She wrinkled her nose.

"This is good," he said after a few bites.

"I know. The key is using salted butter."

He watched her as he opened his water and took a sip. It felt nice having him at her table. It almost felt like they were friends, like he wasn't sitting there with a warrant in his pocket.

"You ever heard the name Beatrice Moore?"

Courtney returned her attention to her sandwich. "No."

"What about Beatrice Morris?"

"I don't know anyone named Beatrice. Why?"

He watched her silently.

"Who is she?"

"I'm not sure," he said. "She seems to have left town."

Courtney wasn't following. She nibbled a few chips, waiting for him to explain, but he just kept watching her.

"You said Alvin was working on a big case while you

guys were seeing each other. Was that made up, or do you think he was for real?"

"It was real." She took a swig of water. "It was some trial that had been dragging on for weeks. He was always getting phone calls and e-mails about it on his BlackBerry."

"How do you know?"

She lifted a brow.

"You snooped through his BlackBerry?"

"I was suspicious. He acted strange sometimes. Secretive. I thought it might be another woman."

"What did you find out?"

She pushed her plate away. "That lawyers use way too much jargon. Okay, I'm ready now."

He swallowed the bite he was chewing. He'd polished off the whole sandwich in less than five minutes. "Ready for what?"

"For you to slap on the cuffs."

His eyes narrowed. "Why would I need to handcuff you?"

"Don't you want to search my house? I figured you'd probably cuff me to the chair here. So I don't flee the scene or plant evidence or something."

The corner of his mouth ticked up. "Why would you plant evidence against yourself?"

She shrugged. "I don't know. I'm new at all this criminal stuff. You're going to have to tutor me."

He stood up and took his plate to the sink. She followed him and put hers on the counter beside his. Then she turned and gazed up at him.

She was getting under his skin. The look in his eyes was part annoyance, part attraction. He was probably annoyed with himself for being attracted to her, probably regretting that he'd let her make him dinner. She smiled.

"You think this is a joke?" he asked.

"Not at all."

His face was stern now. "You're being looked at for murder. You might want to remember that."

She crossed her arms. "Not the kind of thing I'd forget."

"You're not out of the woods yet."

"I'm aware of that, thanks."

He reached into his jacket and pulled out a folded piece of paper. "Here's your warrant. And I'll take that computer now."

Courtney lay in bed, staring at the ceiling and thinking about Will. *You're being looked at for murder.* It was impossible to put the words out of her mind, and even more impossible to forget the way he'd said them.

He'd looked tense. And angry. And she couldn't shake the feeling that she was in more trouble than she'd thought.

Ackerman had told her not to worry. He'd said that if they really had the goods on her, they would have charged her soon after they'd recovered her gun. He'd seemed so confident about it, and Courtney had felt reassured. She'd felt even better after Will had come into the salon, and she'd confided in him. It had been a weight off her chest, and she'd felt as though he wanted to help her. She'd felt as though he *would* help her.

Now she wasn't so sure.

He was attracted to her—that much she knew. But the fact that he wouldn't act on his attraction worried her. *You're not out of the woods yet.* Maybe she never would be. Maybe

Will knew it, too, and didn't want to get involved with a woman he'd later have to arrest. Probably not a wise career move for a rookie detective.

Courtney flopped onto her stomach and squeezed her eyes shut. She thought about prison and girl fights and orange jumpsuits. And that wasn't the worst possibility. In this state, even a woman could end up on Death Row.

She couldn't stand it. It couldn't happen. It *wouldn't* happen. But then she thought of Will's face, of how serious he'd looked in that interview room with the police lieutenant and then again tonight in her kitchen, and she knew she was in deep trouble.

Maybe she should run. Maybe she should alter her appearance and change her name and—

*Thud.*

She bolted upright. Was someone on the porch? Amy and Devon had come home earlier. Maybe Amy's boyfriend was back.

*Creak.*

She kicked away the covers and scrambled off the bed. She snatched up her Mace and cast a frantic look around. Should she hide? Call 911? Panic shot through her as she realized her phone was in the kitchen, plugged into the charger.

But her purse was right there on the floor. She swooped down and slung it over her shoulder. She used her free hand to dig around for her scissors and, with the other, gripped the Mace. Slowly, silently, she crept into the hallway.

Her ears strained for any sound. The scissors felt cool and smooth in her hand. She could hear her own heart thumping as she made her way down the corridor. At the doorway between the hall and the living room, she stopped and poked her head around the corner. She stared through the dimness at her front door. She held her breath.

Nothing.

A minute crawled by. Then another.

Without a sound, she eased up to the door and peered through the peephole.

No one. She moved to the living room window and peeked through the blinds. The porch was empty. As was the yard. She surveyed the block in both directions, noting the cars parked along the curb.

Her gaze skimmed over the house across the street, and she let out a breath. They had a Doberman. He barked at everything—every car, every squirrel; the slightest activity on the street set him off. She'd considered him a nuisance before, but at this moment he was her favorite animal. He wasn't making a peep.

So maybe she'd imagined it.

Courtney's stomach loosened with relief. She turned and stared at her darkened living room. The digital display on the cable box cast a greenish glow over her beige carpet. The ice maker rumbled. The smell of grilled cheese hung in the air, and she remembered Will at her table, his presence filling up her kitchen. She wished he was here now to distract her from the night that stretched out ahead.

She took a chenille throw from the armchair and wrapped it around her shoulders. She picked up the remote. Then she curled up in the corner of her sofa and settled in for another endless night.

"Nice gate," Devereaux quipped as Will pulled the Taurus up to the elaborate wrought-iron barrier.

"You should see the house."Will rolled down the window and examined the keypad beside the speaker. He pressed the green button, just like he'd done last time, and after a few moments of static and some garbled words, the gate slid open.

"Great security," Devereaux muttered.

"I know."

"Hey, you been getting any letters lately?"

Will glanced at him. "No." He drove through the gate and up the curving driveway lined with palm trees.

"I've been getting these letters," Devereaux said. "At work. And in my mailbox—"

"You mean sent to your home?"

"Some of them."

"What do they say?"

He shook his head. "Ah, they don't make much sense. They're pretty kooky, really. I just figured they were related to one of our cases. You haven't been getting anything?"

"No."

Devereaux sighed. "Maybe it's the Goodwin thing. Cernak's been taking a lot of heat for it."

The lieutenant had been taking a lot of heat for all of their cases, as far as Will could tell. In the last two weeks alone their department had caught seven homicides. Austin wasn't used to such a high murder rate, and the public seemed to be getting antsy. The insanely hot weather and the ongoing media coverage of what they'd dubbed the "killer heat wave"wasn't helping.

At the top of the drive, the palm trees gave way to flower beds filled with tropical plants. The surrounding lawn was so manicured, it could have been a golf course. An enormous fountain occupied the center of the cobblestone parking area just in front of the Mediterranean-style mansion.

"Looks like the first Mrs. Alvin missed her shot," Devereaux said. "Bet she's a bitter woman."

Parked between the fountain and the front door was a low-slung silver Lotus. Will pulled up right behind it, and Devereaux whistled.

"So, you follow up on the ex?" Will asked, cutting the engine.

"I did a phone dump on her. Rachel Alvin's made sixteen calls to Wilkers and Riley since the day of the murder. All to the direct line of their top probate attorney. I got the guy on the phone, but he wouldn't tell me what they talked about."

"Maybe she's eager to get her hands on that trust fund," Will said.

They got out of the Taurus. Devereaux admired the Lotus while Will memorized its license plate. The detective drove a vintage black Ford Mustang, and Will figured him for a car nut.

"So, what's this one like?" Devereaux asked as they mounted the steps leading to the front door.

"Polite," Will said, and reached for the bell.

He'd been expecting a maid again, but this time Claire Alvin answered her own door. She wore a caramel-colored suit and had a leopard-print scarf tied around her neck. Will put her diamond earrings at about three carats each.

"Detective Hodges." She stepped back and motioned him into the marble foyer.

The air smelled sweet, and he noticed a crystal vase filled with white roses sitting on the grand piano in the living room.

He also noticed the gray-haired lawyer slouched casually against the doorframe with his hands tucked in his pockets.

"I don't believe we've met," Mrs. Alvin said, offering Devereaux her hand. They exchanged greetings, and then she gestured toward Alvin's law partner. "And have you met Peter Riley?"

Riley stepped forward and shook hands with Devereaux. "At my office," he said, and turned to Will. "Although I don't believe you were there."

Will shook the guy's hand, wondering what he was doing here today. The man had a wife and kids, and it seemed odd for him to be dropping in on Alvin's widow on a Monday afternoon.

"Nice seeing you guys." He nodded. "I was just leaving."

When he was gone, Mrs. Alvin led them into the living room filled with antique-looking furniture. This wasn't the Texas Bucks style, but something more feminine that reeked of money and trips to Europe. The room had an impressive view of Lake Travis, which was busy with boats and Jet Skis.

"I assume you're here to update me on the case," she said, gesturing for them to sit down. She looked at Will, and he could see that beneath the cool smile, she knew they weren't just here to "update" her. This woman was sharp enough to know she'd made the suspect list.

Will sat down on the overstuffed white couch. He scooted forward on the cushion so he wouldn't sink into the giant pillows.

"We're working lots of leads," Devereaux assured her, "and we've developed some promising information."

She sank gracefully into an armchair and crossed her legs.

Devereaux tilted his head to the side. "And how are things going for you?"

Will didn't buy the sympathetic friend routine, and he could tell the widow didn't either.

She smiled thinly. "As well as can be expected. Now, why don't you tell me when you plan to arrest the bitch who shot my husband?"

Devereaux's eyebrows arched, and she turned her chilly gaze on Will. "Detective?"

"It's not that simple," he replied.

"She was in the car, wasn't she? It was her gun."

Devereaux sent him a look. How did she know about the gun? The recovery of the weapon hadn't made the papers.

"Ma'am," Will said, "do you mind if I ask where you're getting your information?"

Instead of answering, she turned to Devereaux. "She's crazy, you know. She took a hammer to the Carrera last winter. You guys must have known about it. John spent all night down at the police station trying to hush everything up."

Devereaux glanced at Will, clearly surprised.

"What? You think I don't know about her?" she sneered. "John was a lot of things, but discreet wasn't one of them. He could never keep his mouth shut about anything. I overheard him talking to his golf buddies about her."

Will stared at her, not sure what to say to that. He cleared his throat. "Mrs. Alvin, the investigation is ongoing—"

"Don't give me that." She stood up. "I want that woman arrested. She's dangerous. Who knows how many families she's destroyed? She needs to be locked up."

Will and Devereaux both stood. This interview was de-
teriorating, rapidly.

"I can tell you we're working 'round the clock." Devereaux's Louisiana drawl was more pronounced now. Will
wondered if he was kicking it up a notch to try to soothe
her. "We have to do everything by the book so that it holds
up in court."

She glared at him, then turned toward Will.

"And what's all this going on at John's office? You already
know who killed him. What good does it do to go dredging
up all this personal information?"

"Ma'am?" Devereaux pretended not to understand.

"You detectives, running around interviewing all John's
colleagues and friends. It's invasive! You think I need you
people stirring up gossip all over town about our marital
problems? I've got a daughter to think about!"

Will tried to look contrite. "We apologize if our methods upset you. But we have to be thorough—"

"Is that what Riley was here about?" Devereaux cut in.
"Gossip at the office?"

She looked at Devereaux. "No, as a matter of fact. He
was here on a sales call."

"Excuse me?"

She glowered at Will, all traces of the genteel lady gone.
"*Sales.* He's afraid my family's company is going to switch
counsel now that John is dead. He's worried about losing
his firm's biggest client. He's worried about his money."
Her chin was quivering now, and her hands balled into fists
at her sides. "Am I the only one who gives a damn about
John? Am I the only one who wants to see someone pun-

ished? I don't want to hear any more about your methods. I want an arrest!"

They were out on the driveway inside of two minutes. The Lotus was gone.

"That went well," Devereaux said.

Will slid behind the wheel. "What next?"

Devereaux rolled down the window and rested his elbow on the door. "Ah, I dunno. A hundred degrees. Sunny. Seems like perfect weather for a jog in Zilker Park."

Courtney stood in tree pose on her yoga mat, trying to cleanse her body of all the tension and caffeine it had absorbed this afternoon. She'd left work early and gone to an Internet café to try to make some sense of everything that was happening.

Slowly, she eased into toe stand, mimicking the instructor. Rivulets of sweat slid down her neck as she strained to hold the position. Her T-shirt was soaked; her leggings were damp. Bikram yoga was relaxing and revitalizing, but the temperature was a bitch.

She took a deep breath and tried to put all things David-related out of her mind. The afternoon had been a waste. She'd spent hours poring over legal journals and newspaper articles, and she'd learned nothing useful except that she wasn't cut out for detective work. She felt a new appreciation for Will, spending his time puzzling over clues and running down leads.

Of course, his job entailed more than staring at a computer. He went to crime scenes. He carried a gun. It was all very *Law & Order*, very exciting. Too exciting for Courtney.

After last week, she didn't want to get near a crime scene or a dead body ever again.

She stretched out on her back and breathed deeply. One by one, she moved through the floor poses. She tried to clear her mind. She tried to just *be*. She let her muscles go lax and felt the heat flow through her as she shifted into the final pose. This was the part she loved most—this tranquil, fluid moment in which she felt at peace.

It ended too soon.

*"Namaste."* Her instructor nodded serenely as Courtney trailed her classmates out of the studio.

She stood on the sidewalk, and the traffic noises brought her back to earth. Unbelievably, the muggy evening air was cooler than it had been inside the studio. She tucked the mat under her arm and set off on the three-block walk home. It was almost dark. She passed the Laundromat and the noodle shop, and her thoughts turned to ways to fill her evening. Maybe she should get carryout and invite Fiona over. Or maybe she should call Jordan and see if she was up for a drink.

She turned onto Oak Trail, weighing the pros and cons of each option. A night with Jordan would be fun, but she'd blow too much money. A night with Fiona would be cheap, but she'd spend the whole time pretending to be fine so her sister wouldn't worry about her.

Courtney glanced down the street. Her blood ran cold.

That black SUV. It had been parked there last night, after she'd heard the noise. She forced her feet to keep moving, forced her face to look neutral. She recognized the shape of the car and the black-tinted windows. It wasn't a car she'd seen around before yesterday, and she realized now that it didn't belong.

Her gaze darted around. Her duplex was dark. Not a sound on the street. The driveway was empty, just as it had been when she'd left.

She couldn't go home. She didn't know why, exactly, but she had that tickly feeling between her shoulder blades like she'd had back at Zilker Park. Someone was watching her.

This wasn't good. She was exposed. She didn't have a purse, or a phone, or a tube of Mace. She certainly didn't have her Beretta. Instead, she had a house key laced to her sneaker, a rubber mat tucked under her arm, and a water bottle clutched in her hand.

She turned around and set a brisk pace for the doughnut shop. The tickling increased until she was *certain* someone was watching her. She glanced around desperately. No traffic. No pedestrians. The doughnut shop was a beacon, but it seemed miles away.

An engine grumbled to life behind her. Courtney's heart skittered. Could it really be—

The grumble became a roar. She broke into a sprint, dropping everything as she raced for the salvation of the neon sign. Her legs strained. The noise closed in.

She darted to the side, up onto the sidewalk. She glanced over her shoulder.

Black car. Silver grill. *Moving closer!*

She lunged left again, dodged a lamppost. Her feet barely touched the pavement. She raced for the light. Almost there, almost there, almost there. Brakes squealed behind her, and she screamed.

Will's phone vibrated as he exited the police station. He checked the display, but didn't know the number.

"Hodges."

"Where are you?"

He knew the voice. "Leaving work."

"I need you to meet me. Right now."

Will neared his truck and shook his keys loose from his pocket. Courtney sounded stressed. "Meet you where?"

"You need to hurry. I thought he was gone, but then he looped back around, and I think he might have—"

"Whoa, there. Who's gone?"

"This guy. This *truck* that tried to run me down—"

"*What?* Where the hell are you?" He jumped behind the wheel.

"At the doughnut store near my house—"

"Are you inside?"

"Yes. But I think he's still out there, and I need you to hurry. What? Just a *minute!* God, would you chill *out?*"

"What?"

"Not you. There's this guy here. I'm on his phone. I need you to get here fast. I can describe the car. I didn't see the license plate, but maybe—"

"Are you hurt?"

"No, but I'm freaked out! It's the same black Tahoe from last night. It was on my street after I heard a noise on my porch and—"

"Did you call the police?"

"Huh? No. Look, I've got to go now. This guy's a little *touchy* about his goddamn iPhone. Hey, do you mind, here? This is the police." Her voice faded, and Will heard arguing in the background. "I've got to go, Will. Please hurry."

She clicked off.

Will tossed his phone onto the seat beside him and pressed the gas. He sped through a yellow light and picked up I-35 for several miles until he reached Courtney's neighborhood. A few intersections later, the doughnut shop came into view. He hit a pothole as he whipped into the parking lot.

Courtney stood in front of the entrance with her arms crossed. Will pulled up beside her, and she jerked open the passenger-side door.

"Finally! What took you so long?"

"Where's this vehicle?"

"It's a black Escalade."

"You said Tahoe."

"It's an Escalade. I got a good look at when it went by the second time." She pointed to the street just north of Oak Trail. "Go that way. I think he circled the block. Maybe we can sneak up on him."

Doubtful. But Will followed her directions anyway, just to ease her nerves.

"You say he tried to run you *down?*"

"Yes."

"You're sure he was aiming for you? He wasn't just speeding?"

She shot him a scorching look.

"Hey, I'm just asking."

"Turn left here. Maybe we can find him."

"If he really was trying to hurt you, he'll be long gone by now."

"Yeah, well, humor me."

He glanced at her. She wore workout gear, and she was soaking wet.

"You been swimming?"

She gave him an annoyed look. "Yoga. Can you step on it, please?"

He stepped on it, but he didn't see any black Escalades or Tahoes anywhere near her house.

"I couldn't get the license plate," she said. "He was going too fast when he drove by."

"And you saw him from the doughnut shop?"

She scanned the surrounding area. "I spotted him when I was walking home. He was parked near my house, and I remembered seeing that exact car on my street last night."

"Are you sure? A Tahoe looks nothing like an Escalade."

"I'm sure."

"You get a look at the driver?"

"No."

Will circled the block again. Then he wove through the neighborhood for ten more minutes, but saw nothing remarkable. He turned down Oak Trail again, pulled up to her house, and stopped.

"Tell me about the noise on your porch."

She took a deep breath. "I was trying to sleep last night. And I heard this *thud*. Like a footstep."

"Why didn't you call me?"

She shot him a "yeah, right" look, which pissed him off.

"Did you call anybody?"

"I got out of bed to check it out, but there was no one there."

Will shoved open his door and got out. "Stay here. And lock the door behind me."

He did a quick inspection of the premises as her neighbor's dog barked its head off. When he returned to the Suburban, she leaned over to pull up his door lock.

"No sign of any disturbance." He slid into the driver's seat but didn't close the door. "We should check around inside, just to be sure."

She glanced up and down the street, and a little worry line appeared between her eyebrows. "I don't want to go in yet."

"Okay." He didn't blame her for being spooked. "When do you want to go in?"

"Later."

"Where's Amy?"

"Visiting relatives this week." She met his gaze. "I'm starving. Are you?"

"No." Actually, he was famished.

"Well, I'm hungry. Let's go get a pizza."

"A pizza."

"Dough? Cheese? Assorted toppings?"

He should leave now. Or he should take her inside to inspect her house, and then he should leave.

Instead, he started the engine. "I think I saw a Home

Slice up the street," he said, pulling away from the curb.

"I'm not sitting in a restaurant like this."

He flicked a glance at her. "Why not?"

"I'm dripping with sweat. But we can do a to-go order and take it back to your place."

Will gritted his teeth. His apartment was the very last place he wanted Courtney Glass and her form-fitting yoga pants. "Not an option."

"Why?"

"Because."

"Because you're a cop?"

"Yes."

She scoffed. "So you're not allowed to have a woman over?"

He didn't answer. He spotted the sign for Home Slice and put on his turn signal.

"You ate dinner at my house just the other night."

Will pulled into the pizza joint and parked the truck. "That was different."

She crossed her arms over her breasts. "Why?"

The difference was intent. He hadn't planned to have dinner at her house; it had just happened. But if he took her home now, it would be a different scenario and most likely a different outcome.

"You're smelling a little ripe, too," she said, eyeing his shorts and T-shirt. "Looks like you came from the gym. I thought you said you were at work."

"I was at Zilker earlier, jogging." He cut the engine and turned to look at her.

She had her head tipped to the side, and he could practically see her wheels turning. "What time?"

"About three-thirty."

"Interesting. And was this work or recreation?"

"Work."

"And did you learn anything?"

"Plenty."

She leaned forward, anxious now. "Is it good or bad?"

It was both, but he didn't plan to talk to her about it. At least, not yet.

He pushed his door open, and the scent of pizza wafted inside, straining every bit of his resolve. "Come on. You said you wanted pizza."

"I also said I'm in no shape for a restaurant. Get us one to go."

"Courtney—"

"I like thin crust."

"This is a bad idea."

She smiled. "And extra pepperoni."

Nathan pulled up to the sixties-era ranch house and took a good look around. This guy must be doing well. Last he'd checked, linguistics professors didn't make enough bank to live in Tarrytown, but maybe he had other sources of income. Nathan got out of the Mustang, locked it, and walked up the sidewalk, scooping up a plastic newspaper bag as he went. He reached the front door and didn't see a bell, so he gave a sharp knock.

He waited. He leaned closer to the door and heard music inside, something familiar that he couldn't quite place. He crossed some flagstones to the driveway. A white Mercedes was parked in front of the garage, which was closed. The car was old—mid-eighties, he guessed—but looked well maintained. A bluish light flickered against the shiny sedan, and Nathan saw that it was coming from a window just off the driveway. Someone had a TV on inside. Nathan walked past the car and found the back door. He peered through the glass into a laundry room, beyond which he could see into a well-lit kitchen. The music sounded like it was coming from a television in the family room. Finally, he placed it. *The Godfather.*

Nathan rapped on the window and waited. He slipped the plastic bag off the paper and read today's date just above the headline.

He looked inside the house again, cupping his hand against the glare of the porch light but taking care now not to touch the glass.

"Dr. Pembry?" he shouted, and knocked again.

His gaze fell on the laundry room floor, where a pile of clothes had been dumped beside the dryer. He saw T-shirts and socks, wadded blue jeans, and bath towels.

"Son of a bitch," he muttered, looking closely at the towels.

One of them was smeared with something dark, and in a heartbeat he knew what it was.

Blood.

It took all Will's self-discipline to hang a left on Oak Trail and deliver Courtney right back to her house. He watched her shoulders go rigid as he parked.

"I don't want to be here," she said, holding the pizza box in her lap with white-knuckled hands.

"You have to go in sometime. Now's better than later. I'll check everything out for you."

Without replying, she pushed open the door and jumped out. He followed her up the sidewalk, scanning the area for anything suspicious. When they reached the door, she shoved the box at him and bent down to untie a key from her shoelace. Then she unlocked the door and pushed it open.

He entered first and immediately recognized the scent she'd had on at the hair salon—probably her perfume.

She flipped on a light, and he deposited the pizza box on the coffee table.

"Do a walk-through with me," he said. "See if anything looks out of place."

He thought she'd object, but then she brushed past him and led him down the hallway to the back. He followed her into the bedroom and stood there as she glanced around.

"Looks fine," she said, apparently not surprised by the cosmetics blanketing the desk or the clothes strewn across the bed.

She yanked open a few dresser drawers, and he averted his eyes, but not before learning that she had a very interesting collection of lingerie. He wandered to the open closet and saw a tightly packed rack of clothes. Beneath it was a neat row of shoes, some of which he'd seen before.

"Everything's okay," she announced.

He walked out of the room and found the bathroom. The shower curtain was pulled back, revealing a spotless bathtub and a small window made of privacy glass. He checked the lock and found it rusty, but secure.

He turned and saw her standing in the doorway with her arms crossed. Without a word, she turned her back on him and walked into the kitchen. He followed and checked the windows and the back door, but found nothing out of the ordinary.

"Guess everything's fine," she said, but something in her voice told him nothing was fine.

Will leaned back against the counter and watched her. She looked rattled. And tired, like she hadn't had a good night's rest in days. She looked like a woman trying very hard to hold it together.

"I need to clean up." She brushed past him and glanced over her shoulder. "Don't eat all the pizza."

When she was gone, he stood there in her dimly lit kitchen and tried to figure out what he was doing here. He tried to tell himself he was here because of his case, but that was bullshit. He was here out of concern for her. His suspect. A suspect he knew was manipulating him to help get herself out of trouble. He didn't believe she'd killed Alvin—especially not after what he'd learned today in the park—but he believed she was involved in something that had *gotten* Alvin killed. And he believed she knew way more than she was telling him.

Will walked into the living room and sat down on the sofa. He heard the shower running and imagined Courtney all lathered up with soap or shower gel or whatever it was she used that smelled so good. He imagined her naked—which he'd been doing a lot lately—and had the urge to go join her in there and let her manipulate him all she wanted.

To distract himself, he opened the pizza box. The sight and smell of thin-crust double pepperoni made his mouth water and made him almost forget the Courtney-smell that permeated her house. He reached for a slice, then checked himself and closed the lid. Instead, he picked up the remote and surfed around until he found a ball game.

The Astros were taking on the Diamondbacks in Phoenix, and his team was up 4–0 in the fifth inning. He nestled back against the brightly colored throw pillows and watched the D-backs' best pitcher throw it wide. He sat through an entire inning, ignoring his growling stomach.

"You're a 'Stros fan?"

He glanced up. She stood behind the sofa now in a T-shirt and faded jeans.

"Yeah. You?"

"My grandfather brainwashed me," she said, twisting her damp hair into a sloppy knot. "He's been a rabid fan ever since Nolan Ryan."

She sank onto the sofa beside him and popped up the box lid. She helped herself to a piece of pizza. "So what happened in Zilker?"

He scooted closer to her and reached for a slice. "Devereaux and I went out there about three-thirty. We were trying to drum up some regulars, maybe someone we missed when we canvassed the area last week."

He took a bite of pizza, which was no longer piping hot, but still good.

"And?" Courtney had tomato sauce on the corner of her mouth, but he didn't tell her.

"Devereaux found someone. You remember seeing a man in running shorts go by about three-thirty? Says he had earphones on?"

She shook her head.

"Well, he claims to have noticed you sitting in the Buick. Alone."

She arched her eyebrows.

"He also claims to have seen a black Cadillac SUV parked at a meter about a quarter mile down the trail. He says the engine was idling."

"A Cadillac SUV?" She leaned forward. "You mean an Escalade? Did it have chrome running boards?"

"We're getting into those details." He didn't tell her that the witness was certain it had been an Escalade. Or that the witness also said he'd jogged past a man in a navy track-suit heading the opposite direction farther up the trail. He claimed to remember the guy clearly because he'd thought his clothing was odd, given the weather.

Courtney dropped her pizza on the coffee table and eased back against the pillows. She closed her eyes and let out a deep breath. "Thank you," she said.

"For what?"

She opened her eyes, and they looked shiny. "For being the first person to reassure me that I'm not crazy."

"You're not crazy."

She sat forward. "Did the dog-walker lady see it, too? The Cadillac?"

"Hard to say," Will said. "We can't seem to find her any-where."

Her eyes widened. "You're kidding."

"Afraid not. Her name's Beatrice Moore, supposedly. And she seems to have disappeared. The address she gave the patrol officer turned out to be bogus."

"Oh my God, I *told* you!" She leaned forward and gripped his arm. "It's a setup! With my Beretta, and the messages, and David. It's all connected. You believe me now, don't you?"

He couldn't answer her. He looked down and focused on his pizza.

"Will?"

"We're still checking out this new witness. Hoping to get more information. So far, he seems pretty credible."

She sank back against the cushions and stared into space. "They're trying to kill me." He heard the tremor in her voice. "Whoever killed David wants me dead, too. That's what's happening, isn't it?"

"You need to be careful." He gave her a harsh look. "Any chance you could stay with a relative? Your grandfather or your sister, maybe?"

"My grandfather's in a nursing home," she said. "And Fiona would be a last resort. She lives with her fiancé in this tiny little place. I'd be a total third wheel."

"Guy's a cop, right?"

"Ex-cop."

"Yeah, well that sounds like a good place for you right now."

"I'll think about it," she said.

The D-backs hit a homer, and the stadium erupted into cheers. Will watched the batter round the bases and tie up the game. The pizza had lost its appeal, and Will closed the box. Courtney tucked her legs underneath her and rested her head on the sofa arm, and for a while they simply stared at the television.

She was getting to him. Maybe it was her looks or her go-to-hell attitude or that vulnerability he kept glimpsing underneath it all. Whatever it was, it made him lose sight of all the reasons he needed to stay away from her.

Houston brought in their star reliever, and two pitches

later, the D-backs knocked another one over the wall. He glanced at Courtney, but her eyes were closed now.

He should take off. He should go home and catch a few winks of sleep before oh-dark-hundred when his phone always seemed to ring. But he didn't have the heart to leave her right now.

His phone vibrated on the table where he'd put it with his car keys. He shot a glance at Courtney, but she didn't move.

He grabbed the phone. "Hodges."

"It's Devereaux. I need you at 162 Tarry Trail, ASAP."

Will got up and stepped into the kitchen. "What's going on?"

"We've got a situation. Remember those letters I told you about?"

"What about them?"

"I tracked down the guy who was writing them. Some UT professor who lives in Tarrytown."

Will glanced into the living room at Courtney. She looked childlike curled up there on the sofa. Barely half an inning, and she was honest-to-God fast asleep.

"What's the situation, Devereaux? I'm tied up here."

"Well, get untied. I'm at the prof's house, and it looks like a crime scene."

# CHAPTER

# 9

Will pulled up to the professor's house and parked behind an unmarked crime-scene van. Someone was keeping a lid on whatever was going on here. Devereaux's Mustang sat farther up the street, and there wasn't a single marked vehicle in sight.

*Name no one man,* Will thought, remembering a line from one of Devereaux's letters. It didn't make sense to him. Devereaux had shown him the notes, all scrawled in pen on yellow legal paper. Will had studied them carefully, but they all looked like disjointed ramblings. Devereaux was convinced they had to do with the Alvin case, though, because he'd started receiving them only a few days after the murder.

He met Will at the gate leading to the yard, which had a swimming pool no one had cleaned in ages. "Over here," he said, and Will followed him across the patio to an open back door.

Cernak stood just inside talking to a neighborhood constable. The door frame was dusty with fingerprint powder. Will glanced around for a patrol officer, or whoever was keeping the crime-scene log, but didn't see one.

"What is this?" Will asked.

Devereaux ushered him into the living room, where a

DVD player was stuck on the opening menu of *The God-father*.

"I traced one of those letters to a P.O. box over at Mail N Such north of campus. Box belongs to this guy Pembry."

Will scanned the room, taking in details. High-quality furniture, but simple. Masculine. The place looked tidy except for a dirty ashtray and an open bottle of liquor sitting on the counter that divided the kitchen from the living area.

"So where's the professor?"

"Great question," Devereaux said. "I showed up here to talk to him, and no one's home. The TV's on, and the back door is wide open."

"So why is this a crime scene?"

Devereaux nodded toward the kitchen, where two techs were labeling a paper evidence bag.

"Dried blood. Lots of it. On a towel in the laundry room. I saw it through the windowpane at the back door."

"So maybe he cut himself shaving."

"Look around, Hodges. What else do you see?"

Will looked around, annoyed at being treated like a rookie. He was new to homicide, but he wasn't new to police work. Still, he played along. He noticed the half-finished drink on the end table beside the big leather arm-chair. He walked across the room and looked at the bottle on the counter. Dewar's. Five Winston Reds filled the ash-tray beside the phone. Four of them had been smoked down to the last quarter inch, and one had burned clear down to the filter, leaving a long cylinder of ash. People tended to be very consistent with their cigarette habits.

"He's on the phone, smoking," Will ventured. "Someone

comes to the back door, or maybe he hears something in the backyard. He goes to see about it, opens the door, someone enters the house."

Devereaux nodded for him to continue. Will let his gaze roam slowly around the room. Nothing looked broken, no obvious signs of struggle. What was he overlooking here? He took a whiff of air but didn't detect any gunpowder. His gaze paused on the armchair positioned in front of the TV.

The coffee table sat at a slight angle, just inches away from the entertainment cabinet. Eight feet of space separated it from the armchair, making it impossible for anyone to prop their feet up or use it to rest a drink.

Will visually combed the room again, noting the drapes that matched the sofa upholstery, the framed art on the walls, the bookshelves filled with hardback volumes and trinkets, even a silk plant. Someone, at some point, had taken the trouble to decorate this place.

"It's the rug," he said. "There should be a rug here, but it's missing."

"Exactly," Devereaux said. "And so is Pembry."

Courtney woke up with the sun in her face and a crick in her neck. She smelled turpentine and remembered where she was. She stared for a minute at the skylight in her sister's living room and cursed Will Hodges for dragging her over here last night. He'd practically dumped her on Fiona's doorstep before taking off to attend to something "important"—some dead body somewhere, most likely.

Courtney squirmed up onto her elbows and tried to orient herself. The living room curtains were closed, but given the blue patch of sky above her and the brightness of the room, she guessed it was at least eight. Jack would have left for work already, but Fiona still would be around. Courtney's arrival late last night with a grim-looking homicide cop had caused a stir, and Courtney had no doubt her sister would be in full worrywart mode.

Pans clanged.

Courtney kicked off the quilt and shuffled into the kitchen. Fiona stood at the stove, melting butter in a skillet. She glanced up as Courtney plopped into a chair beside the breakfast table.

"Morning," Fiona said cheerfully.

"Morning."

"You want breakfast? I'm making French toast."

"Just coffee, thanks." Courtney pinched her neck, trying to alleviate the kink. Fiona wore one of her boring beige pantsuits, meaning she planned to spend her day around cops and robbers. Her gleaming strawberry blond hair was tucked neatly away in a ponytail. Unlike Courtney, Fiona didn't like to draw attention to her sex appeal, even though she had it in spades.

"What time is it?" Courtney asked.

"Eight-thirty. Jack already went in."

Courtney mustered some energy and followed the aroma of expensive caffeine to the coffeepot. Her sister never cheaped out when it came to coffee. Courtney pulled a mug down from a cabinet and poured herself a cup. Meanwhile, Fiona got out eggs and orange juice. She poured a glass and put it on the counter beside Courtney.

"Here."

"Thanks," Courtney said, annoyed. "So. Another rape case?"

"I don't know. Lieutenant Cernak just left me a voice mail. I'm supposed to interview someone at nine."

Courtney closed her eyes and savored the breakfast blend. Fiona busied herself at the stove, which was her way of coping with stress. It was their pattern: Courtney's life spun out of control; Fiona hovered and tried to act maternal.

Courtney wasn't up for a fight this morning, so she took her coffee into the next room, which had a cement floor and unpainted Sheetrock lining the walls. Light flooded the space through two huge skylights. In the center of the room, on a worn drop cloth, stood a paint-spattered easel.

"This is coming along," she said.

"Yeah, they're almost done."

The art studio, which recently had been added to the back of the little house, was Jack's wedding present to Fiona.

It was love, the kind neither of them had ever expected to find when they were kids growing up in L.A. The Glass sisters were realists. And yet, Fiona had found someone. Someone good and solid and head over heels in love with her. Just looking at the studio made Courtney's chest ache. She was insanely happy for her sister and also a tiny bit jealous.

Courtney walked the perimeter of the room and checked out the canvases leaned up against the walls. When she wasn't drawing rapists and murderers, her sister painted nature scenes. Back in California, she'd gone through a desert phase, but lately she'd been into water.

"Breakfast is ready."

Courtney returned to the kitchen and sat down beside a plate of French toast and cantaloupe, which she had no intention of eating. Fiona put the pan in the sink, grabbed a piece of toast for herself, and picked up her car keys.

"Are you sure you're okay with the bus?" she asked. "I can swing back by here around ten-thirty if you need a ride to Bella Donna."

"I'm fine. My first client's at noon, so I'm just going to hang out." Fiona bit her lip, and Courtney headed off her next comment. "I'll keep the doors locked."

"And the alarm on."

"And the alarm on," she promised. "Hey, can I use your computer? I need to check e-mail."

"Sure. And there's lunch meat in the fridge."

"I know."

"Well . . . bye." Fiona headed for the door, and Courtney dutifully followed her and secured the bolt behind her.

On the way back to her coffee, she caught a glimpse of herself in a mirror on the breakfast-room wall. Her eyes were puffy and her complexion sallow. She sighed. Then she opened up Fiona's pantry and rummaged around until she found some oatmeal. She took out a mixing bowl and a wooden spoon and started whipping it together with water and an egg white.

The bell sounded, and Courtney's hand froze.

She padded silently through the living room and parted the gauzy curtains covering the front window. A tan Suburban was parked at the curb.

Courtney glanced regretfully at her jeans and rumpled T-shirt. Her bra was sitting with her purse and shoes beside the sofa, but she doubted Will would notice. She threw the bolt and pulled open the door.

"Hey."

He looked her up and down, and she saw him notice. "Hi. Can I come in?"

"Sure." She stepped back to let him in. "You look like you slept in your car."

He grunted something and brushed past her. He wore the same clothes he'd had on yesterday, right down to the worn Nikes.

"That coffee?"

"Yeah. We've got breakfast, too, if you're hungry." She led him into the kitchen and took down another mug from the cabinet.

He stood beside the counter and watched her pour his coffee.

"Let me guess," she said. "You were on a stakeout?"

"Something like that."

So he didn't want to talk about it. She could understand. Fiona was that way sometimes about her really bad cases.

"Black?"

"Yeah."

She handed him the cup, then went to the table to refill her own. When she turned back around, he had a perplexed expression on his face.

"That's breakfast?" he asked.

She looked at his goopy finger and smiled. "It's a mask."

"A what?"

"For my face." She handed him a dish towel. "Breakfast is on the table. Have at it."

He sat down in front of the French toast and doused it with syrup. The man must burn zillions of calories a day. She watched his back muscles strain against the T-shirt and wondered when he found time to work out.

She joined him at the table and squared her shoulders. "Is this a social visit?"

He looked at her warily and forked up a bite. "No."

She lifted a brow. "Too bad. I have the morning off, and you need a shower."

He reached for his coffee, and she actually saw a blush creeping up his neck. He was fun to tease. It would be even more fun if he teased back.

"I have some more questions for you."

"Okay." She picked up a chunk of his cantaloupe and popped it into her mouth.

"You ever heard of a Martin Pembry?"

The cantaloupe was sweet and juicy, and she stole another chunk. "I don't think so."

"Professor Pembry? From the University of Texas?"

She felt a prick of irritation. "I didn't go to college. But surely you know that, right? It's all in my file?"

He pulled a piece of paper from his pocket and unfolded it to reveal a copy of what looked like a driver's license photograph. He showed to her. "He was a linguistics professor. A PhD."

*"Was."* She glanced at the picture. "So that means he's dead?"

Will sighed. "Most likely."

Whatever that meant.

"Look, I don't know him. I didn't kill him last night, either, if that's what you're thinking. You get to be my alibi this time."

He gave her a sharp look as he tucked the paper back in his pocket. Then he shoveled up some more French toast. "You should cut the jokes, Courtney. This is serious."

"Thanks for the reminder." She crossed her arms. "Why are you asking me about this? Is it related to David?"

"Devereaux thinks so." He guzzled the last of his coffee and stood up. "I need to get home and clean up. What are you doing today?"

"Oh, you know. Plotting my next crime spree."

He put his hands on his hips and gave her the scary look again. He was going to make a great dad someday. She felt sorry for his teenage girls, if he ever had any.

"I'm working," she said finally. "From noon to six. I'll be taking the bus."

"Be careful. And if anything strange happens, call me."

"Okay."

"I mean it. Anything weird. Even if it's just a feeling. Your body's conditioned to pick up on cues you may not even register consciously. If you get a funny feeling about something, just get somewhere safe and pick up the phone."

She gazed up at him and didn't know what to say. He was worried about her. When her sister acted like this, she felt insulted. But with Will, she felt touched.

He glanced at his watch, and she stood up. "Thanks for dropping in," she said. "I'll call you if anything happens. Where will *you* be today?"

"Downtown." He walked to the door. "I'll try to get your computer back to you this afternoon, if I can."

She opened the door for him. "You're finished with it? What did you find out?"

He turned to face her. "You were right about the e-mail messages. They weren't from Alvin. Or at least, they probably weren't."

"Where were they from?"

"A public library near the capitol. The messages were routed through Alvin's law firm by someone who knows something about technology."

Courtney gnawed her lip. That sounded sophisticated. And frightening. Hitmen and technology experts, disappearing witnesses and dead professors. What on earth was this about? And what did it have to do with her?

She shuddered, and Will noticed.

"Be careful," he said. "And remember to trust your gut."

She put on a brave face as he left, and then collapsed on the sofa. She trusted her gut. And it was telling her to call in sick to work and hide under the bed.

Instead, she went back to her coffee. She couldn't call in sick. She needed the money.

She picked up the newspaper that Fiona and Jack had abandoned on the breakfast table. She skimmed the front page, looking for any mention of something involving a UT professor. Nothing. She reached for the Metro section and scanned the headlines.

A photograph at the bottom of the page caught her eye.

"Memorial Fund Honors Slain Cyclist."

Courtney's heart skipped. She recognized the woman. She was plump. Thirtyish. She had a brunette bob and flawless ivory skin. Eve Caldwell, according to the caption. The name wasn't familiar, but Courtney knew she'd seen her before, and she knew she'd been with David at the time. Where was it? Where had they been? Courtney stared at the photograph and tried to visualize it.

The Randolph Hotel.

Eve Caldwell had been glaring at Courtney from across the bar the last time she'd met David there. This woman had been the one to set off Courtney's alarm bells, the one to make her think David was seeing someone else. Later, she'd snooped through his pockets and his BlackBerry for evidence. . . .

Courtney dropped into a chair and gazed down at the picture. Eve Caldwell, whoever she was, was dead. And David was dead. And someone was trying to kill her.

What was this about?

She bent over the article and scoured it for information. Eve Caldwell had been thirty-two. And according to the story, she'd been killed in a cycling accident on Loop 360 last week. This article wasn't about the accident, though; it focused on some scholarship fund that had been set up in her honor. A memorial service would be held today.

Courtney curled her fingers around her coffee mug and stared out the window. Slain cyclist. Murdered attorney. Dead professor.

Dead hairstylist.

She wanted to run. She wanted just to jump into her car and take off. Where would she go? She had no idea. And if she didn't, no one else would either.

But she didn't have a car. And she didn't know the first thing about hiding.

Courtney rested her head in her hands and took a deep breath. This was crazy, whatever this was. What was her connection to all these dead people? No wonder Cernak believed she was guilty—she was at the vortex of something, and it kept getting worse. Just wait until he found out about Walter, and that she'd been investigated for murder once before. He'd have a warrant out for her in no time.

Courtney stood up. She couldn't just sit here, locked

away in her sister's house. She needed to do something, to figure out what was going on. She was linked to these deaths, whether she wanted to be or not, and she might be the only one who could connect the dots.

She checked the kitchen clock and made a decision. She was going to take Will's advice today and follow her gut. She was going to call in sick.

But she had no intention of hiding under the bed.


"What's she doing here?"

Nathan turned around to see Hodges standing behind him, gazing at the video monitor. The screen showed real-time footage of Fiona Glass conducting an interview.

"Cernak called her in," Nathan said, muting the volume. "She's talking to Pembry's neighbor. He says he was taking out the trash when he saw an SUV backing into the professor's driveway two nights ago, between seven and eight."

Hodges stepped further into the room. "Cernak wanted to use her? What if it turns out to be connected to the Alvin case?"

Nathan shrugged. "It's his call. Anyway, he's skeptical about the connection. Or at least he was. He might change his mind when he sees the first drawing." Nathan handed Hodges a sketch, the one Fiona had completed just a few minutes ago.

"Who's this?" Hodges asked.

"The man this neighbor saw getting out of the SUV. White male. Mid-forties. Short, stocky build."

"Sounds like the guy our jogger spotted in Zilker," Hodges said.

"That's what I'm thinking, too. And the vehicle fits."

Cernak stopped in the doorway of the cramped little room. His gaze flicked to the screen. "She's still at it?"

Hodges passed him the drawing.

Cernak frowned down at it. "This is it? So, what's she drawing now?"

"Hands," Nathan said.

"Hands?"

Nathan turned to the monitor and watched Fiona work. The witness was smiling, comfortable. He'd been in there more than an hour now and had hardly stopped talking. Fiona always said the key to a good sketch was the interview, and Nathan knew her interview skills were unparalleled.

"Witness insisted he couldn't see the guy behind the wheel—"

"How do we know it was a guy?" Hodges asked.

Nathan smiled. "That's what Fiona wanted to know, too. Turns out, he caught a brief glimpse of the hands on the steering wheel. Didn't even realize it till she started asking him questions about it."

Cernak muttered something and shook his head. The lieutenant wasn't a big believer in soft skills. He liked Fiona's work product, but he didn't always trust her methods.

Fiona turned her drawing board, sharing her sketch with the witness. He nodded eagerly, and said something. Nathan turned the volume up, but it sounded like the interview was ending. Fiona sprayed fixative on the drawing and shook the man's hand. Then she ushered him out of the room and handed him over to a uniform so he could fill out some paperwork.

"I don't like this," Cernak said, just as Fiona poked her head into the observation room.

"Finished," she said, giving Nathan the second drawing.

Unlike her usual sketches, this one showed the driver's-side door of a vehicle and, through the window, a pair of hands on the steering wheel. The driver wore a distinctive ring on his left pinky. Fiona had drawn a close-up of it on the lower left corner of the paper. It was chunky and square-shaped. Men tended to wear the same jewelry on a day-to-day basis, so it was a good detail to have.

"This a diamond?" Nathan passed the picture to Cernak.

"Something that looks like one, anyway," Fiona said. "The witness said he noticed it because it caught the light."

"This is helpful," Nathan said, stating the obvious, mainly because Cernak was scowling at the drawing. The lieutenant would be thinking Fiona's sketch was both good and bad. The good part—they now had a lead in the Pembry case. The bad part—that lead suggested a connection to the Alvin homicide, which meant the evidentiary value of Fiona's drawing had just evaporated. They could never use her pictures to help solve a case in which her sister was a suspect.

At least, they couldn't openly use the drawings.

Nathan exchanged glances with Hodges. Like it or not, Fiona had just established a link. The next challenge was to figure out what that link meant.

Cernak returned the sketch to Nathan. "Circulate this within the department," he snapped. "But one word of this leaks to the press, and it's your ass."

Courtney slid onto a stool and propped an elbow on the bar. She glanced around the room, then let her gaze settle on the bartender, who had been watching her since she'd stepped into the Lariat Lounge.

He placed a napkin in front of her and gave her a long, lingering look that she recognized. He was going to hit on her if one of the patrons here didn't beat him to it. "What can I do for you?"

"Cape Cod." She smiled. "With a twist, please."

While he made the drink, she let her gaze comb the room, picking up details she'd never noticed before because she'd been too busy noticing David. About a dozen small, candlelit tables filled the floor in front of the stage. There was seating along the sides, too, a series of rectangular tables positioned in front of a leather bench seat tucked against the wall. A handful of couples sat there now, talking in low voices and sipping cocktails. Most of the men looked like wealthy business travelers. Most of the women looked like arm candy.

"Here you go."

Courtney turned to the bartender and shifted her shoulders strategically to make sure she had his attention. For tonight she'd chosen a black baby-doll dress with spaghetti straps.

"Thank you." She smiled up at him. He had the tall-dark-and-handsome thing going, and he knew it, too. "I used to come here all the time, but I don't remember you. Are you new here?"

"Three years." He didn't smile, but he gave her that slow, appraising look.

She held out her hand. "I'm Courtney."

He shook it. "Jason."

She stirred her drink with the slender red straw and took a sip. She turned her head slightly and gazed out at the tables as several more couples arrived and settled into chairs. "You guys are pretty busy tonight."

"It's the singer." He nodded toward the microphone set up on stage next to a gleaming black piano. "Lucinda Mason. Maybe you've heard of her?"

"I don't keep up with the music scene."

A cocktail waitress appeared at the other end of the bar. "Just a sec." Jason winked at Courtney and walked over to fill the order. While he was gone, Courtney took her purse from her lap and placed it on the bar beside her drink. She unzipped the bronze leather clutch, which matched her sling backs, and pulled out a clipped photograph.

Jason took care of a few customers and then made his way back and slid a bowl of cashews in front of her.

"Listen, Jason, I'm trying to find someone." She tapped a red fingernail on the newspaper photo of Eve Caldwell. "You ever seen her in here before?"

He glanced down at the picture. "Sure."

"Guess this is my lucky night. When did you last see her?"

"She was around a lot for a while. Haven't seen her lately, though."

"Who was she with?"

He propped his hip against the counter and cocked his head to the side. "Same guy as you."

Courtney's breath caught. "Are you sure?"

"He's a lawyer, right? Rich big shot. Lousy tipper."

"That's him."

"I haven't seen him around lately." He nodded at the photograph. "Her either."

*That's because they're dead.*

Courtney tried to keep her smile in place as she tucked the clipping back into her purse. "You ever see either of them here with anyone else?"

"Besides you? No."

Courtney sipped her drink, and for a few moments they traded sultry looks. Another waitress approached, and he went off to fill an order.

Courtney pivoted her stool to face the stage. No sign of the singer yet, but the room had filled in. Many of the men had that sly look about them that told Courtney they were here with someone they shouldn't be. How had she missed it before? How had she sat here, in this very bar, and not realized she was being played by a cheap-tipping lawyer in a three-thousand-dollar suit? Just thinking about it made her chest burn. And then all that burning anger was replaced with fear as she glanced around the bar and realized two of the people who used to come here were dead now. And maybe there were more.

What was the connection between this hotel and these deaths? Was David the connection? Was she? She turned her attention back to the bar, but continued to watch people come and go in the mirror behind the liquor bottles.

Jason cleared her glass away and filled a new one with ice. He spent a few moments mixing Grey Goose and cranberry juice, and she wondered whether he'd remembered her brand from months ago, or whether it was just a lucky guess. He seemed to have a sharp memory.

He placed the drink in front of her and leaned a palm on the bar. "So I take it you're mad at your boyfriend."

"You're observant."

He leaned closer. "I could help you forget about him, if you want."

She gazed up at him, and couldn't help but smile. It had been six months, but she hadn't lost her touch. She could make an attractive man want her. But the only man she *wanted* to want her at this particular moment was immune to her.

Or he pretended to be, at least.

"That's very tempting." She took a twenty out of her purse and placed it beside her untouched drink. "I'll have to let you know."

He spotted her immediately. She was standing beside the valet guy and showing him something from her purse. Will pulled up to the valet stand, thrust the Suburban into park, and got out.

"'Scuse us." He took her arm and towed her away from the college kid who stood there, gaping.

"What the *hell*, Will?"

He jerked the passenger door open. "Get in."

She shoved her little purse under her arm and fisted a hand on her hip. "Ex*cuse* me? Did you just *haul* me across the sidewalk? Are you freaking crazy?"

"Get in," he repeated.

"No."

He stepped closer and glared down at her with his full-on, no-holds-barred death stare, and she didn't even flinch, damn it. "I'm warning you, Courtney. I'm in a bad mood, and I've got no patience for games right now. Get your butt in the car."

She waited a beat, staring at him. Then miraculously, she obeyed.

He closed her door and went around to the driver's side. "I thought I told you to stay at your sister's."

"I'm not under house arrest. I can go wherever I want."

"Hey, did it ever occur to you that you're not investigating this case? The police are? And maybe it's not smart to run around town asking questions like you're Nancy Drew?"

She opened up a little makeup mirror and reapplied her lipstick. Her mouth was fire engine red tonight. But he should think of it as a Stop sign.

She finished with the lipstick and shoved it back in her purse. "Maybe if you guys would *solve* the case, I wouldn't have to investigate for you. And maybe you should be *grateful* I'm helping you instead of complaining."

He shook his head and looked away. Then he started the Suburban and left the Randolph behind them. It was after nine. He was going on two days without sleep and twelve hours without fuel, and now he had Courtney to deal with before he could catch up on either.

"How'd you find me, anyway?"

He thought about telling her he'd developed a source at the hotel, that the female desk clerk he'd interviewed had agreed to call him if she ever saw Beatrice Morris, or any other women associated with Alvin. But Courtney didn't need to know all that.

"I'm keeping tabs on you," he told her. "And someone else most likely is, too. You said you were going to be careful."

"I am. But I'm also being practical. Did you know David was seeing a woman named Eve Caldwell?"

"No," he said, marginally interested now. "Who is she?"

"A thirty-two-year-old real estate agent. Graduate of UT. Where are we going?"

"To your sister's."

"I don't want to go there. Take a left at this stoplight."

"Why?"

"I want to show you something."

"No, why don't you want to go to your sister's?"

She shot him an annoyed look, and he thought she was going to dodge the question. "I'm not comfortable there," she said, surprising him.

"She's your sister."

"She's also engaged. Three's a crowd, okay? We're turning here."

He pulled up to the intersection and sighed. He didn't have time for this. And whatever it was, it was probably a bad idea.

"It's relevant to the case," she said. "I swear."

He looked at her, all shiny and enticing on his torn vinyl

upholstery. Then he put on the turn signal. "I've lived in countries where you could get arrested for that outfit. You might want to think about keeping a lower profile."

She rolled her eyes. "Gimme a break."

"I'm not kidding." He eyed her legs. The dress was too short. And those shoes—

She crossed her legs, and he glanced up to find her looking at him. He shifted his attention back to the road, and the light turned green.

"Where are we going?"

"Highway 360," she said, "south of the bridge."

"Who'd you talk to at the Randolph?"

"Lots of people," she said. "Both the bartender and the valet remember David and this woman Eve."

"Okay, so he was a womanizer. So what?"

"So she's dead."

Will gritted his teeth. He flicked a glance at her. "Since when?"

"Last Tuesday."

Will followed the curvy road through the hills of west Austin. He kept a lookout for deer in his peripheral vision. He also kept lookout for a tail, but they weren't being followed.

"How'd she die?" he asked. "APD's not working an Eve Caldwell case."

"It was a 'cycling accident,' according to the paper. But I don't believe that."

"Where was the accident?"

"I'll show you. Turn right at the next light."

Will maneuvered into the turn lane, not happy about the pain in his skull. He'd had a low-grade headache for days now, and he knew it was from his certainty that Courtney was in the middle of something lethal.

And he needed to figure out what it was, soon.

"So," she said, "you're new to Austin, right?"

"Three weeks."

"Then you probably don't know this, but we're getting on one of the most scenic bike routes in town, called Capital of Texas Highway. Very popular with the yellow-shirt set, especially in the spring. Everything's blanketed with bluebonnets."

It was too dark to admire the landscape, but through a dip in the hills, Will caught a glimpse of the downtown skyline, dominated by the capitol dome and the UT clock tower. The road cut a deep, curving path through the limestone, and Will slowed as it sloped downward.

"Just up here," Courtney said. "Stop before the exit."

Will pulled onto the paved shoulder and rolled to a stop. Even at this late hour, he saw the reflectors of a few bikers on the opposite side of the divided highway.

Courtney pushed open her door and hopped out. Will did the same. She made her way down the incline, and Will's shoes crunched on the gravel as he followed her. The Suburban headlights threw their long, black shadows over the asphalt.

Courtney stopped and looked around for a moment. "There it is."

"What?"

"The cross. This is where she went off the road." She picked her way down the grassy slope, away from the headlight beams. Will pulled a penlight from his pocket and illuminated a white cross surrounded by fresh bouquets of

yellow and white flowers. "According to the accident investigators, she was riding early in the morning. There were no
witnesses, but they think she hit this hill, lost control of the
bike, and skidded off into the ravine there. She wasn't wearing a helmet."

Will peered over the ledge into the darkened gully lined
with rocks. "That could do it."

"Except that her friends don't believe it."

"What?"

"That she'd go out without a helmet."

A fresh wave of annoyance washed over him. "When
did you talk to her friends?"

"At her memorial service. It was this afternoon."

"You went to her *funeral* and interviewed her friends?"
He took her elbow and turned her to face him."

"I think she was murdered. I think she was killed and
dumped in that ravine. Or maybe she was driven off the
road—"

"Goddamn it, you're not an investigator!"

She glanced down at his grip on her arm, and he
dropped it.

"Eve *never* went out without a helmet," she persisted.
"And then the day she does, she has a fatal crash? It's too
coincidental. I mean, look at that!" She gestured toward the
gully. "It's got to be fifty feet from the highway. How did
she end up there? She was an experienced cyclist. The road
was dry. She never should have lost control, and she never
should have been out there without a helmet."

"Courtney—"

"She was seeing David the same time I was, back in
January. I remember noticing her at the Randolph and get-

ting jealous. I thought she had a thing for him. And then she was killed the day after he was." She turned to look at the makeshift memorial. She looked so *sad* standing there. And she hadn't even known this woman.

"You know, I hadn't been to a funeral since my dad died." Her voice was quiet. "Now I've been to two in one week."

He reached out to touch her before he could help himself. She glanced up at him.

"Let's go," he said, turning away.

He trudged back to the truck and heard her footsteps behind him. He pulled open her door.

"What should we do now?"

"*We* aren't doing anything." He nudged her inside. "You're going to your sister's, and I'm going to check out this lead."

After a second night on Fiona's sofa, Courtney officially needed a chiropractor. The closest thing her budget would allow was the massage therapist at Bella Donna, and she resolved to hit her up for a free neck rub during one of her breaks today. Kneading her shoulder, Courtney made her way into the kitchen, where Jack sat at the breakfast table.

"Hi."

He looked up from his newspaper. In a white button-down and black slacks, he looked too conservative for her artistic sister. But then, Fiona and Jack had been a case of opposites attract.

"Coffee's strong," he said, and Courtney realized she must look like crap. She needed to spend some extra time with her mirror today.

She got down a mug and poured some coffee. "Fiona's gone already?"

"Six A.M.," he said. "Convenience-store holdup."

"Don't they have security cameras?"

Jack got up to refill his coffee, and Courtney added cream to hers. "This one wasn't working, apparently."

Courtney dropped into a chair and eyed her future brother-in-law across the kitchen. She'd never had a brother. Or a father, really. The only male role model in her life had been her granddad. She wondered what it would be like to have a normal family.

"Fiona's worried about you," he said over his coffee mug.

"I know."

"I'm worried about you, too."

She sighed.

"What would you think about taking a vacation for a few weeks? Maybe visit some of your friends back in California? Or go check out the coast? Padre Island's only a five-hour drive."

"That's a nice idea, but I can't afford the travel or the time off."

"Fiona and I want to pay for it."

A lump rose up in her throat. Jack and Fiona didn't have money to spare, either. All their savings had gone into their house and their upcoming wedding.

"Thank you," she said. "But I couldn't do that. And anyway, I shouldn't. The police told me to stay in town."

Jack set his coffee aside. "I've been doing some poking around."

"Me, too."

He gave her a stern look. "This thing is complex, involving

multiple actors and multiple incidents. That means it's expensive. Someone burglarized your house. Someone routed messages to your computer. Someone planted a witness in the park, and possibly at the Randolph Hotel, to implicate you in this. Someone tried to commit a double murder. Someone else drove that person to the scene. And now there's this missing professor, who Nathan thinks is connected to your case. Do you see what I'm getting at here?"

"I'm in the middle of something awful. Thanks, I caught that." Courtney took a deep breath, no longer interested in telling him about Eve Caldwell.

"At first, we were just worried about you getting charged. Now we're worried about you getting hurt."

"So am I."

Jack gazed at her with his gray-blue eyes. He looked concerned. Brotherly. Courtney's stomach twisted, as she realized this was new for her. She'd mostly dealt with men as lovers or enemies, not friends or family.

"I know you think Fiona worries too much, but it's because she loves you."

"I know." Courtney stood up now and patted Jack's shoulder. "And I'm being careful. I promise."

"Running around investigating this thing isn't being careful."

Gwen Stefani sang out from the kitchen counter, and Courtney welcomed the interruption. She crossed the tile floor and reached for her cell phone. It was Will's number.

"Hello?"

"What time do you need to be at work?"

She checked the clock on the microwave. "About an hour. Why?"

"I'm coming to get you."

Two weeks ago, she'd been a loner, and now she was surrounded by protective alpha males. "You don't need to do that. I can catch the bus."

"Give me forty minutes. And wait inside."

He clicked off, and Courtney dropped the phone back in her purse.

Jack, the clever detective, had picked up everything. "Hodges?"

"Yep."

He frowned. "You need to be careful with him. He's investigating you. You shouldn't trust him."

"Thanks *so* much for your concern." She couldn't say why his comments needled her, but they did. Jack had barely even met Will, just a brief exchange the other night.

"Nathan, you can trust," he continued. "He's a friend before he's a cop. Hodges is new. This is his first murder case, and he's probably trying to prove himself, so be cautious about what you tell him."

Courtney glanced at the clock, and Jack caught the hint.

"Lock up behind me." He snagged his keys off the counter and put his coffee mug in the sink. "And wait inside for your ride."

The surgically enhanced receptionist was on the phone when Will arrived at Bella Donna that afternoon, so he ignored her and showed himself to the back. Courtney stood at her work station, arranging brushes and combs in a drawer.

"Hi."

Her startled gaze met his in the mirror. "Hi."

"I need your help with something. You free?"

She turned around to face him and crossed her arms. "I've got a client at three."

"Can you cancel?"

"No."

"How about getting someone to cover for you?"

She watched him for a moment. Then she glanced at her watch and sighed. "Let me see what I can do."

She disappeared down a corridor, leaving Will standing in the middle of the salon while women in various stages of transformation watched him curiously. He turned his attention to Courtney's work space. It was clean. Immaculate, even—not so much as a wisp of hair on the floor. Hardly any personal touches, he noticed—just a photograph tucked into the bottom corner of the mirror. Will bent closer to study it. The picture showed Courtney and Fiona, both in sweaters and jeans, kneeling beside a snowman and grinning out at the camera.

"Ready."

He looked up. Courtney had her backpack slung over her shoulder and a shiny red purse clutched in her hand.

They left the frigid salon for the humid outdoors, and he darted his gaze around as he walked her to the Suburban. Courtney tossed her bags onto the floor and scooted in, then smoothed her skirt over her legs. Today she wore a white sundress and had her hair pulled back in a ponytail. The dress was very fifties housewife, but somehow those red high heels sent his mind in a different direction.

"I'm off for the day," she announced when he got behind the wheel. "Got my last two appointments covered."

"How'd you manage that?"

They exited the parking lot and she leaned over to play with the radio station. "I told them we had a date tonight, but you couldn't wait for me."

He looked at her.

"They think you're my hot new boyfriend." She sat back in the seat and glanced at him. "What? You expect me to tell them you're a homicide cop? That I'm under investigation? No, thanks."

He hung a left and maneuvered his way through the afternoon traffic. He glanced at her again, and she was grinning.

"What?" he asked.

"Nothing."

"Why are you laughing?"

"It's just that my boss didn't believe me. She said you didn't look like my type. So I told her you were really good in bed."

Will gritted his teeth.

"She recommended some erotic massage oil, so if the mood strikes you—"

"Jesus, Courtney."

"I'm just kidding. God. You're so uptight. Where are we going anyway?"

"A car wash."

She glanced around. "Okay. And you need me why, exactly?"

"I want to show you something. Meantime, flip through these." Will reached into the back and pulled a manila file from the floor. Inside were several Xerox copies showing an array of mug shots and driver's license photos. Placed amid the pictures was the driver's license photo of the Zilker Park jogger and a mug shot of Alvin's former brother-in-law, who had a rap sheet.

"Are these suspects?" She flipped through the pages.

"I can't comment on that."

She rolled her eyes. "Well, what am I looking for?"

"Just tell me if you recognize anyone. Maybe someone from the Randolph Hotel. Or anywhere else. Just someone you've seen around."

Beatrice Moore, a.k.a. Beatrice Morris, was still missing in action. Her account of events in Zilker Park contradicted the jogger's, so someone was lying. As for Alvin's former brother-in-law, he'd done two years for aggravated burglary not so long ago. The guy had had a drug problem, but was supposedly clean now, according to his parole officer. His physical description didn't completely match the jogger's description or the description given by Pembry's neighbor, but it didn't rule him out either. Will wanted to see if Courtney recognized him.

But she skimmed right over his mug shot without comment. She reached the bottom of the stack and found the copy of Fiona's drawing.

"My sister drew this." She held it up, pointing to the initials at the edge of the picture, alongside the date stamp.

"That's right."

"Who is it?"

"We don't know. He look familiar to you?"

She gazed down at the sketch and shook her head. "Not at all."

Will turned into the lot of a fast-food restaurant adjacent to Bubbles Hand Car Wash and Detailing. He slipped into a space facing the service bays, where the brother of Alvin's ex-wife stood making notes on a clipboard. He wore wrap-around sunglasses, but maybe his build or his mannerisms would strike a chord with Courtney. Will pulled some mini-binoculars off of the backseat and handed them to her.

"Okay, see those three guys manning the entrance bays? Look at them closely. Tell me if you recognize anyone."

She took the binoculars and turned to look at the men. "Which one?" she asked, adjusting the lenses.

"Just tell me if any of them look familiar. You remember one of them from the Zilker that day? Maybe you've seen someone at the Randolph or lurking around?"

Will waited.

"Well, the middle one. He's wearing sunglasses, but . . ."

"Yeah?"

"He looks like one of those pictures you just showed me."

"Okay. But have you seen him anywhere else? Watch the way he moves. Look at his body."

She handed back the binoculars. "It's not him."

"You're sure."

"Totally. He's too tall."

Will studied her face. She seemed certain. And he should probably take her word for it. Years of interviews had taught him that the most accurate judges of height were taller-than-average single women. They could nail a man's height in an instant because they made a habit of noticing.

But even if Courtney didn't recognize this guy as her attacker, the man might still be involved. Maybe he'd been hired by Rachel Alvin to drive the car, and someone else carried out the actual hit. Nathan planned to follow up on this lead tomorrow by bringing the guy in.

"You think someone hired that man to kill David?" she asked.

"I can't comment on that."

But that was exactly what he thought. Alvin's ex-wife had been pestering Wilkers & Riley on a daily basis since Alvin's death. And she'd made a large withdrawal from a stock account just weeks before the murder.

It would have fit together nicely, except for the other possible victims. Even if she'd wanted her ex-husband dead, why would Rachel Alvin have Courtney killed, too? And what was the connection between Alvin's murder and Pembry's disappearance? And—if Courtney's theory had merit—the death of Eve Caldwell?

This investigation was a bitch. His first homicide case, and it was a goddamn mess.

Will backed out of the space and left the parking lot.

"Thanks for your help," he said.

"Yeah, right. This was a waste of time."

He blew out a sigh.

"You know, you look tired. And your color's bad."

His color?

"Your eyes are bloodshot, too." She seemed genuinely concerned. "I've got the afternoon off now. Want to go hang out somewhere? We could walk on the lake or something."

"I can't."

"What about later? You could use a night off."

Not with her, he couldn't.

He glanced over. He'd never met a woman so confident with men. She was practically asking him out, and he felt flattered. And tempted.

But he couldn't do a damn thing about it. Why didn't she get that?

Maybe she did, and she didn't care. She wanted to lure him in, manipulate him into seeing the case from a different perspective.

Shit, he was thinking like Webb now. This wasn't some femme fatale, this was Courtney. He knew she wasn't capable of murder. But he didn't have proof. And she was still a suspect.

She gazed at him expectantly.

"I can't," he said.

She glanced away.

"Now's not a good time—"

"Forget it. I understand." She kept her face turned away from him. "Anyway, I've got to meet up with Fiona later. She's having a dress fitting."

"She needs you at her dress fitting?"

"It's her wedding dress. I told her I'd go."

"Sounds fun," he lied.

She shot him a look.

"Okay, you're right, it sounds boring. Why can't she do it herself?"

"She's my sister."

Will shook his head. He didn't have a sister. And if he had, he still wouldn't have gone with her to try on clothes.

He pulled up to a light and the car fell silent. He cleared his throat. "So . . . you going to Fiona's then? Or back to work?"

"Just take me to Fiona's," she said crisply. "I'll hang out with her."

• • •

"I keep coming back to the money," Devereaux said.

Will watched his partner across the conference table littered with Styrofoam cups and sandwiches. They had given up their Saturday to go over leads they'd developed. Will had just told the group about the Caldwell woman.

"Someone with bucks is behind this thing," Devereaux continued. "And Courtney Glass only has a couple thousand dollars to her name, so it's not her."

"Yeah, how do you know?" Webb asked. "Maybe it wasn't a paid hit. Maybe she went on a rampage and killed her ex along with his new girlfriend. She seems like the jealous type."

Will clenched his teeth, wondering once again why Webb couldn't let go of the jealous mistress angle.

Cernak turned to Will. "Courtney Glass have an alibi for the morning of the bike accident?"

Highly doubtful, as it had happened at the crack of dawn. "I'll check," he said.

"There are two sources of money in Alvin's universe," Devereaux stated. "His wife's family and his law practice."

Cernak frowned. "What was his last big case, again? That pharmaceutical thing?"

"Diet pills," Will said.

"But that was what, six months ago? What else you got?"

Will flopped open his file and looked at the information he'd gleaned from Alvin's paralegal. "He spent pretty much all of last year on the drug thing. The trial was in January. Since then, he's done some minor stuff here and there, but mostly he's been coasting."

"Hitting the links," Webb quipped, "and picking up bimbos."

Will kept his face carefully blank. "The woman who tried the case with him seems to be coasting, too. Same with the two founding partners. According to the paralegals, the only people doing any real work over there are the support staff and the associates."

Cernak scowled, and Will knew what he was probably thinking. It sounded more like bitching from disgruntled employees than evidence of criminal activity.

"I checked out the drug case," Will said, shuffling through a notepad. "It was a product-liability suit over some diet pills that allegedly killed a woman. She was an investment banker, mother of two. Her family sued and got sixty million, mostly punitive damages. Firm's chunk of that would have been twenty-four. But the plaintiff took a discounted settlement to sidestep the appeals process, so it ended up being fifty-one million total, twenty and change to the firm."

"Why the discount?" Webb asked.

"I don't know."

"Appeals take forever," Cernak put in. "The family was probably sick of waiting around, wanted less money sooner. Happens all the time."

"Or maybe there was some weakness in their case," Devereaux said, "something that made them think they'd lose on appeal. If you go through with an appeal, there's the chance of reversal, right? That's a lot of money at stake."

Everyone looked nonplussed by the theory, but Will resolved to check into it.

"What about something tax-related?" Devereaux suggested, looking at Will. "You turn up any red flags with the IRS, either for Alvin or the firm?"

Will shook his head. "Nothing."

Webb snorted. "Yeah, that's 'cause half the guys over there practice tax law. If they're doing anything illegal, the feds'll be the last to know about it."

"Okay, so back to the Weenie Queenie." Devereaux tipped back in his chair. "Say she wanted to off her husband and his girlfriends. She's got plenty of money to do it, and probably some people who could help her. Daddy still runs the business, right?"

"Right," Will confirmed.

"So maybe he hired some thugs to help get rid of his daughter's problem." Devereaux looked at Webb. "You check out those bank accounts?"

"Nothing unusual," he said.

Will pushed away the remnants of his soggy Italian sub and glanced at Cernak. The lieutenant seemed to live on takeout food and coffee, and he looked it—a mere heartbeat away from a triple bypass. The media attention this case was getting probably wasn't helping matters. Plus—and this might be the biggest stressor of all—Devereaux had learned that the chief of police played golf with Alvin's father-in-law. Obviously, the family was anxious for a breakthrough, and Cernak probably wanted nothing more than to make an arrest and toss this case over to the D.A.

"What about your professor? That guy Pembry?" Webb asked Devereaux. "He know Alvin or his wife?"

"Can't find a social connection," Devereaux said. "Although I *did* find an article about Alvin sitting in the guy's study. It was a profile from a few months back. He'd torn it out of a magazine."

"How about Rachel Alvin's brother?" Cernak asked Devereaux. "You were checking him out?"

"Still am," Devereaux said. "But that money withdrawal didn't amount to anything. Turns out she used it to put a down payment on a car for her kid. But I think we should keep following the funds. This thing must be costing someone some money."

Webb sighed. "I'll hit the law firm again, see if I get anything new."

"I'll keep looking into the shooter angle," Will said, deciding it was time to check back in with the vice squad. They were supposed to be asking around with their CIs about the possibility of a hired gun.

"Check back with Courtney Glass, too." Cernak ordered Will. "See what she knows about Alvin's business dealings."

"I already asked her," Will said.

"Yeah, well, ask again. She was sleeping with the guy; she probably knows a hell of a lot more about him than we ever will."

Courtney glanced impatiently through the salon's front window. Will was late. Very. If she hadn't been wearing four-inch heels, she would have hoofed it to the bus stop by now.

"Are you sure I don't have any messages?"

Jasmine looked up from her game of computer solitaire. "Nobody since that cancellation at two."

Courtney checked her phone for the tenth time. Then she waltzed over to the mirror. She'd actually taken the trouble to freshen up for this man, and he couldn't even get here on time. And this chauffeur thing was *his* idea, not hers. She undid an extra button on her blouse, just to spite him.

"Here he is," Jasmine said.

Courtney looked through the window as Will's hulking

Suburban pulled up to the curb. The mere sight of it made her smile, but she quickly erased the expression and pushed through the salon's front doors. Will met her halfway up the sidewalk and gave her a stern look that said she should have waited inside.

The passenger door squealed like a pig when he jerked it open.

"How old is this thing?" she asked.

"Eighteen years."

"God, it's a *piece*." She glanced around the interior, secretly liking the rust spots on the floor beneath her feet.

"Your ride has an armadillo painted on the side of it."

She smiled up at him. "Yes, but at least it comes on time."

He slammed the door with another squeal, and she watched him walk around to the driver's side. He wore tan cargo pants, a black T-shirt, and work boots today, and Courtney got the distinct impression she was about to be ambushed.

"Where are we going?" she asked as he pulled away from the curb.

"What makes you think we're going somewhere?"

"You're not in your detective costume. Where'd you hide your gun?"

"You'll never know." The side of his mouth curled up, and Courtney felt a rush of warmth. He was teasing her. She wanted to kiss him.

"So where are we going?" she repeated.

"Baseball game."

*"Baseball?"*

He cleared his throat. "I got tickets to the Round Rock Express. They're a Triple-A team—"

"I know who the Express are. You're asking me to a game with you? Like, on a date?" She couldn't help smiling, especially when he looked uneasy with the label.

"You sounded like you were tired of your sister's place, so I thought maybe you needed a night out." He shrugged. "I know I could use one."

Her smile widened. A baseball game. For the first time in weeks, she had something fun to do with her evening. And for the first time in months, that something included a man.

She let her gaze drift over him again, admiring his ripped body in that T-shirt. She knew he could see her doing it, even though his eyes were on the road.

"I like the commando look," she said. "It suits you better than the business clothes. Any chance you'll swing me by my house to throw on some jeans?"

He glanced at her. "You're wearing jeans."

"These are dressy jeans."

"Dressy jeans?" He looked afraid of her jeans now.

"They're too tight to be comfortable and they cost a fortune. And this shirt is satin. Not exactly baseball game attire."

"Game starts in twenty minutes. We're already going to miss the first inning."

Courtney sighed and gazed out at the road. She supposed she could make do. At least she'd be off her feet. She nestled her head back against the cheap upholstery and felt the tension in her shoulders start to dissolve. She was going to a baseball game. She was going on a date.

And most surprising of all, she was going with a cop.

CHAPTER

# II

The ballpark smelled like funnel cakes and hot dogs. Will glanced around at all the families and young couples, but he didn't see any women besides Courtney wearing dress-up jeans.

"You want a drink?" He put his hand on the small of her back and steered her through the mob. They passed food vendors, margarita machines, and about a hundred beer stands.

"Let's claim some seats first. I take it we're in general admission?"

"Behind home plate."

Her mouth dropped open. "You're kidding!"

"Someone at work hooked me up."

"Oh my God!" She seized his arm. "We'll be able to see the pitches!"

He smiled to himself as they waded through people. She had some tomboy mixed in with the glamour girl, apparently. She quickened her pace until they got to Section 119.

"This way," he said, leading her down a few steps to their row. They were pretty high up, but they had a great view of the diamond. Courtney spotted their empty seats and squeezed her denim-clad butt past a row of spectators.

"This is amazing." She plunked herself down and

beamed up at him. "I can't believe we're behind the plate."

Will settled next to her, not too put out by the fact that they had to squeeze together a little. He was more relaxed now that he wasn't at work. And Courtney seemed more like a casual girlfriend than a suspect in his investigation.

The investigation he'd brought her here to talk about. He felt a stab of guilt. It was manipulative, inviting her out like this just to pump her for information. But people opened up more when they were comfortable. And a ballpark was about the most comfortable place Will could think of.

"What's wrong?" she asked.

"Nothing. Why?"

"You're frowning." She patted his knee. "Loosen up. You're off the clock. When was the last time you took a day off, anyway?"

He hadn't had a day off since he'd started. Hell, he'd barely had a full night's sleep. He'd come into this job determined to hit the ground running.

"Let me buy you a beer." She stood up and flagged a vendor. "Since you got the tickets."

Will watched the beer guy maim a few dozen people's feet in his rush to get to Courtney. Grumbles rippled through the rows behind them as he stood there, making change for Courtney's twenty and stealing glimpses down her shirt.

She sat down and handed him a cup full of foamy beer. "Cheers," she said. "I haven't been to a ball game in years."

"You used to go a lot?"

"Sometimes." She slurped the head. "I dated a guy back in L.A. who was a huge Angels fan. He had season tickets."

Will looked out at the field, needing a change of subject. The Express had their best pitcher up.

"This guy's good," he told her. "Wait till you see his slider."

They watched the next few at bats without talking. She didn't have the need to fill every silence. It was refreshing. Unlike the heat this evening, which was oppressive.

Will glanced at Courtney. The sun reflected off the auburn streaks in her hair. Perspiration misted her chest, and he wondered if he'd ruined her shirt by not letting her change clothes.

The Oklahoma RedHawks hit a triple, and a groan went up from the stands. Courtney lifted her hair off the back of her neck and twisted it into a knot.

"It'll cool off soon," he said, checking the sky. "I bet it drops fifteen degrees soon as the sun sets."

She tore her gaze away from the game and smiled at him. "I don't mind, really. There's a nice breeze."

He felt guilty again, watching her guard come down. It didn't seem like the right moment to bring up a murder case, so he decided to ask about her family.

"So you and Fiona seem pretty close."

She glanced at him, then back at the field. "I guess."

"You guys get along?"

She scoffed. "We'd walk through fire for each other."

"Yeah, but do you get along?"

Her gaze settled on him. "Sometimes. Sometimes not. We're really different."

He sipped his beer. It was ice-cold, just like it needed to be in this heat.

She looked at him. "You have any sisters?"

"Brothers. Two."

"Are you close?"

"Ah, not really. I haven't seen them much these last few years. They're both active duty."

Her eyebrows tipped up. "Your whole *family's* in the army?"

"Was. My dad's retired now."

"And your mom?"

"She died when I was sixteen."

Courtney's face fell. "How'd she die?"

Will shifted in his seat. How had they gotten around to this? He was here to interview *her*. "Leukemia."

"I'm sorry," she said, and her eyes looked sincere.

Shit, was she going to ask him about his mom now? He didn't want to go there.

But she didn't either, apparently, because she turned her attention back to the field. The RedHawks scored another run, and Courtney swore under her breath. She was into the game, and he decided to drop the personal stuff for a while.

They spent the next few innings making small talk about baseball. Courtney knew a lot about the sport, and although she didn't keep up with the Express, she was pretty current when it came to the Rangers and the Astros.

An Express hitter knocked one into the lawn, and everyone stood up and cheered. Courtney put two fingers in her mouth and let out a piercing whistle. She turned and smiled at him.

"Hey, are you hungry?" She looked back over her shoulder as the crowd settled down again. "Those hot dogs smell really good."

"I'll get us some dinner," he said, standing up. It would give him a chance to regroup. "You want another beer, too?"

"That's perfect."

"Ketchup? Mustard?"

She pulled some money out of her back pocket, but he waved it off. "It's on me," he said.

"Everything but onions." She smiled. "And I mean everything, even jalapeños, if they have any."

He escaped to the concession line. *Everything but onions.* Her smile let him know she was thinking about kissing him later.

And why did he feel like he was in high school all of a sudden?

This was pathetic. He needed to get back on track. He was here for information, and this softball approach wasn't working. He needed to be direct, even though he was pretty sure a direct conversation was going to throw a bucket of cold water on the flirty Courtney he was enjoying so much.

But she was a straightforward woman, so he needed just to come right out and ask her about Alvin. What did she know about his law firm? His marriage? His business dealings? What secrets had he spilled during their pillow talk? He needed information, and Courtney had been a deep well of it so far.

Will got the dogs and loaded them up with everything. Then he made his way back down to their seats. She was twisted around, talking to the trio of guys sitting behind her, who'd no doubt been checking out her fancy, silver-studded pockets for five innings.

"Will!" She waved excitedly when she saw him. "You missed the chicken dance."

Thank God. He let her help him with the food, and soon they were chomping on hot dogs as he considered his new approach. But it wasn't going to work. They were hemmed in by baseball fans, and the ones directly behind them were splitting their attention between Courtney and the game.

"Let's walk around," he said. "We haven't seen the park yet."

They took their hot dogs up to the concourse level and started circling the field. It was a nice ballpark. Very family-oriented, with lots of kid activities set up behind the outfield. They headed toward a moonwalk and a rock-climbing wall where half-wasted guys were attempting to impress their dates.

Courtney polished off her dinner. "I *love* stadium hot dogs." She licked her fingers. "There's something better about them."

Will took another bite of his, but he wasn't hungry anymore. He pitched it into a trash can as they walked past.

"So I have a question for you, but you can't lie." She gave him a coy smile, and he felt a prickle of unease.

"What?"

"Did you know it was my birthday?"

It was her birthday? Shit. It was her birthday. He remembered now, noticing the DOB on her paperwork the day they'd first met.

"You're twenty-seven today," he said, not really answering.

She stopped and caught his hand, grinning. "And he evades the question. You didn't know, did you? When you asked me out tonight?"

"I didn't know." God, he was a jerk. She thought this was a date.

She tugged him forward. "It's okay. I'm glad you were honest. You get brownie points anyway. I haven't been on a date in ages."

Will glanced at her as she walked beside him. Her hand was warm and soft around his, and he didn't really believe she hadn't been on a date in ages. "How come?" he asked.

"I don't know." She sighed. "David kind of soured me on relationships. I'm off men. Or at least, I'm trying. I thought about switching teams for a while, but it would never work."

Will floundered for a response. This woman could never *switch teams*. It would be a crime against mankind.

She squeezed his hand, and he saw that she was laughing at him. "You blush at the oddest moments."

He cleared his throat. "So anyway." Great start. "I've been talking to Devereaux."

"Uh-huh?"

"He thinks we need to focus on the money."

"The money." Courtney tossed her hot-dog wrapper in a trash can. She turned to face him and slid her hands into her back pockets. "You're talking about David's money?"

"Sort of. See, so far, everything is pretty complicated. There're lots of people involved, which probably means deep pockets somewhere."

"You sound like Jack."

"Jack?"

"Fiona's fiancé. He's an investigator with the D.A.'s office."

Will wasn't thrilled about some D.A. guy sniffing around their case, but he let it go. "Anyway, I wanted to get your input. You think Alvin might have been involved in some sort of sketchy business venture? Maybe a deal gone bad?"

She frowned. "I have no idea."

"He owe anyone money, that you know of? Maybe he had a gambling debt?"

She glanced up at him. The sparkle had gone out of her eyes, and he could tell she wasn't happy about this new topic. "He never talked about gambling."

"Betting? Horses? Maybe a sports team?"

"No."

Will shoved aside his frustration. He remembered the letter Nathan had shown him, the one from Pembry. "What about someone named Dr. Awkward? You ever meet anyone by that name?"

"Dr. Awkward? It sounds like a nickname."

"Could be. He ever mention a doctor to you at all? Maybe a business acquaintance?"

She paused a moment, gazing out at the field. "We didn't spend much time talking."

Right. He'd had that coming, but it still felt like a kick in the gut. "What about his cases?"

"He might have mentioned stuff in passing, but nothing I remember."

"Okay. How about real estate deals? Eve Caldwell worked for the biggest real estate agency in town, so—"

"Look, I don't know anything about his business." She crossed her arms. "I was his girlfriend, not his wife. Why don't you ask her all these questions?"

Her look was icy, and he realized the reference to Alvin's *other* mistress might have been a little callous. "I'm just trying to put the facts together. I thought you could help."

She scoffed. "You know, if you wanted to interrogate me, why didn't you just drive me straight down to the police station? You didn't have to waste your time bringing me to a ball game."

"I'm not interrogating you. I just wanted to ask—"

"Forget it." She turned around. "Let's go, okay? I've had enough baseball for one night."

Courtney lay on her sister's sofa, trying to ignore the low creaking sounds coming from across the house. They were trying to be quiet. She knew that. More than once, she'd heard Fiona shush him, but still, it was an antique wrought-iron bed, and the house was tiny.

Music. That would help. Courtney grabbed her backpack off the floor and rummaged through it. The interior of the bag suddenly lit up as the first few beats of "Hollaback Girl" sounded from her phone.

"Hello?"

"Hi." It was Will. "Did I wake you?"

"Unfortunately, no."

The other end was silent as he deciphered this. She tossed off the blanket and walked to the other side of the living room, away from the bedroom.

"Where are you?" she asked.

"Driving home from the station."

So, he'd gone back into work following the baseball game. What had he done, transcribed their conversation? Entered an audiotape into evidence? Her temper started to fester.

"I called to tell you I'm sorry," he said. "For earlier. I didn't just invite you out to interview you—"

"Yes, you did."

Pause. "Okay, I did. But I feel bad about it, and I want to apologize."

She bit her lip. If there was anything that got to her about this man, it was his earnestness.

She heard a familiar noise outside and walked to the front window. "Where are you?"

"On my way home."

"No, but where, exactly?"

A few seconds went by. "I just passed your house, actually. Fiona's house. I wanted to check things out on my way home—"

"Come back."

Will pulled up to the curb, certain he was making a mistake and equally certain he wasn't going to do a damn thing about it. The front porch light went off. Then the door opened, and Courtney slipped out.

He got out of the Suburban and closed the door as softly as he could. She met him halfway down the sidewalk. He couldn't really read her expression in the darkness, but he could see that she wore some silky black nightshirt that stopped about midthigh.

"Hi," she whispered.

"Hi."

She held up a six-pack. Then she took his hand and led him back to the house. They settled onto the front stoop. For the second time that night, he felt like he was in high school, only this time, he'd snuck out of the house at night to visit his girlfriend, and she'd stolen her dad's beer.

She passed him an icy bottle. He twisted the top off and handed it back to her, then took one for himself.

"I hope you like Corona," she said. "No limes."

"This is good."

Her bottle clinked against his. "Here's to sucky birthdays." She tipped it back, and he watched her. The breeze lifted little strands of her hair off her shoulders.

"I'm sorry about earlier."

"You said that already. Let's forget it." She picked up his free hand. "What brings you out here so late, Detective Hodges?"

He glanced up and down the street. Everything seemed quiet. Fiona and Jack lived in a middle-class neighborhood with residents who mowed their lawns regularly and went to bed at a reasonable hour.

"Just wanted to do a drive-by."

She gazed at him. He wondered what she was thinking. He wondered what she thought of *him*.

God, he was an idiot. He swigged his beer and looked down the street.

She bumped her knee against his.

He bumped hers back.

Then she rested her head on his shoulder, and he felt a pang of longing so strong he couldn't breathe.

He took another sip and floundered for something to say.

"So. How'd the fitting thing go? I never asked you."

"Fine," she said. "Better than I expected, in fact. Her dress is perfect for her."

"Are you in the wedding?"

"I'm a bridesmaid. No chiffon, thank God."

Her hair smelled good again, and he looked away.

"Courtney . . . ?"

"Hmm?"

"I'm sorry about the timing here. If things were different—"

"Stop apologizing. I'm allergic to guilt."

"I like you a lot."

"Did you hear what I said?"

"I know you're innocent."

She pulled her hand away and rested her beer on the steps. He couldn't see her face in the dimness, but he felt the tension in her body. She was pissed. Great.

And he didn't blame her.

He shouldn't be here, having this conversation. Everything about tonight had been wrong. Yes, he'd been ordered to interview her again, to pump her for information. But he hadn't been told to let it get personal. He hadn't been told to check up on her every night, to take on the role of her personal bodyguard.

He was no longer objective, and that meant he should drop the case. But the thought of leaving her fate in the hands of Webb or Cernak or even Devereaux didn't sit well.

He took one last swig and put down his beer. It was time to leave.

"Will?"

He turned and looked at her. *Now* he could see her face. Now she looked worried and vulnerable, and he could feel that she wanted something. She leaned over and kissed him. Her mouth felt hot and soft again, and he parted her lips with his tongue so he could taste her—that tart, sweet woman taste he remembered from the first time. And then his hands were in her hair, holding her in place while he kissed her and she drew him in even deeper. She whimpered, and he pulled her up, off the ground, into his lap, and his hands slid over all that cool, thin fabric until he found her breasts. She raked her fingernails over his scalp and pressed herself against him until he couldn't think of anything but how much he wanted to have her, every inch of her. She smelled good, she tasted good, and the warm weight of her was better than anything he could remember.

Something buzzed, and they jerked apart.

She stared down at him. "It's you," she whispered.

Reality crashed in, and he shifted her off his legs so he could fish the phone out of his pocket.

"Hodges."

Courtney stood up and turned around. She wouldn't look at him.

"We got a robbery-homicide on Willow and Fifteenth. Can you get there?"

"Yes," he told Devereaux.

"Good. And if you're still interviewing our suspect, you need to cut her loose. You got me?"

Will took a deep breath, then blew it out. "Yeah."

# CHAPTER

# 12

Nathan followed Hodges past the stainless steel name-plate to the sleek glass counter. The receptionist's smile faded as they walked up, and Nathan knew Hodges had been making a pest of himself here for the past week.

"We're here to see Jim Wilkers," the rookie told her.

A stiff nod. "Have a seat, Detectives."

Nathan wandered over to a window that had an impressive view of Town Lake while Hodges went to the stainless steel coffeemaker and poured himself a cup. "Hey, pour me some, too, would you?"

Hodges took a gulp of coffee and sank onto the couch.

Nathan stared at him. Hodges took another sip and looked up. "What?"

"You hard of hearing, man?"

"Who, me?"

"No, the other asshole sitting there ignoring me."

Hodges darted his gaze around the empty waiting room. Then he nodded slightly.

"War injury?"

"Left ear's sixty percent."

Nathan crossed his arms and looked at him. How had he made it through his police physical? This guy was one enigma after another. And probably the biggest mystery was why a cop with so much potential would piss his career away for a woman.

"So, how'd it go with Courtney last night?"

Hodges glanced up from his coffee cup. Cleared his throat. "It was okay."

"You get any new leads?"

He shrugged. "A few things to check out."

"We both know she didn't do it."

His partner's face remained blank.

"But she's Cernak's favorite," Nathan continued.

"Why?"

Nathan shrugged. "He likes things simple. He plays the odds. Female victim, look at the boyfriend, the husband. Male victim, it's usually a business deal gone bad or a jilted lover. Lot a times, that's how it works out."

Hodges shook his head and peered into his coffee cup again. The glass mug had W&R etched on the side.

"So, you like this girl?"

Hodges glanced up at the question, his face much too neutral.

"If you like her," Nathan said, "do her a favor and don't fuck up her case. You get too involved, you get your ass reassigned, and it'll be all Webb. You think that's gonna help her? So leave her alone."

"Mr. Wilkers will see you now, gentlemen."

Nathan shifted his attention to the receptionist. She stood stiffly in the doorway and her voice was even chillier than the air-conditioning. Nathan followed her down a long hallway. She bypassed several windowed conference rooms and then opened a door.

"He'll just be a moment."

"What, no window?" Nathan asked, sinking into a black leather chair at the end of the table.

She glared at him and then turned to Hodges. "Can I get you anything?" She glanced pointedly at his coffee mug.

"No, thank you."

Nathan let her almost get the door closed. "Wait!" She turned around, and he smiled. "I'll have some of that water, please. With the bubbles in it."

Her lips pressed together, and she pulled the door shut. Hodges looked at him from across the room. He hadn't claimed a chair yet.

"I'm surprised you wanted to come," Hodges said. "I thought you were buried today."

"Ah, nothing that couldn't wait."

Hodges watched him closely, and Nathan knew he was trying to pin down his motive. Nathan wasn't even officially *on* this case, but he'd put in more hours so far than anyone.

This was a peach of a case, no matter how you sliced it. And although he hadn't kept the lieutenant up to speed on everything he was doing, he knew Cernak was getting antsy with his involvement. But Nathan didn't give a damn. He wouldn't watch Courtney Glass go down in flames for a murder bought and paid for by someone else.

The door opened and Wilkers stepped into the room, accompanied by the firm's other senior partner, Peter Riley.

"Hey, what do you know? Two for the price of one." Nathan thrust out his hand, but didn't get up. Both men shook it and then lowered themselves into chairs on the side of the table facing the door. Hodges finally picked a seat at the other end of the table.

Wilkers got right down to business. "Detectives. We've been cooperative to this point, but this is getting ridiculous. As you well know, our time is money."

Nathan shook his head. "Sorry, guys. These things take a while."

"But didn't you recover a gun?" Wilkers asked. "We heard you were on the brink of an arrest."

"I'm afraid we can't comment on that," Hodges said, stepping up.

Nathan watched jaws tighten and arms fold over chests. For a couple of guys who used jury consultants on a regular basis to interpret body language, they needed a refresher course.

"And just what is it you want with us?" Riley asked.

Hodges pulled a notepad out of his pocket and shuffled through it. "This won't take long. It's just a formality, really. I need to ask about cars."

The men exchanged looks.

"What kind of vehicle do you drive?" Hodges held his pen poised above his notepad. "Mr. Wilkers?"

"A BMW 550. Black."

Hodges scribbled. "And the license plate on that? You know it offhand?"

Wilkers recited some numbers and looked annoyed.

"And your wife, sir? Oh, wait. Sorry, you're not married. Is that your only vehicle?"

"Yes."

"And Mr. Riley, what about you?"

"A silver Lotus Elise," he said tightly. "I believe you've seen it."

Hodges scrawled something in his pad. "And the tag?"

"G-H-F-3–9–5."

"And your wife's car?"

Riley was getting ticked now. Everyone knew all this information was available on a computer at the police station.

"A white Lexus. I don't know the plate off the top of my head, but I can have my secretary look it up."

"Thanks, that'd be great. Either of you fellas own a Cadillac?" He turned to Wilkers.

"No."

"No," Riley said, and sighed.

"You sure? I mean the SUV, not the sedan. It would be an Escalade."

"No," Riley said.

"Mr. Wilkers?"

"No."

Hodges sighed and jotted down a few more things. "Okeydokey. That should do it."

He stood up, and both men looked surprised. Nathan stood, too, repressing a smile. Hodges had them off balance.

"That's it?" Wilkers asked warily.

"That's it." Hodges reached for the door and pulled it open. Nathan exited first and walked a few steps down the hallway to an open doorway. A young woman sat at the desk inside the office, tapping away on her computer keyboard. It was the blond litigator, Lindsey Kahn. Nathan remembered her from the funeral.

"Oh, just one more thing, Mr. Wilkers. You own shares in an oil company?"

"What? No."

"You sure? Maybe it's not an oil company, exactly, but a limited partnership that owns mineral rights on some land in east Texas. TW Enterprises?"

Nathan kept his eyes on the woman and his back to Wilkers as he waited to hear his response.

"Yes. I own a *share* of the company, if that's what you mean."

"And does *it* own a Cadillac? A black Escalade?"

The attorney's fingers paused on the keyboard. Her nail polish matched her tailored red suit, and Nathan could practically feel the tension coming off of her.

"TW Enterprises owns lots of things in lots of places. I'd have to check."

"That'd be great, thanks. You ready?"

Nathan turned and saw his partner walking toward the exit. He smiled at the two lawyers. "Thanks for your time, fellas. We'll see ourselves out."

Will had nailed it. Jim Wilkers was hiding something, and he'd just moved to the top of Will's suspect list. Feeling like he'd finally made some headway in this case, he bypassed the elevator and took the steps up to his department two at a time.

"Hodges!"

He stopped short at Cernak's office.

His boss stood behind his desk, hanging up the phone. "I been looking for you." He plopped into his chair. "Close the door."

Will stepped inside and pulled the door shut. The lieutenant always looked unhappy, but this morning his expression was set to extra grim. Will noticed the newspaper

on the desk opened to a front-page story about another homicide last night.

"Take a seat." Cernak picked up a file from beneath the newspaper. "Have a look at this."

Will took the file. His phone buzzed, and he jerked it out of his pocket. Courtney. Shit. He turned it off and shoved it back into his pants.

The file contained a stack of paperwork from LAPD, and Will's gut tightened as he skimmed through the pages.

"Girl's got a rap sheet," Cernak said. "DUI, possession, public indecency. There's a juvie record, too, but it's sealed."

Will slid the file back across the desk. Skinny dipping and smoking pot on a public beach didn't make someone a murderer. But he didn't want to rush to Courtney's defense.

"You're spending a lot of time with our lead suspect," Cernak stated.

"You told me to question her."

"And did you get anything, or did you get distracted? I need to know where your head is, Hodges, because I'm *this* close to arresting her." He held up two fingers a half inch apart. "I don't need any headaches from the D.A.'s office if it turns out she was sleeping with one of my cops."

"In that case, sir, I should be reassigned." Will's tongue felt thick as he said the words.

"You're sleeping with her?" Cernak looked genuinely surprised now, and Will realized he'd overstated what he knew.

But it didn't matter. The gist of it was right; Will had lost his objectivity when it came to Courtney.

"No." Will cleared his throat. "But you could say I have a conflict of interest. Sir."

Cernak leaned back in his chair and watched him skeptically. "Okay. I appreciate your honesty." He nodded at the door. "You're off the case, then. And you're free to go."

Go? He was getting axed? Will stood up, numbly, and for the first time he realized how much he wanted this job. He'd spent years getting here, and now he'd blown it.

"Go back to your other cases," Cernak said sharply. "We got no shortage of shit for you to do around here. But watch your step, Hodges. You're walking on thin ice."

Courtney spotted Will at the mall entrance, holding the door for a woman with a stroller. She saw him notice her and felt a swell of satisfaction when his gaze went straight to her legs.

But then he saw her packages and scowled.

He stopped in front of her and planted his hands on his hips. "You called me away from work for shopping?"

She tipped her head to the side and looked at him. "What's with you?"

Shaking his head, he took the Macy's bags containing Fiona and Jack's wedding present, plus a new pair of sandals that had been on sale. He headed back out the door. Courtney followed him, getting annoyed as he outpaced her across the parking lot. He reached the Suburban and tossed her bags in the backseat.

"Careful! That stuff's breakable."

"You want someone who cares, hire a chauffeur."

She halted, stung, and watched him slide behind the wheel. Two nights ago, she'd been in his lap, and now he was treating her like crap.

Why had he even come here?

Maybe he was just responding to the bait. She'd left two messages on his voice mail this afternoon, and she'd been purposely vague: *I thought of something about the shooter.*

Courtney shrugged off the hurt and went around to the passenger's side. "Look, I don't know what your problem is, but don't take it out on me."

He shot backward out of the space, and she braced a hand on the dashboard.

"So, you got me here," he said. "Talk. Meter's running."

She secured the seat belt over her black tank dress and crossed her legs. "Well, it was something I noticed yesterday. I was doing highlights for this client who really likes to chat."

He sighed, and she felt her temper welling up. "Hey, you want this or not? I don't have to help you guys."

"What's the lead?" he asked irritably.

Okay, so he'd had a bad morning. It was Monday; she could give him some leeway. She took a deep breath and decided to start over.

"This client has a thick accent. Very Boston. And it jogged my memory. It made me think of the guy's voice."

He sent her a sideways glance. "You're saying the shooter's got a Boston accent."

"I think so. Or maybe somewhere near there. Northeast, for sure. He didn't say a whole lot, but the accent was distinctive. I remember now."

He stared straight ahead, and she watched his jaw twitch.

"It's not a bad lead," he said. "I'll tell Webb."

"Webb?"

"He's in charge of your case now."

Panic shot through her. "But what about you?"

"I've been reassigned."

"But—"

"Drop it, Courtney." He glared at her. He hadn't just had a bad morning; he was angry at *her*. This was a recent development.

It had happened since the baseball game. Since their kiss on the porch.

Courtney looked out the window, and the fear took hold. Nathan was on her side, but he wasn't on her case officially. Will was on her side, but he'd been reassigned now. That left Webb and Cernak to determine her future. And if they believed she was the killer, they weren't going to be out there looking for someone else.

But someone else might be looking for *her*.

Her stomach churned. Saliva pooled in her mouth, and she swallowed it down. What was she going to do?

"Where to?" Will asked. His voice sounded softer now, and he must have known what she was thinking about.

"Just take me to Fiona's."

He drove silently to her sister's house, maneuvering through rush-hour traffic without so much as a four-letter word. He pulled up to the curb and parked.

"Thanks for the lead," he said without looking at her. "I'll pass it along."

She watched him for a moment. He wasn't telling her something. Big surprise. But she could tell that whatever it was had him very stressed out.

"Will . . . are you all right?"

He flicked a glance at her. "Fine."

But he wasn't.

She wanted to invite him in. Or even better, she wanted him to ask her to dinner so they could talk about everything. But his tension level was ratcheted up to eleven, and it was pretty clear he wanted to be alone.

Fine. She'd offered herself to this man twice now, and she wasn't going to do it again.

She reached into the back and collected her shopping bags. She pushed open the door, and he caught her arm.

She glanced back at him. He didn't say anything, but his look was intense.

"What?" she asked.

"Be careful."

"I am."

And then he let her go.

Courtney spent Tuesday morning in a cranky mood, partly because she'd had a lousy night's sleep, but mostly because of Will. Despite her protests, he'd insisted on taxiing her to work again, which had made for an awkward car ride and an even more awkward good-bye. Courtney had opted for silence, and Will had gone with a brief nod and a "take care" as she'd climbed out of the truck.

She tried to work off her bitchiness with her scissors. Her 10:30 client had long, layered tresses that required lots of snipping and a twenty-minute blow-dry. And she didn't talk much, thank God. Courtney was in no mood to play therapist.

As she swept up for her 11:30, her thoughts returned to the baseball game. She couldn't stop thinking about what Will had said.

Had David revealed something to her that could explain

all this? She'd been scouring her memories, trying to come up with some conversation in which he'd given her a clue about some shady deal he was mixed up in. But he hadn't talked much about his business. He'd told her a little about the trial he was working on, but it had all been pretty high level. It was some diet pill lawsuit. Courtney remembered, because he'd asked her if she'd ever used the drug, and he'd looked disappointed when she'd said no.

How had she missed so many signs he was an insensitive pig?

"Your next appointment just called. She's got the flu."

Courtney looked up at Jasmine. "She want to reschedule?"

"Said she'd call back tomorrow."

Courtney sighed. Her 11:30 had been a generous tipper, and she'd been scheduled for full highlights. At least she'd canceled. Courtney hated it when people showed up hacking up a lung, spreading germs everywhere.

"I'm going to lunch," she announced abruptly. She snatched her purse from the cabinet where she'd stowed it and breezed past Jasmine. "I'll be back for my one-fifteen."

It was another scorching day, but Courtney welcomed the sun on her face as she left Bella Donna. She'd been cooped up indoors too much lately. She needed to get out. She waited for a few minutes at the corner and hopped a bus to the UT campus. Her favorite Internet café was on Guadalupe Street, and she had some research to do.

Two chai lattes later, she was bleary-eyed from looking at news clips and legal articles. God, the law was boring. She didn't know how people could stand it.

Of course, maybe the fees helped. The lawyers' cut of

David's last big trial had been twenty million. Even after David had shared the fee with his firm and the other litigator who'd tried the case with him, he'd taken home over five million, according to the *Central Texas Bar Bulletin*.

Courtney's eyes were glazing over, so she closed out of the text page and clicked over to some video sites. After entering a few keywords, she opened up a thirty-second sound bite from the local ABC affiliate. David stood on the steps of the courthouse in his favorite navy suit as eager reporters shoved microphones in his face.

"The jury's message today was clear," he announced. "The American public won't stand for big business profiting from the deaths of innocent people. Justice has prevailed—"

Courtney clicked Pause. She leaned forward and squinted at the screen. Who were these people walking down the steps, behind David? She clicked back to the beginning of the sound bite.

"—innocent people. Justice has prevailed—"

*Pause.*

It was Eve Caldwell. And that professor whose picture Will had shown her. They were exiting the courthouse as David's trial wrapped up.

They were part of the trial.

Courtney's blood chilled as the idea sank in. This was about the case. This was about sixty million dollars. Will had been right. The pockets involved here were very, very deep.

Her fingers shook on the keyboard now as she searched for more snippets of video. She couldn't find anything, but she had to learn more. Were Eve and the professor witnesses in the trial? Were they plaintiffs?

Were they jurors?

Had David been *sleeping* with a juror in his case?

"Oh my God," Courtney whispered, staring at the screen. That could be it. Maybe he'd rigged the jury. Maybe he'd fixed the outcome.

Courtney shot up from her seat and grabbed her purse. She logged off the computer and stuffed her credit card back into her bag. She had to get out of here. She had to tell Will. She rushed out of the café and glanced down the street.

"Dammit!" She stomped her foot as the bus she wanted pulled away from the corner three blocks up.

But she could call him. She didn't have to go anywhere; she could just call him. She whipped out her phone and stepped back from the curb. She scrolled through her speed-dial list as a car rolled to a stop beside her.

A black Escalade.

The door pushed open.

# CHAPTER

# 13

Courtney stared, slack-jawed, at the man getting out of the car. Gray eyes. Bulky. He was looking at *her*.

He lunged, and she leapt back. A flash of metal appeared in his hand, and Courtney's heart flip-flopped.

"Gun!" she shrieked, ducking into the doorway.

She heard a commotion behind her as she yanked open the door and stumbled back inside the coffee shop. She scrambled past the row of computer terminals, bumping into chairs and tripping over backpacks on the floor. She glanced frantically over her shoulder, but the doorway was empty.

A streak of black shot past the window as the Escalade peeled away from the corner. They were on the move.

She caught a flash of motion as the café's side door flung open.

Him. Coming after her. Her gaze dropped to his hands. One was tucked inside his tracksuit, along with something pointy.

She spun on her heel and elbowed her way through people milling around the coffee bar.

"Help!" she screamed, and people looked at her like she was nuts. She glanced behind her, but the man was gone.

Where'd he go?

She raced past the cash register to the restroom corridor, where she knew there was a back exit. She pushed through the door, jumping with surprise when an alarm howled in her ear.

She stood there, panting. An alarm was good. Weren't you supposed to scream "fire" if you ever got attacked? She glanced up and down the alley and wished a cop or security guard would come running.

He appeared at the end of the alley. The door clicked shut behind her. She whirled around and tried it.

*Locked!*

Her gaze darted back. The man charged toward her.

She bolted the other direction, slipping and sliding over the slick pavement. She dashed past a Dumpster, inhaling the rank smell of garbage as her heart thundered.

"Help! Fire!"

Another glance over her shoulder. He reached inside his pocket.

She spotted a doorway up ahead, propped open with a milk crate. She raced for it, and his footsteps thudded behind her, gaining, gaining. She reached the door and tripped though the opening. On a burst of inspiration, she kicked the crate back into the alley, hoping this door locked automatically, too.

She was in a kitchen, between a vat of dirty dishes and a big stove. She smelled cooking oil.

The door jerked open, and a giant hand seized her arm. Shrieking, she kicked back at him. With her other hand, she grabbed hold of something on the stove. A wok. She flung it backward.

He bellowed and doubled over. She bolted away from

him, plowing through people in aprons and hairnets. She ran past stainless steel sinks and counters, then burst through the first door she spotted and ended up in a dark, empty room. She stopped to let her eyes adjust. A dining room. And it wasn't empty—there were tables scattered around and people hunched over plates of food. Voices hushed. Chopsticks froze. Pairs of startled eyes gazed up at her. She stood there, gasping for breath.

A tall rectangle of light flashed as the kitchen door swung open.

"Fire!" she screamed, sprinting for the entrance. She jerked open the door and ran into the blinding sunshine. A sidewalk. A sandwich shop. An Urban Outfitters. She was on Guadalupe again.

She raced down the sidewalk, elbowing through the endless students and backpacks, even passing someone gliding along on in-line skates.

She hazarded a glance back, and a horn blared. She halted in the middle of an intersection. The car honked again, and she jumped out of the way. She looked around desperately for a cop or a phone.

She had a phone.

She plunged her hand into her bag and groped for it. Where was her phone? She could never find it when she needed it most. She darted her gaze around. Where was the Escalade? She needed to get out of here. She needed safety.

Brakes hissed as an orange-and-white bus pulled up to the corner two blocks away. A student shuttle. She dashed toward it. Her heart pounded. Her calves burned. The straps of her high-heeled sandals bit into her skin.

She heard the door close, saw the brake lights go black.

"Wait!"

The bus groaned forward, and she slapped the side. *"Wait!"*

It stopped.

The doors popped open.

She grabbed the handrail and heaved herself inside.

Will picked his way up the vine-covered hillside, trying to put the images out of his mind. The kudzu tangled around his ankles, and he felt like it was tangled around his neck, too, depriving him of even this hot, stagnant air.

"You okay?" Devereaux asked from behind him.

"Yeah."

They reached the top of the ravine where a slight breeze rustled leaves. Will stepped over to an oak tree and scraped the soles of his shoes on the trunk to get rid of the mud.

"It's the heat," his partner said. "All those weeks in the sun. You sure you're okay?"

"Yeah." Actually, he wanted to hurl, and he probably would if Devereaux didn't shut up soon.

"ME'll probably rush the autopsy. I'll need you to check missing kid reports. See what we can turn up."

Will swallowed the bile in his throat and tried to ignore the sweat streaming down his back. Devereaux scraped his shoes on the same tree, and then they trudged back to the Taurus, which was parked on the shoulder of this isolated stretch of road. The crime-scene van sat a few hundred feet north of them, closer to the slimy creek bed where the body had been found.

Will's phone vibrated, and he checked the screen. Courtney. Damn. He'd missed two calls from her, but he didn't want to tell Devereaux that. He walked away from the Taurus until he was sure he was out of earshot, then dialed her back.

"It's me. What's up?"

"Where have you *been?*" she demanded.

"I'm in the middle of something. What do you need?"

Silence.

"Courtney? What's wrong?"

"Nothing." But her voice sounded funny when she said it.

"Why did you call?"

"I had a problem. But I've got it handled."

She had it handled. How come he didn't believe that?

"What kind of problem?"

"Hodges! We gotta get moving." Devereaux waved him over.

"Are you working?" she asked.

"I'm at a crime scene. What kind of problem?"

"Forget it. It's fine now. When do you get off? I need to talk to you about something."

Her voiced sounded weird still—like she was upset, but trying to hide it. He wanted to know what her problem was that was "fine" and "handled."

"I have no idea," he said. "Probably late. You need to catch a ride with your sister."

Pause.

"Are you really okay?" he asked.

"I'm fine."

"You don't sound fine."

"Hodges!"

"You're busy," she said. "We can talk later."

• • •

Alex Lovell loved a cheap thrill.

She loved to feel her muscles tense and her pulse race as she waited to get what she needed, just how she needed it.

Her fingers tightened on the wireless mouse. She stared at the screen. She held her breath.

"*Yes!*" she hissed, closing her eyes.

She opened them again and smiled at the computer.

"Well, well, Mr. Klem. What do we have here?" Alex skimmed the list of numbers, looking for the precise combination that would tell her her hunch had been right.

And it had. Of course. If there was one thing Alex knew, it was that people were predictable. And the quickest way to find them was to follow their vices.

Which, in the case of Ronald Klem, was cyberporn.

Alex searched the website some more, looking for the address associated with his online account. The site was protected by security screens, but nothing too complicated. A few more clicks, and Alex had what she wanted.

"Hel*lo*, deadbeat."

She jotted down the information on the pad beside her phone and leaned back in her chair. Now came the fun part of her job. She got to call up the former Mrs. Klem and tell her her ex-husband—who'd fallen off the radar after their last court date, and who owed eighteen months of back child support—was kicking it in Jacksonville, Florida.

Alex clucked her tongue at the ease of it all. She picked up the phone.

A bell sounded in the front office, and she glanced at the monitor to her right. She had a visitor. Alex studied the black-and-white image. She checked her watch. She'd planned to knock off early today, but that plan was about to change. This visitor had that look about her that told Alex she had a problem, and whatever it was wasn't going to wait. Alex put her computer to sleep and walked out front to meet her.

She stood in the center of Alex's unimpressive reception room, looking decidedly unimpressed. She was a few years younger, probably mid-twenties. She had an outfit and a body to die for, with the exception of her feet. They were scraped and dirty, and apparently had been roaming downtown Austin without the benefit of shoes. Alex noted the heeled sandal sticking out of her oversize purse.

"Is this Lovell Solutions?" the woman asked.

"It is."

Alex watched as her gaze skimmed over the threadbare couch, the moving boxes, and the Mr. Coffee balanced atop a folding chair. Alex had moved her office here three months ago, but she hadn't found time to unpack. It didn't matter, really, because she conducted the vast majority of her business via computer. Alex had clients she'd never even seen, although she knew their e-mail addresses and cell phone numbers by heart.

The woman's gaze met hers. "I'm Courtney Glass."

"Alexandra Lovell."

Courtney walked over to a teetering stack of software manuals. She flipped the top one open. Alex noticed the tremor in her hands and wondered if she was strung out on something.

"How'd you get this address?" Alex asked, more out of curiosity than annoyance. Her company's address wasn't printed on her business cards.

"Sandra Summers is a client of mine."

Alex pursed her lips. Sandra Summers was a TV anchorwoman whom Alex had helped with a pesky fan problem last spring.

"How's Sandra?" Alex asked, wondering what Courtney did for her, and guessing it wasn't her taxes.

"Fine." Courtney walked to the other side of the room. With a trembling finger, she parted the miniblinds and peered through them.

Did she think she'd been followed here?

She turned to Alex. "You charge by the hour?"

"Depends. Sometime it's the project."

"I've got a project for you, but I need it done fast."

"I'm pretty booked up right now."

"This is important."

"How important?"

Courtney dropped her purse on the couch and glanced up, and Alex saw the fear in her eyes. "I need your help."

"With what?"

"Making someone disappear."

Nathan knew what they were dealing with the moment he saw that Thomas the Tank Engine blanket.

"Bones show a history of fractures." The medical examiner turned toward the X-ray clipped to the light board and used his pen as a pointer. "We've got a broken humerus. I'm estimating six months old. Never properly set."

"What about this?"

Beside him, Hodges pointed to a view of the rib cage.

"Good eye, Detective." The ME indicated the second rib up on the left side. "That's a hairline fracture. I'd estimate three to six months old, but it's hard to say for sure."

Nathan crossed his arms. These were the cases that made him thankful he lived in a death-penalty state. He looked at the medical examiner. "This is a closet case."

"By the looks of it, yes. Especially with the missing lower central incisor. It would have been a permanent tooth. It was knocked out well before the time of the skull fracture that caused death."

"A closet case?" Hodges asked.

"Given the signs of ongoing abuse and malnutrition, it's likely this child suffered for years at the hands of his caretaker," the ME said. "The abuse and neglect would have been so severe, it never would have escaped notice of a teacher, which leads me to believe this child wasn't in school. He'd probably been secreted away by his parent in a closet or attic."

"You're assuming he's school age," Hodges pointed out. "The body looks pretty small."

"I believe you're looking at the remains of a seven-year-old boy."

"*Seven?* The kid couldn't have been more than forty inches tall!"

It was the most emotion Nathan had ever heard in his partner's voice.

"It's the malnutrition." The ME turned to Nathan. "Also, there's the blanket. When we see remains wrapped up carefully in a blanket like that, it points to the mother. She's responsible for, or complicit in, the abuse. And the actual killing, if I had to guess."

Hodges shook his head. "Who *does* that?"

"Someone terribly insecure."

All three heads turned in unison. Fiona Glass stood in the doorway with her art case clutched in her hand. Her gaze was riveted on the X-rays. Nathan had heard Cernak on the phone with her earlier, requesting a postmortem drawing so they could get an ID.

Fiona stepped closer to the light board and stared up at the film showing the tiny fractured skull. Her lips compressed into a thin line.

"You think you'll really be able to get a picture?" Hodges sounded skeptical.

"I'm going to try." She turned to the ME. "I'll need the blanket and the clothing. And any other personal items that accompanied the remains. I'll do drawings of everything. It's important to get as much information as possible out to the public to help prompt recognition."

She looked again at the film. She had a strange expression on her face—a mix of anger and revulsion.

And she hadn't even seen the body yet.

Nathan hated the task that lay ahead of her. He hated that time after time she got called in on the most horrific cases. Cops were expected to deal with the worst shit society could dish out, but Fiona was different—not as jaded as she needed to be. He'd probably never get comfortable asking for her help, although he didn't know how he'd ever do without her. He couldn't count the number of cases they'd managed to close because of her work.

"No missing person's report that you could find?" she asked.

"Nothing that's a match," Hodges said.

Yet another reason why Nathan knew they were looking for the child's mom and whatever dirtbag guy she happened to be living with. It might be the biological father, but Nathan suspected they'd find it was the stepdad or the boyfriend, someone who didn't care much for another man's kid hanging around.

"The mother won't come forward," Fiona said with certainty. "She's too weak. What we need is a concerned relative who hasn't seen this child in a while."

Nathan stared at the X-ray. He loathed any homicide involving a child, but this one in particular got to him. Who were these women who sat by and let their kids get knocked around? They were worse than their men. People said maternal instincts came naturally, but Nathan had seen way too many counterexamples over the years.

"I'll get you your drawing; you get it on the news." Fiona turned to him with somber eyes. "Our best hope is that this child's got a grandmother somewhere."

Someone was in Will's apartment.

He wasn't sure what, exactly, tipped him off, but he knew someone was there. He stood outside the door for a full minute, listening, before sliding his key into the lock. His right hand curled around the grip of his Glock, and his left slowly turned the key. Soundlessly, he pushed open the door.

The apartment was dark, just as he'd left it. The only light shone down from the microwave above the stove. It was quiet. He stepped over the threshold and paused in the foyer.

He smelled Chinese food.

Something moved to his right. He pulled his gun and whirled—

"Omigod, you scared me!"

Courtney.

She stood in his bathroom doorway, silhouetted against the yellow light. "I didn't hear you come in," she said, stepping into the living room.

He stared at her over the sofa and confirmed his initial impression that she was wrapped in his beige bath towel. He shoved his gun back into the holster, embarrassed now. "How'd you get in here?"

She shrugged. "It was easy." She turned and sauntered into his bedroom, and he noticed the flower tattoo on the back of her shoulder.

Easy. Getting into his locked apartment.

"I'll be out in a minute." She switched on a lamp. "Just let me get dressed."

The bedroom door thumped shut, and he stood there, staring at it.

Courtney Glass was in his bedroom.

In a towel.

Will scanned the apartment again, certain now about the Chinese-food smell. He walked into the kitchen and flipped on the light. The counters were vacant, as was the table. He opened the fridge. His usual array of beer and Gatorade stared back at him. Everything looked exactly as he'd left it except—

The bedroom door opened and out came Courtney. She was barefoot and bare-legged, and she wore a zip-up black sweatshirt over frayed cutoffs.

"Have you eaten?" she asked, breezing into the kitchen.

"Time out. How'd you get in here?"

"Your landlady downstairs." She pulled open the oven and took out a small white carton. "You like kung pao chicken?"

"My landlord let you in here?"

"Now, before you get pissed, let me just say that she's a sweet old lady." She removed several more cartons from the oven and lined them up on the counter. "I told her it was our anniversary and I was here to surprise you."

Will tossed his keys on the counter beside the food. "And she believed that? She's never even seen you before."

Courtney smiled up at him. "I can be very convincing."

He stared down at her, both annoyed and impressed. He was annoyed that she was here, in his kitchen, all wet and flirty. He was impressed that she'd tracked down his address.

"How'd you find out where I live?"

Her smiled widened. "Now *that* was the hard part. You're not listed."

"I know."

"I had to hire a detective."

"Seriously, how'd you find me?"

"Seriously, you'll never know." She started opening cartons. "I pegged you for a beef man, but you can share my chicken if you want. I also got egg rolls and wonton soup."

"Courtney."

She turned and pulled open a cabinet above the coffeemaker. "Where are your plates?"

"Courtney, you can't stay here."

She found the plates—all four of them—and got down two, along with a pair of cereal bowls. "You want steamed rice with yours?"

He took her by the elbow and turned her around to face him. Just touching her arm reminded him why she needed to go. "You can't stay here."

"Who said anything about staying? This is dinner. Consider it a thanks for the baseball tickets."

Something was wrong. This morning she'd been bitchy as hell and now here she was bringing him dinner.

And parking her stuff in his bedroom.

Under any other circumstances, he wouldn't have minded. In fact, given his recent dry spell, he should have been overjoyed to find a half-naked woman waiting for him when he got home from work.

But this wasn't just any woman. And today hadn't been just any day at work, either. He was in a foul mood. He was drained. His patience was at an all-time low, along with his willpower.

"What happened?" he asked.

"Nothing."

He clenched his teeth. Counted to three mentally. "Then why aren't you at your sister's?"

She pulled her arm away and searched a few drawers until she found the flatware. "I can't go there tonight. I don't feel safe about it."

"Tell me what happened."

She scooped chicken onto the plates. "Let's talk about it later. Right now, I just need to relax."

She needed to relax, and he needed her to leave. Will emptied his pockets onto the counter and blew out a sigh.

"If you want a drink," she said, "there are a couple beers in the fridge."

"I know. I bought the damn things."

"Why don't you have one? I hear you've had a rough day."

Will rubbed the back of his neck, trying to rub out the tension. She'd talked to Devereaux, then. Or Fiona. Probably Devereaux, and the son of a bitch had given her his address.

She pulled open the refrigerator and took out a Bud Longneck. She used her sweatshirt hem to twist off the top and then handed him the bottle.

"There's an Astros game on tonight. It's probably started."

"Courtney." He set the beer on the counter. "This isn't a hotel. We can eat dinner, but then I'm taking you to your sister's."

There. He'd said it. She wasn't spending the night here, no matter how good she looked in that zipper thing.

"Fine." She shrugged, as if she could take it or leave it. Then she picked up a plate and carried it into the living room. She sat on the sofa and flipped on the TV.

He let out a breath, both relieved and disappointed that she hadn't put up more of a fight. "I've got to clean up."

He grabbed some clothes from his room and ducked into the bathroom that was still steamy from her shower. It smelled like perfume, too, which just added to his mood. What did she do, bathe in that stuff? He'd probably go to work tomorrow smelling like a woman.

This was so screwed up. APD had caught ten murder cases in the past three weeks, and the prime suspect in one of them was on Will's couch watching baseball.

And his partner knew about it. Whatever credibility he'd been trying to build with his new colleagues was trashed. He'd likely be yanked off the homicide squad tomorrow and given some desk-jockey job.

Will set the shower to scalding and tried to scrub off the death stench that clung to his skin. After a good ten minutes, he figured he'd done the best he could both cleaning up and avoiding the problem in his living room.

How was he going to get rid of her?

He toweled off and yanked on some clothes. As he buttoned his jeans, his gaze landed on the pair of gold hoop earrings sitting beside the sink. He'd seen them this morning when he'd driven Courtney to work. She'd been wearing a dress, too, and those man-killer shoes, and he remembered feeling a flare of resentment over the idea that some guy might come sit in her chair today and think about touching her while she cut his hair.

Just like he had done.

Will yanked on a T-shirt and made his way back into the kitchen. The apartment was dark again, except for the television. He picked up the beer and took a gulp. Courtney had left chopsticks out for him, but he dragged open a drawer and got a fork. Then he grabbed his plate of cold food and joined her on the couch.

"Do you have transportation?" he asked.

"A friend dropped me off."

He plunked his plate on the table without comment.

"The Astros are winning," she said, trying to distract him with her sunny mood. "Hey, perk up. If it makes you feel any better, I had a crappy afternoon, too."

He sneered. "What, someone have a bad hair day?"

Courtney got up and went into the bedroom. A moment later, she was striding toward the door with a duffel bag slung over her shoulder.

Shit.

She jerked the door open as he shot up from the couch.

"Wait," he said, shoving the door closed with his palm.

"*Move.*" Her cheeks were flushed with anger, but her eyes glistened.

"I'm sorry."

"Apology accepted. Now *move.*" She pulled the door, but he kept leaning. "You're a jerk, you know that? And I probably make better money than you do, so you can just save the condescending bullshit!"

"I didn't mean that like it sounded."

"You think your job's so great? At least I make people feel good about themselves. When was the last time you did that?"

"Probably never," he admitted, hoping she'd stay mad and not let those tears leak out. "I'm sorry."

"Yeah, well good for you." She pulled the knob again, but he kept his palm flat on the door.

"Move."

"I told you I'm sorry."

She crossed her arms and looked at the floor. Her cheeks stayed dry, but he could see her chin quivering. Jesus, was she going to cry over this? Obviously, he'd underestimated the severity of her bad day.

Either that or she was seriously touchy about her job.

Courtney acted so tough all the time, he hadn't realized he could hurt her feelings. Or maybe he had, but he'd been so desperate for her to leave, he hadn't cared.

He hooked his finger through the strap of her bag and tugged it off her shoulder. "Don't go."

She took a deep breath, and he kissed the top of her head. It was damp and sweet-smelling, and he kissed it again. She looked up at him, and he lost whatever scrap of resolve he'd had left.

"Please?" He kissed her mouth. "I want you to stay."

# CHAPTER
## 15

Courtney wanted to enjoy the kiss, but she was too distracted by the hurt. His words cut. She'd known they were from different worlds, but she hadn't realized he thought of her with contempt.

She pulled away. "Stop."

He stopped, although she could see the frustration on his face.

"Please forget what I said. You're right, I'm a jerk."

Instead of kissing her again, he pulled her against his big, hard chest, right next to his heart.

Of all the things he could have done, this was the worst. Until he wrapped his thick arms around her and held her there, in his protective cocoon.

She closed her eyes and sighed. This was *so* dangerous. And *so* not her. She'd come running to this man for protection, and now here he was protecting her. Offering shelter and safety.

And something even more tempting, judging by the ridge pressed against her stomach.

And she wanted all of it so much she ached. How had she become like this? She'd never been dependent on a man. She'd never been like her mother. But on a day when she'd been more terrified than she'd ever been in her life, more afraid of the future than ever before, she'd gone running straight to a guy to make it all better.

She felt the slight rock of his hips against hers, and realized she'd been pushing against him. Her arms went up around his neck. His hands slid slowly down over her back to cup her bottom.

He kissed her temple. "What is this stuff?" Still holding her, he turned her away from the door and started easing her back into the living room.

"What stuff?" Her toes barely touched the floor as he lifted her, pressing her against him as he walked.

"That perfume." But then his mouth was on hers, preventing her from answering. He was hurried and hungry, and the thrill of it shot through her as she realized this was a first. *He* wanted *her*. Before it had been her flirting and seducing—sometimes jokingly, sometimes not.

But this seduction was all him, and it was totally serious. She heard the high rasp of her zipper being lowered, followed by a moan deep in his chest.

"I knew you'd have something good under here."

She glanced down at her sheer black bra and watched his giant palms slide over her breasts. She was busty, but not quite enough to fill those hands. It was one of the things she liked about him—she was no lightweight, but still he was so much bigger than she was. It made her feel feminine.

"It's not perfume," she told him now, as his thumbs stroked over her. Lord, she'd missed this. Something firm hit the back of her thighs, and she realized he'd backed her against the sofa arm.

"Whatever it is, I love it. And that black thing, too. Hold on."

She toppled backward and he fell on top, the full weight of him crushing her into the sofa. She squealed with delight.

"I have to see the rest of it," he said, pushing up now with one arm to let her breathe. She loved the way his muscles strained the fabric of his T-shirt. She had the sudden urge to sink her teeth into him, and then she smiled at herself. That was a completely new desire for her. She must be starved for a man.

"Please?" His finger trailed down to her belly button, and he looked into her eyes.

She reached up and hooked an arm around his neck. "Yes," she whispered, and kissed him.

Another rasp of zipper, and she felt her shorts slide over her hips. She watched his eyes heat in the flicker of the television as the baseball game droned on. Then he kissed his way up her body, murmuring something, but she was too busy licking and nipping at his neck to make sense of it all. Then his hand cupped her and a sharp bolt of pleasure speared through her.

"Oh my God." She clutched her arms around his neck, pressing as close as she could, never wanting it to end. Instead of ending, it went on and on, and she grasped and pulled at him, frantic to get close, to feel every part of him closer and closer. He touched her everywhere while she closed her eyes and combed her fingers through his short, bristly hair. Finally, she shuddered violently and went limp underneath him.

His hand gentled and stroked, then gradually trailed up to wrap around her waist.

"Oh my God," she whispered again, utterly lax. It was

like yoga. Only the sated, hot flowing was so much deeper and so much better than ever before.

He kissed her temple and rested his forehead against hers. Their skin was slick with sweat, and she didn't know whether it was his or hers.

"You okay?" he whispered.

"Yeah."

"Just checking."

She felt a powerful surge upward as he lifted her off the sofa. He carried her into the bedroom and laid her down on his bed. The mattress was firm, like she'd expected when she first saw it, and she smiled up at him as he eased down beside her.

"You look happy," he said.

Her smile widened. She picked up his big hand and kissed the palm. He had a long, jagged scar there that she'd noticed days before, but now wasn't the time to ask about it. "I like your hands," she said instead.

He lifted an eyebrow and dipped his head down to kiss her breast. "My hands, huh?" His breath was hot against her skin, making her entire body tighten. He kissed her breasts and her collarbone and her throat. She felt the pressure building again, and she hooked her calf around the back of his knee to bring him closer. She rocked her hips against him, and felt the evidence of his immense patience. He'd made the first part all about her and she loved him for it. It seemed such a minor thing, but in her whole life, no one had done that. She'd never realized it until now.

She pulled back from the kiss and looked up into his face, at the intensity of his gaze. He looked so somber now, as if he'd sensed her seriousness, too. Whatever this was, it wasn't a joke. Beads of sweat formed at his temples, and she knew he was working to control himself. The idea made her urgent for him, and she arched against him and pulled his mouth down to hers.

His kiss became forceful, and she responded the same way. She wrestled with his T-shirt as he tugged at her bra and panties. She popped the front hook and had no idea what happened to the rest, but then they were naked except for his jeans. She raced her hands down the button fly as a drawer beside the bed scraped open. He hurried to cover himself and then pushed her thighs apart.

Tears sprang into her eyes at the shock of him. She wrapped her arms tightly around his neck and tried not to cry out. She wanted this, and she didn't want him to know it hurt her.

"Wrap your legs around me."

She did, and felt relieved at the fit. And then the pain was gone, and it was just him and heat and the awesome power of what he was doing to her. She never wanted to let him go. She'd never felt like this, like she was *joined* so completely with someone. Like they were one thing, together, and he could touch every cell of her body, and the feeling went on and on until she thought she would die.

"Courtney." His voice was hoarse. "Honey, are you . . . ?"

She couldn't breathe, she couldn't talk, and she answered him the only way she could. *Yes.*

And after a final, burning moment, they collapsed together.

Alex waltzed into APD headquarters and did what she always did when she didn't belong somewhere—she faked it. She walked briskly down the corridor, stopped briefly for a drink at the water fountain, and then pretended to be taking a cell-phone call until she spotted a mid-twenties guy with some sort of tag hanging around his neck. By the scruffy, harried look of him, she decided he was a print reporter and followed him through a set of double doors to a chest-high counter. Once there, he joined several other young, newshound-looking people culling through metal trays of police reports. Alex joined them and tried to look bored. If they knew she wasn't one of their ranks, they didn't mention it. And anyway, the thing she wanted was public information.

But it wasn't in the trays. Finally, she stepped up to the Plexiglas window and cleared her throat to get the attention of the woman seated at a desk behind the counter.

"Excuse me. I'm looking for an incident report from earlier this week."

The woman stood up and stepped over. "Date and address," she intoned. "Incident number, if you got it."

"I don't."

"Date and address."

"Actually, it's a missing person's report. For a Dr. Martin Pembry? You know where I could find it?"

The woman's gaze sharpened, and she glanced over Alex's shoulder at the information junkies behind her.

"Have a seat," she said, and nodded at the bank of chairs beside the door. The woman disappeared down a hallway, and Alex wandered back over to the trays of paper. She thumbed through the reports one by one and pretended to be interested.

A trickle of unease traveled down Alex's spine, and

she turned around. A dark-haired man was slouched against the nearest doorway, watching her. He stepped forward.

"Hey, there."

"Hello," she said. Did she need a press pass to be in here? She was pretty sure this room was open to the public.

"I'm Nathan Devereaux." He held out a hand, and she caught a glimpse of the holster beneath his jacket. "Alex Lovell." She shook his hand firmly, and he smiled.

"Nice to meet you, Alex." He jerked his head in the direction of the hallway. "This way."

She followed him down the long corridor and took the opportunity to check him out. He had thick, dark hair—a little shaggy around the ears—and a navy jacket that looked like it had seen better days, but that stretched nicely over a muscular back. He wasn't exceptionally tall, but he had a confident walk.

And when it led her right out a side door, to a flight of concrete stairs, she stopped in her tracks. He stopped, too, and turned casually around to face her.

"Just thought we'd get some air. A little crowded in there, don't you think?"

He had a low southern drawl, and she guessed he used it to put people at ease. It wasn't working with her, though.

"What is it you want, Mr. Devereaux?"

"Nathan. And I was thinking we could go get a drink." He nodded in the direction of Red River Street, where a neon sign advertised a dubious-looking barbecue joint.

"Why would I go get a drink with you?"

A slow smile spread across his face. "I have something you want."

It was either the worst come-on in history, or he knew something about Martin Pembry.

She shrugged. "Let's go." The place was within blocks of a police station, and she wasn't riding in a car with him. How dangerous could it be?

They walked in step, and Alex suddenly felt self-conscious about her clothes. She was wearing the same outfit she'd had on when Courtney Glass had appeared in her office—faded blue jeans, a snug ACL Fest T-shirt, and worn cross trainers. But the Smokin' Pig didn't exactly look like a five-star establishment. It smelled heavenly, though, like hickory and campfires.

He held the door for her, and she decided he wasn't just a cop, he was a detective. He looked the part, with his cheap business casual and his alert blue eyes that noticed everything but didn't react.

She picked a table for two in the bar area.

He pulled her chair out, and she smirked. "Is this a date?" she asked.

"Nah, I don't date other detectives." He took the seat across from her.

"What makes you think I'm a detective?"

"You're not a PI?"

She tipped her head to the side. "I asked what makes you *think* that?"

He shrugged. "Experience. You've got that bad-ass, don't-follow-the-rules look about you. And you've got a purse full of gadgets."

She jerked her head back, amazed. "How do you know what's in my purse?"

"I'm psychic."

A waitress stopped by their table, and Devereaux smiled up at her. "Two Shiner Bocks, please. A glass for the lady."

Alex crossed her arms. This guy was too cocky for her tastes. "I don't drink beer, thanks."

He leaned back in his chair. "Charlie on the X-ray machine's a buddy a mine. He saw you come in."

Okay, this was getting creepy. Charlie on X-ray was sharing the contents of her purse with some detective? And they'd sent him down to talk to her about Martin Pembry? She was starting to believe Courtney Glass was right—there was a major conspiracy going on here. She'd thought the woman's story sounded over the top, but now she had to wonder.

"What do you know about Martin Pembry?" she asked.

"I know that he's missing. And the press hasn't caught wind of it yet, which makes me wonder how you found out."

"If the guy's missing, why isn't his family sounding some alarms? He's a UT professor, right? It should be all over the news."

Their beers arrived, and he waited for her to take a sip before tipping back his bottle. Old-fashioned manners seemed ingrained in the guy. She wondered if he was a true southern gentleman, or if the accent was just his shtick.

"He's divorced," he told her. "Plus, he's on sabbatical. He was supposed to leave for England next week, as a matter of fact. Wasn't putting in face time at the university."

Alex sipped her beer again and wondered why he was telling her all this. In her experience cops didn't share information just for the heck of it, and certainly not with outsiders. He must think she knew something.

"I have a client who thinks she's in danger from the

same people who may have made Pembry disappear. She seems legit, but I'm trying to check out her story."

"You're a skeptic, huh?"

Alex shrugged. "It's standard." She'd had people try to hire her to help them flee the police, or kidnap their children, or get money out of the country. She didn't take those clients. And she didn't break the law.

Sometimes she just bent it a little.

"So this client wants you to run security for her?"

"Sort of."

His gaze traveled over her, taking in her petite frame. Alex's curly, dark hair was in a ponytail today, which she knew made her look even younger than she normally did.

"You employ bodyguards, I take it?"

"I'm not going into any more detail about my client," she said. "I just need to know if this Pembry thing is real. She also gave me the name of some woman she thinks was killed in a staged bike accident."

"Eve Caldwell."

Her surprise must have been visible on her face.

"Your client isn't crazy," he said. "We just reclassified that incident today as a homicide."

Alex suppressed a shudder. Courtney Glass wasn't nuts. This wasn't some wild story.

Which meant her life really *was* in jeopardy. And Alex would have to make good on her promise to help protect her from whoever it was who wanted her dead.

Devereaux leaned forward on his elbows. "Listen, Alex. I need to know who your client is."

"I can't say."

"Can't or won't?"

"Won't."

He didn't react to this, except to lean back in his chair. He watched her for a long moment, and she started to get uncomfortable.

"I'd like to show you something," he said. "I can almost guarantee it will be of interest to your client. But if I do, I need you to tell me who that person is. I can't protect someone if I don't even know they're in harm's way."

Alex sipped her beer and considered the offer. She didn't want to reveal her client's identity, but this was an unusual case. The timeline was short. She needed all the information she could get, and she needed it now.

"Okay," she said. What did she have to lose? If everything went as planned, Courtney Glass would be long gone by tomorrow morning anyway. Who cared what APD knew about her? With Alex's help, she'd be invisible.

"Don't go anywhere." Devereaux got to his feet. "I'll be back before you finish that beer you didn't want."

Courtney lay against him, her hair still damp from the shower. He twisted and untwisted a lock of it around his finger. He'd figured it out finally. It wasn't perfume that made her smell so good—it was something she put in her hair.

She shifted, sliding her thigh higher up on his body, and tipped her head up to look at him. "Hi."

"Hi."

"You're really quiet."

"I'm recovering," he said, although that was a gross understatement. He felt like a bomb had gone off in his bed. He'd never be the same.

"Are you in trouble now?" she asked.

"What do you mean?"

"I mean, is there supposed to be some kind of line between you and me because of the case?"

He slid his hand over her hip, up the length of her thigh, then back down again. "I'm so far over the line, I can't see it from here."

She propped up on an elbow, and his attention was drawn to her plump, white breasts.

"Are you sorry I came over?"

"I don't know." It wasn't the nicest thing to say, but it was the truth. He could lose his job for this, a job he'd spent years earning the chance to do. "We just made everything a lot more complicated."

She gazed down at him, and he was relieved she didn't look hurt. She stroked her hand over his chest, tracing the muscles. She seemed to like touching him, and she could do it until the cows came home, as far as he was concerned.

"I'm not sorry," she said.

She settled back down against his side, all curves and heat, and he decided he wasn't sorry, either. No matter what happened. But he wasn't ready to tell her that.

She lifted his hand and turned it palm up, and he knew what she was going to say.

"What happened to your hand?"

"Stupid accident," he said. "Drunk at a party. Tripped and fell on a glass bottle."

"Hmm." She traced the silvery scar with her index finger. Her finger trailed over his wrist to another scar on his forearm. "And this?"

He tensed as her finger sought out yet a third faint scar

near his elbow. He started to say something, then stopped himself. It felt strange, lying to her. She'd lied to him over and over, but he felt like they were past that now. Some sort of trust had developed between them, and it seemed wrong to break it.

"It's something from when you were a soldier, isn't it?"

He glanced down at her.

"It's okay if you don't want to talk about it," she said. She pressed a kiss into his palm, and something twisted inside him. "I have stuff like that, too."

She nestled closer and tucked her head against his chest. Her ear was right next to his heart, and he wondered if she could hear it pounding, if she could sense how uncomfortable he was. He'd never been tempted to talk about this, especially not with a woman. But something about her leaving it alone made him think maybe she'd understand better than most.

He tightened his hold around her. "Tell me about your day."

Now she was the one to tense up.

"I was at a crime scene when you called, or I would have picked up," he said, combing a hand through her hair.

"The closet case?"

"Fiona told you?"

She sighed against his skin. "Yeah. She was really upset about it. I spoke with her on the phone."

"So what happened this afternoon?"

"Someone tried to kill me."

He bolted upright. *"What?"*

"They came after me at the Internet café—"

"Did you call the police?"

"I called you."

She lay there, looking up at him, and he was skewered by guilt. She'd called *him*. And he'd been too busy to deal with it.

"What happened?" he demanded, searching her for signs of injury.

She sat up and scooted back against the pillows. Then she pulled the sheet up and tucked it around her. "I was doing some research at an Internet café. I found this video clip—"

"You were attacked at a *coffee shop?*"

"Just outside. The black Escalade pulled up and—"

"Goddamn it, what were you doing there?"

"I was researching something."

He clenched his teeth and tried to rein in his temper. If he overreacted now, she wouldn't tell him the full story. "And then what?"

He listened, grinding his teeth to nubs, as she told him about being chased through restaurants and down alleyways until she was lucky enough to hop on a bus without getting gunned down by some thug, probably the same thug who'd tried to kill her at Zilker Park. Will watched her recount everything, amazed that she could be so calm right now. He wanted to take someone apart.

"So that's why I came here," she said now. "I didn't want to lead them to Fiona. Or to Amy and Devon. I didn't want to go anywhere but here."

"You need to report this. We need to talk to my lieutenant—"

"Fine, I'll do all that. But maybe tomorrow, okay? I

don't want to think about it right now. I just want to be here."

He closed his eyes briefly, realizing now just how badly he'd screwed this up. He'd let this get personal. And now he was going to have a hell of a time doing his job. How could he protect her—not to mention clear her name—if he couldn't even listen to her talk without going ballistic over the danger she was in?

He clasped her shoulder. "I'm going to get you some police protection."

"Okay."

"I'll talk to Cernak, see what we can set up, all right?" Even if it had to be him, and Nathan, and whoever else he could drum up—he was going to get someone on her twenty-four/seven. "This isn't going to happen again."

"Okay."

He studied her face in the lamplight. She looked way too nonchalant about this, as if it didn't matter what he did.

She leaned forward, and the sheet dropped away. "Let's worry about this tomorrow." She kissed him.

"We should go in tonight."

"Tomorrow." She kissed him again and slid onto his lap.

"First thing, Courtney. I mean it."

She settled herself on top of him and draped her arms over his shoulders. "First thing."

Nathan made it back to the barbecue joint in record time. He sat down in front of the pretty PI and noticed her beer was exactly the level it had been when he left. She was stubborn, and he wouldn't be surprised if she left it sitting there, untouched, just to piss him off.

"Is this a top-secret file?" she asked, and nodded at his thick brown folder.

"Not really." He pulled out several large Ziploc bags containing yellow sheets of legal paper. He selected the first letter he'd received and placed it in front of her.

"Any of that gibberish mean anything to you?"

She pulled the page closer and hunched over it, resting her elbows on the table. "'No evil I did, I live on'? What's it mean?"

"I don't know."

Her finger went to the bottom of the page where someone—presumably Martin Pembry—had sketched a fairly good depiction of Lady Justice. She was blindfolded and holding a scale.

"'Level, madam, level!'"

"I think he's referring to the scale," Nathan said, somewhat proud to have made the connection.

Alex frowned down at the page. It wasn't so much a letter as it was a collection of phrases and doodles. All of the notes he'd received from the professor—two at work and two at home—had been similar. All yellow sheets of legal paper, folded up and stuffed into business envelopes with MR. DEVEREAUX, HOMICIDE UNIT printed neatly on the front above an address.

Alex tapped her finger on something scrawled in the margin beside what looked like a caricature of a bald man with glasses. "Who's 'Dr. Awkward'?"

"Got me. I thought you might know. Sounds like maybe

a nickname. He mentions someone named Sarah there, too. Is that your client?"

She didn't say anything, just stared at the page. He watched her face, searching for a clue, but she gave nothing away.

"Or maybe your client's a doctor?" he asked.

"Oh, my God." She looked up at him, her eyes bright with excitement. "This guy's a professor, right? Does he teach English?"

Nathan frowned. "Linguistics. Why?"

"It's a palindrome."

"A who?"

"A palindrome," she said, turning the page around for him to see. "It reads the same forward and backward. 'Harass selfless Sarah.' See? And this one here: 'Evil is a name of a foeman, as I live.'"

"Holy shit," Nathan muttered, gazing down at the page. It seemed so obvious now. He'd read these things over and over and never spotted it. He glanced up at Alex. "How did you know that?"

"I grew up in a family of crossword freaks." She grinned. "We played Scrabble every Sunday. Let me see another one."

He slid another page to her, feeling a little dizzy. He knew what it was now, but what did it mean? And why had some guy mailed all this to a homicide detective right before he disappeared?

"A lot of these seem to reference good and evil," she said. "And those are the Scales of Justice, right? In that picture?"

"That's what I thought, too."

"Look, what do you make of this: 'Now Eve we're here we've won.'? Is he talking about Eve Caldwell?"

"I assume," he said. "Even her name is whatever you called it."

"A palindrome. Damn, you're right."

"Listen, Alex." He gave her a hard stare. "This is more than a word game. I've got three murders here, all potentially connected. If your client is someone named Sarah, or if she's a doctor, she could be in serious danger."

She sat back and pushed the paper away. "Her name isn't Sarah. And she's not a doctor."

"Is she related to Eve?"

"No."

"I need you to tell me—"

"Her name's Courtney Glass."

Courtney, of course. He supposed he didn't blame her for going out on her own to get help. APD sure as shit wasn't helping her any. If it were up to Webb, she'd be under arrest right now. And Cernak was a breath away from charging her in the Alvin homicide. He had the gun and the GSR test, plus the media and the chief and the hot-dog heiress's legal team breathing down his neck and demanding an arrest. Nathan knew it was just a matter of time before the lieutenant bowed to all the pressure.

Unless he or Hodges could come up with a more viable suspect.

"She told me something else you might find interesting." Alex looked at her watch. "I'll pass it along, and then I've got to get going."

Nathan nodded.

"There was some big lawsuit her ex-boyfriend was

working on. David Alvin? She found a video clip on the Internet that showed Eve Caldwell and Pembry exiting the courthouse the day the trial wrapped up. She thinks all this is about that trial."

Nathan absorbed every syllable she said. He couldn't believe a woman PI was sitting here cracking this case open for him. With the help of a hairdresser. It was humbling as hell.

She checked her watch again. "I've got to go. I've still got work to do tonight."

"Of course you do."

She stood up and pulled a wallet out of that cavernous purse. "What do I owe you for the beer?"

Nathan shook his head and laughed. "Not a goddamn thing."

Courtney lay sprawled on Will's bed, eyes closed, breath even, until she heard the soft thud of the bathroom door and the hiss of running water. She got out of bed and quickly pulled on her clothes. She shoved her feet into flip-flops and picked up the duffel bag she'd packed in the wee hours of last night, while Will lay sleeping and spent after yet another round of lovemaking. He'd insisted on setting the alarm for six, insisted that they needed to rush straight to headquarters this morning and put a plan in place to deal with the threat against her.

But she had her own plan.

She crept into the kitchen and lifted the set of keys from the counter. Darting a glance at the bathroom, she worked the Chevy key free from the chain.

Her stomach knotted. If he walked out here right now, she'd never be able to explain herself. She'd never be able to look him in the eye and convince him that she had to do this, that she didn't have a choice.

He thought she did. He thought he could pull a few strings, get her set up with some sort of security detail, and that would solve everything. He also thought he could clear her name.

But Courtney knew differently. This thing was going

to get worse, and even Nathan, a veteran on the force with a lot more clout than Will, wouldn't be able to pull enough strings. That lieutenant had her in his sights, and yesterday had illustrated all too vividly that somebody else did, too. She didn't intend to sit around waiting for a man to shield her from danger. Her freedom was at stake. And her safety. And the safety of her sister, and her neighbors, and anyone else who happened to be nearby next time some hired gun came looking.

Her gaze fell on the pen sitting beside the phone, and her heart squeezed. Maybe she should leave a note. Maybe she should explain herself, try to lessen the impact of what she was about to do, because she knew he'd be hurt. He was an ex-soldier and a cop, a man who'd obviously seen more than his share of bad things, but he had feelings, too. And this was a betrayal, no getting around it. They had bonded last night. In between the groping and the moaning, they'd had some quiet, gentle moments of understanding. She'd never had that with anyone, and she felt guilty now for running away. She reached for the pen.

The pipes went silent, and she froze. She glanced at the bathroom door. It remained shut.

She tiptoed across the apartment, silently unlocked the door, and slipped out.

Making someone disappear in the digital age was no easy task, but Alex relished it. She sat at her computer, her fingers flying over the keyboard, while she spoke with Courtney's telephone company.

"Thank you for holding. How can I help you this morning?"

"Hi, this is Courtney Bass. I hate to bother you, but I've got my last bill sitting here, and I notice you guys still have my name wrong. It's 'Bass,' not 'Glass.' I called about this last month."

"I'm sorry about that. Let me pull up your account. Are you calling from home?"

"No, actually, I'm at a friend's place. Let me give you my number." Alex recited Courtney's home phone number.

"Just to confirm, Ms. Bass, could I have the last four digits of your social security number?"

"Sure thing. That's 4-3-1-0."

"Hmm . . . That doesn't match my record. Could I have your mother's maiden name, please?"

"It's McCowen. Sounds like my whole file's messed up. I guess I got the new guy on data entry, huh?"

"We'll take care of it for you, Ms. Bass. Just give me your full social."

Alex rattled off a number ending in 4-3-1-0 and listened to the clack of computer keys as the customer service rep changed the record.

"Thanks for calling, Ms. Bass. We've got it all straightened out now. And is there anything else we can help you with today?"

"That'll do it, thanks."

Alex disconnected and smiled with satisfaction. She planned to call back again tomorrow to tell them she'd been getting obscene phone calls and that she wanted a new number, which would further muddy the waters. Whichever skip tracer went looking for Courtney's phone records was going to have a bitch of a time tracking them down.

Locating someone was all about resources—namely

time and money. The more time and money eaten up by the search for a person, the lower the likelihood of success. According to Courtney, the people after her had no shortage of funds. But Alex could make their job time consuming and tedious as hell, giving Courtney a chance to get underground.

Alex moved on to the next item on her list: the cable company.

"Hello, this is Courtney Glass. I'm moving and I need to disconnect my service."

"Are you calling from home?"

"No, actually."

"I'll need your social security number, please, to access your account."

Alex recited Courtney's actual social and waited for the rep to pull up her file.

"Thank you, Ms. Glass. And when would you like your service disconnect?"

"I'm moving tomorrow," Alex said. "So let's do it as soon as possible."

"We'll put you down for tomorrow, then. And I'm showing a balance of eighty-two dollars and fifty cents on your account. We'll need a forwarding address where we can send the bill."

"Certainly," Alex said, and gave her a P.O. box in Nashville.

"Will that be all today?"

"That's it, thanks."

"Thank you for calling, Miss Glass. And good luck with your move."

Alex made phone calls until all Courtney's records with

her Austin-based utilities were in shambles. In some cases, she altered Courtney's name, providing any PI who came looking with a potential alias he'd have to track down. In other cases, she had the service canceled completely and the final bill forwarded to the Tennessee P.O. box.

Next, Alex got on the phone with several airlines and had their frequent-flyer accounts altered so they no longer had a record of the various flights Courtney Jane Glass had taken over the past ten years. One less clue for someone to follow in the search for her.

Finally, Alex pulled up the website for an apartment locator in Nashville. She'd get the firm searching for an apartment, which would generate a credit check linked to Courtney's social. Someone looking for her would see that she was using a Nashville-based apartment finder.

The phone rang and Alex checked the number. She punched speakerphone.

"Lovell Solutions."

"Alex, it's Nathan Devereaux." A pause. "Am I on speakerphone?"

"Yep." Alex kept typing while Nathan mumbled an obscenity. Most people hated speakerphone.

"I need to reach Courtney."

"Then why are you calling me?"

"Don't get cute, Alex. Where is she?"

Alex entered one of her many e-mail addresses, along with Courtney's name, in the Contact Us section of the website. She'd bet she had an agent on the phone to her within the hour.

"I don't know," she said patiently. "But even if I did, I wouldn't tell you."

"You helped her leave town, didn't you? Listen, I need to track her down, ASAP. She's wanted by the police."

Alex pondered this news briefly, then decided he was lying. Every last thing Courtney had told her had checked out.

"I have no idea where she is," Alex said, and it was more or less true.

"This is serious. You could lose your license—"

"If you see Courtney, give her my best. I've gotta go."

Alex disconnected and called Courtney.

"Do you have any active warrants I need to know about?"

"No."

"Good. Just checking." Alex left the apartment finder site and clicked onto Greyhound.com. "I'm almost done here. You all right?"

"Yes."

"Okay, I'll call you in ten."

Courtney hung up the phone and stared through the tinted-glass window of the juice bar. She watched the morning commuters race past—in their cars, on their phones—oblivious to one another in their rush to get to work. Buses hissed to a halt, loading and unloading. Bicycles whizzed by. Noise enveloped her as the juice bar filled up with health-conscious Austinites ordering veggie frappés with a shot of wheatgrass.

She was surrounded by people, yet she'd never felt more alone.

She thought of Will's hands. They were big and strong and callused—from lifting weights, she guessed. They were scarred. They were warm and knowing, too, and she remembered the precise feel of them gliding over her skin. Heat pooled inside her, and she bit her lip.

Maybe she should stay.

A woman pulled up to a stoplight in a battered white Pontiac with the windows rolled down, and Courtney thought of another Pontiac from years ago.

She remembered standing in the driveway of their rented house just a few short weeks after her father's funeral. Fiona had been holding their cat, Twix, and crying while their mother crammed boxes and suitcases into the car. It was time to get a move on, time to make a fresh start, and pets weren't allowed where they were going. Fiona had begged and sobbed, but their mom had insisted. Twix would stay behind with Grandpa.

Their mother had been right. The dumpy apartment where they'd ended up in North Hollywood hadn't allowed cats, or dogs, or even birds. It had been the first of many dumpy apartments with a no-pets policy and the first of many stops on their mother's soggy, self-destructive journey.

Courtney watched the Pontiac disappear and wondered if she was making a mistake. She didn't really have to run.

Her phone vibrated on the table. She checked the display to make sure it wasn't Will again. She'd ignored three calls from him in the past two hours.

But it was Alex.

"Okay, phase one is finished. Are you at home?"

"I didn't go home. I just—" Courtney paused, trying to think of a way to explain the feeling of foreboding she'd had the moment she'd turned onto her street. "Something felt off, so I didn't stop there. I'll just make do with what I've got now."

"All right, then, just forget your stuff. We're into phase two."

She recalled the three phases Alex had detailed at her office yesterday: misinformation, disinformation, and reformation. Courtney had expected the process to include getting a fake identity, but Alex had talked her out of that. Buying one was illegal, for one thing, and she could end up with a worse identity than the one she had now. Better to stick with her own identity, but fly well under the radar.

"I've got you headed to Tennessee," Alex said.

"All right."

"Some of your bills have been rerouted to a P.O. box in Nashville leased by a friend of mine."

"Will they accept my mail?"

"It doesn't matter. We're just leaving crumbs here."

"Okay." Courtney's stomach clenched. She was really doing it. She was really disappearing. She was leaving behind her job and her sister and Will—

"You sound hesitant. Are you sure you're up for this?"

Courtney thought of Will. She thought of the look on his face last night when he'd pulled her bag off her shoulder and asked her to stay. He was in her head now, saying the same thing over and over.

She could stay. She didn't have to be like her mother. Her mom had never faced her problems, but had gone from man to man and place to place in a vain attempt to outrun herself.

"Courtney?"

A shiny black Escalade rolled past Bella Donna and turned into the neighboring parking lot.

Her stomach fell out.

"Courtney, are you there?"

"They're across the street. At the salon." Her throat went dry, and she hunched down in her chair, even though she was separated from them by a four-lane street and a pane of tinted glass.

"Are you sure it's them?"

"It's them."

The driver backed the Escalade into a space just beside a Dumpster. They were waiting for her, confirming her very worst fears.

"Can you get a plate number?" Alex wanted to know.

"It's too far away."

"Okay, forget it. Just get out of there. Did you get the money order?"

"Yes." Courtney collected her purse and the little duffel bag she'd stowed at her feet.

"Drop it in the mail this morning, along with your ATM card. You left a few hundred bucks in there, right?"

"Right, but why do you need—"

"For a decoy. I'm going to FedEx it to friends in various parts of the Southeast. Have them make some withdrawals, make it look like you're on the move."

"Oh." Courtney shouldered her bags and felt confident suddenly. She'd clearly hired a PI who knew what she was doing.

"Get yourself to the bus station, like we talked about, okay? You need to be on the ten-twenty heading north to Dallas. Then buy a ticket for the four-thirty to Memphis."

"Okay." Courtney made her way past the carrot-drinkers to the back door of the restaurant. Will's Suburban was parked out back beside a trash bin, right where she'd left it.

"And you're sure about this now?" Alex asked. "Once we get to phase three, it's going to be tough to go back."

"I know." Courtney took a deep breath and summoned her courage. The Escalade was less than a hundred feet away, and although she couldn't see it, she felt its presence.

"When we hang up, you need to ditch the phone."

Courtney pulled Will's key from her pocket. "I know."

"That's it then. Good luck."

"Thanks."

"And watch your back."

"This is starting to make sense."

Will cut a glance at Devereaux, who was in the passenger's seat of the Taurus with a file open in his lap.

"What's that?"

"This jury list." Devereaux held it up. "Eve Caldwell was the forewoman. There were ten men on the jury and only two women. Maybe that's what Pembry meant when he said, 'Evil is a name of a foeman, as I live.' Get it? Corrupt foreman? Maybe he saw her death in the paper, and Alvin's, and he was trying to send me a message."

Will gripped the steering wheel. He was having a hard time focusing on this shit today. All he could think of was Courtney.

But Devereaux wouldn't let up. "He also wrote, 'Draw nine men inward.' Maybe she drew them in, convinced them to rule for the plaintiffs. The court records show it was a ten-two split."

"You said nine men," Will pointed out.

"Yeah, but Pembry voted for the defense. So did this woman, Sarah Schumacher. Holy crap, 'Harass selfless Sarah.' It all fits! Pembry and Sarah were taking heat for not voting with Eve and everyone else."

Devereaux's face was animated with excitement, and Will wanted to pound it. He couldn't care less about any of this right now. He wanted to find Courtney. They'd been by her house, and her sister's, and the salon, but they hadn't found a trace of her.

"We should drop by this woman's office," Will said. "Twist her arm some."

"I already twisted it."

"Then we should twist it some more."

Devereaux shot him a warning look. Hell, Will didn't mean they should hurt her—just lean on her a little. Will could be very intimidating when he wanted to be.

Right now, for instance.

He'd had a hot ball of anger in his gut ever since he'd gotten out of the shower to find his bed empty and his truck gone. He'd stood in his parking lot, cursing a blue streak and feeling like a horse's ass. He should have seen it coming. It was just the sort of move he should have expected from Courtney, and he was the world's biggest idiot for not spotting it a mile away and coming up with a countermaneuver.

Will blamed the sex. Just a few hours in bed with her had cooked his brain.

"What did Fiona say?"

"I told you," Devereaux said. "She has no idea."

"Maybe she's lying."

"Maybe she's not."

"But how could she just take off like that? How far does she expect to get on a few thousand dollars?"

"She could sell your truck."

Will gritted his teeth, infuriated by the thought. "She doesn't have the title," he said. "And she won't get shit for it anyway. It's got close to two hundred thousand miles on it."

"You sure she didn't snake the title?"

"I'm sure." Practically shaking with fury, Will had checked his file box before calling a goddamn taxi to take him to work.

"Let's head back to the station," Devereaux said. "I've got to show all this to Cernak. You and Webb need to check out the plaintiff who collected all that money, see if anything sends up a red flag. And then there're the lawyers. I don't like a one of 'em. We need to take a closer look at their finances."

"I'm sure they're all squeaky clean," Will grumbled.

"Well, we know Alvin was bent. The question is, was he a lone operator, or was someone else in on it?"

Will wended his way back to headquarters, trying to come up with a plan of action for the afternoon. No way he intended to spend it interviewing a bunch of attorneys. He needed Courtney, and he needed her now. Amy Harris had told him she hadn't seen Courtney in a week, but she *had* seen a black Escalade parked on their street the other day.

Someone was gunning for Courtney, and if she did a poor job of hiding, he had every chance of finding her before Will did.

Will whipped the car into a parking space and jumped

out. Maybe he'd take the afternoon off and strike out on his own. Not the most impressive move from a rookie detective, but Will wasn't feeling all that concerned with Cernak's opinion of him at the moment. The guy was still calling Courtney a "person of interest" in Alvin's murder, even though anyone with half a brain could see she was a target, not the shooter, for fuck's sake.

"Calm down," Devereaux told him as they entered the back door.

"I'm calm."

"You look like you're about to throttle someone. Just relax, okay? We'll find her. And I won't tell anyone you're boning her, so you can quit worrying about that, too."

Will shot him a glare. It was no accident Devereaux had used the term Will had used when they'd first started working this case and Will had thought his partner had a thing for Fiona.

"Hey, when's that wedding?" Will asked.

"What, Jack and Fiona's?"

"Yeah."

"About a month from now. Why?"

They rode the elevator up to their floor, and an idea took root in Will's head. "Courtney's her only family, right? Besides the grandfather? There's no way she'll miss that wedding."

Devereaux grunted something as they made their way through the maze of cubicles. They both were thinking the same thing, probably—a month was a long time for someone on the run. If they didn't locate Courtney before then, they might never locate her at all.

Will got to his desk and loosened his tie. He opened his

drawer and grabbed a handful of aspirin from the bottle he'd started keeping there, then jumped on his phone to check messages. Six calls, but none from Courtney.

"Long time no see."

He looked up to see a bulldog-like mug peering over the wall to his cube.

"Thought you guys went for lunch," Webb said. "Where you been all afternoon?"

"Working."

"Oh, yeah? Well, while you guys was jacking around, we got a break in the Alvin case." Webb stepped into Will's cube and tossed a fax on his desk.

"What's this?" Will asked.

"Walter Greene."

"Who's he?"

"A minister in Los Angeles. Died in a house fire 'bout five years ago."

Will jerked his tie free from his collar and stuffed it into his coat pocket. Devereaux walked up behind him, saving him from having to deal with Webb's crap. The man was a blowhard.

"What's he got to do with anything?" Devereaux picked up the fax, and Will clicked open his e-mail on the off chance Courtney had sent him a message.

"Looked like a kitchen fire at first, but the guys over there figured it for arson. Then the ME pulled a couple slugs from the victim's skull, whole thing became a homicide investigation."

Will's in-box was full, but nothing from Courtney. He clicked out before Webb could get nosy reading over his shoulder. "What's it got to do with us?"

Webb smiled. "Homicide dick out there heard about our background check, called me up with this lead."

"What lead?" Will watched Webb's smile widen and got a sick, greasy feeling in the pit of his stomach.

"It's our girl Courtney again. They never could prove it, but the cops out there swear she offed the guy."

Courtney stared at her reflection in the smudged bathroom mirror. Her next bus left in twenty-five minutes, and there was no more putting this off.

A strange calm settled over her, and she studied her image with a critical eye.

She wasn't beautiful, by any stretch. She had faint freckles dusting her nose, and her chin was too pointy to suit her face. She had good lips, though. And a clear complexion. She combed her fingers through her hair and let it fan out over her shoulders. Will liked her hair. He hadn't said so, but she could tell from the way he'd played with it all last night, like a kid suddenly given a toy he'd always wanted. They'd made love three times, and after each time he'd lain there, stroking his hand through her hair, until she'd practically purred from the pleasure of it.

She pushed the thought away and picked up one of her claret-colored locks. She'd never gone blond before. It was the one color she'd never tried, mainly because it was clichéd, but also because to pull it off she'd have to color her brows, too, which would be an ongoing pain in the butt. But with hazel eyes and fair skin, she knew she could make it work.

The door burst open, and Courtney jumped back, startled. It was a woman and two kids. Courtney took a deep breath and told herself to calm down; she'd been a bundle of nerves all day.

She watched in the mirror as the mom checked the cleanliness of the stalls and shepherded each girl into one. The children looked about four and seven, and the mother looked almost as young as Courtney.

"Don't touch the potty," she told them. "It flushes by itself."

Courtney watched the girls finish up and dutifully cross the bathroom to wash their hands. The mother stood at the sink, dispensing soap and towels, then pulling a Wet Wipe from her purse to clean something red and gooey off the younger girl's face.

"No more sweets." She straightened her daughter's hair bows. "You'll be bouncing off the walls by the time we get to Gram's house."

Courtney's chest tightened as they left the bathroom. How strange would it have been to have had a mother like that? And if she and Fiona *had* had a mom like that, how would things be different?

Would Fiona be a carefree painter today, instead of a forensic artist who drew rapists and murderers? Would she be a friend to Courtney, instead of the pseudo-mom she'd been most of her life? Would she be married already, with kids of her own?

Would Courtney?

She almost laughed at the thought. But the urge came with a twinge of pain because she knew, deep down, she'd never written off the idea completely. So what if she'd had a crappy childhood? Who hadn't? She could still have a family. She could be happy someday.

Just maybe not today.

The door swung open again, and a trio of women bustled in. Courtney ducked into a stall and unzipped her duffel. She took out her square cosmetics case and hung it on the door so that the top formed a flat surface. She got out her large folding mirror and positioned it on the case. She doused her hair with Evian and used a wide-tooth comb to work it through. With well-practiced movements, she scooped a layer of hair on top of her head, then dug a clip from her pocket and secured it in place. She waited for the restroom to go silent again, and then she took out her scissors.

Wisps of hair fell on the floor as she broke the cardinal rule of haircutting. *Shh-shh. Shh-shh.* Her beautiful hair rained down. *Shh-shh.* The floor was a carpet of wine-colored locks. *Shh-shh.* And with every snip, she thought of Will's hands.

Will gave in to the urge to stop by Courtney's house one more time on his way home from work. He'd been by twice already today, and each time he'd stood on her porch as her neighbor's dog went nutso and her door went unanswered.

He pulled the Taurus into the driveway behind Amy Harris's car. He wondered if the violence-prone boyfriend had been around since his run-in with the police. Will thought of Amy's little boy, Devon, and he thought of the pitiful remains sitting unidentified in the morgue tonight. Will knew, after catching that case, he'd never look at a domestic in quite the same way.

He went up to the door and rang the bell. A television could be heard from the Harris side of the duplex, but

Courtney's side was silent. Will looked in the front window, but the blinds were closed tightly. He walked around the house and checked the back door. Locked. He tromped through some weeds to the side yard. He pulled out a penlight and checked the bathroom window.

It was open.

His pulse spiked as his flashlight illuminated shards of glass all over the ground. Someone had busted out the pane, then undone the lock and gone in, it looked like.

Careful not to crunch the glass in case there might be fingerprints, Will picked his way back to the front porch and rang Amy's bell. She answered the door in a bathrobe.

"Ma'am. Looks like there's been a break-in next door."

Her eyes widened, and she leaned her head out to look at Courtney's front door.

"Bathroom window's busted," he explained. "I need to check it out. You wouldn't happen to have a key, would you?"

"Yes, I do, but—you're saying we had a *burglar?* I've been here all evening. I never heard a thing."

Will filed that away as she hurried off to get the key. Maybe the break-in had occurred last night, while Courtney was at his place.

Or maybe it had happened today, and Courtney had been inside.

Amy reappeared, and Will grabbed the key from her. He jammed it into the lock. He shoved the door open and stumbled over something as he entered the apartment.

# CHAPTER

## 17

A sofa cushion?

Will flipped on the light and scanned the room.

"Oh my *gosh!*" Amy yelped.

The place had been tossed. Thoroughly.

"Get back inside," Will ordered. "Lock the door and call APD."

Will unholstered his weapon and moved briskly down the hallway. He came to the closed door of the bedroom and hesitated a moment, dread clogging his throat. He pushed it open. He turned on the light.

They'd spent time in here—drawers overturned, closet ransacked, clothes strewn everywhere.

"Courtney?" The word was a croak as he forced himself to step into the room, to peer over the bed, to check the closet ...

He rushed into the bathroom, where the shower curtain had been pulled back. A brown shoeprint marred the porcelain tub. The contents of Courtney's medicine cabinet littered the floor, jars of cosmetics smashed and spilled across the linoleum.

He hustled back into the kitchen and did a thorough sweep. The pantry stood open. The refrigerator, too. Will jerked open the door to the utility room to find only a heap of household cleaners pulled from a cabinet.

She wasn't here.

But had she been? Had she been rolled up in a rug, like Pembry, and dragged off someplace to be dumped?

She didn't have any rugs.

He went room to room, checking for anything missing—a bedspread, a shower curtain, a blanket, even. Nothing missing, as far as he could tell.

He holstered his weapon and called Devereaux.

"I'm at Courtney's."

"You bringing her in?" Devereaux asked, and Will remembered the arrest warrant. Cernak had pressured the D.A. to have a judge issue it this evening. It was so absurd, Will could hardly get his mind around it.

"She's not here," Will said, surveying the mess with a pain in his chest. "But someone's been here. The place has been ransacked. Drawers, closets, everything. I'm talking empty cereal boxes."

The phone in his hand was silent as Devereaux absorbed this.

"Someone's looking for something."

"No shit," Will said.

"Something besides Courtney. Any idea what it is?"

"Hell if I know. But by the looks of this place, I don't think they found it. Whoever did this was frustrated." Will eyed the painting of a desert landscape that had been pulled down from the wall and slashed with a blade. "And pissed."

"Maybe we'll get some prints," Devereaux said hopefully.

But Will wasn't optimistic. He noticed the air vent that had been unscrewed, the filter that had been pulled out and taken apart. Whoever had been here knew what he was doing and would have worn gloves.

"Hodges? You there?"

"I'm here."

"Keep an eye on those crime-scene techs, when they show up. We need a lead."

"I hear you."

"We need IDs. And we need to catch up with these guys before they catch up to Courtney."

Alex pulled into a parking space in front of her office and tugged her cell phone free from her purse. She composed a brief text message to a client and pressed Send.

A tap on the window made her jump. A barrel-chested man stood beside the door. He flashed a gold detective's shield.

She cracked the door an inch. "Yes?"

"Will Hodges, APD. I need a word."

Goddamn it.

She got out of the car, leaned back against the door, and crossed her arms. "I'm running late." She glanced at her watch. "What can I do for you?"

"I'm looking for a client of yours. Courtney Glass."

Alex kept her face neutral, but she was kicking herself mentally for opening up to Nathan Devereaux. What was it about that man? Half a drink and half an hour of that sexy drawl, and she'd spilled her guts to him.

"I'm afraid I can't discuss—"

"I have an arrest warrant for her." He eased closer, until

he invaded her space with his huge chest. "She's wanted for murder," he added, as if this would scare her.

Although, actually, it did. Alex made a habit of avoiding dirty cases. If some woman showed up and claimed that her husband was after her, that she needed to disappear, Alex demanded police reports or hospital records. If a guy called up and asked her to track down some woman who'd made off with his bank account, Alex ran a background check to see what she was dealing with. She didn't take on criminals, and she sure as heck didn't take on murderers.

"Show me the warrant," she said.

"What?"

"You say you have a warrant? Produce it."

"I don't have it in hand—"

"Then I've got no information for you." She started to walk away, but he blocked her path and leaned his hand against the side of her car.

"Aiding and abetting is serious. You could lose your license, you know."

Alex bit her tongue, using all her restraint not to tell off the big man with the badge and the gun.

She gazed up at him. His eyes were dark and dangerous-looking. This cop wanted his man. Or his woman, in this case. There was a certain desperation in his eyes that made Alex look more closely.

Was it possible . . . ? No, it couldn't be. . . . But was it even *remotely* possible this man was the "friend" Courtney had stayed with last night? Was this the guy whose apartment Alex had taken her to with a duffel and a bag of Chinese food?

No way.

Courtney Glass was ballsy, but not enough to sleep with a cop who was investigating her for murder.

Unless maybe—

"Where is she?" His hand balled into a fist against the car, and Alex realized she wasn't imagining things. This man was desperate to find her, and it was personal.

But that didn't make it okay. Lots of guys were desperate to track down the women who'd walked out on them. Sometimes they did it with shotguns.

"I don't know," Alex said. "I have no way to reach her. But I might be able to pass a message along, if she happens to contact me."

He stepped back and raked his hands through his short hair. "Just tell her—damn it, just tell her to call me." He pulled a card from his pocket and thrust it at Alex. "Day or night. I have to talk to her. And same goes for you. If you hear anything, I need you to call me. That's my cell number."

Alex shrugged and slipped the card into her pocket. "I'll see what I can do."

"Tell me one thing."

She looked up at him, and there it was again—that urgency.

"Is she okay? Do you know? Someone trashed her house yesterday, and no one's seen her."

Alex's eyebrows tipped up, and the detective seemed to hold his breath.

"I spoke with her yesterday around midmorning. She sounded fine." Alex could tell from his face that she hadn't answered his question.

He blew out a sigh. Nodded. "Thanks. And I mean it about that number. Anytime, day or night."

• • •

Will's XO presented Fiona's drawings to an alert press corp. The meeting room was packed as reporters from news outlets across the state recorded every detail of the story. Will scanned the eager faces, not bothering to conceal his disgust. Their young John Doe had slipped through the cracks all his life, only to capture the attention of a sympathetic public now that his body had been destroyed beyond recognition.

Will cut a glance at Fiona, who stood just a few feet away, stiff and somber in her black pantsuit. She looked stressed. Tired. Probably a lot like Will looked after spending a sleepless night on his sofa with his phone in his lap.

Will straightened his spine and ignored the frustration burning in his belly. Once upon a time he'd stood for hours, not moving, in the biting winds of the Korengal Valley, his gaze fixed on a distant stretch of highway, usually some supply route that needed protection from terrorist insurgents.

He could take a few minutes in front of a crew of reporters.

The key was to clear his mind and focus on the task at hand, in this case an unidentified boy and the people who'd killed him.

But every time he thought of that, his mind went to Courtney. And Walter Greene. And the inch-thick file he'd had copied and overnighted from Los Angeles yesterday afternoon. It wasn't Greene's case file—which took up two entire boxes, according to the LAPD clerk he'd managed to get on the phone. No, this file was all about Courtney and her probable—but not provable—involvement in Greene's murder.

The sea of reporters rose up and surged toward the exits.

It was over. Will spotted Fiona trying to make a break for it, and caught up to her in a few strides.

"Wait." He clamped a hand on her shoulder and watched her eyes flare with annoyance. She didn't want to talk to him. Well, too bad. He steered her through the door and down the corridor until they were alone in the relative privacy of the vending machine alcove.

She turned to face him. "I haven't seen her."

"Have you talked to her?"

"No."

Will watched her, gauging her honesty. "Have you had an e-mail? Anything?"

"No." Fiona's eyes brightened with tears, and he knew she was telling the truth. She hadn't heard from her sister. She was just as scared as he was.

"Do you have anything I can go on? Maybe some friends or relatives I can look up?"

Fiona looked down, and he could sense the conflict inside her. She looked up again. "Tell me why I should help you arrest her."

"That wasn't my idea."

She scoffed. "Whose was it?"

"It came from higher up," Will said, wishing he could be more candid.

"Cernak has his head up his butt." She clenched her hands into fists. "Did he even *talk* to that jogger from the park? Who does he think those two men were? And does he know about what happened to my sister's house?"

"I don't know—"

"Does he think she did that *herself*? It's like he's got blinders on!"

"I know, I know." Will stepped closer and lowered his voice. "And I agree with you. I'm working an entirely different theory of this case. But I need to find Courtney. Skipping out on an arrest warrant isn't doing her story any good."

"Her *story*? You act like she made it up! You act like she's guilty!"

"She looks guilty if she runs, and you know it. I need to find her. You need to help me."

Fiona looked down and chewed her lip.

"Is there a friend somewhere? An ex-boyfriend, maybe? She doesn't have much money, so she couldn't have gone far without help."

Fiona shook her head.

"You didn't lend her money, did you?"

"No." She looked at him again, and she seemed to have decided something. "I didn't give her a dime. But my passport's missing."

"Your passport." His stomach sank.

"I'm not sure she has it, but—" She shook her head. "I don't know. She sort of looks like me. I think maybe she plans to leave the country."

Will stared at the television, too tired to move and too tired to sleep. The Yankees were up against the Red Sox, but if someone held a gun to Will's head, he couldn't have told them the score.

He reached over and pecked at the laptop sitting beside him on the couch. No new mail. He checked the battery on his phone.

He swigged his beer.

He'd come home from work and decided to get tanked.

He was doing a damn fine job of it, judging by the six empty bottles lined up on his coffee table.

Walter Fucking Greene.

Ordained minister. Youth director. Spiritual leader with a fondness for single moms and troubled kids. Will had spent the past three hours imagining how he'd kill the guy if he weren't already dead.

According to the file from California, Greene had spent four years married to a Denise McCowen Glass, a part-time waitress and mother of two. Police had been called out to the couple's house several times, including once for an altercation involving a broken whiskey bottle. Denise had claimed her husband tried to hit her with it, but the husband said it had shattered against the wall when his wife tried to wrestle it from his hand. Then she'd gone after him with a pistol, getting a shot off and prompting a 911 call.

The police report favored the minister's side of things. Greene said his wife was a recovering alcoholic, and he intended to get her back into a treatment program as soon as possible. According to the report, he'd asked the cops not to arrest his wife but to pray for her instead.

The 911 call had been placed by Fiona Glass, age fourteen. Courtney Glass, eleven, had been present at the scene.

Also in the file was the write-up from a later incident in which a twenty-two-year-old Courtney "accidentally" rearended Greene's car. Three times. In a movie theater parking lot. A witness said the driver seemed "crazy" and "drunk," but a Breathalyzer came up clean. Greene declined to press charges, saying it was a family matter, although he and Courtney's mom would have been divorced for years by then.

Two weeks later, Greene burned to a crisp in his house with a couple of .22-caliber slugs embedded in his skull, and police hauled Courtney in for questioning.

Will glanced at his watch. It was after eleven. Tomorrow was a new day, and provided he didn't get his ass called out to some crime scene at three in the morning, Will planned to spend it at the posh offices of Wilkers & Riley. He'd interview everyone. Again. Especially the lawyers he'd missed, the ones Webb had talked to when they'd first made the rounds. And then Will would go talk to the plaintiff, a millionaire widower. He'd take another crack at everyone until he found someone who looked good for rigging a jury and then hiring a pair of hitmen to tie up loose ends.

Another day of interviews. Another day of lies and half-truths and separating the important ones out from the crap. People lied about everything, and only some of it mattered.

The phone rang, and Will sloshed beer on his shirt as he lunged to answer it.

"Hello?"

Silence.

"Hello?" He flipped the TV off and listened. He could have sworn he heard breathing.

"Courtney . . . talk to me."

The line went dead.

# CHAPTER

# 18

*Name no one man.* Will gazed at his computer, unable to get that damn phrase out of his head.

Will was fried. He'd spent all day at his desk, including more than an hour on the phone with an attorney. The guy was a childhood buddy, and he'd given Will a crash course in litigation as Will had taken pages of notes. He thumbed through the notes now, unable to shake the feeling that somewhere in all this legal mumbo jumbo was the key to Alvin's murder.

The LivTech case had been a product-liability suit, which was tried in federal court. The players included the family of a dead stockbroker, one judge, fourteen jurors—twelve regulars plus two alternates—and an army of attorneys on both sides, although the actual courtroom participation had been limited to a select few.

The victim's family took home more than thirty million dollars when the case settled prior to appeal. Wilkers & Riley's cut of the settlement had been twenty mil, with five going to each of the two litigators. Will stared at his notepad and the numbers started swirling together. His paltry salary paled in comparison, and he knew Courtney had been right when she'd said she probably made more money than he did.

Courtney invaded his brain again, and Will glanced at his phone. She'd been gone a week now, and each one of the days had been a month.

"You still here?"

Will glanced up to see Devereaux standing beside his cubicle. "Still here."

"How was Dallas?"

"Dead end."

After receiving a call to come get his Suburban from an impound lot near the bus station in Austin, Will had tracked down a Greyhound worker who remembered selling Courtney a ticket to Dallas last week. So Will had driven his ass to the Dallas bus station, but the trip had been a waste of time.

"You check the security tapes up there?" Devereaux asked.

"Yeah."

"Hmm. I bet she's got some tricks up her sleeve. Woman's a beautician. She can probably change her looks at the drop of a hat."

"No kidding."

"I talked to Fiona again," Devereaux said, ignoring the sarcasm. "Still nothing."

Will squeezed his pencil. Fiona was the most promising link, and it amazed him that Courtney hadn't reached out to her. In fact, he wasn't sure he believed it. But Fiona kept telling Devereaux she hadn't heard a thing, and Devereaux seemed to be buying it.

"You know, you look like shit," his partner said. "How 'bout we get some dinner over at the Smokin' Pig?"

Will's gaze dropped to his notes. "I keep coming back to

the trial. Two litigators, a man and a woman. Lindsey Kahn. You remember her from the funeral?"

Devereaux sighed, obviously realizing Will wasn't going to be lured away from his desk even though it was nearly ten. He dragged a chair over from a neighboring cube and plopped into it.

"Yeah, I remember her. Blonde. Hot. So what?"

"So she's the youngest partner at the firm. The least experienced litigator they have, yet they hand her their most important case. Her and Alvin."

Devereaux crossed his arms. "So juries like attractive lawyers. What's the mystery there? Lots of businesses put their best faces out front."

Will tapped his pencil. "But what if it was carefully calculated? A man and a woman. The jury foreman isn't chosen until the end of the trial, during deliberations. So what if Wilkers and Riley hedged its bets?"

"You mean put something out there for everyone?"

"Right." Will leaned forward. "The jurors heard hours and hours of boring testimony from doctors and scientists and drug experts. It would have been miserable. They would have welcomed a distraction. Shit, Pembry was so bored, he was doodling pictures and dreaming up word puzzles."

"Okay, they were bored. So what?"

"So then the deliberations lasted eight days," Will continued, "interrupted by a weekend. What if the lawyers found out who the foreman, or woman, was going to be, and then moved in as soon as it was decided and tried to influence the outcome of the case?"

Devereaux frowned. "But why just the forewoman? They needed ten people on their side to win."

"Yeah, but the foreman is key. It's usually someone persuasive. Someone influential with the other jurors. Eve Caldwell was in sales, so she fits. Now, this group was made up of mostly men, so you'd think they'd end up with a male foreman. So they dangle Kahn out there. But then Caldwell gets picked, and Alvin moves in on her."

"That's a serious offense," Devereaux pointed out. "It's not just disbarment. Both those lawyers could go to jail for jury tampering in a federal case."

Will shrugged. "Sixty mil is serious money."

"Also, it's a risky plan. What if the jury foreman or fore-woman or whatever wasn't the type to fall for it? What if it was some dried-up old librarian still in love with her husband?"

"I thought about that," Will said. "But maybe they weren't just manipulating Eve Caldwell. Maybe Kahn was busy, too, meeting up with some of the male jurors after hours. It was a nine-week trial. Maybe they didn't wait until the deliberations to begin targeting people, seeing what kind of favor they could rustle up."

"And what do the crooked jurors get out of it?"

"Sex. Flattery. A break from the monotony."

Devereaux leaned back in his chair and seemed to think about it. "You've been to that law firm a dozen times. We've been all over their finances, their backgrounds. Nothing looks amiss."

"Maybe we're the only ones really looking," Will said bitterly. It still burned him up that Cernak had gotten an arrest warrant for Courtney. He and Webb had already made up their minds; they weren't interested in any other theories. "Why go after the lawyers when they've got the jealous mistress angle tied up with a bow?"

"What about the plaintiff? Out of everyone, that broker's husband benefited the most from this thing."

"Guy looks clean as a whistle. Fact, he gave half the money to some charity foundation already." Will sighed and rubbed his eyes. "But, shit, I don't know. Maybe that's just another smoke screen."

"You sound pretty cynical."

"I am. You know, you expect the plaintiffs' attorneys to be all about standing up for the little guy. But they're just as greedy as the corporations. It's bullshit. It's all about money. All these deaths over some pile of money."

Devereaux stood up, grabbed Will's cell phone off the desk, and held it out him. "Come on. You've been here long enough. Let's get some dinner."

Will checked the message icon on his computer before packing it up for the night.

Devereaux led the way through the dimly lit maze of cubes. "We'll find her," he insisted.

Will felt the weight of his phone in his pocket and said nothing.

He bolted upright and checked the clock. Four fifty-eight. He grabbed the phone off his nightstand.

"Hodges."

"I just got a call from a homicide cop I know down in Corpus."

Will's brain snapped to attention. They'd found her.

"They found him," Devereaux said.

"Who?"

"Martin Pembry."

Two minutes later, Will stood in front of his bathroom mirror and gulped down a handful of aspirin. Going to the Smokin' Pig with Devereaux had been a mistake. Will felt hung over and he looked like it, too—a long way from the prime condition he'd been in when he reported for duty in Austin less than two months ago. He threw on some shorts and sneakers.

The pounding in his head echoed his soles on the pavement as he wended his way toward the Y. It was five miles north, which would take forty minutes, given his sluggish pace. Their gym opened at 6:00, and Will would punish himself with an hour of weights before heading into work.

The case had taken a turn.

Corpus Christi investigators said it was a homicide. Scavengers had made a mess of the corpse, but a credit card found on the body belonged to Martin D. Pembry. Before being dumped in Laguna Madre, the man had been garroted with a length of barbed wire.

Will's headache raged as he made his way up Congress Avenue toward the spotlighted capitol dome. The humidity was like a blanket already, and he knew it was going to be a bitch of a day.

Pembry was dead. Executed, mostly likely by the same goons out looking for Courtney. The only bright component of this bleak news was that his murder went a long way toward clearing Courtney's name. The jealous mistress theory was strained way past the point of credulity now, and the case would have to be reexamined as part of a bigger crime spree, a crime spree being orchestrated by someone with money and power and determination.

Will pounded out the miles, grimly satisfied to be making headway on at least part of his mission—exonerating Courtney. The other part—actually finding her before someone else did—was no further along.

His heart pumped in his chest, and he thought of her body underneath him in bed. He wanted her back. He wanted her safe. He wanted her every way imaginable, and with a ferocity that scared him. He'd never felt this way about anyone, and he couldn't believe he was feeling this way now about a woman with purple hair and a rap sheet. About a woman he was *investigating*.

He still couldn't believe she'd run away. And he'd been so blinded by lust, he hadn't seen it coming.

She'd covered her trail well, too, and every tracking technique Will could think of had failed to produce a solid lead. It was beyond frustrating, except for the fact that if Will was having this much trouble finding her, somebody else must be, too. He was beginning to think Fiona's passport theory had merit.

Sweat streamed down his face and arms. Mile three, and he still felt like shit. This was pathetic. He was a soldier, for Christ's sake. He was better than this.

He was a soldier.

And even though he really wasn't anymore, the mind-set had been hammered into him through years of training. He wouldn't turn loose of it. He couldn't. He never wanted to be one of those burned-out old cops who let his body go to hell and his life slide into a bottle.

He had a mission: find and retrieve. And he would approach it the way he approached every mission—with the knowledge that failure was not an option.

# CHAPTER
# 19

Lindsey Kahn exited her office building and walked north on Rio Grande. Nathan predicted she was destined for the sandwich shop two blocks away and smiled slightly to himself when she veered into the café and lined up with dozens of other yuppies seeking midday eats.

He hung back and perused a menu as she ordered. She paid with plastic, collected a number from the cashier, and filled a cup with Diet Coke, no ice. She tucked herself into a booth, pulled a phone from her purse, and started checking messages.

Nathan made his move.

"Hey, there."

She looked up, startled, as he slid into the seat across from her. Her gaze darted around anxiously.

"Nathan Devereaux." He pushed a business card across the table to her, but she didn't look at it.

"I know who you are."

"We need to talk."

He studied her up close for the first time. She had a certain toughness about her, despite the blond hair and the cream suit. Her purse and shoes were cream, too. Very feminine, but the outfit didn't hide the edge.

She sighed. Then she zipped the phone back into her

purse and folded her hands in front of her. She gave him a look that said, "Bring it," but her tightly clasped hands said something else.

"You've been avoiding me."

"I have?"

"You have."

Another sigh. "What can I do for you, Detective?"

"I want to talk about the LivTech case."

A server appeared with a bowl of minestrone and a breadstick that smelled like garlic.

"Thank you," she said to the server. Then to Nathan, "The transcript's a public record. You can read about it."

"True enough. Thing is, I'm more interested in what's happened since the trial."

She scooped up a spoonful, and he admired her for ordering red soup while wearing an outfit like that. "Which means?"

He leaned back in the booth. "A dead attorney. Two dead jurors. Kind of weird, don't you think?"

She dabbed her mouth with a napkin and some of that pink lipstick rubbed off. "I wasn't aware there were two dead jurors."

"Martin Pembry washed up on the shores of Laguna Madre yesterday morning." He shrugged. "I'd think you'd be getting a little jumpy."

"Jumpy?"

"'Bout your safety."

She reached for her drink. Her gaze was nonchalant, but she gripped the cup too hard.

"I can get you protection. If you'll give me an idea what's happening, I can line something up."

She looked away. "What makes you think I need protection?"

"Don't you? Isn't that why you've been leaving work every night at five? Going straight home, locking the doors up tight?" Her gaze snapped to his, and he continued. "Security guard at your condo seems extra cautious about your visitors these days. You telling me you didn't give him a heads-up?"

She'd gone rigid at his words. Maybe she didn't like the idea he was watching her. Maybe she didn't like the idea someone else might be, too.

She picked up her purse and slid from the booth. "I have nothing more to discuss, Detective."

He looked up at her. "You could be next, you know. You'd be smart to talk to me, let me help you."

"Thanks, but I can take care of myself."

She turned and walked away. Nathan watched her go, then looked at the abandoned soup. She'd hardly touched it.

But his business card was gone.

Fiona's wedding day was blue and bright and full of promise.

Especially for Will.

He watched the smiling couple emerge from the church, followed by a crowd of guests. Fifty-two, by his count—not a tiny wedding, but not nearly large enough for Will to drop in unnoticed.

From his blind across the street, he watched Devereaux and all the other guests head for their cars. The ceremony had been simple, with a minimum of fluff. Fiona wore a knee-length white dress, no veil, no train. She wore a smile, too, and it flickered for just a moment as she gazed up and down the street, as if looking for someone.

After the couple left the church, Will retrieved his Chevy from a nearby parking garage and made his way across town. The reception was at their house, where Courtney had stayed and where Will had wolfed down breakfast five weeks before. Will had staked out the location ahead of time and found an empty house on the street just behind Fiona's. He backed into that driveway now and angled his Suburban under the shadow of a massive oak tree. Fiona's backyard was visible through the chain-link fence across the street. Will cut the engine. He waited.

The September sun was hot, and they'd planned an indoor party. Guests were mingling, though, and little clusters kept forming on the back deck as people stepped outside to have a private conversation or maybe a smoke. Will's skin turned damp beneath his black T-shirt. His boots felt heavy. He took a cool swill of Gatorade and continued to watch and wait.

*Hurry up and wait.*

His phone vibrated in the pocket of his jeans. Devereaux. Damn, had he spotted him out here?

"Where are you?" Devereaux demanded. "I thought you were on shift today."

"I'm off the clock. Why?"

"I'm at the station. You won't believe what just came in."

Will's chest tightened, but he didn't say a word.

"You remember that lady lawyer? Tried the drug case with Alvin?"

"Lindsey Kahn," Will said. "What about her?"

"I went to visit her yesterday on a hunch. She's been dodging me for days. Anyway, I gave her my business card, and now her boyfriend just called and said she never came home from work yesterday."

Will's skin went cold. "She's missing?"

"Her car's at her health club, but no one's seen her since yesterday at five."

Some movement across the street caught Will's eye. A flash of white . . .

*Shit.*

"Anyway, the boyfriend's worried. Says she's been nervous lately. Paranoid about her safety all the time."

Will cursed himself as Fiona walked up the driveway. She yanked open the passenger door with a squeak, and Will winced as she slid her immaculate white dress over his ratty upholstery. She closed the door.

"I'll call you later," he told Devereaux, and hung up.

For a moment, they simply looked at each other. Then her attention shifted across the street, where her wedding reception was in full swing.

"Congratulations," he said lamely.

"Thanks." She cast a glance around the truck and seemed intrigued instead of horrified. "This thing's big. I'm surprised I didn't see you at the church."

"I was on foot."

Her gaze lingered on the backseat, and he winced again as she picked up the file there. She dropped it into her lap. Her lips pressed into a thin line as she flipped through the pages. She paused on an autopsy photo of Walter Greene. The remains were charred, but someone in Fiona's line of work would know precisely what she was looking at.

Will watched her and waited. She flipped through the

pages and stopped on an incident report—one of several domestic disturbances contained in the folder.

"Mom married him during one of her dry phases," she muttered. "Said he helped her find God."

She continued to thumb through the papers and paused on a mug shot of Courtney at age eighteen. She'd been picked up on a DUI, and she looked it. Fiona frowned at the picture.

"I shouldn't have moved out," she said.

Will didn't respond.

"Sometimes I wonder how things would be different—"

"Don't."

She glanced up.

He reached over and gently closed the file. He took it from her lap and dropped it onto the backseat. No one should have to think about this crap on her wedding day.

She looked down at her lap now and twisted her wedding ring. "I don't think she killed him."

Will didn't say anything. The evidence was inconclusive, but the motive and the opportunity were pretty overwhelming.

Fiona cleared her throat. "I don't know what set her off, really. She wouldn't talk about him. I think she saw him somewhere unexpectedly, and she just snapped. It was a Friday, I remember. I dropped by her apartment. She'd made these flyers, and that weekend she snuck into his church and put them in all the hymnals."

Will didn't respond. One of the flyers was stuck in the file somewhere. *Rev. Walter Greene: pedophile.* They were printed on fluorescent orange paper and would have been impossible to miss in the middle of a church service.

Fiona gazed over at her house. "Why don't you come in with me? Join the party?"

He looked at the deck where people were laughing and drinking. The last place Fiona should be right now was in his stuffy Suburban.

"She's not coming."

His head whipped around. "You talked to her?"

"She called this morning."

Will couldn't breathe. It felt like a sandbag was sitting on his chest.

Fiona looked out the window. "She didn't say where she was or anything."

"What did she say?"

"That she loved me. That she was doing fine, settling in. But she wished she could be here."

Will stared at her. Courtney was alive. She'd called her sister, but she hadn't called him.

She was alive.

Fiona looked at him, and the stress of these past few weeks was visible again in her face. "She's a tough person to care about. You should know that up front."

He laughed. He couldn't help it.

"What?"

He shook his head. "You make it sound like I have a choice."

He felt her gaze boring into him, that protective sister gaze. She wanted to know what he felt for Courtney. She wanted to know his intentions. But he didn't want to explain himself to Fiona. Hell, he didn't even understand it. All he knew was Courtney had him tangled up, and the only way he'd get untangled was if he found her. Guilty or innocent, he didn't really care anymore. He just needed her back. He needed her safe.

"So will you come in?" she asked.

"Thanks, but I can't."

"Why not? Why sit out here melting, when you could be inside having crab cakes?"

"I'm not dressed for it."

She scoffed. "This is Austin. If you're wearing shoes, you're dressed for it."

"I can't leave my weapon." And he couldn't exactly waltz into her party with a Glock hanging out of his jeans.

"Stuff it in your boot and come on." She jerked her head toward the door. "I married a cop, remember? Half the people in there are packing."

He smiled slightly.

"Come on, I insist."

He glanced up at Fiona's house again and made a decision.

"Okay, thanks."

She smiled. And then she surprised him by leaning over and pecking him on the cheek.

"I see why she likes you," she said, and got out.

He tucked his gun into his boot and followed her across the street to a narrow stone path between her house and her back neighbor's. She picked her way over the cobblestones and pulled open a back door.

He followed her inside and felt a blast of cold air. It was dark. They were in a bedroom. He remembered Courtney's stuff piled beside the couch and decided it must be the master because they didn't have a guest bedroom. Fiona opened the door to the hallway and nearly bumped into her new husband.

"Hi." She stood on tiptoes and kissed him. "Look who I found."

Will stepped into the hallway as Jack eyed him with hostility.

Fiona squeezed Jack's hand. "Why don't you get Will a drink? I need to check on the food."

She disappeared, and Jack crossed his arms.

"Congratulations." Will held out his hand, and Jack hesitated a moment before shaking it.

"You want a beer? Wine?"

"Beer," Will said. "Whatever you got."

They headed into the living room, where people were chatting and laughing and drinking. A buffet table had been set up in Fiona's art studio. Bunches of brightly colored flowers filled vases all over the house, and some sort of jazz-sounding music floated from the speakers. It was a festive, low-key party, and Will felt bad for crashing it.

Jack handed him a cold glass of beer and then disappeared to talk to his invited guests.

Will wasn't much for parties. He didn't like small talk. He nodded at a few people he recognized from APD, then busied himself admiring the vibrant paintings lining the walls. These would be Fiona's landscapes and waterscapes. He recalled the desert picture from Courtney's house. Last time he'd seen it, it had been lying on her living room floor, slashed.

Will glanced through the gauzy curtains to the deck outside, where Fiona and Jack stood visiting with their friends.

Will wandered into the kitchen and set his glass on the counter beside the sink. He wove his way through people and asked a woman if she knew where the bathroom was—an inane question in a house this size. He ducked inside the room, locked the door, and then opened the second bathroom door that adjoined the master bedroom. He made a beeline for the dresser, where he'd spotted a woman's purse when he'd first entered the house. He found Fiona's cell phone and scrolled through the call history: local, local, local . . . an out of state number ending in four successive digits. That would be a pay phone.

And that would be Courtney.

# CHAPTER

# 20

Courtney tipped her head back and let the sun warm her cheeks. The last remnants of yesterday's thunderstorm had blown through the valley, leaving the sky clear and the air so fresh she could almost taste it.

"Six needs a refill, C.J."

Courtney snapped out of her daze and watched Renee disappear into the kitchen with a tray. She glanced at table six and saw that they did, indeed, need more drinks. She grabbed a pitcher of tea from the beverage stand and made her way across the deck that looked out over Silver Creek Canyon.

Courtney fixed a smile on her face and poured tea. "How is everything?" she asked, using the tone she'd picked up from Renee. *I hope you're enjoying your meal. I'm not at all annoyed to be waiting on snotty rich people. Some of you actually tip well.*

"We need a check," the man said curtly, and looked at his watch. "When's that tour leave?"

"Two-thirty." His wife replied, forking up her last bite of grilled salmon salad with sugar-free raspberry vinaigrette. "We've got plenty of time."

"Not if you're navigating, we don't."

The wife rolled her eyes, and Courtney pretended not to hear as she cleared dishes.

"Was your trout good, I hope?" Courtney asked, although the guy had practically licked his plate clean. The Silver Creek Inn's pecan-encrusted rainbow trout was legendary, or so she had been told to tell customers.

The man just grunted and handed her a credit card.

"I'll get this right out." *You pompous prick.*

She took the plates into the kitchen and slid them into the bin with all the rest. The lunch rush was ending, and Pedro stood at the sink, working double-time with his hose of scalding water.

Courtney stepped over to the computer and pulled up the order. She swiped the prick's credit card and thought of all the little conveniences she used to take for granted—paying with credit, hopping on the computer at work to check e-mail, picking up the phone and calling Jordan or Fiona whenever she wanted. . . .

"Pauline needs to see you up front," Renee said as she swept past.

"What for?"

"No idea."

Courtney dropped off six's bill and checked her other tables' drinks before hiking across the deck, through the lobby, and behind the reception counter to Pauline's office. Her boss sat at her desk, talking on the phone. She looked up and smiled over her reading glasses when Courtney walked in.

"That's right." She held up a finger, telling Courtney to wait. "I recommend Theo's Fishing Tours. They're based in Santa Fe, but they're real big up here, too."

Courtney stepped inside the office but didn't sit down in the overstuffed armchair by the door. Offices made her uncomfortable now. As did paperwork, and men in uniform, and security cameras. She carefully avoided them. It was a new way of thinking about the world.

"That's early for the snow," Pauline was saying, "but there's still plenty to do. . . . Uh-huh . . . Absolutely."

Courtney watched her boss and suppressed a sigh. Her platinum-colored helmet hair added decades to her age, and for the umpteenth time, Courtney's hands itched for her scissors. Courtney combed her fingers through her stacked blond bob—which she still wasn't used to—and glanced away.

"All right, then. We'll see you in November." Pauline hung up and sighed. "I swear, some people can't make a *decision*. So." She smiled and rested her elbows on the desk. "How's it going, hon? How's the lunch crowd?"

"Good. Hardly a lull since breakfast."

Pauline's smiled widened. "Music to my ears." She picked up an envelope and held it out.

"What's that?"

"Payday."

Courtney glanced at the envelope uneasily. Did it have a check inside it? Made out to whom? When Courtney had responded to the ad posted at the local grocery store, she'd agreed to work for tips only, if she could get a break on lodging. Pauline had agreed immediately. She'd given her a small room at the back of the property and promised to keep her name off the books.

Courtney cleared her throat. "I thought we said—"

"It's cash." Pauline pushed the envelope at her. "I pay everyone in cash." She winked. "Makes things easier."

She took the envelope. "Thanks, but—"

"You been working your tail off. And you're good, too. You deserve more than just tips."

Courtney bit her lip. She'd never met anyone so straight-forward and *nice*. From day one, Pauline had treated her with kindness and compassion, and Courtney was pretty sure it was because the woman thought she was on the run from a husband or boyfriend somewhere. But she'd never asked, and Courtney hadn't volunteered a different story.

"Nice earrings," Pauline said, nodding at Courtney's new dangles.

"I bought them in the gift shop."

"I know." She shook her head, and her own earrings jiggled. "They're pretty. Just not what I'd expect for you."

Courtney tipped her head. "Why?"

She laughed. "Because you're such a tomboy! You dress like my son."

Courtney gazed down at her flannel shirt and jeans and clunky boots. The outdoorsy look didn't come easily for her, but at least someone was buying it.

"Anyway, thanks for your work this week," Pauline continued. "You've been a huge help with the film festival crowd. Hopefully, we'll calm down a little before Thanksgiving, give you a chance to settle in."

Courtney smiled stiffly. Yet another thing that made her uncomfortable—talking about her future. If things went well money-wise, she'd be nowhere near Silver Creek by the time Thanksgiving rolled around. She had her next destination all picked out. Fiona's passport would help her get there.

Courtney returned to the restaurant, and the pace slowed down as tourists headed into the mountains to catch up on the hiking and fishing they'd missed due to yesterday's rain. When her shift finally ended, she slipped her tips into her pocket, took off her apron, and left the inn behind her. She'd walk into town today. She needed groceries and a change of scenery. Living near her workplace was convenient, but stifling at times.

Her boots sank into the soft earth as she plodded down the dirt road leading to the highway. The inn occupied a spruce-covered hillside overlooking Silver Creek Canyon. The view was spectacular—so good, in fact, it attracted travelers from all over. People would turn off Highway 25 to catch some scenery, then decide to stay a night. Then another. The canyon was magical like that—it could lure a person in. It had lured Courtney from the moment she'd seen it. She'd stood in the town's tiny bus depot and gazed out the window at the narrow fall of water cascading down the wall at the far end of the canyon. She'd been mesmerized. And what had started out as a day trip from Santa Fe had turned into a three-week stay.

Courtney was glad. It was better here. She felt safe, tucked away in the San Juan Mountains. And since she'd changed her mind about seeking work at a salon, she didn't need proximity to those luxury resorts, anyway. Silver Creek was lower profile, a little farther off the beaten path.

The dirt road met the highway, and the town of Silver Creek came into view. Her pace quickened as she planned out her errands. First, the grocery. Then the bookstore. She needed another travel guide, and she wouldn't mind a new magazine to keep her busy this evening. Her tiny room didn't have a television, or even a decent view. But it had privacy, which was just what Courtney wanted.

She stopped at one of the town's three traffic lights and waited. No more jaywalking, as even the most minor brush with law enforcement could become a problem. She rolled her shoulders to ease the soreness. She'd stop by the drug-store, too, and pick up a heat patch. She was used to being on her feet all day, but those trays were killing her. Her arms felt like noodles.

She remembered Will's arms, and her gaze shifted from the grocery store to the gas station where she'd stopped yes-terday to call Fiona. She realized now why Alex had been so adamant about not making calls. They were addictive. Just a few minutes of her sister's voice, and she wanted more. She wanted to talk to Jordan, too. And Will. And even Amy.

The light changed, and she crossed the intersection. She especially wanted to talk to Will. But the last time she'd heard his voice, she'd started aching inside, and the feeling had persisted for days. She couldn't do that again.

Especially not now. Not with a warrant out there, and Will sworn to uphold the law. He felt something for her, but whatever it was didn't trump his commitment to his job. She knew that. She could deal with it. Just like she could deal with walking away from him and whatever crazy thing they'd started at his house that night. It was one night. It was over.

It wasn't love.

At least, she didn't think so. It couldn't be. It wasn't pos-sible to love someone after just a few weeks. After just one night.

What she felt was loneliness.

She thought of his solid body under her hands. She thought of *his* hands.

Loneliness. With maybe some lust mixed in.

Courtney cut a glance at the pay phone. Her feet slowed. It was late afternoon, almost evening in Texas. Just one phone call . . .

*Not a trace,* Alex had told her. *Not a single trace, or you're blown.*

Courtney tore her gaze away and kept walking.

Some clients were a hell of a lot more trouble than they were worth. Courtney Glass was quickly turning into one of those clients.

Alex watched on her video monitor as Nathan Devereaux strolled though the door to Lovell Solutions and gazed directly into her security cam. He smiled slightly. She murmured a phrase that was sure to make her grandmother roll in her grave.

By the time she stepped out of her office and into her reception room—which hadn't improved since Courtney's visit—she had her arms crossed and her mind made up. She'd tell him nothing.

"Mornin'." He gave her the full smile now, along with the accent. It wasn't a Texas accent. She hadn't placed it yet, but it was definitely someplace in the South.

"You're wasting your time here," she said. "I won't divulge the whereabouts of my client."

He lifted an eyebrow and wandered over to the Mr. Coffee. "Mind?" He took an NPR mug from a box she hadn't finished unpacking and poured himself a cup.

"I'm not here about Courtney." He propped a shoulder against the wall and looked at her.

"Why are you here?"

He took a sip. Nodded. "Damn, that's good."

"Why are you here, Detective? I've got work to do."

"I bet you do. You must stay busy, huh? Woman with your skills?" His gaze roamed the room, pausing on the enormous computer box that had been delivered yesterday. She was in the process of upgrading all her systems.

"I make a living," she said.

"You use a lot of computers?"

She shrugged. "They come in handy. If you know what you're doing."

He took another sip. "I'm not much on computers, myself. Spend most of my time out in the field."

She wasn't surprised. Nathan Devereaux struck her as a talented detective. At the very least, he had a way with people. She'd guess he got most of his leads by conducting face-to-face interviews, not mining databases or cruising the Net.

"Why are you here?" she asked for the third time.

He pushed off the wall and stepped closer until she was looking right up into his face. Alex was short, and it didn't take much for a man to tower over her. She'd learned not to let it intimidate her.

He smiled. "You're very businesslike."

"I'm running a business."

"So I noticed."

He was standing so close, she could see the flecks of gray in his blue eyes. His hair was dark and scruffy and just the kind she'd like to run her fingers through during sex.

"I have a challenge for you," he said.

She lifted an eyebrow in question.

"It's a skip trace."

"Why don't you do it?" she asked. "You've probably got better resources than I have."

"Possibly. Thing is, I have no time. Zero. It's for a case

that isn't even mine, really." He glanced around her office. "And I have a feeling you'd do it quicker than we would anyway."

She tried not to feel smug, but he'd given her some nice compliments in the space of five minutes. All part of his charm, probably. "Who is it?" she asked.

"Lindsey Ann Kahn. Thirty-five. Single. She's a junior partner over at Wilkers and Riley."

"She worked the LivTech trial with Alvin."

He nodded.

"You didn't tell me you weren't on that case."

He shrugged. "It's a technicality, really."

She crossed her arms. "It'll cost you a thousand dollars."

He whistled. "You're steep."

"Take it or leave it. I've got more than enough work." Actually, she didn't at the moment, but he didn't need to know that.

He took another gulp of coffee and looked pensive. "I'll take it. But for that price, I need a quick turnaround. She was last seen Friday afternoon leaving work. Her car was parked at her health club as of Friday night. She wasn't seen or heard from all weekend. I need to know where she went."

"What if she's dead?"

"That's entirely possible. But she might have gone some-place on her own steam."

Alex had to admit, she was intrigued. And a thousand dollars would do wonders for her bottom line this month. She'd given Courtney Glass a bargain-basement rate be-cause she'd liked her spunk and felt bad about her predica-ment. She shouldn't have been so soft.

"Okay, I'll do it."

He nodded, as if he'd expected this. "Good. I'll check back in twenty-four hours, see what you've got."

"That's not a lot of time."

He smiled and handed her his empty mug. "Should be plenty for you."

When he was gone, she stood in the middle of her reception room and decided it was time to get serious. She was charging someone a thousand dollars for probably a day's work. It was time to get her act together and start looking professional. The office decor could wait, but she needed her new computer up and running pronto.

She found a utility knife in a crate of office supplies and cut open the cardboard box. It was packed in pieces of Styrofoam, of course. She pulled at the giant block. It didn't budge. She tugged and wrestled with it, but nothing moved. She turned the box on its side and heard the door open behind her. Devereaux must have forgotten something. He could lend her a hand with this damn thing.

She turned around. The man standing in her doorway wore a ski mask. In his hand was a Sig Sauer, just like the one Alex had stashed in her desk drawer.

About twenty feet away.

She tried to speak, but her voice wouldn't work. Her heart galloped in her chest as she looked at his gun.

He turned and locked the door, and she slipped the utility knife into her back pocket.

He crossed the room and shoved her roughly into her office and into a chair. Bloodshot gray eyes peered through the mask at her.

"We can do this hard or easy," he said. "Your pick."

She felt the bulk of the knife in her pocket. She had to time this right or—

"Where's Courtney Glass?"

"Who?"

His fist connected with her cheek, and her teeth rattled. "That was my left hook. You wanna try my right?"

Tears stung her eyes, and she felt dizzy. Shocked. She tried to think. "I don't know—"

The butt of the pistol drew back. She jerked sideways, but the blow came anyway, and her world went black.


Will left his Suburban at a campground on the outskirts of town and hiked in through the forest that blanketed the canyon's southwest side. A stranger in a dinged-up battle cruiser of a car would attract attention, and attention was something he did not need at the moment. Just about everything he'd done in the past two days was, if not illegal, something that could get him fired. But Will was Special Forces before he was a cop, and the teams had their own MO. It called for knowing the mission, adapting, and breaking the rules when necessary, provided you had a damn good reason.

And snatching Courtney out of a killer's sights was a damn good reason.

Will picked his way through a dense thicket of vines on the forest floor. He moved among the ponderosa pines, pinions, and junipers—all trees he knew well from training ops conducted in the Colorado Rockies. He could hide in these woods for days, not making a sound or leaving a trace, as he waited for his target to appear. He could, but he hoped he wouldn't have to. His equipment at present included a

Glock, a cell phone, and a PowerBar, and his truck was paid up at the campground for two days.

This wouldn't take two days, though. Two hours maybe, if he guessed right. It was two o'clock on a Monday. Whatever Courtney did in this town, she probably did it during the day, which meant her shift likely ended in the late afternoon or evening. Unless she was a waitress, in which case she might go on about that time, but if so, she'd have mornings free, and he'd catch her tomorrow.

Money was key. He wondered how she was getting it. The amount she'd had when she left Austin wouldn't have gotten her far, so she would have taken a job by now— probably something cash-only. Will had checked with the state board, and Courtney hadn't applied for a New Mexico cosmetology license, or applied to have hers transferred. So if she was working in a salon, she was doing it illegally. But he didn't figure she'd do that, not after all the effort she'd made to cover her tracks. He figured she was doing something low profile, maybe cleaning hotel rooms or waiting tables. Or maybe she'd shacked up with some rich family whose kids needed a nanny, although that was doubtful. That sort of job required references.

Will chose his steps carefully. It had rained recently. The ground felt spongy and unreliable, and it took extra effort not to leave footprints everywhere. He probably didn't need to be so cautious, but the training was ingrained.

He hiked uphill, then down, descending the steep slope that hugged the town's main road. Through the trees, he glimpsed all the predictable marks of moneyed civilization: a sporting goods store with fly-fishing rods in the window, a coffee shop, a gift boutique with a sale on turquoise jewelry. He walked another fifty yards, until he saw what he was looking for: a grocery store—the town's only one, if his research proved accurate. And a gas station. It had a pay phone out front, a phone Will had made inquiries about yesterday under the pretext of being a repairman.

Will glanced around until he spied a fallen log concealed by a layer of branches. He eased himself behind the cover and checked the view. He could see the phone, the coffee shop, and the entrance to the grocery store. If Courtney was within ten miles of here, he predicted she'd stop at one of those three places before sundown. And if she didn't, he'd watch for her tomorrow, maybe nose around a bit. He had her picture in his pocket, but he intended to save it for a last resort. She'd probably altered her appearance since she'd left Texas, and an out-of-towner flashing around a picture was sure to generate gossip.

Will took a deep breath of damp, forest air and checked his watch. He had a good five hours before dusk, although the woods would go dark before everything else did.

*Hurry up and wait.*

Feeling like a soldier for the first time in years, he blended himself into the foliage and settled in.

Alex opened her eyes and winced. Too much light. Stabbing pain. She closed her eyes again and tried to think. Her head felt swollen. Her lip stung.

She braced herself for the pain and tried again. She squinted at the brightness and scanned her surroundings. Was he here? Was she alone? Where *was* she, anyway? Her gaze fell on an overturned box of files, and she realized she was in her office. A tornado had hit. She was on the floor, on her side, surrounded by the wreckage that had once been her desk.

She sat up and wanted to puke. She closed her eyes until the feeling passed, and when she opened them again, things looked worse. Everything was topsy-turvy. Her computer was gone. *Her computer.* The whir of the ceiling fan overhead made her notice the relative quiet.

She was alone.

Her arms throbbed. They were secured behind her. She tried to pull them apart, but they were bound with something.

Alex blew out a breath. She tried to think of a plan. She knew, instinctively, that she shouldn't stand, so she maneuvered onto her knees and let herself sit there a moment, adjusting to the new position.

Her head hurt. A lot. Her arms, too, but she didn't think they were broken. Her gaze moved over the carnage of her office and landed at last on the black desk phone sitting upside down on the floor. Slowly, painfully, she made her way over to it on her knees. Then she flipped the phone over and stared down at it. Her brain felt fuzzy. She looked at the numbers for a moment, turned her back to the phone, and craned her head around so she could see to dial. She punched speakerphone as the call connected.

"Nine-one-one. Please state your emergency."

"Um . . ." She looked around. "I'm at my office. I've been attacked." Her voice broke as she realized she could be dead right now. She muddled through the details with the operator. Then she disconnected.

Help was coming. She was alive. But the shaking was worse now, like her body was waking up and realizing what had happened. She glanced back at the phone again. She remembered Nathan calling, nearly a month ago, looking for Courtney Glass, just like the ski-mask guy. Twisting herself around again, she found the arrow button and searched through the call history. She got to the right date and found the digits. She pressed Redial and then Speakerphone and waited.

"Devereaux."

She couldn't talk.

"Hello?"

"Nathan?" Suddenly her cheeks were wet and her nose was running. She couldn't get her hands up to wipe away the snot.

"Alex? What's wrong?"

She took a deep breath and tried to get control. "He was here—"

"*Who?*"

"That guy. Looking for Courtney. He took my computer and—"

"Are you *hurt?*"

"Yes. No. Not too bad, I think—"

"I'll be right there."

Will shook off the drowsiness. He checked his watch. Three hours, and no sign of Courtney. He shifted, ever so slightly, and got the blood flowing in his legs. The lack of sleep was taking a toll. Since getting his hands on Fiona's phone, he'd been occupied nonstop, first running down the pay phone lead and then with driving his ass across Texas and New Mexico. A plane would have been faster, but he hadn't wanted a paper trail. So he'd driven.

And driven. And now he could barely keep his eyes open.

*Focus.* He forced his attention back to the coffee shop, the most popular destination in town, evidently. Another baseball cap guy walked out carrying an overpriced drink, and Will added a notch to his mental tally. Coffee shop, nine. Grocery store, seven. Gas station, four. Pay phone, zilch.

His phone vibrated, and he checked the number. He weighed the risk of talking to Devereaux versus the benefit of gaining information.

"Yeah," he said quietly.

"Where are you?"

"Busy. What's up?"

"Christ, Hodges. You picked a hell of a day to call in sick, you know that? I'm in the hospital right now with Alex Lovell."

"The PI?"

"The PI. She took a beating off some ski-mask guy at her office this morning. He came in looking for Courtney, and the sonovabitch gave her a concussion. A split lip, too. She's a mess—"

"Did she give up Courtney?"

Pause. "Hey, she's okay, by the way. Thanks for asking. And she didn't *give up* Courtney, but the asshole took her computer, so it's possible he's got a location. Alex said they traded e-mails maybe a week ago. Luckily, we got the perp on videotape, and we're working on an ID, so—"

"I'll call you later."

Will hung up and squinted at the woman crossing the street. She was blond. She wore flannel. She was heading for the grocery store, and she looked all wrong except . . .

That walk. He'd know it anywhere. She wore jeans and hiking boots, but that walk was all spike heels and attitude. She entered the exit door, and Will's heart gave a kick.

He eased from the cover of the blind.

Courtney pushed up on her palms and arched into cobra pose on the narrow balcony just outside her room. She gazed at the sky. It had gone dark already as dusk settled over the canyon. She took a deep, cleansing breath, and allowed herself one more moment of tranquility before she went inside for a shower.

A flicker of movement caught her eye.

She scanned the pine-covered hillside. Was someone . . . ? No, it was a squirrel. She took another deep breath and told herself to relax. She'd been jumpy all day.

She stood up and stretched her arms above her head. She felt warm. Loose. Rejuvenated after her half hour routine. It wasn't as vigorous as Bikram yoga, which required a 105-degree room, but it made her feel good.

She pulled her towel off the banister and blotted her face. A breeze rippled over the hillside, and the pines swayed. She scanned the woods again, letting her gaze pause on all the deep, dark shadows. There was no one out there.

She tugged the sliding-glass door open and went inside. Several bags of groceries sat on the bed, and she culled through them. She found soap and a razor, and went into the bathroom to clean up.

The water pressure was low again, so she didn't linger. It was no secret why Pauline offered these rooms to staffers—they were minuscule, had outdated plumbing, and faced the hillside instead of the canyon. Plus they needed a makeover.

Courtney whisked back the orange-and-aqua shower curtain and wrapped a towel around her body.

She went into the bedroom and rummaged through the dresser. Hmm . . . flannel nightshirt or cotton? Neither of her Walmart purchases held much appeal. She was homesick for her wardrobe, for something cool and silky to slip over her skin tonight. She settled for some lace undies and a black tank top. She dropped the towel and dressed, then opened the minifridge and searched for some dinner.

More tantalizing choices—yogurt, apples, or the remaining half of the club sandwich she'd had for dinner yesterday. The menu at the inn was getting repetitive, so she reached for an apple.

A draft tickled her skin, and she turned around. The drapes fluttered near the balcony. She'd left the door open?

A shadow shifted in the corner. She jumped backward.

"Hello, C.J."

W ill.
      She dropped the apple on her foot, and it rolled under the bed.

"How did you get here?"

He stepped closer. "Drove."

"No, but . . ." She stared up at him. Several days' worth of beard covered his jaw, and something dangerous flashed in his eyes.

"But how'd you get *in*?"

"It wasn't locked."

She turned toward the balcony. It had to be ten feet off the ground—

He shoved a pair of jeans into her hands. "Get dressed. We're leaving."

"*What?*"

"We're leaving. Now."

"I'm not leaving. I'm not going anywhere!"

But he wasn't listening. He snagged her backpack off the chair and stuffed her purse inside it. Then he went in the bathroom and she heard her toiletries being shoveled off the counter.

"Wait. *Wait!*" She stalked in behind him, but the bathroom wasn't large enough for both of them, and she was squeezed up against the wall. She'd forgotten how big he was.

He zipped her pack and shouldered it. "We need to get moving."

He took her arm and pulled her toward the door just as someone knocked.

They halted and looked at each other.

He was here. She couldn't believe it, except that his hand was clamped around her elbow like a vice. He gazed down at her, and his face was so beautifully familiar, and she wanted to hug him. *He'd come after her.* There was something miraculous about that, something that made her throat tighten and her eyes sting.

"Ask who it is." He spoke so low, she could barely hear.

She cleared her throat. "Who is it?"

"It's me."

Pauline. She shook Will's grip off and cracked the door. "Hi." Courtney was half naked and had wet hair, and she hoped Pauline would figure she'd interrupted her shower.

"Sorry to bother you, C.J., but you had an urgent message from your sister. She said for you to call home."

How had Fiona known where to find her? Had Will told her?

"Thanks." Courtney forced a smile. "I'll take care of it."

She closed the door and turned around, and Will was right there behind her, his arms crossed over his chest.

She couldn't believe he was *here*, in Silver Creek. They stood there gazing at each other in the lamplight, and four weeks of emotion crackled between them. He was angry. And something else, too, something she recognized instantly as his gaze slid over her bare legs and up again. Her pulse jumped, and he eased forward.

He clamped her arm again, and she thought he was pulling her toward the bed, but he kept going, to the sliding-glass door that stood open.

"This way."

"It's two stories up!"

"I'll help you." He grabbed her jeans off the bed and shoved them at her yet a second time, and she knew if she didn't put them on, she'd be wandering around the woods in bikini underwear.

She pulled on the pants. Will watched her zip up and fasten the snap. She started to slide her feet into flip-flops.

"Get your hiking boots."

Her eyes narrowed. How long had he been watching her? She retrieved her Timberland boots from the closet and quickly put them on over the dirty socks she'd left stuffed inside them.

Then she followed him out onto the balcony. "Can't we use the door like normal people?"

"No."

"Why not?"

In answer to her question, another knock sounded across the room.

"Don't worry, I'll catch you."

She watched, shocked, as he stepped over the railing and pivoted his body. Then dropped into the darkness and landed with a soft thump.

Hel*lo*? No way was she flinging herself off a balcony! She peered over the railing at him and shook her head.

He nodded and motioned her down.

She shook her head again.

He nodded yes.

The knock came again, harder.

What was this? She hadn't had a visitor in weeks, and now her room was Grand Central Station. She gazed back at the door, then down at Will, who looked extremely impatient.

Fine. This wasn't the craziest thing she'd ever done, but it was up there, maybe top ten. She hoisted herself onto the railing and swung her legs over. He positioned himself beneath her and held out his arms.

"If you drop me," she hissed down, "I'll never forgive you." Then she closed her eyes and pushed off.

He caught her. Just like that. And she was tucked up against his chest, staring up at him, wondering what the hell sort of danger she was in that had him driving nine hundred miles and jumping off balconies.

Then he dropped one of his arms, and her feet hit the ground. He took her hand and pulled her toward the woods.

"Where are we going?" she asked.

"Anywhere but here."

He towed Courtney behind him, cursing mentally every time he heard the *snap* and *crunch* of her footsteps. They might as well have been hiking through the woods with a tambourine. With her hand tightly in his, he skirted the perimeter of the property until he saw the inviting glow of the Silver Creek Inn visitors' entrance.

He turned to Courtney. "Stay here. If you're gone when I get back, I *will* find you, and I *will* be pissed."

Before she could respond, he slipped into the woods and approached the portico where several vehicles were parked, presumably awaiting check-in. The minivan had been there earlier, when Will first scoped out the hotel, but the teal Chrysler Sebring was a new arrival. Will spotted a sticker on the bumper and confirmed his suspicion that it was a rental car. He considered approaching it to check it out, maybe get a glimpse of any paperwork inside, but then a woman and young girl exited the hotel lobby and walked toward the minivan.

Will had two choices. He could get back to Courtney or he could go after whoever it was who'd come looking for her. The last option was tempting. Alarmingly so. He could envision himself snapping someone's neck in these woods, and the fact that he really wanted to scared him. But his mission was find and retrieve. And the thing he'd spent four weeks finding could be getting lost again at this very moment.

Another tourist stepped out of the hotel. He carried a fishing rod and tackle box, and Will made up his mind. There were too many civilians around here to risk a confrontation.

He retraced his steps and found Courtney exactly where he'd left her, in a clump of trees southwest of the inn.

"Hey," he whispered.

She jumped and whirled around. Then she punched him in the arm. "Don't *do* that!"

"Keep your voice down."

"Where did you *go?*"

"Reconnaissance." He took her hand again and started back into the woods, but she jerked herself free.

"Tell me what's going on." She was whispering, but she was angry.

"Later."

"I need a phone. I have to call Fiona."

"Why?"

"There's some emergency going on at home."

He pulled her deeper into the trees and lowered his voice. "Did you tell Fiona you were here?" he asked.

"No, I thought you did."

"And were you expecting company? Tonight at your room?"

"No. I don't know anyone here except my boss and my coworkers."

He exhaled, surprised at his relief. He'd prepared himself for the possibility that she'd met someone here.

"There's no emergency," he said.

"How do you know?"

"I'll explain later. Right now we need to get going." He took her hand—more firmly this time—and pulled her through the forest. "Try not to sound like a herd of elephants."

Sufficiently insulted, she followed him through the trees and foliage more quietly than before. They didn't speak. Her breath came faster as they moved uphill, away from the road, but she kept up. He heard little noises every now and then and knew she was getting all scratched up. Why couldn't she have picked a long-sleeved shirt tonight? Or long underwear, for that matter? That little lacy thing was becoming a distraction as they raced through the woods together, her panting behind him in the dark.

They neared the campground, and he slowed the pace

so he could pay closer attention. He led her down a hillside to the northwest corner of the camping area, where his Chevy waited. He scanned the vicinity and noted three new vehicles since this afternoon: two aluminum campers, both hitched to pickups, and a full-size RV. With their cook stoves and lanterns, the people hanging around looked like legitimate tourists. Will dug his keys out of his pocket and led Courtney to the passenger's side of the Suburban. He unlocked the door for her and held it open. She climbed in without a word.

His temper resurfaced as he went around to the driver's side. He'd had this thing thirteen years, even bothering to store it at his uncle's deer lease while he'd been OCONUS. Will wasn't sentimental about much in his life, but this truck meant something to him. Maybe because he'd earned the money for it working his ass off two summers in a row. Or maybe because as a teenager, he'd gotten lucky in the back of it more times than he could count. But whatever the reason, it still irked him that Courtney had swiped it out from under his nose.

He slid behind the wheel and looked at her. "You owe me two hundred bucks."

She stared at him. She had little cuts on her face from crashing through the woods, and he started to feel guilty. But then she crossed her arms and looked ahead. "Nice greeting."

"Nice exit," he retorted, and instantly regretted it. All the way up here, he'd promised himself he wouldn't go there. He didn't want to talk about her walking out because it just pissed him off.

"I never stole your *money*," she said.

"Stole my truck." He started it up. "Same thing."

"Borrowed. Not *stole*."

"Yeah, well it cost me two hundred bucks to get it back, so you owe me."

She pursed those pretty lips of hers. Everything about her looked so goddamn familiar. Except her hair. He couldn't believe she was a blonde.

"How did you find me?"

"It wasn't that hard."

"Bullshit. It was the phone call, wasn't it? You tapped Fiona's phone. I hope you had a warrant, because if you didn't, she'll sue your butt off."

He almost laughed. She thought he was scared of a *lawsuit*? He rested an elbow on the seat and leaned toward her. "Running was a bad idea, Courtney. All you did was make things worse."

She looked at him with disdain. Then she turned away. "You smell like dirt."

Shaking his head, he put the truck in gear. He drove across the campground and turned east onto the highway.

"How do you know there's no emergency?" she asked.

He glanced over at her. Even in the dimness, he could see the worry on her face. She probably thought something had happened to Fiona. He felt oddly satisfied to see her fear, to watch her get a taste of what it was like to be twisted up with worry, like her sister had been these past four weeks. Like he had been.

*She's a tough person to care about.* Will swallowed down the bitterness, and he shifted his gaze to the road.

"It was most likely a ploy," he told her. "Someone got a tip-off you were in town. Probably checked out likely places you'd be staying. When they found someone who fit, they left you a message, then the manager pointed them straight to your door."

"Who would do all that?"

"Same people who killed Alvin. And Eve Caldwell. And Martin Pembry, and probably that other attorney, Lindsey Kahn."

The road stretched out before them, along with the silence. She was safe. She was right here. But he still didn't feel right, yet. There was too much that needed saying, but saying things—especially emotional things—wasn't something he did well.

Or ever.

She turned to look out the window and sighed wistfully. "I liked Silver Creek."

"Why?"

She shrugged. "It was beautiful. And quiet."

"Hell of a place to hide."

She turned to look at him. "What do you mean?"

"It's a *box* canyon, Courtney. It's a nightmare. One way in. One way out." He gritted his teeth, still annoyed that she'd picked such a place. The damn town was surrounded by three walls of rock. Scenic, yes, but a literal dead end if someone had found her there.

Which they had.

Will thought back to the Sebring. Whoever had come calling tonight had missed his mark by about two minutes. It was much too close a call.

"Am I under arrest?"

He cut a glance at her. "Maybe."

"What does that mean? Fiona said there was a warrant."

"It means behave yourself or I'll haul you to the nearest jail."

She rolled her eyes and huffed out a breath, and his pulse picked up for some reason. He'd missed that attitude of hers, and seeing it again was doing funny things to him. He wanted to pull over right now and drag her into his lap. He wanted to pull over right now and spank some sense into her.

Instead, he drove. And drove. He felt her sitting just inches away from him, getting more anxious by the minute. She didn't like her new predicament, and he'd bet anything she was plotting a way to get out of it.

The juncture finally appeared, and he turned south on the four-lane highway that would lead them to I-40.

She shook her head. "This is illegal, you know. You haven't read me my rights."

"You're not under arrest." There wasn't even a warrant out on her anymore, but he kept that to himself. He'd have no trouble coming up with a reason to arrest her. If he pushed the right buttons, it would take him about two seconds to have her on assaulting a police officer.

"So what the hell is this? I'm being held against my will. It's unlawful imprisonment."

"Yeah, sorry 'bout that. Maybe I should have left you back in the canyon, see how long you would have lasted against some hired gun."

He flipped on the radio and turned the dial until he got a staticky country-music station. He hadn't realized how angry he was until now. Four weeks of agonizing, and now that he finally had her safe, he wanted to yell at her. This was going to be a long drive. He checked the speedometer, then the clock. He was eager to put some distance between the Suburban and Silver Creek. He also needed to make sure they weren't being followed.

He thought back to Devereaux's call. They had the ski-mask guy on videotape, which put Courtney completely in the clear. Now they just had to find the guy—or guys—and pin down who'd hired him. Will's bet was Wilkers, whose east Texas company owned a black Cadillac Escalade and who had profited handsomely from the LivTech case.

Will turned the music down. "Did Fiona tell you some-one trashed your house?"

She glanced at him apprehensively, then looked out the window. "Yes."

"What were they looking for?"

She didn't speak.

"And why would they come all the way to New Mexico to silence you?"

She cringed at his blunt statement. "I guess because of Eve Caldwell. I can put her with David at the time of the trial. They were exchanging e-mails. That's lawyer miscon-duct, or jury tampering, or whatever you call it."

"Both," he said. "It's grounds for the verdict to be over-turned. That's twenty million dollars in legal fees on the line. Not to mention disbarment, jail time."

"So I guess someone's afraid—oh my God, I just thought of something."

He glanced over. Her eyes were huge. "What?"

"Those e-mails," she said. "I told you how I snooped through David's e-mail? I didn't have time to read them right then, so I just forwarded everything to myself."

"You forwarded *his* messages to yourself?"

"What if he found out I did that? And maybe told someone, and that's what they were looking for? They don't just want *me*. They think I have his messages."

"Do you?"

"I have no idea. Maybe. This was, like, seven months ago. Do they stay in your in-box that long?"

"Depends." Will was already thinking of how long it would take them to find a place where she could check. Where was her laptop? But then he remembered it had been searched already.

"We ran your computer," he said. "Nothing like that came up."

She shook her head. "It wouldn't. This happened in the middle of the day, on my lunch break. David was in the shower while I was looking through his BlackBerry, and I didn't have much time, so I forwarded his messages to myself at work. They'd be in my in-box at Bella, only that's probably been shut down by now, since I left."

Will gripped the steering wheel, and not just because he didn't like the image of her having a nooner with Alvin. "This is exactly why running was a bad idea, Courtney. We could have gotten to all this weeks ago if you'd just let us interview you."

"You mean arrest me and charge me with murder?" She scoffed. "No, thanks. Your lieutenant hates me. He's had it in for me from day one."

"It's different now. We've got video of a guy in a ski mask entering Alex Lovell's workplace. He beat her up, trying to get to you. It corroborates everything you've been saying."

"*What?* Why didn't you tell me?"

"I'm telling you now. You've been a little hard to reach lately."

"Is she all right?"

"She's fine," he lied, then felt guilty. "He tossed her office, gave her a bloody lip."

"Oh my God."

She was upset now, and Will regretted bringing it up. But she needed to know he wasn't dragging her back to Austin to face charges. He was dragging her back to Austin to clear her name.

And he was dragging her back to the place where someone was actively trying to kill her.

Which was why he intended to be on her like her shadow. She needed protection, and he would provide it. He just had to get *her* to believe that.

He pressed on through the darkness. She got quiet and leaned her head against the window. He wondered what she was thinking but didn't want to ask. She might turn around and ask him the same thing, and then he'd be screwed.

*I'm thinking it's so good to see you again it hurts. I'm thinking I love listening to you argue with me, and I thought I'd lost you, and now I never want to let you out of my sight.*

He glanced at her and saw that her eyes were closed. Maybe she was asleep. Or, more likely, ignoring him.

The Suburban vibrated with its familiar hum. Yellow stripes flew past in a rhythm that threatened to hypnotize him. He shook off the feeling and turned up the AC.

She turned it down.

He turned it up again.

"I'm *freezing*," she said, rubbing her bare arms.

"Yeah, well, I'm tired."

"Why don't I drive? You can take a nap."

He snorted.

"What?"

"You're not driving anywhere."

Her eyebrows arched. "What do you think I'm going to do, kidnap you?"

"I have no idea what you'll do. I just know that I don't trust you. And you're not driving my truck."

"Stubborn," she muttered, and then shut up again.

The minutes slid by. Then the hours. The mountains became foothills, and then the desert stretched out in all directions, the vast flatness dotted with lights here and there. The yellow lines kept coming, and Will's eyelids drooped. He ran through baseball stats in his head in an effort to stay alert. Suddenly the tires buzzed over the shoulder, and he jerked the wheel left. *Shit.*

"Why don't you just shoot us both now? Get it over with?"

He glanced at her. "Sorry."

"When was the last time you slept?"

He trained his gaze back on the highway and didn't answer.

"It's nearly one o'clock. Let's stop for the night."

He shot her a scathing look.

"What? Look, there's a motel up ahead. I saw a sign a few miles back. We can sleep a few hours, then get back on the road."

It was about the sorriest plan he'd ever heard. Except for

the sleep part. That part would be good. Problem was, he knew she had no intention of sleeping. She'd get him to pull over and then she'd take the first opportunity to make a run for it, which, in this middle-of-nowhereville location probably meant hitching a ride with some trucker.

"Will?"

He ignored her and kept going. But then he shifted in his seat when he noticed the gas gauge had dropped to a quarter tank. They'd have to stop at some point.

An exit sign loomed ahead. Gas. Food. Lodging.

"Come on, Will. You look beat."

He slid a glance at her.

"I know I am," she said reasonably, "and I got a good eight hours last night. Let's pull over."

"Gas and coffee. That's it."

"And we can switch drivers. You can take a nap."

"Not happening."

He pulled off the highway and quickly found the gas station. The convenience store adjacent to it was dark, but the pumps were lit up like a stadium. Will pulled up to one and realized his mistake. He'd been so tired, he'd forgotten he needed to use cash, not credit. Credit would leave a trail. He had a wallet full of twenties, but that wouldn't do him much good here.

He sighed and rubbed the bridge of his nose. "Hey, you wouldn't happen to have a credit card, would you? That has some name on it that has nothing to do with you?"

"What, you mean like an alias? That sounds illegal."

Her tone grated on him. God*damn* he needed sleep. "Don't push me. Do you have a card or not?"

"Not."

He muttered something particularly shocking, and she didn't look shocked at all.

"Let's call it a night." She nodded at the motel across the street. "We can gas up in the morning."

Will gazed tiredly at the Desert Dreams Motel. The neon sign announced a vacancy, and a light glowed in the front office.

Fuck it.

He was out of gas in every sense of the word. He needed a nap. Not to mention a shower and a few thousand calories to get his system cranked up again before he faced another ten hours behind the wheel.

He drove across the highway and pulled into the motel. Courtney's happiness at this turn of events was palpable.

"Four hours," he said firmly. "I want us gassed up and on the road by daybreak. And don't even think about going anywhere."

She tipped her head to the side and pretended to be confused. "We're in the middle of a desert. Where on earth would I go?"

The tiny room smelled like cigarettes. Courtney sat on the edge of the bed as Will turned on the shower. After a few minutes, steam drifted into the room and she glanced over her shoulder just in time to see him step naked under the showerhead.

He caught her eye in the mirror. "I'm watching you. And if you think I'd be embarrassed to go after you buck naked, you're wrong."

She let her gaze drop to his bare butt, which looked even better than she'd remembered. She lifted an eyebrow.

"Forget it. I don't fall for the same shit twice." He ducked his head under the stream, and she turned away so he wouldn't see her expression.

The same shit? What was that supposed to mean? Did he think she'd slept with him to . . . what? Distract him? Influence the investigation?

Fuming, she stood up and flipped on the TV. Besides the predictable lineup of pay-per-view porn, she found infomercials and televangelists. She switched off the power and unlaced her boots. She kicked them to the floor and shimmied out of her jeans. Then she pulled down the tacky bedspread, stretched out on the bed, and closed her eyes.

The water shut off. He stepped into the room, and she heard a towel being tossed over a chair. Next, she heard denim against skin as his jeans went on. Then there was the gentle *thunk* of something on the floor near his side of the bed. His gun? The mattress dipped, and she rolled into him.

"Hey!"

"Sorry." He was sprawled out on his stomach, diagonal across the bed, with his feet hanging off. His right elbow was practically in her face, and his eyes were closed.

He was going to *sleep?* No way. She was half naked here, and she'd seen the way he'd looked at her at the inn.

Suddenly, he pushed up on his palms, reached into his back pocket, and pulled out a pair of handcuffs.

"Forgot something." The cool metal clamped over her wrist just as she jerked backward.

"Ouch!"

He flopped onto his back and clamped the empty silver bracelet on his left hand.

"*What* are you doing?"

He closed his eyes and settled back against the pillows. "Combat nap."

She stared down at him, at his bare, perfect torso and the smirk on his face. She nearly bit a hole in her tongue to keep from screaming.

"You have three seconds," she said calmly.

"To what?" He opened his eyes and reached for the lamp. The room went dark, except for the blue glow from the vacancy sign in the parking lot.

"To take these things off or I will *claw* you to pieces."

He lifted one eyelid. "I'd love to see you try."

"Will—"

"Go for it." He rolled onto his side and flung his free arm over her, pinning her against the mattress.

And then she got it. He was baiting her. He wanted her to start a wrestling match with him, which she'd lose, of course. This was revenge. This was him exerting control over her after she'd walked out on him without a word. What was it he'd said earlier? *Nice exit?* She'd hurt his feelings, and rather than admit it, he was doing this macho power play. What he really wanted was sex, obviously—the same thing every man always wanted. She glanced at his chest, rising and falling. There were those arms again, those arms she'd missed. Something heated inside her, and she knew sex wasn't far from what she wanted, too.

But the handcuffs pissed her off.

They weren't about preventing an escape, they were about his being a Neanderthal.

Weren't they?

His breath came deep and even, and she frowned at him. Was he really *asleep?*

No way he'd gone to sleep so quickly.

But his arm was heavy on her rib cage, and he was totally, completely immobile, except for that breathing.

She turned and stared at the wall, feeling angry and confused and *frustrated* all at the same time. She thought about all the lonely, restless nights she'd endured over the past month. She'd never minded sleeping by herself before, but that had changed recently. She'd felt so *alone*. All those endless hours in that cramped little room at the back of the inn. No TV. No friends. Nothing to keep her company besides books and yoga and her depressing thoughts.

She didn't want to run.

She didn't want to spend every day looking over her shoulder.

In Austin she'd felt terrified, but in Silver Creek she'd felt isolated beyond belief. Alienated from everyone and everything around her.

Empty.

And when Will had shown up, she'd felt a deep, drowning sense of pure *relief* that someone cared enough to come. She'd felt wanted, for the first time in her life, and now she was terrified for a new reason.

He'd come for her.

He was angry, and hurt, and probably humiliated, but he'd come anyway. And it wasn't about his job. She knew that. If this were official police business, he would have come with a local sheriff or maybe sent a bounty hunter.

But he'd come by himself. For her. And now he planned to force her back to Texas to face all her worst fears.

He must know about Walter.

Fiona had said she thought that's what the arrest warrant

was about—Walter's unsolved murder and her presumed involvement. If she'd killed one man, why not two?

And if Will knew about Walter, he knew about her past. And if he knew about her past, he knew about her record, maybe even the juvenile stuff that was supposed to be sealed. And if he knew about all that, it was even more astonishing—and more terrifying—that he was here now, conked out beside her in some dumpy motel room.

"Hey." His voice was husky.

She swallowed the lump in her throat and glanced over at him. "Hey, what?"

His eyes were dark and luminous in the bluish light. His brow furrowed. "Are you crying?"

She turned away and pressed her cheek into the pillow. She *was* crying. She didn't know why. She didn't want to try to explain, either.

His arm tightened around her waist and pulled her closer. He pressed a kiss against her shoulder, and she tensed.

A kiss. It was almost like a truce. It was a peace offering. She turned toward him, and then his mouth was against hers, and it tasted so good, she wanted to drink him in. His cuffed hand was pressed awkwardly between them, but his free hand reached for her cheek and slid into her hair. She wedged her leg between his and scooted herself closer, close enough to feel that hard body from her thighs to her breasts.

He wanted her.

He didn't want to sleep; he wanted her. The knowledge made her thrilled and scared and giddy all at the same time. Whatever had happened, whatever she'd done, this man wanted her, right here, this instant. She kissed him and pressed into him. She breathed in his warm, male scent until the pain in her chest eased and the loneliness of the past four weeks faded away.

He rolled onto his back and sighed. He muttered a curse under his breath as he dug something from his pocket, and then she heard the *snick* of the handcuffs coming off. She was free again.

"I'm going to regret this," he said quietly to the ceiling.

She propped on her elbow and gazed down at him. "Why?"

Instead of answering, he reached over and hauled her on top of him. All her breath whooshed out, and she barely had time to catch it before he reached up and pulled her head down to his.

He made her dizzy. One hand tunneled into her hair and the other gripped her bottom, pulling her against him while he kissed her until there was nothing but his mouth and his steely body beneath her. He tasted like *him*, and she hadn't known how much she'd missed it until just this moment.

And then he sat up, and she started to fall back, but he caught her around the waist. She nestled onto his lap, and his eyes went black, and he pulled her cotton tank top over her head and tossed it on the floor. And then he was kissing her again, taking away all her breath and all her thoughts except him. He felt so good—his mouth and his hands, even the scrape of his beard against the tender swell of her breast was like heaven. She tipped her head back and shivered at the pleasure of it. They were here. Together. It still didn't quite feel real, but it *was* real. Her fingers in his hair were real. His palms sliding over her thighs were real. His mouth against her throat was good and hot and very real.

"I missed you," she whispered, and then he pulled back and looked at her, and she felt a rush of panic. She shouldn't have said that. It was too close to what she wanted to say, and he knew.

But then everything shifted suddenly, and she was on her back with him staring down at her. She wrapped her legs around him and arched against him, and he groaned, and she knew he wasn't thinking about words anymore.

And then it *was* a wrestling match, only not really because it wasn't a contest, but a frantic race to the same finish. There was something fierce about him, and even angry, as they pulled and clutched at each other, jerking and yanking on clothes until everything was a heap on the floor, and their skin was slick against each other's and they were fused together in every possible way.

"Look at me."

His voice was like a growl, and she opened her eyes and gazed up at him, wondering at the tension in his face and his shoulders as he rocked into her. He was trying to say something, something with his body, something he didn't have the words for, as he drove himself into her. And then she was shaking and shattering, her whole world breaking apart, as the full, brutal force of it hit her.

# CHAPTER

## 22

He rolled off her, onto his back, and she stared at him in the darkness as reality sank in. He loved her . . . or something. That's what this was about. That's why he'd come all this way. His chest rose and fell in the dimness as his breath came back, but he didn't look at her. Finally, he got up and ducked into the bathroom.

She gazed at the ceiling. Her heart hammered, and her lungs seemed to shrink, like she was having a panic attack, only she didn't know for sure because she'd never had one before. She glanced at the nightstand, where he'd left his keys. She glanced at the door, where he'd secured the chain. She bit her lip and wondered how long it would take him to drift off again.

"Don't even think about it."

He stood in the bathroom doorway, gazing down at her, his shadow huge and intimidating. Or it would be to most people. She wasn't intimidated because she knew he'd never lay a hand on her.

"Think about what?" she asked.

"Taking off." He pulled back the sheets and blankets and slid into bed, then lifted her legs and pulled her under the covers with him. The sheets felt cool, and his body was warm as he tucked her head against his chest.

He knew she wanted to run. Did he know she felt panicked, too? Did he know why? Her heart was beating a million miles an hour. Maybe he could hear it right there in the dark.

He stroked a hand down her back and up. Then down, then back up to tangle in her hair. She'd cut it chin-length, which was a completely new style for her. She'd had long hair since high school.

"Blond, huh?"

She closed her eyes and tried to think only about his fingers in her hair. "Uh-huh."

He pressed a kiss against the top of her head, but didn't comment.

"You don't like blondes?"

"Not particularly."

"All guys like blondes. It's a proven fact."

He shrugged. "I like redheads."

She smiled in the darkness and felt herself relax. The slow, steady beat of his heart against her ear was helping. This felt good. Friendly. She could worry about the other stuff later.

His hand trailed down her back again, and she sighed.

"Courtney?" His voice was low.

"Hmm?"

"You don't need to be scared."

She tensed. "Scared?"

"Of tomorrow."

"What happens tomorrow?"

His hand settled on her hip. "We get back to Austin."

The panic was back, full force, and she sat up. The sheet dropped, and she pulled it up to cover herself. "How can you be sure?"

He watched her calmly. "Because I can."

"Can you control your lieutenant? Can you control some assassins who want to kill me?"

God, what was she doing here? She eyed the keys again and tried to think of a way out.

He sat up and leaned back against the headboard. "I can't control anyone but me. And I'm not going to let anyone hurt you."

"But they could still arrest me and put me in jail, right? If they run out of suspects? They think I'm a murderer, Will."

He pulled her against his chest and wrapped his arms around her. "Everybody knows you didn't kill Alvin."

"I didn't kill anyone! I didn't kill Walter, either."

His arms tightened. "I wouldn't blame you if you had."

"I didn't."

"I know."

And then it got quiet, and the only sound was their breathing and the soft hum of the vending machine outside their door. He knew. He knew everything about her, and he was here anyway. It didn't make sense.

And she knew he meant what he said about protecting her, but that might not be enough. He couldn't control a whole police department. He couldn't control a team of killers. The stakes were high—millions of dollars high—and way too many people would be much better off with her dead.

"Stop worrying," he whispered. He laced his fingers through hers and rested their hands on his lap, on top of the blanket. She turned his hand over and looked at it. She traced the jagged silver scar across his palm. She trailed her finger up to the one at his wrist.

"It's from bone fragments."

She looked up at him.

"It happened in Afghanistan."

She gazed back down at his hand, puzzled now.

He cleared his throat. "It was one of those crazy days. Everything was fine, but then it all went to shit, all at once, before you could even react. One minute was routine, and the next was this bloodbath."

She didn't say anything. In an odd way, she could relate. The day David died had started out so normal, and then everything turned upside down.

"It was the end of the tour," he said. "That was the worst part. Twelve fucking days left."

He paused, and she could feel his muscles tighten. She waited.

"We were on this pass through the mountains. Real narrow, you know? Not much more than an animal trail, really, but it was the quickest way through. We'd been over it a couple times. Locals used it. Everything seemed fine, and then boom."

"You got shot?"

"Land mine. Two, actually. Guys up front took the brunt of it. I was in back, humping extra gear, but it knocked me right off my feet. Just picked me up and dropped me flat on my ass."

He stopped again, and she held his hand, running her thumb over the scar.

"Dust was everywhere, guys screaming to get down, get cover. Then bullets were flying. It was an ambush. Soon as I could move, I got behind a rock and returned fire. Then

I looked off to my right and saw Denton—this guy from Mississippi, twenty-three. He was lying there in the dirt, bleeding like a faucet. His whole leg was gone, and he was just lying there, not ten yards away."

She squeezed his hand. "What happened?"

"I made a run for it. Grabbed him and dragged him behind some rocks. It was bad, though. The blood was pumping out. I tried to get a tourniquet around it, but there wasn't much left to secure it to, so I just started pressing on the wound, stuffing anything I could in there, bandages, clothes, whatever I could get my hands on. Blood seeped through all of it, but I just kept pressing and plunging my hand in there, trying to get the blood to stop. Whole time, he's screaming at me to just let him bleed out. He can't go home without his leg."

"Did you let him?"

"No. It seemed like forever, but finally we got some air cover. We got a chopper in there, got our team the hell out before it could get any worse. Not that it could, really. Out of six guys, we'd just lost three, plus Denton's leg."

"He made it back?"

"Thanks to me." Will's voice sounded bitter. "Got a great homecoming, too. Came back just in time to find out his wife was seeing someone else, had already filed for divorce."

"That's awful."

He shrugged. "Happens a lot. The stress. The absence. It puts a lot on a marriage."

She looked down at their hands now, and had so many questions, but she didn't want to ask them yet. She wondered why he'd signed up for a job like that.

"Are you glad you're back now?"

"Sometimes. Sometimes it's weird. Everything's so nice over here, and people don't even realize it. They take it for granted." His chest lifted, and he let out a deep sigh. "I'm glad to be away from all the killing, though. It gets to you. I can't explain it. It's like you get numb to it. I never wanted to be numb. That's why I didn't re-up."

"So why'd you decide to be a cop?"

He glanced down at her. "A detective. I set out to be a homicide detective, not just a cop."

"Why?" It seemed a strange career move for a man who was sick of seeing death.

He shook his head. "I don't know."

"Yes, you do."

He paused. "I guess I wanted it to matter. Each person. Every time. For me, it's like if one person doesn't matter, then there's no point."

She looked down and brushed her thumb over his palm. He trusted her, despite what he'd said before. He trusted her, or he wouldn't be telling her all this. Now it was her turn to trust him, too. But that panic was still there, nibbling at her.

"Let's get some sleep." He kissed her head. "I've got ten hours of driving tomorrow."

They slid down under the sheets, and he rolled her against him.

"Why don't you let me drive?" she asked again.

He hitched her thigh up over his belly and gave a contented sigh. "Not a chance."

Nathan heard the arguing as he neared Room 822 and recognized Alex's voice, clear as a bell, above the nurse's.

"This is absurd," she said. "You can't *prohibit* access. That's the point of an *open* network."

"I got doctor's orders. You're not allowed to use that in here. You're supposed to be resting."

Nathan stood in the doorway and watched Alex—who looked like she'd been hit by a baseball bat—glower at the nurse who was unplugging her computer cord. He cleared his throat, and she looked up.

"Thank *God!* I've been trying you all morning. Why'd you turn off your cell?"

"I was in a deposition," he said.

The nurse bustled past and shot him a glare. Evidently she'd given up trying to separate Alex from her laptop.

Nathan stepped toward the bed and rested his hand on the metal rail. She looked so frail underneath that hospital gown, and that purple goose egg on the side of her face made him want to throttle someone.

Or at least throw a few people in jail.

Her fingers flew over the keyboard as she continued working. She had files fanned out beside her, and a cell phone, and she seemed to have set up shop for the morning.

"Aren't you being discharged today?" He secretly hoped not, or at least not without some powerful meds.

She glanced up from whatever she was doing. "Noon, supposedly. That's *if* I don't get kicked out first by Nurse Ratched. I swear to God, that woman—"

"What'd you find out?" he interrupted.

She set her computer aside, finally. "I had a friend of mine run down that skip trace."

Nathan's lip twitched with amusement. "You're telling me you subbed out my job from your hospital bed?"

"You got a problem with that?"

"Nope."

"Good." She sighed. "But you're not going to like what he found."

Will felt itchy.

He sat with his back to the wall, scanning the greasy-spoon diner for the source of the threat. He scrutinized every dough-bellied trucker and leathery ranch hand who walked into the place, but he couldn't pinpoint it.

Still, something was off. His senses had been twitching since the moment they'd stepped out of their room at the Desert Dreams Motel. Courtney had wanted breakfast immediately, but Will had insisted they get on the road. He couldn't explain the gut-deep feeling that they needed to leave town, but he'd followed it. That same instinct had helped him dodge a bullet a time or two over the years.

"You gonna eat that?"

He glanced at Courtney, who sat directly across from him in the red vinyl booth. She was showered and rested and looking at his bacon with lust in her eyes.

They'd been here twenty minutes, and already she'd cleaned her plate. His gaze skimmed over her sinewy arms, left bare in that yoga getup. She seemed thinner now than she had before. Stronger, too.

He forked up some huevos rancheros. "What, they didn't have food in Silver Creek?"

"Waitressing killed my appetite." She nodded at his plate. "Come on. Don't you wanna share?"

He leaned back and draped an arm over the booth. "Depends."

"On what?"

"On what you're offering."

She crossed her arms. "Are you bartering with bacon?"

"Yep."

"You're flirting."

"Yep."

She gave him that half smile he loved. "In that case, you can have whatever you like."

He scooped up all three strips and dumped them on her plate as the waitress stopped by with their bill. He picked it up.

"Whoa." She chomped right into the bacon. "Flirting *and* paying? Is this a date?"

"This is breakfast." Her left hand was sitting beside her plate, and he covered it with his. "But I *would* like to take you out on a date soon."

She stopped chewing and gazed down at their hands. She swallowed. He watched her reaction closely, because he'd guessed it would be this way. They'd spent the night together naked—fine, no problem. But his wanting to hold her hand and take her out made her nervous.

"Okay," she said.

"Okay."

They looked at each other for a moment, and then he slid his cell phone across the table toward her. "You should probably call your sister."

"Why?" she asked, seeming relieved by the change of subject.

"Just to check in."

"She's in Florida," Courtney said. "I doubt she wants to hear from me on her honeymoon."

"I bet she would. She's been worried about you."

"When did you talk to her last?"

"At her wedding."

She gaped at him. "You went to the *wedding?*"

"I sort of dropped in."

"How was it? How did she look?"

He heard the envy in her voice. "It was fine."

"But how did she *look?* What was her hair like?"

He frowned. "I don't know."

"You saw her, didn't you? Was it in an updo? A chignon? God, don't tell me she had a beehive!"

"I have no idea what you just said."

She rolled her eyes.

"She looked pretty," he offered. "Her dress was nice."

"*I* was supposed to do her hair. She probably did it herself, probably one of her damn French braids."

"So you want to call her or not?"

She gnawed on the bacon. "Not yet. She'll just give me the third degree. I'll wait until we get home."

Home. He liked hearing the word from her.

"Okay, then try Jordan again," he said. "We need her to try to log in and find out about your e-mail account at Bella."

She picked up another strip of bacon. "You know, I've been thinking about David."

Will tensed.

"He wasn't very discreet," she said. "He liked to brag about stuff. I wouldn't be surprised if other people knew about our affair, maybe even his wife."

"Yeah. And?"

"So, what if he lost interest in Eve after the trial ended, and what if, out of spite, she threatened to report his misconduct to a judge or someone? The verdict could get overturned."

"Blackmail," Will said. "I've been thinking along those same lines. That might make someone who got a piece of that award want to get rid of Alvin and anything else that could put their money at risk."

"Like me," she said. "Maybe he even told someone I'd found those e-mails."

"Pembry was a problem, too, especially when he started stopping by the station, leaving notes for cops. His little messages probably got him killed."

The words came out harsher than he'd intended, and Courtney looked worried.

She tugged her hand away from his and downed her last sip of orange juice. "I'll try Jordan. She's probably at work by now."

"Good idea," Will said, pulling an envelope from his back pocket.

"Hey! That's my money!"

He fished out a twenty from the stash he'd found on her bureau back at the inn. "Just keeping it safe till we get to Austin."

"That's stealing!" She made a grab for the envelope, but he jerked it away, out of her reach.

"Thanks for breakfast, C.J." He winked. "Now make that phone call."

She thrust her chin out, but didn't say anything. Then she picked up the phone and dialed. "You have definite trust issues."

He lifted an eyebrow and slipped the money back in his pocket.

"Jordan? Hi, it's me."

Will heard the squeal from across the table.

"Yeah, I know. . . . Uh-huh . . . It's been a trip."

The diner was noisy with the breakfast crowd, and Courtney hunched over the phone, straining to listen. "Huh? I can't hear you. . . ." She looked up at Will and jerked her head toward the back of the restaurant. "*Restroom,*" she mouthed and got up. She took her purse with her, but not her backpack, and he knew she wouldn't get far. Not without money.

*You have definite trust issues.*

He trusted her. Mostly. But he was practical, too. Courtney was the most impulsive woman he'd ever known. If she got spooked, she might make a run for it, and he didn't intend to give her the chance.

Will polished off the rest of his eggs and drained his coffee. He checked his watch. Maybe he should call Devereaux and get an update. If the man was any kind of detective—which he was—he would have figured out by now that Will's sick day wasn't a sick day at all, but a quest to find Courtney. Will needed to tell him where things stood and see if any progress had been made on the investigation since yesterday.

Courtney had his phone, though. He drummed his fingers on the table and waited.

A man slid out of a booth up front and tucked a newspaper under his arm. He wore jeans, a flannel shirt, and a cap—like almost every other man in here—but something didn't fit.

Will watched him through the window as he crossed the parking lot. Something about the guy bugged him, and he couldn't make the thought go anywhere.

Where was Courtney?

He glanced impatiently over his shoulder to the REST-ROOMS sign at the back of the diner. She'd been gone too long. Irritated at his own paranoia, he patted his pocket and felt the reassuring bulge of his key. Maybe she was in there putting on makeup or something.

A rig grumbled across the parking lot, and Will watched it turn onto the highway.

The hair on the back of his neck stood up. Something was wrong. Where the hell *was* she? He slid out of the booth and strode to the back of the restaurant. The narrow hallway leading to the bathrooms was empty. Will pushed open the door marked WOMEN and startled some lady at the sink.

"Courtney?" He checked under the stalls. Nothing.

Buzzing with adrenaline now, he opened the men's and took a quick look around. Empty.

"Shit!"

He pushed out the back exit and found himself in a gravel parking lot beside a rusted Dumpster. *"Courtney!"*

An eighteen-wheeler roared down the highway as he scanned the desolate landscape surrounding the restaurant.

It wasn't possible. Not this time. She wouldn't run out on him now.

Would she?

She didn't even have any money. But, shit, maybe she didn't need any. Maybe she'd simply smiled up at some trucker and asked for a ride.

But she wouldn't do that.

Would she?

"God*damn* it!"

He scanned the horizon. The Texas panhandle stretched for miles in every direction. No cars, no trucks. No Courtney.

She watched Will through a gap in the weathered fence slats. The smell of garbage surrounded her as she listened to him curse.

The arm tightened around her neck, choking her even more. She whimpered, and it tightened again, while at the same time the gun barrel pressed against her temple swung around to point at Will.

She sucked air through her nostrils and smothered the urge to scream, to make even the slightest sound.

*Don't look. Don't look. Don't look.* She stared at Will's back and sent the message with her mind.

The arm around her neck remained strong and thick. The arm pointed at Will remained steady.

*Turn around! Go inside!*

The gun arm lifted fractionally, and she squeezed her eyes shut. She couldn't watch this. Not again.

Suddenly her windpipe opened, and she took a dizzy step backward. Will was gone. And just as she realized it, a hand clamped around her arm and dragged her backward.

"Not a word, or I swear, I'll blow your fucking brains out."

He pulled her out from behind the Dumpster, and she glanced desperately around the parking lot. A few empty trucks sat near the highway, but no one was outside. The man hauled her around the corner of the building to a green sedan. He shoved her into the front passenger's seat, slammed the door, and then opened the back door and slid in behind her.

Courtney reached for the handle, but the lock snapped down. She jerked her head around. A woman sat in the driver's seat, smiling at her.

"Hello, Courtney."

"Who the hell are you?"

# CHAPTER
## 23

Will checked the ladies' room again. Then the men's. He strode back toward the dining room, but a familiar sound made him stop.

His phone. He did a 360.

"Courtney?" He opened a door marked EMPLOYEES ONLY. Supply closet. The sound came again, from the corridor leading to the exit. There, on the floor beside a dust mop, was his cell phone.

He snatched it up while at the same time plowing through the restaurant's back entrance.

"Courtney!"

His gut clenched. She hadn't gone willingly. Wherever she'd gone ...

He pivoted toward the Dumpster, the source of that putrid odor. He shoved the noisy phone into his pocket and approached it with feet that felt like cinder blocks. A padlock secured the rusty hatch. Gripping the metal lip of the box, he heaved himself up.

And peered down into a rancid heap of garbage.

He dropped to the ground and bent over, nearly sick with relief.

His phone started up again, and he yanked it from his pocket. Devereaux.

*"What?"*

"We got a problem."

*No joke,* Will thought, as he raced around the side of the restaurant to the parking lot in front.

"Lindsey Kahn is in New Mexico," Devereaux said.

Shit. That explained a few things.

"So is Courtney."

"I know," Will told him. "I'm here, too."

"With Courtney?"

"No," Will said. He unlocked his truck and hitched himself behind the wheel. *Damn it,* which way? The highway stretched endlessly in both directions.

"Lindsey Kahn's in a Chrysler Sebring, and she's not alone," Devereaux said. "There's a man with her."

"How do you know?"

"I just got off the phone with the rental-car people in Albuquerque. We've ID'd the guy on Alex Lovell's surveillance video. Name's Mick O'Donnell. He's an ex-con suspected of two professional hits in Boston. Rental car people say he looks like the man they saw with Lindsey. This guy rented the car under an alias, but he was dumb enough to use Lindsey's cell phone as a contact number."

To the east, a couple of trucks disappeared into the glare of the morning sun. To the west, nothing but miles of highway and a faint green dot fading over the rise.

The Sebring.

"Hodges? You there?"

He skidded onto the highway. "I'm here." He stomped on the gas and pleaded with his oldest friend in the world. Thirty-five, forty, fifty. He slapped the wheel, and she gave a mighty lurch forward.

"What's going on? What are you doing?"

"I'm going after Courtney."

Courtney watched the woman barreling down the road. She wore a diamond Rolex and a black Juicy Couture tracksuit, and she had a head full of expensive blond highlights. She looked like half of Courtney's clients, except for the crazed gleam in her eyes.

"You thought you could hide from me?" She turned to Courtney, taking her attention off the road. "Let me tell you something. Information is king. *Information,* all right? You don't have it, you get left behind. Are you listening?"

Courtney was sort of listening, but mostly she was trying not to hyperventilate. That gun in the backseat was pointed straight at her head, and this woman was doing ninety-five miles an hour. What if she hit a bump?

She glared at Courtney. "Are you *hearing me?*"

She gulped. "Yes."

"Do you think I worked my way through college washing *dishes* so I could get *disbarred?* You think I let motherfucking Wilkers pimp me out so I could *lose?*" She pounded a fist on her leg. "It's *my* money. I *earned* it. I earned everything, and I'm not going to lose it all now because of you!"

Courtney stared at her. She was unhinged. Or maybe on something.

Music emanated from the backseat, and the woman reached back—still pushing one hundred—to dig a phone out of a Louis Vuitton purse.

She snapped it open. "You have him?" Pause. "Good." She checked her watch. "Okay, got it."

Have who? *Will?* Courtney's terror multiplied.

"Up here on the right's good," the man in back said, and Courtney turned toward him. His belly spilled over his jeans. She looked into his bloodshot gray eyes and knew he was the ski-mask guy from the park.

The one who'd killed David.

The one who'd tried to kill *her*.

And she'd Maced him, and thrown a wok of hot oil on him, and given him the slip at least half a dozen times. And now he looked pissed.

The woman jerked the wheel right and then they *did* hit a bump, and Courtney held her breath, certain she was about to be decapitated by a bullet from that gun. They lurched over dip after dip, and then the land flattened out and they were flying across a huge expanse of dust.

"Where are we going?" she croaked.

By way of answer, the woman pointed the car toward what looked like some sort of abandoned outbuilding. As they neared it, Courtney saw tumbleweeds bouncing across the dusty plains. *Tumbleweeds.* She glanced around, frantic. There was nothing. *No one* who would see whatever was about to happen.

Where was Will?

The car skidded to a halt beside the shed. She thrust it in Park and turned to Courtney.

"You are nobody, do you understand? Nothing! Except for one tiny piece of information that you will give to me if you ever want to see your boyfriend again."

Courtney was going to puke. "Where is he?" And then she regretted the question, because the crazy bitch smiled.

"Wouldn't you like to know that?" She reached into the backseat and jerked a computer bag from the floor.

Courtney watched, baffled, as she whipped out a sleek silver notebook and powered up.

And then she understood. The e-mails.

"We're going on a little treasure hunt," Juicy Woman said cheerfully. "*You* have the map—those e-mails between Eve and John. *I* get to keep the treasure. Are you getting this now? I'm not returning a dime of that money. I earned it!"

Courtney eyed the computer with dread. There was no way she was going to get a signal out here. Did this lunatic realize that? And was she going to flip out when she did? She glanced over her shoulder, at the man in back, but he wasn't watching the screen. He was watching Courtney with some serious hostility in his eyes.

He hadn't forgotten the Mace.

"Goddamn it!" The woman jabbed a manicured fingernail at the Enter key. "What is *wrong* with this?" She stared at it a moment, and Courtney noticed the tremor in her body. She was definitely on something.

"Fine!" Her gaze snapped up to meet Courtney's. She grabbed the purse from the backseat and pulled out a gun, a giant black cannon that was completely at odds with her French manicure.

"Forget the computer. You can just *tell* me your password. But know this: if you lie, we will kill him. Do you understand me?"

Courtney nodded.

"The password!"

Will swerved off the highway where the cloud of dust had begun to settle. About half a mile off sat a small, dilapidated building. The Sebring had disappeared behind it.

Will jumped out of the truck and left the door open, in case the sound carried. Two people, probably armed. He took out his Glock, checked the clip, and set off.

"The password!" she screamed again.

What could she say? If she told her, would she pull the trigger? The password was her only leverage, her only means of buying herself time.

"It's my birthday."

"*What?*"

"My birthday. That's my password. On my computer at work." Oh God, oh God, oh God. Where was Will? Where was anybody? How long could she draw this out?

The woman sighed, annoyed. "And what is your birthday?"

"August twenty-second."

She frowned, obviously wondering how this would translate into a password. "What year?" she demanded.

"Not the date," Courtney said. "The sign."

"The *sign?*"

"The zodiac sign. I'm a Leo."

"That's your password? *Leo?* It's only three letters!"

God, where was Will? Where was help?

"*Is that it?*"

Courtney glanced at the man in the back, still pointing the gun. She glanced at the black cannon. The hands holding it weren't steady, but at this distance, it wouldn't matter. Courtney was in the passenger seat, she realized, just like David had been.

And Will was going to find her. He was going to see her, *dead*, just like she'd seen David, only she hadn't loved

David, but she loved Will, and he loved *her*, and he'd never get over it.

"Out of the car." The woman jerked the gun toward the door.

They were going to march her into the field and shoot her. But at least she'd have a chance. Maybe she could make a run for it.

"*Out!*"

She unlocked the door and scrambled out.

Will crouched low, behind the one scrap of cover within fifty yards of this place—a freaking cactus. A small one at that. But the targets weren't watching him—they were too absorbed with Courtney.

She stumbled out. She cast a terrified look around, searching for him, he knew, and his gut twisted. The woman barked an order, and the man raised his weapon.

Will murmured a prayer and took aim.

*Pop!*

Courtney dropped to the ground and covered her head with her hands.

"*Shit!*"

The man with the gun was on the ground, too, clutching his knee and writhing on his back.

Glass shattered, and Courtney registered another, closer shot, from the car.

Juicy Bitch was shooting. Courtney searched desperately for cover. A dark blur burst up from the ground.

*Will!*

"Get down!" Will raced past the man beside Courtney

and kicked his gun out of reach, then dove into the car.

Courtney tripped to her feet just as the injured man made a lunge for the gun. Courtney snatched it up.

"Freeze!" Will boomed.

She whirled around. Will had the blonde facedown beside the car, his knee planted in her spine, while his gun pointed at the man wobbling to his feet. The guy's bulging eyes zeroed in on the weapon in Courtney's hand. Panicked, she rushed over and kicked him in the kneecap, and he crumpled to the ground again, howling.

And then Will was on him, flipping him onto his stomach and jerking his arms behind his back. He glanced at Courtney. "Take his belt off."

She gaped at him.

"His *belt*, Courtney!"

She put down the gun and stumbled over. She cast an anxious look at the woman handcuffed and whimpering beside the car. Her face was coated in dust.

Will held the man's hands tightly together and helped her flip him over so she could access the belt. She unbuckled it and gave a few hard yanks until she'd freed it from his pants. She handed it to Will, who quickly secured the guy's wrists with it. The man spewed obscenities at both of them while Will stripped off his T-shirt and went to work on the gory knee.

Courtney stood there, panting and staring down at him. He was so calm, so efficient. Meanwhile, her heart was galloping out of her chest, and her legs felt like rubber. She sank to her knees.

Will glanced at her. "You okay?"

She nodded dumbly.

With a bloodied hand, he pulled a phone from his pocket and tossed it at her. She watched it hit the ground in front of her, completely incapable of a reaction.

"Call 911," he said. "We need the sheriff here."

She looked at the phone. She looked at Will. He was so calm. So confident. He was a soldier on a battlefield, unfazed by bullets and blood and everything else. She was a terrified civilian about to heave up her omelet.

With a shaking hand, she picked up the phone.

"Drop it."

A man walked out from behind the shed. He had a gun aimed at Courtney as he approached them. A diamond sparked on his finger, and she remembered Fiona's suspect sketch.

She met Will's gaze. She spotted the pistol tucked into his jeans.

"Hands up, or I blow her away."

Courtney sucked in air as the metal barrel jabbed into her neck.

"Now."

This man wasn't fat. Or bulky, even. He had a completely average build, but his dull, emotionless voice chilled her. He was all business.

Will raised his bloodied hands above his head as the fat guy continued to moan and clutch his knee.

"Stand up," the gunman ordered. "Both of you."

They rose to their feet. Courtney's legs were shaking so badly, she thought she might fall, but the gun pressed against her neck had a steadying effect.

"Glock on the ground," he told Will, then positioned Courtney right in front of him, in case Will tried to get a shot off. The man's hand clenched her arm. His sour breath tickled her cheek, just above the spot where the gun pressed into her skin. Courtney's throat went dry.

Slowly, Will pulled his gun free from his jeans and lowered it to the ground.

"One wrong move, and I kill her."

Will stared over her shoulder with flat, cold eyes. "You do it, you're fucking dead."

She heard the low chuckle behind her.

Something beside the car caught her eye. The woman had managed to get to her feet now. She leaned against the car, coughing and scowling at Will, whose cuffs she was wearing.

"You, over there." The man gave Courtney a mighty shove in the direction of the empty field. "You, too."

They both walked into the open field. Will caught her eye and seemed to be trying to tell her something, but she didn't understand. Her teeth chattered. Her chest hurt. She could hardly walk on her wobbly legs.

"On your knees."

She thought he was talking to her, but she glanced back, and he was looking at Will.

*"Now!"*

Will lowered himself to his knees. The man left Courtney's side and made a wide arc to stand right behind him.

She choked out a sob.

"Hands behind your head."

Will complied, and a wail tore from her chest. He met her gaze. "Don't look," he said, and her heart caved in. But she couldn't look away. *No, no, no!* She pleaded with her eyes.

The man raised the gun.

And in a lightning flash, Will lunged sideways and swept his legs around, toppling the gunman.

A shot pierced the air. Courtney dropped to her stomach, screaming. The two men's bodies thrashed and tangled together in the dirt.

Where was the *gun?*

Then Will was on top, straddling the man and pounding his face, over and over, as if he'd never stop.

A flash of black caught Courtney's attention as the woman lunged for Will's abandoned Glock, but she was cuffed, and Courtney got there first.

"Stop!" Courtney shrieked and pointed the gun at her. The woman's eyes widened, and she stepped backward. Courtney whirled toward Will, who was still punching away at the man beneath him. "Stop!"

Will glanced up. He jumped to his feet and grabbed the second weapon from the ground, where it had fallen in the struggle. He pointed it at his attacker, whose nose was broken and bleeding.

"Roll over! Facedown!"

The man rolled over.

Will glanced at Courtney. "Get hers." He nodded at the black gun sitting on the ground near Courtney. She retrieved it and went to Will. He stood there, panting and alive, and she wanted to crumble at his feet and cry, but she just held out the guns. He tucked the big one into his jeans and left her with the Glock. He kept the other weapon trained on the figure lying facedown before him.

Will took a deep breath and gazed down at the man who'd nearly executed him just seconds ago.

"You're under arrest."

# CHAPTER
# 24

They spent the better part of the day giving statements and filling out forms at a rural sheriff's department west of Amarillo. By late afternoon, Courtney was so exhausted, her vision blurred. She sat in a molded plastic chair in the hallway outside the sheriff's office and waited for Will to finish up what looked like a painful phone conversation with Cernak back in Austin. By the sound of it, the lieutenant was none too happy about his detective's recent field trip.

Finally, Will ended the call, traded some brief parting words with the sheriff, and came to stand in front of her.

"Ready?"

"Ready."

She had no idea what she was ready for, beyond getting out of this dustbowl they'd been stranded in. She followed him to the Suburban and gratefully climbed inside.

"Where to?" she asked, when he was behind the wheel.

"Home."

Nine hours of driving. Was he out of his mind?

Her gaze skimmed over the three-day beard, the dirty jeans, and too-tight Red Raiders T-shirt that was an apparent loaner from some sheriff's deputy, and decided he was.

But for once, she didn't feel like arguing. She settled her

cheek against the window and watched the flatlands glide by. She fell asleep.

When she awoke, they were in Abilene, and Will was gassing up for the final leg of their journey. She watched the dollars tick off at the pump and came to the groggy realization that in addition to her life, she owed him at least half a dozen tanks of gas.

Will disappeared into the convenience store and returned with two twenty-four-ounce Cokes and two hot dogs. He passed her a dog loaded with everything, including jalapeños, before starting up the truck again and getting on the freeway.

"Want me to drive?"

"No."

The next four hours were silent and uncomfortable as Courtney awoke to the new reality that lay ahead of her.

She had no job. She had no car. She had no utilities. Although she did, at least, have a duplex apartment, as her rent was paid up through October. But much of her stuff had been destroyed by Lindsey Kahn's thugs. Fiona, in her infinite selflessness, had cleaned up the mess as best she could a month ago. But the thought of returning to the house on Oak Trail made her spirits sink.

Will, too, was in a black mood. He didn't say a word for three hours, and Courtney waited for him to share whatever was on his mind, but he just stared ahead at the road. Finally, she couldn't stand it.

"Did you get fired?"

He slid a glance at her. "No."

"Then what's wrong?"

"Nothing."

Nothing. Right. They'd almost died this morning, and nothing was wrong.

She crossed her arms and gazed out the window until they were well inside the city limits. Will passed the exit leading to her neighborhood, then Fiona's, and then got off at the one leading to his apartment.

"Where are we going?"

"Home."

She started to protest, but really, she had no energy. She sat silently as he pulled into his apartment complex and found a space.

He cut the engine and turned to look at her. She saw the muscle twitching in his jaw, and held her breath, waiting.

"I'm sorry."

*He* was sorry? "Why?" she asked.

He shook his head. "I didn't hear the car. The second gunman. I didn't hear him drive up."

"Neither did I," she said. "It was chaos. I could barely think straight."

"I saw him back at the diner, too. I saw his ring, the one Fiona drew, but it didn't register then." He looked her in the eye. "I'm sorry. I almost got us both killed."

"Don't apologize to *me*. If it weren't for you, I'd most likely be dead in a hotel room in New Mexico right now. I'm the one who should be sorry for dragging you into this—"

"You didn't drag me. It was my job."

The words were like a slap. His *job*. It hadn't felt like a job last night. They'd lain together in that desert motel, and it had felt like what brought him to her was much more than a job.

She should know better than to get too hopeful about a relationship. Any relationship, even one with Will.

He sighed. "Let's get inside. I'm beat."

That, at least, she could agree with. Courtney trudged up the stairs behind him, amazed that he'd spent the entire nine-hour drive torturing himself over not hearing that car. She hadn't heard it, either, but he seemed to think he had some special obligation to be Superman just because he had a badge.

At his door, he stooped to pick up a blue Tupperware container.

"What's that?" she asked, frowning.

"Nothing."

She followed him into the apartment and sank down on the sofa. He flipped on the TV and found a baseball game.

"You want a shower?" he asked.

"Definitely."

"Go ahead. I have to make some calls."

Courtney showered, lathering her skin with Will's Dial soap—which she knew would dry it, but that smelled like him. She washed her hair and wrapped herself in a towel. When she stepped out of the bathroom, Will was still on the phone with Devereaux or some other detective, from the sound of things, and she lay down on the bed to wait for him.

She didn't have any clean clothes.

But before her mind could tackle that problem, she was fast asleep.

When she awoke, she was tucked under the sheets, and Will was standing beside the closet, pulling on a shirt. Light peeked through the miniblinds covering the windows.

"What time is it?" Her eyes felt gritty. She searched for a clock.

"Seven-thirty."

She sat up, confused. Where was her towel?

He slipped a belt into his pants and came around to her side of the bed.

"Amy Harris brought some stuff over this morning. She's coming back around ten to give you a ride. You have a meeting with your attorney at ten-thirty." He buckled his belt as she tried to clear the cobwebs from her brain.

"Who called Ackerman?" she asked.

"I did." He planted a kiss on her head and went back to his closet to pick up his shoes.

"Am I under arrest?" She said it without thinking, voicing one of the many fears that had been lurking in her dreams. The others involved choke holds and desolate fields and black guns.

"No. But your attorney needs to help you sort this out. He can probably trade your cooperation for a dismissal of the charges against you."

"What charges?"

He gazed across the room at her. "Lying. Obstruction. Cernak's trumped up a whole list of stuff, most of it bogus. Talk to your lawyer about it. Then get him to bring you in to talk to Cernak."

"Where will you be?"

"Close by."

He was closer than she'd expected, sitting at the end of the long conference table in another one of APD's interview rooms, only this one was a bit more refined than the two she'd seen before. It actually had padded chairs and a coffee machine.

After several hours of back and forth, and tape-recorded statements, and more forms, Ackerman slid a thin file across the table. The folder contained the e-mails printed out from Courtney's still-functioning account at Bella Donna, and Cernak was clearly pleased to get his hands on it. It was yet another clue proving that the attorneys of Wilkers & Riley had tampered with the jury in the LivTech trial. It was one of the many pieces of evidence that Lindsey Kahn, Jim Wilkers, Peter Riley, and who knew how many others would have to face in a criminal trial.

If they didn't cut a deal first. Being lawyers, Courtney figured they'd try. But given the high-profile nature of both the LivTech case itself and the string of killings, they probably didn't have a chance at any kind of leniency. People hated lawyers to begin with, and lying, cheating, murdering ones weren't likely to garner much sympathy.

Ackerman dropped Courtney off at Will's apartment when it was all over.

"So I guess this is it?" She gazed across the cramped hatchback at the one attorney she didn't despise.

He smiled. "Not quite. I haven't sent you my bill yet."

She winced.

"Don't worry. I'm affordable."

"Yeah, right. Would you accept some of my payment in the form of goods and service?"

He looked wary. "What kind of services?"

"I can definitely improve on that haircut." She smiled to soften the message. "And as soon as I find a new job, I can hook your wife up with some spa treatments."

He laughed and looked relieved. She'd known he was a family man the very first day.

"We'll talk," he said. "I think we can negotiate something."

When Will came home a few hours later, she was already dressed for bed in one of the short, silky things Amy had wisely packed in her bag.

But it didn't stay on for long. Will started stripping off his clothes the instant he walked in the door, and a few minutes later they were tangled naked on the bed. Their lovemaking was frantic and desperate, ending in the most earth-moving climax of her life.

The afterglow was cool and silent.

Courtney took a deep, cleansing breath and opened her eyes. Her reflection stared back at her, a reflection she barely recognized these days. She was back to ebony again, with a few streaks in order to keep it interesting, but her eyes had changed. They were more serious now. Older. And sometimes they'd fill with tears inexplicably in the middle of the day.

Something was wrong with her. She didn't know what, really, just that her emotions were out of control. It was all she could do to hold it together at work every day before going home to Will's apartment, where she almost always had a crying jag before he got home from work. He'd get called out of bed sometimes in the middle of the night, and she'd cry then, too, having flashbacks of him on his knees in that field until she fell asleep on a soggy pillow.

"Courtney?" Someone tapped on the door. "Your three-thirty just showed."

She took another deep breath and fluffed her hair. Then she opened the bathroom door and strode back into the salon. Zen was a hip, high-end day spa in the heart of Austin, and her 3:30 client looked totally out of place here.

She smiled at him. "You came."

Devon shrugged.

"Where's your mom?"

"Next door. She's trying on shoes." He eyed the black leather chair suspiciously. "Do I sit there?"

"Sure, hop up." Courtney patted the chair, and he settled into it.

"Have you decided on a color?

"Green."

"Are you sure? It's Halloween. We could always do black and orange."

"I want green," he said firmly.

"Green it is."

Thirty minutes later, Courtney was standing on the sidewalk in front of the salon, waiting for Will. She felt anxious. Restless. The dread that had been lodged in her stomach since this morning started to expand. She tried to calm herself, tried to give herself a pep talk. What was one more uncomfortable conversation in the scheme of things? She'd been on an emotional roller coaster for weeks. And today was going to be one of the dips.

The Suburban pulled up at precisely 4:00, as they'd agreed. Courtney got in. Will wore his usual gray slacks, white shirt, and dark blazer, but today he had on a tie.

"Hi," she said.

"Hi."

She'd grown accustomed to his aversion to chitchat, and for the most part, it didn't bother her.

They wended their way through downtown. He drummed his fingers on the wheel, then swore under his breath when they missed the light.

"Are we late?"

He glanced at her. "No."

"You seem worried."

"I'm fine." He looked at her again, seeming to notice her presence for the first time. "Are *you* worried?"

She shrugged. "Not really." Although she should be. She was on her way to a meeting with Lieutenant Cernak—one of her least favorite people—two federal investigators, and a U.S. attorney.

She glanced at Will. Tiny beads of perspiration clung to his temples.

"Are you okay?" she asked.

"Fine."

Lie.

"What's going on?"

He glanced at her. "Nothing."

Another lie. Anger gathered in her chest. He was *lying*. It was so obvious. There was something going on. She'd sensed it all week, and she wasn't imagining it. Her stomach churned as she thought of the thing that had been needling her since 9:00 this morning when she'd seen another package sitting on the doorstep. She'd been conflicted all day, and she couldn't stand it anymore.

"Who's Lori?" she blurted.

"Who?"

"Lori. With the *cookies*."

He smiled, and her anger swelled.

"What's so funny?" she demanded.

"You. You said 'cookies' like it's a venereal disease."

"Who is she?"

"She's my neighbor. When did she bring cookies?"

She shot him a heated look.

"What? I helped her hang a picture last weekend."

"Whatever."

They reached the white granite government building, and Will parked at an empty meter. Courtney licked her lips and tried to pretend she wasn't feeling stupid and hurt. Relationships sucked. She'd known it forever. Why did she keep hoping she'd get better at it?

He cut the engine and turned to look at her. "Courtney."

"It doesn't matter. I don't care. Do whatever you want."

"Do whatever I want."

"Sure. Go screw the girl next door if you want to. I don't care."

"You don't care."

She wouldn't look at him. This was unraveling because she was being one of those hysterical women. But she couldn't help it. What was *wrong* with her lately?

"Courtney?"

"I don't care what you do. It's your life."

She turned toward him now, and his gaze was intense.

"I think you do care," he said. "I think you care a lot. I think you care way more than you want to, and you're terrified."

She crossed her arms and looked away.

"That's what's going on, isn't it?" he said. "With the blue

hair and the smoking and the aromatherapy shit all over the apartment. You're trying to push me away."

She crossed her legs and picked some invisible lint off her black miniskirt. "You sound like Dr. Phil."

"Are you?"

She paused. She cleared her throat. "Maybe."

"Well, cut it out. It's pissing me off."

God, what was her problem? She was a nutcase. She was freaking out over some woman with *cookies*. She glanced up at him. "I've never lived with anyone before."

"Well, that makes two of us."

"I keep waiting for the other shoe to drop. I don't know."

"Not everyone's like David, or whoever it is you're comparing me to." He jerked the keys out of the ignition and pushed his door open. "Let's go. We're late now."

She stepped out of the car, and he came around. They started up the wide concrete steps, and he picked up her hand.

She cast a sidelong glance at him, admiring his ramrod straight posture—which always reminded her of his military background—and his way-too-conservative business attire.

"You really don't mind the blue?" she asked.

"I couldn't care less."

"And the aromatherapy?"

"The only thing that bugs me is the smoking." He pulled the glass door open for her, and they stepped into a lobby. "That, I hate."

He led her to an elevator bank and punched the UP button. They waited in silence, and she looked at him again. He tugged on his collar.

The elevator arrived, and they stepped inside. He pressed

the button for the third floor, and they rode up, with him nervously squeezing and unsqueezing her hand the whole way. The doors pinged open, but she didn't move.

There *was* something going on. He was acting totally strange. He was nervous, and he didn't *get* nervous. He could perform triage without even breaking a sweat, and here he was with clammy palms on the way to some informal meeting.

He stepped off the elevator, tugging her with him.

Unless this wasn't an informal meeting. What if this was some kind of setup? Cernak was here. Maybe he wanted to arrest her. Maybe they'd found some new evidence, something new to charge her with.

Her feet slowed as she walked down the long linoleum corridor. She looked at Will, but he had his gaze fixed straight ahead.

She stopped walking and shook off his grip.

"What's going on? You're acting weird."

He turned and looked at her, and his discomfort was written all over his face. He cleared his throat.

"I didn't want to tell you where we were going."

"What do you mean?" she stepped back. "I thought this was a meeting."

"Not really."

She took another step back, but he caught her hand. She looked around, panicked. What was this?

And then she saw it—the door at the end of the hallway with a placard beside it that said MARRIAGE LICENSES.

No way.

She looked at Will. He was gazing down at her patiently.

"Oh my God," she murmured.

He dropped down on one knee and kissed her palm.

"Are we here for a *marriage license?*"

Her heart was thundering now. Now *her* palms were sweating. He was on one knee, for Christ's sake!

"I know you're freaked out," he said. "But it's okay. I understand."

"Oh my God."

He took something out of his pocket and slipped it on her finger. A ring. It was a *ring*. She stared down at the sparkling red ruby flanked by diamonds and felt her throat close up. This had to be a joke. But she looked into his brown eyes, at the seriousness on his face, and knew he wasn't joking at all. He was down on one knee, proposing to her in this hallway.

"When we were in Silver Creek, I told you to jump, and I'd catch you, and you just closed your eyes and did it." He kissed her hand. "I'm asking you to do that again."

She stared down at him, utterly speechless.

"I love you. Please marry me."

And then she noticed someone standing beside her.

Fiona. And Jack. She glanced around at all the bureaucrats who'd stopped what they were doing to smile at her.

She turned to her sister. "You knew about this?"

Fiona smiled and nodded. Jack grinned at her.

Then she looked down at Will again, this giant man who was kneeling before her with his heart in his eyes.

He loved her. He wanted to marry her.

And then she did the most impulsive thing she'd ever done.

She said yes.

Turn the page for a sneak peek at the next
thrilling suspense from Laura Griffin . . .

# FAR
# GONE

Coming soon from Gallery Books

*Three messages.*

*The first to create shock and awe.*

*The second to deliver a terrifying blow—but only to the few who understood it.*

*The third was his favorite. It would be understood by everyone and bolder than they ever imagined.*

# CHAPTER

# I

The messenger pulled up to the stoplight and scanned his surroundings. People streamed up and down the sidewalk, headed to jobs and meetings and classes under the colorless Philadelphia sky. The older ones wore dark overcoats and moved briskly down Market Street, with cell phones pressed to their ears. The younger ones were casual, dressed in jeans and bright-colored scarves and hats. They had backpacks slung over their shoulders and read texts from their friends as they walked.

He glanced at his watch. Eight minutes. He rolled his shoulders to ease the tension as he waited for the light. Three hours ago, he had woken up in a motel parking lot. He'd had a solid night's sleep in the front of the van—which was probably odd, considering his cargo. But years ago, he'd learned how to sleep anywhere.

The car ahead of him rolled forward. A silver Accord, late-model, female driver. She hooked a right, and the man followed, keeping his moves cautious.

A utility crew occupied the left lane, squeezing traffic down to a single line as they tore up the asphalt. The construction was good and bad, he'd decided. Bad because it might throw off his timeline. Good because it added to the chaos and created another reason for him to go unnoticed.

The man surveyed the sidewalks, skimming his gaze over the now-familiar takeout restaurants and shops hawking Liberty Bell replicas to tourists. Another glance at his watch.

Six minutes.

He reached into his jacket to check his weapon, a sleek FN Five-seveN with a twenty-round magazine. The pistol was loaded with nineteen SS195 jacketed hollow-point bullets, one already in the chamber. He was good to go.

Five minutes.

The messenger circled the block again. His stomach growled as he passed a doughnut store for the third time. He scanned the faces along the street, forcing hunger and fear and all distractions out of his mind as he made what he hoped would be his final lap through campus.

The phone beeped from the cup holder. He glanced at the text.

*Red coat. Coming from the trolley stop.*

He spotted her. No hat today, and her blond hair hung loose around her shoulders. Tall black boots. Tight jeans. Short red jacket with a belt at the waist.

He checked his watch. Once again, she was right on time.

Easing the minivan to the curb beside a fire hydrant, he watched her. She hurried toward her destination, gripping the strap of her backpack with a gloved hand. The other hand held a cigarette, and she lifted it to her lips for one last drag as she neared the building.

The cigarette disappointed him. She'd probably taste

like an ashtray, nothing at all like his fantasies. He looked her over for another moment before sliding from the vehicle.

The sound of jackhammers hit him, along with the familiar smell of busted-up concrete. He glanced up and down the block and noted the cop on foot patrol talking to one of the utility workers. Both guys were fat and complacent. Too many doughnuts. The cop would hoof it over here in a few minutes, but by then, it would be too late.

The messenger hit the sidewalk, keeping the brim of his cap low as he watched the woman.

Eye contact. Just an instant, but it sent a sweet jolt of adrenaline through him.

One minute.

He trained his gaze straight ahead as they passed each other. This was it. He reached into his jacket pocket and pulled out two bits of orange foam, which he pressed into his ears. He hung a right and saw the Ford parked in the designated place.

Ten seconds.

He pulled out his second phone. Took a deep breath as he flipped it open.

*Message One: You reap what you sow.* He hit send and braced for the concussion. For a moment, nothing.

And then the earth moved.


Andrea Finch had never been dumped at a barbecue joint, but there was a first time for everything.

Her date looked out of place at the scarred wooden booth in his charcoal-gray suit. He'd come straight from work, as she had. He'd ditched the tie but still seemed overly formal in a restaurant that had paper-towel rolls on every table and classic country drifting from the jukebox.

"So." Nick Mays took a swig of beer. "How was your day?"

Andrea smiled. He sounded like a tired husband, and they'd only been dating a month.

"Fine," she said. "Yours?"

"Fine."

For the dozenth time since she'd sat down, his gaze darted over her shoulder. When his blue eyes met hers again, she felt a twinge of regret. He really *was* a nice-looking man. Good eyes, thick hair. A bit of a beer gut, but she didn't mind, really. His main problem was his oversize ego. Andrea was used to men with big egos. She'd been surrounded by them since she'd entered the police academy, and they'd only multiplied once she earned her detective's badge.

"Listen, Andrea." He glanced over her shoulder again, and she braced for the speech. "These last few weeks, they've really been great."

He was a terrible liar, which was too bad. As an assistant district attorney, he was going to need the skill if he planned to run for his boss's job someday.

He opened his mouth to continue just as a waitress stepped up and beamed a smile at him.

"Y'all ready to order?"

Nick looked pained. But to his credit, he nodded in Andrea's direction. "Andie?"

"I'm good, thanks."

He glanced at the waitress. "Me, too."

"So . . . y'all *won't* be having dinner with us?" Her

overly made-up eyes shifted to Andrea. She tucked a lock of blond hair behind her ear and looked impatient.

"Just the drinks for now." Nick gave her one of his smiles, which seemed to lessen her annoyance as she hustled off. The smile faded as he turned back to Andrea. "So I was saying. These past few weeks. It's been a good time, Andie. You're an interesting girl."

She gritted her teeth. If he insisted on using frat-boy speak, she was going to make this *way* harder for him. She folded her arms over her chest and cast her gaze around the restaurant, letting his comment dangle awkwardly.

The cowbell on the door rattled as a family of four filed outside. Tonight's crowd was thin, even for a Monday. Maybe the weather was keeping people away. Austin was set to get sleet tonight, and her lieutenant had called in extra officers, expecting the roads to be a mess.

"Andrea?"

She looked at him.

"I said, wouldn't you agree with that?"

The cowbell rattled again as a skinny young man stepped through the entrance. He wore a black trench coat and clunky boots. His too-big ears reminded Andrea of her brother.

She looked at Nick. "Agree with what?"

His mouth tightened. "I said it seems like neither of us is looking for something serious right now. So maybe we should cool things down a little."

She glanced across the room as the kid walked toward the double doors leading to the kitchen. She studied the line of his coat, frowning.

"*Andrea.*"

"*What?*" Her attention snapped to Nick.

"Christ, you're not even listening. Have you heard a word I said?"

She glanced at the kitchen, where the clatter of pots and pans had suddenly gone silent. The back of her neck tingled. She slid from the booth.

"Andie?"

"Just a sec."

She strode across the restaurant, her gaze fixed on the double doors. Her heart thudded inexplicably while her mind cataloged info: six-one, one-fifty, blond, blue. She pictured his flushed cheeks and his lanky body in that big coat.

A waiter whisked past her and pushed through the doors to the kitchen. Andrea followed, stumbling into him when he halted in his tracks.

Three people stood motionless against a counter. Their eyes were round with shock, and their mouths hung open.

The kid in the overcoat stood a few yards away, pointing a pistol at them.

His gaze jumped to Andrea and the waiter. "You! Over there!" He jerked his head at the petrified trio.

The waiter made a strangled sound and scuttled out the door they'd just come through.

Andrea didn't move. Her chest tightened as she took in the scene: two waitresses and a cook, all cowering against a counter. Possibly more people in back. The kid was brandishing a Glock 17. It was pointed straight at the woman in the center, Andrea's waitress. She couldn't have been more than eighteen, and the gunman looked almost as young. Andrea noted his skinny neck, his *freckles*. His cheeks were pink—not from cold, as she'd first thought, but emotion.

The look he sent the waitress was like a plea.

"You did this, Haley!"

The woman's eyes widened. Her lips moved, but no words came out.

"This is *your* fault."

Andrea eased her hand beneath her blazer. The kid's arm swung toward her. "You! Get with them!"

She went still.

"Dillon, what are you—"

"Shut up!" The gun swung back toward the waitress. Haley. The trio was just a few short yards away from the gun. Even with no skill whatsoever, anything he fired at that distance would likely be lethal. And who knew how many bullets he had in that thing?

Andrea's heart drummed inside her chest. The smoky smell of barbecue filled the air. The kitchen was warm and steamy, and the walls seemed to be closing in on her as she focused on the gunman.

His back was to a wall lined with coat hooks. She counted four jackets and two ball caps, probably all belonging to the staff. Was anyone else hiding in the back? Had someone called for help?

"*You* did this!" the gunman shouted, and Haley flinched.

Andrea licked her lips. For only the second time in her career, she eased her gun from its holster and prepared to aim it at a person. The weight in her hand felt familiar, almost comforting. But her mouth went dry as her finger slid around the trigger.

*Defuse.*

She thought of everything she'd ever learned about hostage negotiations. She thought of the waiter who'd fled. She thought of Nick. Help had to be on the way by now. But the closest SWAT team was twenty minutes out, and she *knew*, with sickening certainty, that whatever happened here was going to be over in a matter of moments.

"I trusted you, Haley." His voice broke on the last word, and Haley cringed back. "I trusted you, but you're a lying *bitch*!"

"Dillon, please—"

"*Shut up!* Just shut up, okay?"

Ambivalence. She heard it in his voice. She could get control of this.

Andrea raised her weapon. "Dillon, look at me."

To her relief, his gaze veered in her direction. He was crying now, tears streaming down his freckled cheeks, and again he reminded her of her brother. Andrea's stomach clenched as she lined up her sights on his center body mass.

*Establish a command presence.*

"Put the gun down, Dillon. Let's talk this through."

He swung his arm ninety degrees, and Andrea was staring down the barrel of the Glock. All sound disappeared. Her entire world seemed to be sucked by gravity toward that little black hole.

She lifted her gaze to the gunman's face. Dillon. His name was Dillon. And he was eighteen, tops.

Her heart beat crazily. Her mouth felt dry. Hundreds

of times she'd trained to confront an armed assailant. It should have been a no-brainer, pure muscle memory. But she felt paralyzed. Every instinct was screaming for her to find another way.

Dillon's gaze slid to Haley, who seemed to be melting into the Formica counter. The others had inched away from her—a survival instinct that was going to be of little help if this kid let loose with a hail of bullets.

*Loud, repetitive commands.*

"Dillon, look at me." She tried to make her voice firm, but even she could hear the desperation in it. "Put the gun down, Dillon. We'll talk through this."

His gaze met hers again. He rubbed his nose on the shoulder of his coat. Tears and snot glistened on his face.

"I'll kill you, too," he said softly. "Don't think I won't."

"I believe you. But wouldn't it be easier just to talk?" She paused. "Put the gun down, Dillon."

She could see his arm shaking, and—to her dismay—hers began to shake, too. As if she didn't know how to hold her own weapon. As if she didn't work out three times a week to maintain upper-body strength.

As if she didn't have it in her to shoot a frightened kid.

He was disintegrating before her eyes. She could see it. His Adam's apple moved up and down as he swallowed hard.

"You can't stop me." His voice was a thread now, almost a whisper. He shifted his stance back toward Haley, and the stark look on her face told Andrea she'd read his body language.

"I'll do it."

Andrea's pulse roared in her ears. The edges of her

vision blurred. All she saw was that white hand clutching that big black gun. The muscles in his hand shifted as his index finger curled.

"I'll do it. You can't stop me."

Andrea squinted her eye.

*Lord, forgive me.*

She pulled the trigger.